Katseye

Harriet Redfern

Published in 2018 by Ambessa Publishing

First Edition

A CIP catalogue record for this title is available from the British Library.

By the same author

Tabikat 2016

Prologue

10.00
Cheltenian News Radio, Traffic News

There are severe delays on the B4362 at Cleeve Hill to the North of Cheltenham following the closure of the road in both directions. Traffic from Prestbury is being diverted onto Southam Lane towards the A435. Traffic coming from Winchcombe is at a standstill. Cleeve Hill Golf Club at the top of Cleeve Hill is currently inaccessible. Drivers are being advised by police on the road to return towards Cheltenham or Winchcombe and to find alternative routes.

A number of emergency vehicles are in attendance on Cleeve Hill. There is no information as to when the road will re-open. Avoid the area.

10.30
Cheltenian News Radio, News

We are getting reports of a body discovered at the foot of Cleeve Cloud on Cleeve Hill to the North of Cheltenham. Police have closed off the B4362, the route between Prestbury and Winchcombe, causing major traffic queues in both directions.

This is the second year in succession that a body has been found on the day following the end of the Cheltenham Festival. Exactly one year ago, members of the public discovered the battered body of a known criminal alongside the A40 opposite GCHQ. That location is on the other side of Cheltenham from Cleeve Hill and there is no suggestion that the two events are connected.

We understand that the body was discovered by a walker in the area. More information when we get it.

11.00
BBC News, South West

Sophie Wilde, Newsreader

We are picking up reports from local radio in Cheltenham of a body found in suspicious circumstances near the town. Our reporter Max Bennett is at the scene.

What can you tell us, Max?

Max Bennett

Good morning Sophie. I'm standing here on picturesque Cleeve Hill just to the North of Cheltenham. The road here has been closed for some time whilst police and ambulance personnel recover a body which has been found at the bottom of Cleeve Cloud.

Sophie

What and where is Cleeve Cloud, Max?

Max

Cleeve Cloud is a rock face which is a local landmark and popular with climbers. Racing TV viewers will be familiar with it as the backdrop to one of the most popular views of Cheltenham racecourse. The Cotswold Way runs along the ridge of the hill alongside Cleeve Hill golf course. The hill provides panoramic views over Cheltenham and Bishop's Cleeve towards the Malvern Hills and the Bristol Channel. It is popular, not only with walkers and golfers, but with kite flyers, who can take all good advantage of the strong winds on the hilltop. Flying model aircraft or drones is forbidden, but people still do it, I'm told.

My understanding is that the body does not appear to be that of a climber but of someone who seems to have fallen from the edge of the hill above the rock face. It is a sheer drop and there are no fences or barriers alongside the path.

Sophie

So, it could simply be a tragic accident then, Max?

Max

Well it could, of course, Sophie, except that it appears that the body may have been there for some time, certainly since yesterday. Walkers and golfers tend to be in couples or groups, or at least within sight of other people, and no one has reported a person falling or going missing from the golf course or along the footpath. I am told that the police are due to issue a statement later this morning, requesting information from members of the public who may have been in the area at the time.

Sophie

What about the person who found the body, Max? Do we know anything about him or her?

Max

Yes, Sophie, I spoke to someone at Cleeve Hill Golf Club, which is on top of Cleeve Hill, who was in the clubhouse when the body was found. She said that the lady who found the body had asked directions so she could take her dog for a walk along one of the footpaths below the rock face. I understand that this lady is not a local but was visiting the area from Essex. Her husband was about to go out on the course to play golf with friends. After calling 999 on her mobile phone, she contacted her husband to tell him what had happened. There were a number of other passers by waiting with her by that time, other walkers who had seen her on the path.

Sophie

So it looks like there was no attempt to conceal the body then, Max?

Max

That's right Sophie. The lady who found the body told my informant that it was not far from the path. But the ground at the bottom of the rock face is very uneven and overgrown in places, with some quite deep holes and small trees and bushes, so other people could easily have walked fairly nearby without ever seeing the body. This lady only went over there because her dog wouldn't come back when he was called. I am told that the lady is now in the bar in the golf club waiting to be interviewed by the police and the golf course has been closed.

Sophie

Did anyone else at the golf club see anything, Max?

Max

My informant said that the club manager went out and walked across the hill - which is extremely steep, by the way - to the spot above Cleeve Cloud where the dead person might have fallen. When he came back he said that he thought the ground might have been disturbed in one place, as if there had been a scuffle. But the police have cordoned off that area now, as part of the crime scene, so we won't know anything more until they release an official statement later.

Sophie

Thanks Max, we'll come back to you later.

That was Max Bennett in Cheltenham.

12.00
Cheltenian News Radio, Traffic News

One lane of the B4362 between Cheltenham and Winchcombe has now been opened and traffic queues are slowly beginning to disperse. But the area remains congested and is still best avoided.

13.00
Gloucestershire Constabulary Official Statement

A body has been recovered earlier this morning from common land at the foot of Cleeve Cloud on Cleeve Common near Cheltenham. It was discovered by a member of the public at about 0900 and appears to have been there overnight.

The body is of a male aged between 25 and 35 years. Forensic tests are currently being carried out. At this stage the death is being treated as unexplained. If you are aware of anyone from the local area who matches the description of the deceased and who has been missing since last night, please contact Gloucestershire Police in Cheltenham or any local police station.

We would like to hear from anyone who was out and about on the top of Cleeve Hill yesterday afternoon. Please make yourself known to Gloucestershire Police in Cheltenham or to the officers who are still at the crime scene. We are particularly interested in speaking to people who may have been flying a kite, model aircraft or a drone from Cleeve Hill, or who saw another person doing so.

17.00
Gloucestershire Constabulary Official Statement, Update

This statement is issued further to that released earlier today concerning the body recovered from the foot of Cleeve Cloud near Cheltenham this morning. Information received this afternoon from members of the public, together with the results of initial forensic tests and the recovery of items located with the body, indicate that the deceased person was subject to a violent attack prior to his death. The weapon used in the attack has not yet been recovered.

We are interested in hearing from a woman wearing a white jacket or raincoat seen walking yesterday along the footpath above Cleeve Cloud and carrying binoculars. We would also like to trace a man reported to have been flying an orange kite in the shape of a bird on Cleeve Hill at around 3.30 yesterday afternoon. We would emphasise that neither of these two people is suspected of any wrongdoing but may have useful information to help us understand the events leading to the death of this young male on Cleeve Hill.

In the light of further information received today, the death is now being treated as murder.

11 Months Earlier

1

Stevie Stone, horse racing tipster and vlogger to the Smart Girls, stood quietly in the parade ring at Cheltenham racecourse intently watching the big screen. Her long multi-coloured hair, free flowing when she appeared online, was knotted on top of her head and covered with her characteristic burgundy coloured hat. Apart from the fact that she was standing alone, she looked no different than any of the other connections, gathered in little groups around the parade ring, ready to follow the progress of their expensively acquired and nurtured equine possessions over the challenging obstacles of the undulating Cheltenham racecourse.

Stevie could see Merlin ap Rhys, the charismatic and talented Welsh jockey, urging the easy winner of the second race up the final hill to the finishing line. Merlin's mount was Fan Court, a smart young hurdler from the yard of Somerset trainer Ranulph Dicks. Stevie's online tipping guru, Jayce, with the help of the prescient Tabby Cat, had correctly predicted that the horse would win. The Racing Tips for Smart Girls app was still serving its female clientele well.

The fractious weather had not been kind to Cheltenham that Wednesday. In the days leading up to the April meeting at the racecourse, the air had felt mild and warm, with a tantalising promise of the summer yet to come. A light breeze had washed across the green slopes and rocky golden outcrops of the magnificent Cleeve Hill, which presided grandly over Prestbury Park from the North Eastern side. But today, dark and heavy clouds had blown down onto the hilltop, obscuring its warm face and replacing the usually pleasant view with scudding rain showers, sent intermittently on their way by the sharp gusts of an irritable wind. The occasional glimpse of a group of windbent trees along the skyline testified to the conditions to be experienced there by the golfers, walkers and sheep who all frequented the paths and slopes of the summit.

A fierce burst of rain suddenly drenched the parade ring and Stevie quickly grabbed at her hat to prevent it blowing away in the accompanying flurry of wind. On the screen, a triumphant Merlin was turning the handsome head of Fan Court towards the horsewalk. A female figure, which Stevie recognised as that of Sadie Shinkins, yard manager at Sampfield Grange, but today working for the Dicks yard, darted forward up the track to take Fan Court by the bridle. Fan Court jogged towards her, still full of beans despite his recent exertions. Stevie could see Sadie's happy face smiling up at Merlin, who grinned back at her and said something which made Sadie laugh. Beside them, some of the rain soaked crowd cheered and shouted their congratulations to Merlin but others had already scuttled back into the shelter of the grandstand.

Stevie wondered if the triumphant Merlin would agree to answer a few questions for the Racing Tips for Smart Girls vlog. Merlin had been hot property with the Smart Girls ever since Stevie had revealed his relationship with Sadie through the vlog Stevie had produced at the Cheltenham Festival a few weeks ago. Merlin, for his part, had always preferred to keep his options open when it came to women and had not enjoyed being outwitted by Stevie, especially as he still had no idea how she had found out about this interesting part of his private life. Merlin knew full well that he had told Stevie that he did not have a girlfriend, even inviting the Smart Girls to apply for the role, although at the time the statement had made him feel as guilty as Merlin ever felt about anything to do with his enjoyment of his sex life.

There were compensations, though, Merlin thought, as he looked down from his vantage point on the back of the jigjogging Fan Court at Sadie's radiant face. Merlin knew he could hardly complain about his luck in finding such an adoring and willing bedfellow as Sadie. He had certainly enjoyed an exciting time with her during the few months they had been together. And now that Sadie would soon be working for Ranulph Dicks, he would be getting some top quality rides of the equine kind into the bargain.

"You've done a great job with this lad, *cariad*," Merlin called down to Sadie, "Maybe you can get me all ready to race too, later on."

Sadie Shinkins could not help but laugh. Sadie thought she was the luckiest woman in the world at that moment. She was about to start a wonderful new job at a top racing yard, looking after three beautiful horses, one of whom had just won his race today. Mr Dicks had asked James Sampfield Peveril, Sadie's current employer, to let Sadie also join the Dicks team for today so that she could turn out Fan Court and see him in action. And she had the sexiest and most exciting boyfriend any woman could hope for. It was a shame that the forthcoming work assignment at the Dicks yard would last only until Amelia Dicks returned from her trip to Australia. But that was months in the future and she was not going to worry about it now. As for Merlin, she was not allowing herself to think about what would happen if he lost interest in her.

Sadie's only regret at present was that Mr Sampfield, as Sadie and the other yard staff called their employer, had sent their recent Gold Cup runner, Tabikat, back to his former trainer Brendan Meaghan in County Meath. The lordly and talented Tabikat was Merlin's only rival for Sadie's affections, and she had been heartbroken to hear that he was to return to the care of the Irish trainer, not to mention that of his erstwhile groom Claire O'Dowd. There had been some strange confusion about the horse's ownership, which Sadie had not really understood, and it seemed that the current owners, whoever they were, now wanted him back in Ireland. But Merlin was soon due to ride the beautiful horse again at the Punchestown Festival and Mr Sampfield had unexpectedly agreed that Sadie could accompany him there. Sadie had never been to Ireland before and was looking forward to the trip, not to mention the opportunity to see Tabikat again.

Coming up the horsewalk, Fan Court, with his human retinue, passed under the golden stone bridge which preceded the entrance to the parade ring. Sadie could see Mr Dicks and Mr Sampfield standing expectantly with Fan Court's excited owners, a smart looking middle aged couple, ready to welcome them to the victory post in the parade ring. The horses which had come second and third in the race had arrived ahead of them and, notwithstanding the wet and gusty conditions, were being washed down with cold water poured over their coats from yellow buckets. A damp and loyal collection of spectators had braved the miserable conditions to stand on the steppings opposite the winner's circle and cheered loudly as Fan Court made his approach.

Merlin quickly dismounted and started to remove Fan Court's tiny saddle. He was immediately surrounded by the two trainers and the enthusiastic owners, who seemed almost as pleased as if the horse had just won the Cheltenham Gold Cup. Sadie stood to one side, ready to lead the horse around in a small circle, whilst another of Ranulph Dicks' stable staff sluiced Fan Court down, and yet another held one of the brightly coloured buckets under the horse's nose to allow him a well deserved drink. Fan Court gulped briefly from the bucket and then knocked it away contemptuously with his dark nose. The blaze on his forehead, shaped like a bolt of lightning, glistened with water droplets.

As Sadie continued to walk the steaming Fan Court, her eyes narrowed. On the other side of the parade ring, she had spotted Stevie Stone, who seemed to be getting an iPad out of the leather bag which she was carrying over one shoulder. Sadie was not sure that she trusted Stevie. Who did she think she was, telling everyone that Sadie was Merlin's girlfriend on Gold Cup day? Not that the news had done Sadie any harm, but she had had to endure a few cheeky comments from the work riders at Sampfield Grange and the Dicks yard, all of whom were well aware of Merlin's womanising reputation. But Sadie was sure they were all secretly jealous, so she had simply smiled brightly and ignored them.

Someone else in the group had also noticed Stevie Stone's presence in the parade ring. James Sampfield Peveril, known to his friends in the racing world as Sam, had spotted her too. Sam had not seen Stevie since the running of Tabikat in the Gold Cup less than a month earlier. On that occasion, there had been no opportunity to speak to her, but he was still desperate to understand quite what had happened with the talented chaser which had been briefly in his care. On that day, Tabikat had run in the colours of Stevie's deceased mother, Susan Stonehouse, an eleventh hour change which had come as one more in a series of many unwelcome surprises visited upon Sam in the preceding six months. A group of connections had unexpectedly turned up to watch the horse run, including Stevie Stone herself, but they had all become distracted by other events as soon as the race was over, leaving Sam none the wiser as to why they were all there.

Sam's old school friend Frank Stanley, who appeared to have orchestrated many of the mysterious happenings in Sam's life, had promised Sam an explanation of matters relating to Tabikat and his Gold Cup run, and it had been arranged for Frank to visit Sampfield Grange later that month. Sam had many questions to ask, but experience had unfortunately shown him that he would probably not get the answers he wanted.

Prizes were duly presented to Fan Court's owners, to Ranulph Dicks, to Merlin and even to Sadie, whilst the wet crowd thinned out on the steppings. Merlin dutifully provided his comments on Fan Court's performance to a hovering TV interviewer, expressing confidence that the horse would be seen at next year's Festival.

"And what about Tabikat?" asked the smooth voiced interviewer quickly, before Merlin could get away, "How is he? You're riding him again at Punchestown later this month, I believe? Will he be back to run again for the Gold Cup here next year?"

Merlin was too professional to be taken off guard by this unexpected change to the line of questioning.

"Tabikat is fine," he said, "I'm lookin' forward to ridin' 'im again. As for next year, you'll 'ave to ask the trainer."

"The horse is back with Brendan Meaghan in Ireland, is that right?" persisted the interviewer, "He's left Sampfield Grange, then?"

"That's right," said Merlin shortly, "And I'm lookin' forward to ridin' for Mr Meaghan at Punchestown."

Horses were already coming into the ring ready for the next race, so the interviewer, sensing he would find out nothing useful from Merlin, moved away to start his commentary on the new runners. Fan Court's race was history now and Tabikat was far away in Ireland and not of immediate concern.

Fan Court himself was soon on his way back to the stables, accompanied by the Dicks staff. Ranulph Dicks had been invited by the ecstatic owners to celebrate in the Owners and Trainers bar.

"Will you join us too, Mr Sampfield Peveril?" the wife of the couple asked Sam, flashing him an arch smile. She rather liked the look of this country gentleman, with his politely reserved manner and smart brown fedora hat covering still mostly fair hair.

"Thank you, most kind of you, Mrs Todd," responded Sam, grabbing at the said hat as another gust of wind threatened to remove it, "I will follow you shortly, if I may. There is someone I need to speak to first."

"Make sure you come soon, or there'll be no champagne left," trilled Mrs Todd, putting her bejewelled hand on Sam's arm, whilst Mr Todd waited impatiently for her to join him.

As Ranulph Dicks and the Todds walked off in the direction of the Princess Royal stand, Sam turned towards the spot where he had seen Stevie Stone. Perhaps she could answer some of his questions whilst he was awaiting the visit of Frank Stanley later in the month.

But Stevie was no longer standing where he had previously spotted her. Instead, to Sam's exasperation, Stevie appeared to be in animated conversation with a woman who was standing in the Press area alongside the weighing room.

Some seconds earlier, Stevie had been surprised to hear a loud female voice calling out to her from the side of the parade ring.

"Stefanie Stonehouse, I knew it was you!" shouted the young woman, who was clad in a brown leather coat and boots, and was clutching a mobile phone. She had long curly black hair which was blowing around her sharp chinned face in the April breeze. Her dark eyes were staring straight at Stevie.

Stevie looked back at the newcomer, trying to think which members of the media might choose to address her so publicly by her real name. Her heart sank as recognition slowly dawned on her.

"Jessica Moretti!" she called back, hoping that she sounded happy to see the woman who had been such a thorn in everyone's flesh at school. Jessica's teenage character could have been quickly summed up by the words pushy, nosy and spiteful. She had been a bully, the sort who delighted in finding out other people's secrets and then using them to cause embarrassment. She would have made an excellent internet troll had the internet been generally available for such purposes in those days.

Stevie did not remember her old schoolfellow with any pleasure. Still, she thought, as she approached the white rail behind which Jessica was standing, she might have improved with age. A horse about to run in the next race passed along the track between them.

"I suppose I shouldn't have called you that, should I?" Jessica blared, once the horse had gone by, "You're Stevie Stone, racing tipster to the Smart Girls, nowadays, aren't you?"

It wasn't really a question, but Stevie nodded, and called back politely,

"And how about you, Jess? What brings you to Cheltenham races in April? I didn't know you were interested in horseracing."

"I'm not, really," Jessica stated loudly, thereby alienating everyone within earshot, had there been anyone interested enough to be listening. Most people were watching the horses as they were paraded around the large oval ring, and the Press area was otherwise deserted.

"Come out here, Stevie," Jessica continued, " And I'll tell you all about it."

So Stevie went unwillingly to join the other woman on the steppings and learned that Jessica was now a journalist, working for a social media news outlet called Hornblower Online. Stevie had heard of it. It sounded just the job for Jessica, she thought. The seedy outfit specialised in muckraking, researching and creating salacious accounts of the misdoings of politicians and celebrities and other people whose lives might be considered to be public property. It offered rewards to members of the public who could direct its researchers and online bots to suitably scandalous and reputationally damaging activities on the part of these, probably deserving, targets.

Jessica, leaving aside her moral shortcomings, was an extremely capable and outwardly highly engaging person. She had inherited good looks and an apparently sunny disposition from her Italian father together with creative flair and a strong work ethic from her Jewish mother. From both of them, she had also acquired a clever brain and a good memory. Hornblower Online, whose motto boasted *You do the dirt, we dish it up,* had been pleased to acquire her services.

"So why are you here then?" asked Stevie, curious to know what could be of interest to Hornblower Online at an April race meeting at Cheltenham racecourse.

"I'm watching to see who turns up to watch Penalty Kick run in the next race," Jessica told her, "The owner is a Premier League footballer who has been cheating on his wife with his sister-in-law. Hornblower is going to tweet to the world about which one he turns up with here today. If he comes here with both of them, that will be even better."

Stevie thought privately that the unfortunate trio were more likely to be sitting in a corporate box somewhere rather than shivering in the breezy chill of the parade ring, but she kept her views to herself.

"But what about you, Stevie?" Jessica said suddenly, "I was really sorry to hear about your mum and dad. Your mum was such a hero getting that gangster put away last winter. And then your poor dad dying of his injuries. I guess it was all too much for your mum in the end."

Such was Jessica's carefully summarised reference to the suicide of Susan Stonehouse, who had jumped in front of a train at Golders Green Underground station one freezing February morning fourteen months ago. A warning signal flashed up in Stevie's mind. Jessica's conversational gambits were rarely casual or sympathetic. Jessica was after something.

"Yes, it was all a terrible shock," Stevie said, declining to elaborate further.

"She was being harassed by the gangster's family, wasn't she?" Jessica went on, "What a dreadful thing to happen. And what about your sister? How did she take it all? Is she still an item with the rich boy from the banking family?"

"TK's fine," Stevie said, deliberately ignoring the other elements of Jessica's quick fire interrogation.

"Yes, I saw them both here on Gold Cup day," Jessica went on, her relentless narrative not skipping a beat, "And you too. What was all that about, the race card saying your mother was still the owner of the horse? What was its name?"

The warning signals in Stevie's mind flashed brighter and louder. But at least this was one question for which an answer had previously been prepared, although she had not expected the question to come from the long forgotten Jessica Moretti.

"The horse's name is Tabikat," responded Stevie, "When he came over from Ireland, whoever did the new registration information used an old record by mistake. By the time we found out, it was too late to change it. It's been corrected now, if you wanted to look the horse up."

"That must have been upsetting for you," said Jessica, her tone implying that she would not have cared one way or the other if anyone had been distressed by the error, "Who were the other people with you then? Are they the real owners?"

"The trainer invited a few people to watch Tabikat run," Stevie said, apparently thoughtfully, "Some of them were in one of the boxes in the main stand. I brought a couple of them into the parade ring."

"The woman looked a bit like your mum," Jessica pressed on, "Not a relative then? TK and the banking boy seemed to know her. And the man who was with her."

"Like my mum?" Stevie asked, a tone of surprise in her voice, "She was one of the trainer's staff. He just asked me to look after her - and the man who was with her. TK and Danny must have met them before. Maybe in Ireland?"

Much to Stevie's relief, Jessica's attention was suddenly diverted by the shrill sound of her mobile phone. Clamping the phone to her ear, Jessica listened in silence to the caller, then said curtly,

"I'll be right there."

"That was my tog," she told Stevie, "The target's in the Princess Royal stand. Got to go. Nice to see you."

And Jessica turned sharply away up the steppings and was gone.

Notwithstanding the story about the footballer, Stevie was absolutely certain that she herself was the real target of Jessica's interest that day. And, she thought glumly, whatever Jessica's reasons, they were bound to be very good for Jessica and very bad for everyone else.

2

Merlin ap Rhys had rarely worried about anything during his busy and largely fortunate life. Blessed with good health, a confident personality, a prodigious talent with racehorses, a casual success in attracting members of the opposite sex, and an ability to compartmentalise the various elements of his lifestyle, he had had little enough to worry about. Being followed by an ambulance as he carried out his challenging and dangerous work as a jump jockey had never bothered him. Getting injured was an occupational hazard and an unpleasant inconvenience. The possibility of getting so severely injured as to end his career was something he never even considered.

But he had never expected to be blackmailed. He was not even sure that that was what it was.

Following the April meeting in Cheltenham, Merlin had been booked to ride his Cheltenham Gold Cup horse Tabikat once again, this time in the equally competitive race for the Punchestown Gold Cup. The Irish contest, run in the last week of April over a slightly shorter distance than the Cheltenham event, was due to take place on the second day of the famous Punchestown Festival in Ireland.

Merlin had been surprised to be asked to ride the beautiful chaser in the Irish Festival's feature race. Tabikat had been returned to his former trainer Brendan Meaghan in County Meath shortly after his Cheltenham run and Merlin had assumed, wrongly as it turned out, that this would be the end of his association with the talented horse. But it appeared that either the trainer or the owners, whoever they were, had been impressed by Merlin's performance on their valuable possession, and Merlin's agent, Jackson Argyrides, had contacted Merlin in a state of excitement to say that Merlin had been offered the ride on Tabikat at Punchestown.

"That's great, Jacko," Merlin had responded, more pleased than he cared to say, "See if you can get me booked on anythin' else on the other days, will you?"

Jacko had promised to do his best and had indeed found two other rides for Merlin at the Festival.

Sadie, keen to see her erstwhile equine charge once again, had successfully petitioned Mr Sampfield to be allowed to accompany Merlin on the trip. She was now sitting next to Merlin on the crowded Embraer 195 aircraft, full of childish excitement at the novelty of the short flight to Dublin from Cardiff Airport.

Although Tabikat's owners had clearly decided to bypass the Grand National, in which the Gold Cup winner Macalantern had run into a place, Merlin had had a number of bookings to ride for other trainers at the Aintree Festival, which had preceded the April meeting at Cheltenham. And it was there that the trouble had seemingly begun.

Merlin had found the video recording on his mobile phone whilst he and Sadie were waiting to board the flight which would take them to Dublin. They had been sitting in a rather chilly Cardiff Airport, having spent an energetic night at Merlin's cottage in Chepstow. Scrolling idly through his messages, Merlin had found one which appeared to have no text but consisted simply of a video recording. Opening the file, he had suppressed an involuntarily gasp of shock.

The scenes shown in the recording on the screen had been taken in a bedroom at the Adelphi Hotel in Liverpool. Merlin had had no difficulty in recognising the semi-naked and dishevelled couple writhing noisily on the carpet next to the curtain-draped four poster before moving themselves onto the capacious and rumpled bed. Conscious of Sadie squeezed into the seat next to him, he had shut down the recording immediately, and made an excuse to go to men's toilets so he could review it properly.

"I remember 'er as looking better than that," Merlin thought, irrelevantly, as he struggled to understand not only who could have made the recording, but how they had done it. He had been certain that there had been no-one else in the room with them.

Swiftly reviewing the events which had led to the scenes in the pictures, Merlin recalled that he had been invited to a party at the Adelphi Hotel, a grand Edwardian edifice in the centre of Liverpool, by the owner of the spare ride he had picked up unexpectedly in the Aintree Grand National over two weeks ago. The horse's usual jockey had been stood down following a fall in an earlier race and Merlin had been the last minute replacement.

Merlin had had only one previous experience of competing in the world famous contest. On that occasion, his over enthusiastic mount had come to grief at Becher's Brook, quickly getting up and galloping off into the distance leaving Merlin face down in the Aintree mud, his back covered with a heap of green spruce. But this year he had been lucky enough to be handed an experienced chaser which, although unplaced, had completed the race the previous year. Merlin had thought gleefully that he was in with a chance, if not of winning, but of a place at least. In the event, he had brought the aptly named The King's Sorcerer home in fourth place, the horse having proved a classy and intelligent conveyance although it had become outpaced in the hard fought final stages of the race.

The owner, a loud and portly Essex builder, had been thrilled with the result.

"Me an' a few of the lads are 'aving a knees up at the Adelphi later," he had told Merlin, as the predominantly middle-aged lads whooped and cheered around him, "Make sure you're there too. We'll show you how to party!"

Merlin had not taken long to decide to accept the invitation. He had two days ahead of him with no rides, so had judged that he could risk abandoning his usually strict diet and teetotal regime for that night. Sadie had been safely at the other end of the country with the Sampfield Grange team. She had not been at home to watch the race live on television, as she had been out with Mr Sampfield at a point to point meeting, but her sister Kelly and brother-in-law Lewis had watched it in the Sampfield Grange kitchen and had texted her the news of Merlin's success.

ur brill wish I cd kiss u all over xx

Sadie had texted in turn to Merlin.

The party at the Adelphi had turned out to be less fun that Merlin had anticipated. Watching the Essex lads getting staggeringly drunk on champagne and lager - "We only drink stuff with bubbles in it" one had told him - he began to wish he had not accepted the owner's invitation. Champagne and lager contained too many calories even for his night off, so he had stuck to vodka interspersed with a few glasses of water. The exertions of the day and the alcohol had also made him ravenously hungry but no food appeared to be on offer at the Essex lads' boozy spree.

Just as Merlin, having heard that the partygoers were about to move their noisy celebrations to a nightclub, had been thinking he would call it a night, he had realised that an attractive woman in a strappy gold dress was standing next to him in the Adelphi's plush bar. For a second, Merlin had thought Sadie had come unexpectedly to join him. The woman was about her height and had wavy blonde hair and blue eyes. But that was where the resemblance ended. This woman was older and more slightly built than the fit and strong Sadie, and, when she spoke, it was in a soft voice with a local accent.

"Does yez know these people?" she had asked him.

And from that inauspicious beginning had started the events of an evening in which Merlin had not only taken his new female companion to dinner, but had ended up taking a keen part in the athletic bedroom scene which was to be replayed to him in audible and graphic detail on his phone just over two weeks later.

Merlin had shut down the phone and made a determined effort to compose himself. There was no message with the video recording, but he was in no doubt that one would arrive. He had returned to find a rather puzzled Sadie looking around for him, ready to board the flight. Now that the aircraft had taken off, the unfamiliar throbbing hum of its engines had caused Sadie to fall into a doze and Merlin had time to get his thoughts in order.

Why would someone send this recording to him? If it was an attempt at blackmail, it was not a very threatening one. He was unmarried, and, whilst the scenes were clearly embarrassing and might well cost him his current relationship with the loyal Sadie, they were not sufficiently incriminating to induce him to do something against his will. Merlin was no fool and had been quite sure that his companion for the night was an adult and also that she was not so drunk or otherwise incapacitated as to be unaware of what she was doing. Indeed, no-one viewing the video could have possibly thought that the woman was in any way a reluctant participant. She had worn no rings on either of her exquisitely manicured hands. Neither of them had taken drugs so no evidence of any such illegal activity could be shown to any watchers of the recording. When they had eventually parted company early in the morning, she had not asked for any form of payment, merely saying a polite thank you for an enjoyable time and wishing him a safe journey home.

Merlin was quite clear what blackmailers might want from a jockey. Inside information to help punters place advantageous bets on races, or stopping a horse from winning, were the sorts of things desperate riders might be prepared to consider if enough frightening pressure were to be exerted on them. But the contents of this recording hardly fell into that category.

So what was it about, then?

Merlin had a sharp mind and a good sense of self-preservation. He knew he needed to be prepared as well as possible for whatever was going to follow in the next message from the person who had sent the illicit recording. The information on the phone gave no clue as to the sender, whose identity was indicated only by the random collection of letters and numbers.

Merlin tried to bring together such few facts he knew about his partner in the unwelcome video. He recalled that she had plied him with questions about his work as a jockey and that he had been glad to talk about himself in response. Merlin had eventually given in to the temptation to drink champagne with dinner and it had certainly loosened his tongue. As a result he had found out little about her in return. He remembered only that she had told him that her name was Lara, that she lived in Cheshire and that her brother owned a racehorse. Her close fitting dress and skimpy silk underwear were of good quality. The room in which they had spent the night was one of the hotel's more expensive suites and had been booked for her, she said, by a friend who would be joining her the next day. And Merlin had been enjoying himself too much to ask any more questions.

As the aircraft landed smoothly in the afternoon sun at Dublin airport, Merlin decided that he had done enough thinking for one day. Until he had a better understanding of what he was up against, there was little more that he could do to prepare to deal with it. He resolved put it to the back of his mind until that time arrived.

A sharp easterly breeze had sprung up and the late April air felt chill as the arriving passengers descended the aircraft steps. But nothing could spoil Sadie's delight in the sight of her new surroundings.

"I can't wait to see Tabikat again," she enthused to Merlin as they walked into the terminal building, "Aren't you looking forward to riding him?"

Sadie's innocently happy mood was infectious and Merlin felt almost cheerful as they collected the rented car in which they were to drive the short distance to Brendan Meaghan's County Meath yard. The dry wind had cleared the skies into a fading blue as they made their way in the direction of Navan through green farmland towards the dull orange disc of the setting sun.

Brendan Meaghan's yard, inaptly named *An Féarach Beag*, proved to be a large and smart establishment with facilities which outshone even Ranulph Dicks' excellent set up in Somerset. Merlin had expected an old fashioned rural farm, but instead he was greeted with modern white American barns and an equally modern looking slate roofed house and associated outbuildings. Sadie was open mouthed with admiration as Merlin steered the hired Mazda sports car up the lengthy lane which formed the approach to a collection of impressive new buildings set in the middle of extensive open fields. The dull purple of shallow hills provided a distant backdrop, already hiding the lower edge of the rapidly fading sun. On one side of the lane, well kept gallops were laid down and on the other were paddocks in which a few horses were idly cropping the evening grass.

The rather clinical splendour of the racing yard was offset by the noise and calling of the numerous staff working around the stables. A young woman with spectacles and untidy black hair detached herself from the group and came running towards the car, waving a greeting. Sadie recognised her as Claire O'Dowd, the groom who had accompanied Tabikat during his time at Sampfield Grange.

"Hello Claire. Where's Tabikat?" asked Sadie, impatiently jumping out of the car before Merlin was even able to put on the brake.

Standing by the car and breathing in the cool evening air, Merlin watched the two excited women enter one of the nearest barns without a backward glance. A young man clad in blue jeans and a grey sweatshirt came towards him, holding out his hand.

"Mr ap Rhys? Welcome. I'm Declan Meaghan, Assistant Trainer," he said shortly, as Merlin shook the proffered hand.

"Merlin. Pleased to meet you, Declan," replied the jockey. Waving his free hand in the direction of the surrounding estate, he went on, "Great set up you 'ave 'ere. I was expectin' somethin' less modern I 'ave to say. This place 'as a long 'istory I should 'ave thought, but it all looks new."

Declan pulled off his denim cap to reveal a shock of coppery hair. He had clearly heard such comments from visitors before.

"Indeed it does, Merlin," he confirmed, "But the old buildings were all burnt to the ground fifteen years ago now. My father had to start again. We still have pictures indoors. But they are all that's left of the old place now. Want a quick tour, do you, before it gets dark?"

As Merlin and Declan set off in a mud spattered green Japanese SUV in the direction of the gallops beyond the buildings, Sadie was running her hand down Tabikat's soft mahogany coloured nose. Tabikat seemed pleased to see his former Sampfield Grange carer again, and nodded his head up and down, making quiet snorting noises. Claire O'Dowd, who seemed to be equally in love with the beautiful chaser, told Sadie excitedly, "To be sure, he's in top condition. Mr Meaghan has big hopes for him in the Gold Cup race at Punchestown. We all think we can win, so we do."

"I'm sure he can win with Merlin riding him again," Sadie enthused, patting Tabikat on the neck, "You'll be pleased to see him too, won't you, Tabsi?"

"Is that Merlin your boyfriend now?" asked Claire, who had little notion of subtlety, and was genuinely curious about the relationship, "I know you're staying together in the house tonight."

Sadie was not sure how to reply. Superstitiously, she sometimes thought that declaring that Merlin was her official partner might be tempting fate, but it was clearly difficult to reply in the negative when everyone at the Meaghan yard apparently knew that they were sleeping together. She took a deep breath.

"Yes, he is," she told Claire, "And he's really looking forward to riding out on Tabsi in the morning with you all. Is there a horse I can ride for you too?"

"To be sure, we could use the help," Claire told her, "Come and meet some of our horses now. And some of our staff too."

When Brendan Meaghan himself arrived home later that evening, he found Merlin and Sadie in his comfortable living room looking through an album of pictures of the original *An Féarach Beag*. Declan's mother, Doireann, was leading them through the book as though conducting a guided tour.

"And this was the original stable block," she said, pointing to a long and delapidated building with moss covered slates sliding down from the bowed roof. Before it was a large rough cobbled yard with loose boxes along either side. In the centre of the yard stood a young man holding a powerful looking horse by the bridle.

"And that," said Doireann, as if she were a conjuror pulling a rabbit from a hat, "Is Genie Foley, Tabikat's breeder, in the days when he was the stable jockey here. You'll have met him at Cheltenham?"

Sadie and Merlin agreed that they had met Mr Foley. Merlin added that they had met Mrs Foley too, whereupon Doireann frowned slightly, saying that Mrs Foley, if that was really her proper name, had not been part of Genie's life in those days.

"I think Mrs Meaghan must have fancied Mr Foley when they were younger," Sadie said to Merlin, as they undressed for bed in the cosy bedroom which had been assigned to them.

But Merlin was not listening. His eye had been caught by a picture on the front of one of a number of magazines which had been left on a small table in the corner of the room.

"And, just fancy," Sadie went on, oblivious to Merlin's sudden inattention, "Claire thought I might be bored with no TV and said she'd put some magazines in here for me. As if I'd be bored when I've got you with me!"

As soon as Sadie had gone into the bathroom, Merlin snatched up the magazine which lay on the top of the pile.

The magazine was called WOW! and its multi-coloured cover provided a garish run down of the gossipy information and pictures contained within its pages. The main story appeared to be about a glamorous looking woman called Abigail Alvarez, who was attempting to patch up her stormy marriage, a process which included forgiving her Premier League footballer husband his recent affair with her sister.

I still love him! shouted the headline, followed by the statement **Heartbroken Abby forgives them both.**

Merlin had never heard of Abigail Alvarez. But he certainly knew who she was - except that he had called her Lara.

3

Merlin had been booked for two rides on the first day of the Punchestown Festival. Both of them were for a Dorset trainer whose regular jockey was serving out a whip ban. Merlin had ridden for the dour and softly spoken Justin Venn in the past and had found his horses to be tough and well prepared for their races.

Merlin had resolutely put into the back of his mind the unwelcome surprise of seeing Abigail Alvarez's picture in the tawdry gossip rag. He had quickly reasoned that her infidelity to the Argentinian footballer husband she claimed to love so much was her problem, not his. After all, she had given him a false name and he had had no reason to suppose that she was married. A feeling of annoyance at the deliberate deception which had been practised on him was now beginning to creep into his thinking. Stuff her, he thought, she deserves whatever she gets.

The morning ride in the soft chilly air of County Meath had cleared his head and filled him with enthusiasm for the two days ahead. Tabikat had greeted him like an old friend, rubbing his handsome dark head along Merlin's arm, and had worked flawlessly on the gallops under an increasingly threatening iron grey sky. The Meaghan yard had several horses entered at Punchestown races and the string which had ridden out that morning and been a large and impressive one.

Sadie had also enjoyed herself riding a big bay gelding which had been entered in one of the following day's races. The animal, which had the distinctly non-Irish name Le Champignon Sauvage was due to be ridden in that event by Katie Meaghan, Brendan's daughter. Katie was already on her way to Punchestown with her brother Cormac. All of the Meaghan horses which had been entered at the Festival, with the sole exception of Tabikat, would be ridden by Katie and Cormac.

When Sadie had asked Claire O'Dowd, who was riding alongside her on an excitable young chestnut mare, why neither Mr

Meaghan's son nor daughter would be riding Tabikat too, Claire had shrugged.

"Look, we don't know anything about it at all," she had said, "Some agreement between Mr Meaghan and Mr Foley, I think it is. I know they want Tabikat back in England next year so they'll be keeping an English jockey on him."

"Merlin's Welsh," Sadie said, pedantically, not wanting to leave an error uncorrected.

"Well, on that side of the sea then," Claire had conceded as they had broken into a canter at a signal from Declan Meaghan who was driving alongside the string in the green SUV. The horses had pressed forward keenly and begun to fill their capacious lungs with the cold, sharp air. Their noisy breath had trailed in ghostly clouds behind them as they had ascended the shallow slope ahead, their hoofmarks joining the many others already imprinted on the deep rich loam.

After breakfast in the large and noisy household kitchen, in which everyone seemed to communicate by shouting, Merlin and Sadie had left *An Féarach Beag* and continued in their hired car to Punchestown racecourse.

"See you tomorrow, Tabsi," called Sadie, as they sped away down the long lane leading to the main road.

Merlin had never ridden at Punchestown before and had been impressed with the beautiful rural vista which had greeted him on arrival. Now he and Sadie were walking dutifully around the brilliantly green grass of the course. The Spring ground was perfect beneath their feet and Merlin felt confident of a great couple of rides later that afternoon. Pink and white blossom decorated some of the smaller trees at the side of the track, whilst the bare branches of their taller brethren stretched starkly towards the dull grey and grim sky. A sharp easterly breeze rustled through the bright yellow gorse speckled along the banks of the undulating course.

"This is going to be like riding on a roller coaster," giggled Sadie as they tramped determinedly up yet another slope on their circumnavigation of the picturesque track.

Merlin stole a glance at her. Sadie reminded him of a schoolgirl, taking in new experiences with enthusiasm, accepting everything and questioning nothing. Her disingenuous nature coupled with her warm and athletic body was one of the characteristics which still attracted him to her.

"Tell me *cariad*," he said, sliding an arm around her slim waist, "'ave you never thought about bein' a jockey yourself? You're a good rider, you are. 'Orses go well for you. They know you care about 'em and they try 'ard for you."

Sadie flushed crimson. Merlin rarely gave her compliments on her equestrian skills and she was so in awe of his talents that she did not expect praise from him.

"Like Katie Meaghan, you mean?" she responded, "I'd love to be like her."

"Well, you 'ave a think about it," Merlin told her, "Get Mr Sampfield and Mr Dicks to let you ride in some points an' see 'ow you get on. Now Kye's goin' to be a conditional and startin' to go in for the pro races, Mr Sampfield'll need a jockey for the points. Mr Dicks too with Amelia bein' away."

"OK," replied Sadie, "If you think I can do it. Thank you Merlin."

As she planted a big kiss on his cheek, Merlin felt a lump in his throat. Although his original interest in Sadie had been purely sexual, he suddenly realised that he had become dangerously fond of her. And now this business with Abigail Alvarez might spell the end of his relationship with Sadie. He had better make good use of their time at the swish hotel that night, he thought, before he was thoroughly covered with whatever shit was about to hit the fan.

"Come on, *cariad*," he said, kissing her in return, "Let's go and find Mr Venn."

Merlin's two rides for Justin Venn were in the second and fourth races on the first day's impressive card. Rather than wander about alone in the rapidly filling spectators' area, Sadie had arranged to join the *An Féarach Beag* team for the afternoon and so she was able to see the capable Katie Meaghan at close quarters. Watching from the side of the hedged parade ring as Katie was legged up onto a solid and experienced grey gelding, on which she would compete around the banks course in the centre of the open and sweeping parkland of the racing arena, Sadie was entirely unaware that she herself was the object of interest to someone looking from one of the windows of the gabled buildings which stood behind her.

Justin Venn's horse, well prepared though it was, did not prove to be enough of a match for two of the Irish horses competing in Merlin's first race. The perfect ground on the course produced an excellent contest, but Merlin was able only to secure third place in the competitive novice hurdle event. If Justin Venn was disappointed, he did not show it, merely pushing his tweed cap back from his forehead and saying to Merlin,

"'E's done well 'nough, Murrlin. Thur'll be another day for 'im."

Mr Venn seemed hardly more animated when Merlin brought his horse home in first place in the fourth race, which was a Grade 1 chase with a classy field of runners. The race was made more eventful by a shower of hail which suddenly blew down from the gloomy sky and obscured the competitors from view as they entered the back straight to take the two jumps which lay in the dip on that part of the course. By the time the finish was being fought out between Merlin's horse and two other runners, a sharp burst of sunlight had briefly broken through a gap in the charcoal clouds and illuminated the bookies' colourful umbrellas by the finish line. The frantic crowd was mostly yelling for the Irish horses, but a respectful smatter of applause went up as the Venn horse crossed the finish line less than half a length ahead of the locally trained favourite.

Merlin returned to the parade ring to be greeted by triumphant connections and a small smile from the trainer. He had had the horse flat to the boards all the way around the course and had had a niggling concern that the tough and hard galloping creature would not be able to sustain the pace to the end of the race. But the horse had lived up to the Venn's yard reputation for producing hard fighting stayers and it had resolutely refused to be passed in the dying moments of the race.

Justin Venn had spotted Sadie watching them and clapping as he and Merlin accepted their prizes on the windblown platform in the parade ring.

"That the gurrl 'oo led up that Chel'nem Gold Cup 'orrse of your'n? The one you'rr on again tomorrow?" he asked Merlin, "She still with Sampfields?"

Merlin replied in the affirmative, adding that Sadie was about to go to Mr Dicks' yard on their return home.

"You c'd do wurrse than roide furr Dicks," Justin Venn opined, glumly, "An' Oi'll still be 'ere if 'e don' wan' un".

As Merlin and Sadie drove back to the country house hotel together, Merlin reflected contentedly that it had been a good day. Sadie was chatting happily about everything she had seen, including Katie Meaghan's ride in the cross country event and Cormac Meaghan's less successful ride in the race which Merlin had won. The Meaghan staff had been generous in their praise of Merlin's victory, perhaps supposing that taking some of his reflected glory was at least some small consolation for their horse's poorer than expected run.

The upmarket hotel in which Merlin had booked their room for the night proved to be a large and rambling establishment built in dark grey stone in the style of a medieval castle. A curving gravel drive led up to a small iron bridge which spanned an artificial moat in front of the building. Disappointingly, the moat did not extend around the sides and back of the imposing walls and appeared to serve a purely decorative rather than a defensive purpose. A group of paddling water fowl in the water completed the effect.

Sadie, who had not expected anything so grand, was ecstatic as they were shown into a large and spacious bedroom overlooking an ornamental lake on which grey geese and bevies of bobbing mallards ducked and splashed. A large swan took off from the lake surface, its black feet propelling it through the water until it eventually became airborne. Crowded bluebells surrounded the boles of trees overhanging the water whilst flat green parkland extended away into the distance towards the slowly setting sun.

Merlin's first observation about the lavish bedroom was that it had a four poster bed. This grand piece of furniture was draped with green and gold curtains swept back neatly with tasselled ties against the turned wooden posts. Matching cushions had been carefully placed against the plump white pillows and a smooth gold counterpane covered the rest of the bed's surface. Soft white rugs lay on the floor on either side.

The sight of the four poster bed was an unwelcome reminder to Merlin of the disagreeable video recording lurking in his mobile phone. He had checked the phone a few times during the day, but the sender of the video had not yet seen fit to contact him again. Merlin had no illusions but that a further message would arrive at some stage and took advantage of Sadie's preoccupation with the view of the park outside the window to form an assessment of how the recording might have been obtained.

Someone had clearly set up some kind of hidden camera in the bedroom in the Adelphi. As this had not been done when he and Lara, the name by which he was determined to continue to call the woman in the recording, were in the room, it followed that it must have been done in advance. So either Lara herself had put it there, or someone she had been with in the room had done so. Or, he supposed, a member of the hotel staff could have set it up, either because they were a voyeur, or because they were hoping to capture some revealing pictures of the well known female guest with a view to threatening to publish them on social media. So maybe the recording of his sexual encounter with Lara, or Abigail Alvarez or whoever she was, had been an extra stroke of luck for that person. Whoever had done this clearly knew who he was, since they had sent the recording directly to his mobile phone.

The images, Merlin remembered, had been captured from an angle above the foot of the bed. It was a static frame, suggesting that the camera, or whatever had made the images, had been fixed in one place. Taking his iPad from the overnight bag which had been placed carefully on a carved linen chest at the bottom of the bed by the uniformed hotel porter, he held the device above his head so that the camera lens embedded in the casing showed on the screen a view of the bed and part of the floor. No doubt the perpetrator had rigged up something more sophisticated and less obtrusive to make the recording, but the view it showed would be much the same. Standing on the linen chest, Merlin soon found a spot where the iPad screen produced exactly the angle he was seeking.

So engrossed was he in his self imposed task that the sound of Sadie's voice made him jump.

"What on earth are you doing, Merlin?" asked Sadie, who had been following his actions with mystification.

"Just checkin' somethin'," said Merlin vaguely, hastily closing the cover of the smart tablet device.

But Sadie had seen the iPad and the conclusion she immediately reached saved Merlin from finding any explanation.

"Are you thinking of doing a video of us in bed?" Sadie asked, her blue eyes wide with excitement.

"Would you like that, *cariad*?" asked Merlin, slightly surprised at her enthusiasm, but relieved to be let off the hook of thinking up a convincing reason for his behaviour.

"Well, I could keep it to look at when I haven't seen you for a while," Sadie told him, "Then I won't miss you so much."

And so it was that Merlin and Sadie spent the next fifteen minutes building a makeshift camera rig which consisted of an iPad balanced on top of a leather overnight bag placed on a chair which was standing on top of the linen chest at the bottom of the four

36

poster bed. Then, for the second time that month, Merlin gave a convincing performance as the male lead in a blue movie.

"If I ever stop ridin'," he said, as he and Sadie, sprawled naked together amongst the scattered pillows and cushions, reviewed the entertaining recording, "P'rhaps I can make a livin' doin' this."

"You'd be brilliant," Sadie told him.

But Merlin had no time to think further about a future career as a porn star. Another message from the unrecognisable address had just pinged into his Inbox.

4

Six fit, powerful and immaculately turned out horses were circling close to the start for the Punchestown Gold Cup. From his seat on the back of the regal and untroubled Tabikat, Merlin watched his fellow jockeys carefully. Whatever they might have said to each other before the race, there was no guarantee that their running plans would be carried out in the manner expected. The horses sometimes forced unexpected decisions on them, but occasionally the jockeys secretly had something entirely different in mind.

Merlin was familiar with most of the other runners and their riders. Three of them had competed against Tabikat less than six weeks ago for the Cheltenham Gold Cup. Less Than Ross, Stormlighter and Champagne Cork were in the field again today. The victorious Macalantern, however, had gone on to run in the Grand National at Aintree in the hope of achieving a double victory. But his owners had been disappointed in this ambition, although Macalantern had achieved a creditable third place, and the horse had now been put away for the summer somewhere not far away in County Kildare. The two remaining contenders in the Punchestown race were Irish horses against which Merlin had not raced before.

Tabikat had been led up in the parade ring by his *An Féarach Beag* groom, Claire O'Dowd, who had remained completely confident that Tabikat would win the race.

"He'll take to this course just right, you'll see," she had told Merlin, as she had released her hold on the bridle to allow Tabikat to canter away to the start.

Brendan and Declan Meaghan had said much the same thing to Merlin during breakfast at *An Féarach Beag* the previous day. Remembering his experience at Cheltenham, Merlin's question had been whether the ground would be soft enough to suit Tabikat's natural way of running. This concern had been brushed aside by the Meaghans.

"This course is entirely different," had said Brendan, firmly, "You'll be going right handed – not that the horse minds it either way round - and you'll find that there is no hard climb going to the finish. The ground does not need to be soft, just a bit of cut, and you'll have that at Punchestown. And the distance is shorter. There'll not be a bit of bother with it, to be sure."

"It's a great chance for Tabikat," Declan had added, meaningfully, "So we're expecting to see you both first over the finishing line, now."

Merlin had thought briefly of Declan's brother, Cormac Meaghan, already on his way to the racecourse with the Meaghan horses which had been entered on the first day of the Festival. He was sure the family would have preferred Cormac to be Tabikat's rider. A less confident man than Merlin might have been daunted by the prospect of being considered a weaker jockey than Cormac. But Merlin had no such misgivings.

"And what about the owners?" Merlin had asked, still curious about the apparent change in ownership of Tabikat which had taken place, to everyone's surprise, during the Cheltenham Festival itself.

There had been a pause, until Brendan Meaghan had eventually said, "I believe Mrs Foley and some people from the bank will be there tomorrow."

"The bank?" Merlin had asked, becoming aware that silence had fallen in the previously noisy kitchen, as the yard staff listened with sudden attention to his discussion with their employer, "I thought that the 'orse had been moved to a new owner."

"No, no, that was all a mistake," had said Brendan hurriedly, "Some clerical error at the Sampfield Peveril place. The horse is still in the ownership of Levy Brothers International."

"So this Susan Stone'ouse isn't the owner then?" Merlin had persisted, referring to the name which had appeared in the race card that day, "I wore her colours when we ran in the race. Purple with gold stars, it was."

"Well, she did use to be the owner, so I believe," Brendan had replied carefully and had fallen silent.

"So the people who came to see Tabikat run at Cheltenham were from the Levy Brothers bank then?" Merlin had continued, not really sure why he wanted to know.

"Well that I cannot say," Brendan had seemed to want to be finished with the conversation, "You will need to ask Sampfield Peveril about that. The horse was with him then, not me."

Brendan had then got up abruptly from his chair and had called out to his staff that there was work to be done and so the kitchen had quickly emptied. Merlin and Sadie had been left sitting alone at the breakfast table, feeling that there was some mysterious secret which they were not to be told.

"Screw them," Merlin had said, as they stood up to leave, "Makes no difference to me, so long as the 'orse is fit to run. It's a tough ask for 'im so soon after Cheltenham."

In the preliminaries to the Punchestown Gold Cup race, Sadie, with no official role to play on this occasion, had positioned herself amongst the many spectators alongside the part grass, part soft-surfaced parade ring. She had watched Claire leading Tabikat proudly along the black path and had called out a quiet word of encouragement to the horse, which had stalked grandly by, looking straight ahead, dark ears pricked, as if about to go out to do battle with some armoured knight errant on his back. Sadie had fancied that Tabikat had favoured her with a lordly glance and the good natured Claire had certainly smiled and waved.

Remembering the odd conversation at breakfast the previous day, Sadie had watched as Merlin appeared in the parade ring dressed in the blue and gold silks of the Levy Brothers International bank. He had joined a group in the centre of the grassed area which had comprised Brendan and Declan Meaghan and three other people.

Two of them were a young couple, the man dark and bespectacled and dressed in what looked like a business suit, the woman small and pretty with curly dark hair and wearing a well cut red and white patterned dress and matching jacket. The third person was an older woman, dressed less formally, who clearly, from her smiling greeting to him, knew Brendan Meaghan well. Merlin, she could see, had been introduced to all three of them as he came out to join the group.

Sadie had been too far away to hear what was said to Merlin. Tabikat's supporters today were 'Mrs Foley and some people from the bank', so Mr Meaghan had told them. But this lady was not Mrs Foley, a woman who Sadie remembered well, as she had complimented Sadie on her turn out of Tabikat at Cheltenham racecourse.

Sadie, like the entire Meaghan yard, had every confidence that Tabikat and Merlin could win the race. Now that the horses had gone down to the start, the parade ring enclosure had become less crowded as the spectators migrated to the grandstands to watch the race. Sadie knew that the best views of the action were to be seen on the big screen facing the parade ring, so she made no attempt to move from her present position by the hedged fence. The Meaghans and their guests also remained standing where they were, their gazes fixed on the large monitor.

The racecourse commentator, speaking in an understated and flowing Dublin accent, had informed the assembled crowd about the horses before they left the parade ring and went down to the start. As at Cheltenham, Tabikat's name was listed last in the alphabetical list of runners, and he was the last horse to be introduced by the commentator.

"And finally, horse number 6 is Tabikat, ridden by Merlin ap Rhys and trained by Brendan Meaghan. Tabikat has a strong chasing record in both Ireland and England and was last seen in the Cheltenham Gold Cup. Today he is running in the blue and gold colours of Levy Brothers International."

The image of Merlin cantering Tabikat down to the start was replaced by a show of the betting on the race. Tabikat, it appeared, was second favourite, going off at odds of 5/2. The only horse showing shorter was Less Than Ross, who was the 9/10 favourite.

As post time approached, Sadie felt her fists clench involuntarily. The screen was now displaying the horses walking in a tidy group towards the starter who stood atop a small flight of steps with a white flag raised above her head. After what seemed to Sadie like an age, but could have been no more than a few seconds, the flag dropped, and the six horses surged forward like missiles fired from a gun.

"Come on Tabikat, come on Merlin," muttered Sadie under her breath.

"The flag is down and they're off and running with seventeen fences before them," began the commentator, "And it's the outsider Uisce Dorcha which shows first with the field packed in close behind. Champagne Cork is tucked in at the rear, just behind Less Than Ross and Tabikat who race together. Stormlighter and Arthur's Council are just in front of them."

The route to the first plain fence lay over rising ground. Sadie watched as the small field poured over it effortlessly. The track rose further then sloped away towards the second fence, where clumps of bright yellow gorse in the background reflected the sharp April sunshine. Although cold, it was a beautiful bright day with scarcely a breath of the chill breeze which had swept across the course the previous afternoon.

Approaching the second fence, Merlin found that the other jockeys had so far little to say. Intensely competitive though the race was, no-one was yet showing his hand, and everyone seemed content to hunt along with the field, as if it were a training exercise, albeit a highly classy one. They were moving confidently at a good speed. The momentum carried the horses smoothly over the second fence, after which the course began to turn to the right. Tabikat was galloping effortlessly towards the third fence and took off accurately on a long stride, moving slightly ahead of Less Than Ross.

"Those Meaghans were right," Merlin said to himself, as Tabikat also winged the fourth fence and landed with no loss of momentum on the other side, "There's nothing going to touch this 'orse if we can keep this up."

"And as they make the turn towards the two fences which lie before them in the straight," the commentator continued, his voice an even monotone, "The whole field is going well and remains well grouped. Uisce Dorcha continues to lead the way as they pass the grandstand."

Merlin heard the booming surge of cheering as the six horses thundered past the closely gathered spectators and the point of the course which would be the winning line after one more circuit. The track soon ran uphill again, providing a good line to the seventh fence.

As Merlin had expected, the race began to take shape only as the horses approached the eighth fence. The relative positions of the runners as they passed the grandstand had provided few clues as to the likely finishing order, but now the race was moving on towards the further side of the course, a new urgency began to enter proceedings.

So far, none of the jockeys had been anything other than apparently relaxed on their respective contenders. The horses themselves had bounced round the track effortlessly, as would be expected from a field of such calibre, but Merlin could sense that the cracking pace was beginning to tell on the three horses at the head of affairs. He saw their jockeys become slightly more animated, shouting encouragement and giving a few nudges, but not yet going for their whips. They would need them later if they were to have any chance of a win.

"Go frit, Tabikat, *bachgen*," said Merlin softly into the dark ears which were pricked up in front of him, a black line of neatly tied golf ball plaits running back towards him down the horse's neck, "We got this, we 'ave."

"The horses are running downhill now to the two fences in the dip," the commentator was informing the crowd, "The first is a ditch which they all clear well. Tabikat and Less Than Ross are moving forward as they approach the eighth from home. And it seems that the leaders are beginning to tire as they enter the back straight."

The back straight was an uphill section of the course. Most of the jockeys were shouting and yelling now as Uisce Dorcha surrendered the lead and began to drop back through the field. His jockey, who had never expected the horse to win, yelled "Go for it Merlin, you bastard!" as Tabikat hurtled past, his level stride never faltering, his breath sounding in long even snorts.

Three more fences saw the runners back at the point of departure. Merlin was increasingly aware of the stands filled with spectators on the opposite side of the open arena. Riding alongside him still were Less Than Ross and Champagne Cork, the voices of their jockeys urging them forward. Of the three previous leaders, only Stormlighter seemed still to be in touch with them. Merlin could hear his rider's loud encouragement to the horse as it hammered along behind the three which now looked as if they would be in the mix at the finish.

"Coming to this last ditch, there are five fences and four furlongs still to go," announced the commentator, sounding slightly more excited, "There's a battle for the lead between Tabikat and Less Than Ross. Champagne Cork and Stormlighter are still there as they approach the bend".

Sadie had watched Tabikat and Merlin intently throughout the race. Merlin had not moved a muscle and Tabikat had apparently needed little encouragement. They're really enjoying this, thought Sadie, with a pang of envy. In the centre of the parade ring, she could see Tabikat's connections becoming excited. The older woman was jumping up and down, her fingers gripping Brendan Meaghan's arm. The young man in the business suit was asking

44

Declan Meaghan a question, in response to which Declan was nodding furiously and pointing at the screen. The pretty wife was listening intently to what they said.

Over the fourth and fifth fences from home, the commentator informed the crowd, there was no change in the order, although Champagne Cork and Stormlighter were beginning to struggle. And by the time that the horses reached the home turn, it was quite clear to everyone watching, without any need of the commentator's intervention, that the race was now a head to head battle between Tabikat and Less Than Ross.

Both horses flew over the second last, the exertions of the race now beginning to tell on them. But they had both made it up the Cheltenham hill less than six weeks ago, and neither of them was about to give up. Nor were their jockeys, both of whom went for their whips as the final fence loomed.

Merlin could hear the screaming of the crowds. Tabikat was an Irish horse and relatively locally trained, so he knew many of the spectators would be calling the horse's name. The adulation was like nectar to Merlin. His heart was already racing from the exertion of the race, but the hubbub of the crowd, the bright sunny sky and the sensation of the powerful animal forging along underneath him made him feel like a god.

"Show them who's boss!" he yelled at Tabikat as the horse approached the final fence.

Tabikat did not need to be told. He sailed over the last obstacle as if it were the first and swept across the finishing line a full two lengths ahead of Less Than Ross.

"And Tabikat wins the Punchestown Gold Cup," shouted the commentator, sounding animated at last, "Less Than Ross is second, and it's a long way back to Stormlighter in third place."

Merlin, standing in the stirrups, still breathless and panting, pulled Tabikat up as they passed alongside the bookies' brightly coloured umbrellas by the rails. The horse came quickly to a walk, snorted and blew for a few seconds, before his usual demeanour of regal calmness came over him once again. Merlin, by contrast, was shouting and punching the air, as Less Than Ross's jockey trotted the defeated horse over to congratulate the victor.

A dishevelled and excited Claire O'Dowd ran forward from the horsewalk to take Tabikat's bridle.

"Well done, well done, you lovely horse," she told Tabikat, patting him fiercely on the neck, her round face illuminated by a massive smile.

A TV interviewer was approaching Merlin as Claire walked the steaming horse in a circle. The beaten horses were already making their way off the course.

"Well done you, too," the interviewer, a retired jockey, told Claire enthusiastically. He seemed almost as pleased as Merlin with Tabikat's win.

Sadie had been jumping up and down and shrieking Tabikat's name as the final stages of the race had unfolded on the screen. As she watched Merlin giving his comments to the interviewer, she became aware of a sharp-faced woman standing quietly beside her.

"That was exciting," the woman commented to Sadie, sounding anything but excited, "I think you have some connection with the winner, don't you? I saw you with the horse at Cheltenham, if I'm not mistaken?"

Sadie was too overjoyed to ask herself why she should have been recognised by this stranger.

"Yes, Tabikat used to be at our yard until a few weeks ago," she replied.

"You must be very pleased," the woman went on, "My name is Jess, by the way. I'm a friend of Stevie Stone. I saw her with your horse in the parade ring at Cheltenham that day, didn't I?"

"Is Stevie Stone here?" asked Sadie, distractedly, still staring at the screen as Claire began to lead Tabikat and Merlin towards the horsewalk, the interviewer still holding his microphone under Merlin's nose.

"Not today," Jess replied, 'She doesn't cover Irish racing. I guess the smart Irish girls just have to fend for themselves."

The force of the sarcastic comment was entirely lost on Sadie, who did not respond. Attempting to get her attention, Jessica Moretti, who had carefully sought Sadie out that afternoon, went on, "Those people who are with your horse today. Do you know them?"

"Well, two of them are the trainers, Mr Meaghan and his son," Sadie told her, as Tabikat continued along the horsewalk towards the parade ring, preceded by two red coated riders on big grey hunters, "I don't know the others."

"I don't think they were at Cheltenham, were they?" Jessica persisted.

"No, I didn't see them there," Sadie told her, "There was just someone who worked with us at the yard and some people I think Mr Sampfield invited. I don't get involved with the owners much. Mr Sampfield owns most of our horses himself anyway."

Jessica sensed that she was fighting a losing battle with Sadie, who was clearly only half listening to her and keen to get over to the parade ring to meet the horse as it arrived to its triumphant welcome. She risked a stab in the dark.

"Did Mr Sampfield invite Mrs Stonehouse?" she asked quickly, "Wasn't that the lady in the parade ring with him at Cheltenham?"

"I'm sorry, I don't know Mrs Stonehouse," Sadie said hurriedly, "It must have been one of our yard staff you're thinking of, Isabella Hall. Sorry I must go now."

But Jessica had no qualms now about letting Sadie off the hook. As she watched the younger woman running over towards the entrance to the parade ring, where cheering and shouting and loud music could now be heard, Jessica sucked in her breath.

"Isabella Hall," she said quietly to herself, "Now we're getting somewhere."

5

Sam had watched the running of the Punchestown Gold Cup in the comfort of the capacious drawing room at Sampfield Grange. The drawing room was a well furnished and comfortable retreat with long and wide leaded windows which overlooked the rear of the old manor house. Anyone sitting on one of its large sofas would always have a fine view of the Sampfield Grange horses during their daily passage along the narrow track which connected the training yard to the practice jumps and gallops on the hills above.

As at Punchestown, the weather that day at Sampfield Grange was bright and clear. Gone were the strong gusts of the previous day, while the hedgerows and uplands behind the warm stone buildings seemed to have at last awoken from their winter sleep. A green shimmer glowed from the bark and branches of the nearby trees as new buds struggled to form. Bluebells were beginning to appear in clumps along the side of the track, gradually replacing the shivering snowdrops and windblown daffodils which had brightened the route over recent weeks. The sound of sheep and their lambs could be heard, carried on the light breeze from the other side of the house, and mixed with the subdued and repetitive sounds of small songbirds in the hedges and shrubbery of the kitchen garden. The harsh croak of crows cruising the blue and empty skies could occasionally be heard from overhead.

Sam had been as elated by Tabikat's victory as if he had trained the horse for the race himself. The supersize TV screen in the drawing room was a recent purchase, although the carefully concealed satellite dish alongside the far wing of the rambling house had been there for some years, supplying a signal to the kitchen television, on which the race had been watched by Lewis and Kelly, the Sampfield Grange household staff.

During his lifetime, Sam had experienced many hours watching a much older TV set with his mother, as they had reviewed conscientiously recorded performances on the part of the Sampfield Grange horses in point to point races and at numerous horse trials. Stacks of old fashioned, and now useless, video tapes sat in their cardboard cases on the deep shelves behind one of the long sofas. Sam was still finding it hard to accustom himself to the sharpness of the image on the high definition screen as compared with what now seemed to be hopelessly grainy and shaky pictures recorded so carefully in earlier years.

Sam's Australian mother, Geraldine Elliot, had been a top class event rider in her younger years and had continued to ride to the local Charlton Foxhounds until creeping arthritis in her spine and an irreparably damaged hip and knee had eventually forced her permanently onto the ground. Having spent the majority of her life on the back of a horse, Raldi, as she had been known since childhood, had found herself at something of a loose end, her husband Richard having by that time been dead for several years. Much to Sam's dismay at the time, she had interfered relentlessly in his training programmes for the Sampfield Grange horses, until one day she had suddenly announced that she was leaving her home of over fifty years to return to her family in Australia.

It had not been clear to anyone at Sampfield Grange that this was a wise move on Raldi's part, but she had insisted on the plan. So, arrangements had been made with Sam's cousin, Teddy Urquhart, for Raldi to return to the cattle and sheep station in Queensland on which she and her two sisters had been born and raised. Teddy was the son of Raldi's older sister Lucinda and was now in charge of the vast livestock operation. In the face of everyone's misgivings, Raldi had made it safely by air to Brisbane, whence she had been taken off into the outback and into the bosom of her large Australian family, leaving Sam to run Sampfield Grange and its training yard alone.

Raldi herself had been under no illusions that there was little more she could do for her son, who was by then in his forties, and, notwithstanding Raldi's efforts to persuade him to marry, remained single. Raldi had hoped that Sam would somehow grow out of his early love for his schoolfriend, Frank Stanley, but, notwithstanding the number of suitable young women who became part of her son's social circle in the ensuing years, Sam had shown no inclination to choose one of them as his wife. Raldi had

had high hopes for the lively and attractive Helen, the daughter of an eventing friend, but that young woman too had slipped through Raldi's fingers and was now married to Sir John Garratt, a prominent musician and racehorse owner. Raldi had therefore reluctantly decided to retire from the matchmaking battlefield and to leave Sam to solve the problem of his future without her interference.

Raldi had been in Queensland for over two years and her mind had now succumbed to the vicious and unassailable enemy of dementia. Sam sometimes wondered if her sudden decision to return to Australia had been prompted by an early recognition of the onset of the condition and a wish for no-one amongst her friends in England to witness her decline. Her life was now lived much as it had been when she was a child, as though she had never left the cattle station. Sam had given up all attempts to speak to her by telephone or, more recently, through Skype. Raldi did not recognise the name of her son, or even remember that he existed, and Sampfield Grange had been completely wiped from what was left of her memory.

"Aunt Raldi's happy enough," his cousin Teddy had told him during one of their occasional Skype conversations, "Thinks she's a little kid again. We'll look after her just fine, James, don't you worry. Plenty of room for her here."

Sam was saddened to know that his talented, uncompromising and tough mother could not remember any of her long and action packed life in England. But the assurances from Teddy that she was happy had provided him with some consolation for the lost memories, many of which were captured in the now useless video recordings. Like his mother's mind, Sam thought, they were lying there unused, waiting to be covered by a blinding layer of remorseless dust. Kelly ensured that the boxes were regularly cleaned, but they nevertheless remained closed and without purpose.

At least, Sam knew, Raldi had been spared the knowledge that his association with Frank Stanley had been resumed, more than thirty years after Raldi had banished Frank from the house.

Indeed, Frank had been with him only yesterday, avoiding Sam's questions about Isabella Hall, but unexpectedly agreeing to ride out with him in the afternoon. The passionate schoolboy relationship of old was long gone, but Sam now hoped that a friendship of sorts might replace it. And Lady Helen Garratt, as she had become, was still part of his equestrian life, and expecting his assistance with an ambitious project which she had in mind. Sam had a yard full of good horses, not to mention a potentially talented conditional jockey to ride the best of them. Things had moved on rapidly at Sampfield Grange since Raldi had left, he thought, and had at last enabled him to start to come out of the self-created shell in which a combination of dyslexia and disappointed love had caused him to exist for much of his adult life.

Tabikat's race at Punchestown had taken place late on the sunny Spring afternoon. The striking of one of the antique clocks in the hall outside reminded Sam that it was time he went down to the yard. The point to point season would soon be coming to an end and the opportunities for Kye, his soon to be licensed conditional stable jockey, to get a race or two under his belt in the current season were fast diminishing. The Hunter Chase Evening at Cheltenham and the Badminton Horse Trials would soon be over and the Flat racing season was already well under way at racecourses across the country.

Lewis and Kelly were nowhere to be seen as Sam passed through the kitchen with its large, square table at which the work riders clustered to eat their breakfast after the morning rides. Now the room was silent and deserted. Most of the work riders were part-timers, many of them teenagers recruited by Sadie from the farms and villages in the local area, and went home once the morning lots had returned to the yard. The only permanent stable staff nowadays were Sadie, acting as yard manager and head lass, and Kye. A couple of the work riders came back to help after they had finished school in the late afternoon.

Sam had not seen anything of Sadie on the TV screen when he had watched the triumphant return of Tabikat to the parade ring at Punchestown racecourse, although he had quickly recognised

Claire O'Dowd leading the horse towards the winner's station. As he walked along the path which connected the house to the neat square stable yard, he reflected that Merlin had looked as self-confident as ever on Tabikat and wondered whether he would be able to continue to ride the gelding in the future. Sam fully intended that Merlin should be retained as the jockey of Curlew Landings, the talented Sampfield Grange hurdler, once the National Hunt season began again in late Autumn. Curlew had now been put away for the summer after a relatively successful first season as a novice and was currently enjoying himself in the pastures above the stable yard.

Sam recalled too that Sadie would be joining the Dicks yard on her return, leaving Kye and Sam to oversee the Sampfield Grange operation alone. Over the summer, when many more of the horses would be turned away along with Curlew after the end of the season, this was manageable with the assistance of temporary and part time stable staff. But in October, when things started to get busy again, they would need more help. The date of Sadie's return had not been fixed, but was unlikely to be before Christmas, and even then Sam wondered whether Sampfield Grange would provide enough interest for her in the future. He still hoped to take her and Merlin to assist him in the selection of some new horses, perhaps from Eoghan Foley in Ireland, over the summer.

But Kye's ride in Saturday's point to point meeting at Ashfordleigh Downs was the issue which Sam wanted to address with Kye that afternoon. Kye was to be riding Highlander Park, already a successful competitor in point to point races, but whose sole attempt at competing in a Listed race at Newbury earlier in the year had been, to say the least, unsuccessful. Kye himself would soon be ineligible to ride in a point to point race, as his conditional licence as a professional jockey would soon be issued, ready for the coming season.

Sam passed the small yard office, which was now shut and empty, as Bethany, the office manager, had departed for the day. Unlike Isabella Hall, who had lived in the old chauffeur's flat above the garage, Bethany went home each evening to her partner and their new baby.

The two teenage stable hands were filling water buckets and sweeping the stone paving as Sam entered the yard. They both immediately stopped what they were doing and stood looking questioningly at their employer, as though expecting to be told that they had done something wrong.

"Good afternoon," Sam greeted them, shortly, "Where's Kye?"

"He's with Ranger Station, Mr Sampfield, sir," the girl told him, the yellow water hose which she had been using to fill the buckets continuing to sluice water into the drain alongside the stable block.

Sam decided to leave them to their work before much more water was wasted, and with a brief nod, strode on into central area of the yard where he found Kye brushing down an indifferent Ranger Station who was more interested in pulling at a half full haynet tied to the back wall of his box. Ranger Station was a large bay animal who was due to be ridden by Sam's cousin, Gilbert Peveril, on Saturday in one of the Ashfordleigh Down races specifically for older working hunters. But yesterday, Ranger had been hacked around the Sampfield Grange estate by Frank Stanley alongside Sam on his usual mount Caladesi Island.

Kye straightened up as Sam came to the door of the loose box.

"How's Ranger today?" Sam asked, "Are we happy that he's fit for the race on Saturday?"

"No problem, Mr Sampfield," Kye replied promptly, "Ranger knows what he's about and so does Mr Peveril. I think he enjoyed the outing with Mr Stanley too, yesterday."

"Hmm," responded Sam, not wanting to be drawn on the topic of Frank Stanley, "And what about Highlander? He seemed to work well this morning. Do you reckon you have the measure of him now, Kye? He's always been good at points. I think the big occasion at Newbury got him a bit over excited. It will be good for him to get back to something he's more used to."

Sam did not add that the unknown element in Saturday's point to point meeting was the fact that Highlander Park was being ridden in a race for the first time by Kye. Kye's experience as a jockey was limited to a few rides for his former yard in Cheshire and the horses had been of nothing like the quality of Highlander Park, who was locally bred and came from a line of successful pointers. Kye had ridden Highlander many times over the Sampfield Grange practice jumps, but a real competition, with all its strange and unfamiliar elements, including the other horses, was a different challenge altogether. Still, Sam thought, the lad had a good relationship with the horse, who seemed to trust and listen to Kye.

"And Sadie should be back to provide you with support," Sam added, intending his remark to give Kye a degree of additional reassurance, "It will be her last meeting with us at Sampfield Grange before she goes to the Dickses on Sunday."

Kye nodded, and, having firmly bolted shut the door to Ranger Station's box, accompanied his employer on a tour around the yard trying to sound more confident than he really felt as they briefly discussed each of the horses. The two silent stable staff continued work around them with their brooms and water hoses.

Although Kye was looking forward to riding Highlander Park in the competition in three days' time, he was also beginning to feel nervous. Having been granted the unexpected chance of resuming his career as a jockey, he was well aware of how much he had forgotten in the months since he had left the Cheshire yard. Outwardly confident, Kye was highly conscious of his position as an outsider in the Sampfield Grange set up. Everyone else was somehow connected with the Sampfield Peveril family, even if only because they had been born and brought up within a few miles of the Grange. But Kye was from inner city Liverpool and shared nothing in common with any of them other than his love of horses.

Sadie, he thought, was a bit of a mixed blessing as far as support was concerned. She had found him the job at Sampfield Grange in the first place, after meeting him at Wincanton racecourse, but his brief sexual relationship with her had been quickly brought to an end once the self confident Merlin ap Rhys had appeared on the scene. Not that Kye minded that much. There were plenty of other potentially available girls amongst the work riders and their families, he told himself. At least Sadie had been to Ashfordleigh Downs before, and was familiar with the course, so perhaps she would be of more help than not, Kye decided. He had pored over the website associated with the left handed track and memorised its rather erratic course around a large cabbage field and then alongside a drystone wall after passing through a deep dip with a small stream at the bottom. But no amount of theoretical preparation could substitute for actually riding the course.

By the time Sam went indoors, Kelly had returned to the kitchen to prepare an evening meal for herself, Lewis and Kye. Sam was due to spend the evening with Gilbert Peveril and his wife and did not expect to return until late.

"Tabikat did well today, Mr Sampfield," Kelly ventured to comment as Sam entered the kitchen, "I'm sure Sadie will have been there cheering him on. But we didn't see her in the parade ring. There were just some people we didn't know."

This apparently innocuous remark on Kelly's part had been carefully crafted with Lewis in the hope that Mr Sampfield might be induced to say something about the identity of the group of people they had seen on the TV standing with Merlin before he had been legged up on Tabikat. Isabella Hall was clearly not there, nor was the mysterious tall man who had been with her at Cheltenham. And neither had the people at Punchestown looked like the other individuals who had arrived to stand with Mr Sampfield during the televised running of the Cheltenham Gold Cup.

But Kelly and Lewis were destined to be disappointed, as Sam had taken little notice of the Punchestown connections, other than to note the presence of Brendan Meaghan. Agreeing with Kelly that Tabikat had put in an excellent performance and that he had not seen Sadie either, he left Kelly to her work in the kitchen.

"Never mind," said Kelly to Lewis, when he returned to join her in the kitchen, as Sam's black Audi sports car sped off down the lane outside, "We can ask Sadie when she comes back on Friday morning with Merlin."

The three Sampfield Grange staff spent an uneventful evening watching television. Lewis would have preferred to go out with Kye to the pub for a couple of hours, but with Sadie absent and Isabella Hall no longer in the chauffeur's flat, this would have left Kelly alone in charge of the house and the horses in the stable yard. With two horses about to compete on Saturday, Kye was well aware that Mr Sampfield would expect staff to remain on site.

At about 10.00pm, when Kye had already gone back to his cottage by the yard and Lewis and Kelly were thinking of going to bed, the house telephone rang. Picking up the extension in the kitchen, Lewis was surprised to hear the now familiar Australian tones of Teddy Urquhart.

"G' Morning - Lewis, isn't it?" boomed Teddy, as though trying to project his voice forcibly from the other side of the world, "James there, is he?"

"Hello, Mr Urquhart," Lewis replied, "I'm sorry, but Mr Sampfield is out for the evening."

"Get him to call me, will you, when he gets in?" Teddy shouted.

"Yes, of course, Mr Urquhart. Can I tell him what it's about?" asked Lewis, not wanting to lose an opportunity to glean inside information on Sampfield family affairs, "I hope Mrs Sampfield is well?"

"Mrs Sampfield?" Teddy replied, vaguely, "Oh, Aunt Raldi you mean? Yeah, she's ace. Nothing for James to worry about. Just get him to call me before he flakes, will you, Lewis?"

And with that, Lewis had to be content.

6

Sadie had to look at the phone several times before she could believe what she was seeing. A chilly dawn was just beginning to illuminate the eastern sky and a thin line of light had filtered beneath the black blind covering the sloping window of Merlin's extended attic bedroom.

Sadie and Merlin had returned to Merlin's bachelor pad cottage in Chepstow late on the previous evening. Merlin had been still elated by his victory in the Punchestown Gold Cup that afternoon and had graciously accepted the congratulations of a number of fellow passengers who had recognised him on the flight back from Dublin to Cardiff. Sadie had been disappointed that they had had to leave Punchestown racecourse so promptly, an arrangement which meant that she had had hardly any time to say goodbye to Tabikat.

"See you soon, I hope, Tabsi," she had said to the magnificent horse, stroking his dark nose, whilst Claire O'Dowd efficiently prepared him for his journey in the horsebox back to *An Féarach Beag*. Tabikat had merely nodded his handsome head, but Sadie fancied that the flick of one of his ears meant that he had understood her words.

Merlin had been anxious to return to Chepstow that evening for two reasons. The original reason, and the one which he had shared with Sadie, was that he had been booked to ride at Sandown Park on the Friday and Saturday that week. Being at home for one whole day would provide a short rest before his next demanding assignment. The new reason, which he had not entirely shared with Sadie, was that he had decided to replace his mobile phone and the number which went with it. The message which had pinged its way to him on the evening of the previous day had served only to increase his determination to resist any forthcoming attempts to blackmail or pressurise him.

The second message had contained no new information, but had consisted of a particularly compromising still from the video recording made in the Liverpool hotel room. By some feat of malware, the image had now become the phone's wallpaper and screensaver and popped up on the screen every time Merlin made or received a call. Try as he might, Merlin had not been able to delete it. He had also discovered that the file containing the video had been apparently ineradicably inserted into the image catalogue in the phone and that it would start playing at full volume as soon as the file directory was accessed.

After fiddling around unsuccessfully with the phone for a while in the relative safety of the jockey's changing room at Punchestown, Merlin had decided that the simplest line of defence against whatever was going on would be to discard the phone and its SIM card completely. A new phone and a new number would be impossible for the hacker, or blackmailer, or whatever they were, to trace. So he had stuffed the phone into a sock in the bottom of his travelling bag and told Sadie that he had lost it.

"I've let the 'otel and the racecourse know," he had told her untruthfully, "But we'll 'ave to go out an' get a new one in Chepstow tomorrow. I'll get a new number too. Too many people know the old one."

On their arrival at Merlin's home, they had gone straight to bed. Merlin had claimed tiredness and had fallen into a deep sleep almost straight away. Sadie, however, who had done nothing other than to act as race spectator and passenger all day, had been wide awake and had felt slightly annoyed that Merlin seemed uninterested in sex that evening. As she had lain looking up at the ceiling, Sadie had thought of the exciting recording they had made in the Irish hotel the previous evening and wondered whether they could set up something similar tomorrow in Merlin's bedroom.

Sadie had eventually fallen asleep after about an hour of listening to Merlin's even breathing filtering through the darkness of the room. But she had been woken again a few hours later by a familiar and insistent buzzing noise. After a few moments of disorientation, she had traced the source of the noise to Merlin's travelling bag at the foot of the bed.

"It's Merlin's phone," she had realised with relief, "He was wrong about losing it. It must have just fallen into the bottom of his bag."

Sliding quietly out of the bed so as not to disturb Merlin, Sadie had rummaged through the clothes in the bag. She had been mystified to discover the phone wrapped inside a rolled up sock. Releasing the phone from its unconventional container, she had been immediately confronted with a garish image on the screen. The buzzing sound had stopped now and the picture shone eerily at her in the dim dawn light.

Sadie's immediate reaction was that the image was from the recording she and Merlin had made together. It took her just a few seconds to realise her mistake. The male partner of the naked couple was certainly Merlin but the young blonde woman sprawled beneath him was someone she had never seen before. Vomit rose in Sadie's throat as she took in the implications of the picture.

Notwithstanding her adoration of Merlin, there was a limit to what even Sadie was prepared to tolerate. Sadie had always been aware that Merlin might well have other girlfriends, a situation about which she had resolved not to complain, so long as the other girlfriends remained hidden and unknown. But this girlfriend was displayed on the screen of Merlin's phone. Every time he used the phone, he would see her. Did he also see her in his mind when he was making love to me, Sadie wondered, her stomach churning. As she thought of the implications of this, her hand began to shake and she dropped the phone like a hot coal onto the bed, where Merlin, oblivious to the emotional crisis taking place beside him, slept peacefully on.

Gathering together her clothes, Sadie dressed quickly and stuffed her few travelling possessions into the battered rucksack she had brought with her from Sampfield Grange. Looking numbly at Merlin one last time, she crept down the stairs and let herself out of the front door. Awakening birds were singing enthusiastically in the strengthening light as she walked down the hill towards the railway station.

When Merlin awoke two hours later, the train carrying Sadie and a host of anonymous daily commuters was already gliding into the platform at Bristol Temple Meads station. And later that day, Kelly was surprised to observe from the kitchen window Sadie alighting from a minicab in the entrance to the Sampfield Grange stable yard.

Sadie had had plenty of time to think during the somewhat tortuous journey from Chepstow to Sampfield Grange. Once she had recovered from the initial shock of finding the compromising picture on Merlin's mobile phone, she had set her practical mind to considering what she should do next. Sadie had spent most of her life working with horses and understood them very well. Had one of her favourite horses shown some kind of unacceptable behaviour, she would have known exactly what to do. But she had little experience of dealing with, or even understanding, such behaviour in people.

Sadie loved all horses unconditionally, even the difficult and awkward ones, and was prepared to work hard to get the best out of them. This required a combination of strength, patience, tenacity, and a clear message to the horse that bad behaviour was not going to be tolerated. Sadie had read that horses in the wild would give the cold shoulder to members of the herd which displayed antisocial tendencies, quietly excluding them until they conformed to the group norms. She had discovered for herself, when lungeing difficult horses at home, that the action of turning slightly sideways and away from them would often result in the recalcitrant horse coming towards her of its own accord even when it had earlier been plunging about and pulling at the lunge line.

Sadie had no idea whether these tactics would work with people, but they were the best she had. She loved Merlin unconditionally too, but, as with the horses, she was not prepared to tolerate unacceptable behaviour on his part towards her. If he wanted to behave badly, that was up to him, but she would not be party to it.

So, Sadie decided, reluctantly, she would simply give Merlin the cold shoulder, and see whether he responded. In the meantime, she would turn her attention to other, more rewarding, activities and people. She knew that she would miss Merlin terribly, but, as with the horses, she had to get tough and make it clear that she was not prepared to be pushed about by selfish and unruly behaviour.

Whether Sadie's logic was correct, and whether Merlin would have appreciated being compared to an awkward horse, making the plan made Sadie feel as if she was on safer ground, and she began to feel better.

Sadie was determined too that the incident with Merlin should not become generally known amongst either the Sampfield Grange or Dicks staff. The last thing she wanted was people whispering and laughing behind her back. In anticipating this, she had probably done her colleagues a disservice, as doubtless most of them would have been sympathetic. But Sadie did not want people feeling sorry for her either. So she had resolved to tell no-one what had really happened, and to simply stick to the facts as they had been up until the point at which she had found the image on the screen. Already the horrible incident had begun to seem far in the past, although in reality it had happened only a few hours ago.

"You're back a day early!" was Kelly's statement of the obvious when Sadie clumped into the Sampfield Grange kitchen.

"Yeah, I know," Sadie said, dumping her rucksack onto the floor, "Change of plan."

"What happened?" asked Kelly, eagerly, hoping for some gossip to share with Lewis later, "You and Merlin have a row or something?"

"No, nothing like that," Sadie replied, truthfully enough, "We had a great time in Ireland. But Merlin has things to do in Chepstow today. He went and lost his phone at Punchestown too. He's riding at Sandown Park tomorrow and Saturday so he needs to get a new phone before he goes. I wouldn't have seen much of him today. I thought I'd be more use here, helping Kye and Mr Sampfield."

As Kelly opened her mouth to ask more questions, she was, to Sadie's relief, interrupted by Sam coming unexpectedly into the kitchen from the boot room.

"Hello, Sadie," Sam said, without surprise, not having remembered that she had been due to return the following day, "I trust you enjoyed your trip to Ireland. I must congratulate Merlin on his excellent ride on Tabikat. The horse looked completely in control of the race. A very good outcome altogether."

Before Sadie could reply, Sam spoke to Kelly.

"I'm going to be in my study for a while," he told her, "Would you or Lewis bring me coffee?"

And as Kelly turned her attention to dealing with her employer's request, Sadie took the opportunity to escape quickly to the stable yard.

"First hurdle jumped successfully," she said to herself as she opened the door of her small room in the staff cottage and threw her bag onto her narrow bed. And, lying down in the familiar surroundings, she at last fell asleep.

Awaiting the arrival of his coffee in the study, Sam stood looking out of the lead paned window. The Sampfield Grange flock of sheep and lambs in the paddock by the lane were as a mere drop in the vast ocean of his cousin Teddy's Australian livestock operation, he thought.

Sam had arrived home the previous evening shortly after Teddy's call. His first reaction when Lewis had informed him that Mr Urquhart had wanted him to call back immediately had been that something had happened to his mother. In the event, when he had made the return call at what was by then about 7.30am in Queensland, it appeared that Teddy was simply in a hurry to get on with his daily routine.

"I'm in the chopper all day with Leo," Teddy had told Sam by way of explanation, "The stockmen went off yesterday on the horses. We got cattle to move down. Likely take most of the day."

"If my mother is well, what can I do for you, Teddy?" Sam had asked his cousin, wondering why Teddy always felt the need to speak as though addressing a large assembly of people who might be hard of hearing

"My younger boy, Ryan," Teddy had boomed down the line, "Just gone travelling. Bali, Phuket, Angkor Wat, and such places these kids think they need to do some mucking around in before they croak. I told him to go to England too. Said he'd think about it."

"Yes?" Sam had interjected, as Teddy had seemed to pause for breath.

"Fact is, James," Teddy had continued loudly, "Kid seems to have gone off the rails a bit. Finding things here not what he wants in life, he says. We're hoping this bit of a walkabout might set him right again. What I'm asking is, if he comes to England, will you give him a fair go at your place?"

"I should be very glad to have him here," said Sam, "We could use a bit of extra help in the yard later this year. I imagine he is an experienced horseman?"

"Horseman? Yeah, course," Teddy had responded at once, "Everyone here has as much riding as they can handle. Thanks James, that's beaut. I'll tell Ryan to give you a bell."

Just as Sam had thought that Teddy was about to conclude the conversation, his cousin had suddenly added.

"Nearly forgot, James. Tessa wants us to come to England for March and April next year. Says she wants to get out of the heat and catch up with some ace British jumps racing. Fancies seeing the big ones at Cheltenham and Aintree, she reckons."

"I should be very pleased to welcome you both here," Sam had assured his cousin, and, with that, the conversation had come to an end. Sam had no doubt that Lewis had heard every word of it.

Sam was right. Lewis had been hovering on the staircase throughout the conversation and had lost no time in imparting the unexpected haul of gossip to Kelly as soon as he had reached their bedroom, and then to Kye in the kitchen the following morning.

"Mr Urquhart's son going off the rails," Kelly had said, excitedly and for the umpteenth time, "I wonder what that means? Do you think it's drugs? Or a girlfriend he's got pregnant? Or that maybe he's committed a crime? He must be running away from something, don't you think?"

"How old is he?" had asked Kye, who had not been entirely happy to hear that a relative of Mr Sampfield would be joining the Sampfield Grange yard, especially as the potential newcomer had been described as a good horseman. Kye did not want anyone else to come in the way of his opportunities to ride the Sampfield Grange horses in races.

Whilst Kelly and Lewis did not know the answer to this question, as Lewis had pointed out, the unknown Ryan Urquhart must be at least eighteen years old if he had gone off on a world tour, apparently on his own. They would just have to wait to find out, if and when he turned up at Sampfield Grange.

Whilst Sadie was sleeping off the effects of her journey at Sampfield Grange, Merlin was making plans of his own. Having woken up to find that Sadie was no longer in the bed with him, he had quickly noted that her possessions and bag had also disappeared. Initially mystified, Merlin had looked for some kind of explanatory note in either the bedroom or the kitchen downstairs. But there had been nothing.

Returning to the empty bedroom, he had soon spotted his mobile phone lying on the floor, tipped from its previous resting place on the bed when Merlin had thrown back the covers. It had not taken Merlin long to realise that Sadie must have seen the image which had been placed ineradicably on the screen. At first he had not been able to understand how Sadie could have found the carefully hidden phone until he had eventually realised that he had not cancelled the alarm which had woken them the previous two days and which had clearly given out the sound which had enabled Sadie to track down the phone to its hiding place in his bag.

Merlin's initial feeling of annoyance at his own stupidity had been quickly replaced by a black fury. Who the hell were these people who were trying to mess up his life, and why were they doing it? Nothing had been requested of him in any of the unwelcome messages nor had he heard anything at all from Lara or Abigail Alvarez or whoever she was. Was she being sent these images too? Or maybe they were being sent to her husband, the apparently adulterous Argentinian footballer.

Merlin's quick mind had mulled over these questions without success. But one thing had soon become very clear to him. He needed someone who knew what they were doing to look very carefully at the incriminating material and the garbled number from which it was being sent to see if it gave any clues as to the sender. If malware was being installed on his phone, it was being done from a computer. And he knew just the person who could make these investigations on his behalf.

Putting regretful thoughts of the absent Sadie out of his mind, Merlin had been soon knocking loudly on the door of a small camera equipment shop in the pretty central area of Chepstow. It was still early and there were few people about. Certainly the shop was not open, as an angry voice from the other side of the door sharply informed him.

"Bryn!" called Merlin in response, "It's Merlin. I need your 'elp with somethin'. It's urgent."

After some rattling of locks and a door chain, the sun-faded green door had been pulled open, and Merlin had shoved his way in before Bryn could object.

Bryn was a small, skinny man with lowering dark eyebrows which seemed too big for his narrow, pale face. A pair of black rimmed spectacles were sliding down his nose. He ran a pale hand through receding wavy dark hair.

"What's so bloody urgent, then, Merlin?" Bryn had asked crossly, closing the door and replacing the chain.

"I'll show you," Merlin had replied, grimly.

7

Kye carefully steered the larger of the two Sampfield Grange horseboxes through the narrow entrance to the sloping grass parking area at Ashfordleigh Downs point to point course. In the horsebox were Highlander Park and Ranger Station and at Kye's side in the cab was an unusually subdued Sadie.

Kye had had been surprised to find Sadie sleeping in her bedroom at the cottage on the afternoon of the day of her return from Chepstow.

"I thought yez was coming back tomorrow," he had said when she had eventually appeared in the shared sitting room, rubbing the sleep out of her eyes. Sadie had given Kye the same explanation as she had earlier given to her sister, and had then announced that she needed a shower.

Kye had lived and worked with Sadie long enough to know that something was different about her manner. She normally sang loudly, and mostly in tune, when she was in the shower, but that afternoon there had been silence. And then, she had gone straight into her bedroom to get dressed instead of joining him for a chat in the little sitting room with a towel wrapped around her wet hair. Most tellingly, she had not asked after the welfare of any of the Sampfield Grange horses.

Sadie had joined Kye as usual to help at evening stables that day and had come out on the exercise ride the following morning. She had worked Ranger Station alongside Highlander Park over the top line of jumps above the Grange, and, by the end of the morning's riding, had seemed almost like her usual self. But Sadie had soon lapsed into silence once again, and, when Kye had asked her whether she was all right, had simply said that she thought she might have picked up a cold during the trip to Ireland. She had told Kelly the same thing later that day and had taken herself off to bed early, saying that she needed to try to sleep the illness off before the point to point meeting the following day.

Kye had not been fooled for a moment. But, for now, his mounting nerves at the prospect of his ride on Highlander Park that afternoon were his foremost concern. The weather had become unexpectedly warm and the air correspondingly dull and still, so Kye was already perspiring as he and Sadie unloaded the two horses from the box. He could see Mr Sampfield, who had driven to the course ahead of them in the green Range Rover, approaching them from the direction of the small parade ring.

"Good news, Kye," Sam said, as he reached the lorry, "There are a number of withdrawals from your race. You and Highlander are up against only two other runners. That should give Highlander a good look at all the fences. He's not run at this course before, as you know. Come along now, Kye, let's walk round the course, so you know what to expect."

Under Sadie's expert supervision, Highlander Park himself came out of the horsebox in an apparently calm frame of mind and seemed to be unbothered by the unfamiliar surroundings. His travelling companion, Ranger Station, was his usual stolid self and his influence seemed to have had a good effect on the younger horse.

The good weather had brought out a large and colourful crowd, which included many excited and noisy children, as well as a wide variety of dogs. But they were some distance away from the horsebox park, and the two Sampfield Grange horses seemed quite happy to stand quietly by the lorry until it was their turn to go to the parade ring.

Highlander Park was due to run in the second race and Ranger Station in the fourth. From his resumed position in the parking area, Kye could see the runners lining up for the start of the first race. Sadie was sitting in the cab of the horsebox, fiddling with her mobile phone and Mr Sampfield had gone to the members' area to fetch his cousin, Gilbert Peveril, who would be riding Ranger Station.

Kye felt someone touch his elbow.

"Anything doing today, Kye?" asked the pretty, dark haired girl, her head cocked to one side.

It took Kye a second to understand what the young woman was asking.

"No, I'm not into that shit any more, Jackie," he told her in a whisper, "It got a bit hot, so we're giving it a rest."

"Shame," the girl replied, "Let me know if you change your mind. I liked dealing with you."

"Yez'll be the first to know," Kye assured her, privately thinking that nothing would induce him to get back into drug dealing ever again.

"And good luck in your race, Kye," said Jackie, unexpectedly, "I saw your name in the card. Is this your horse? He looks lovely."

"Well, he's Mr Sampfield's horse," Kye responded, relieved at the change of topic of conversation.

As Jackie stroked Highlander Park's smooth neck, she said suddenly, "I'd love to work at your place, Kye. Mr Sampfield has the best horses. Any chance of a job?"

"Not up to me," Kye responded, "Mr Sampfield and Sadie do all the hiring for the yard. Sadie's in the lorry. But she's going to be working for Mr Dicks after tomorrow, so I don't know who's going to decide after that. Maybe ask Mr Sampfield?"

"Ooh, I don't dare speak to him," Jackie replied, "He's dead posh."

"Well, I'll ask him for yez," Kye assured her, "I know he's going to be needing people after Sadie goes."

As Jackie walked away, her mobile phone clamped to her ear, Kye realised that the first race had gone off and that it was time to get Highlander Park to the parade ring. Mr Sampfield and Mr Peveril were approaching across the grassy slope and he heard the sound of Sadie jumping down from the cab of the lorry and slamming the door shut.

Highlander Park's first race at Ashfordleigh Downs turned out to be a rather strange experience for his rookie jockey.

Highlander had behaved perfectly in the parade ring, and Mr Sampfield himself had legged Kye up into the saddle. Sadie had led Highlander round the ring, saying little, but ensuring that the horse had remained calm. The dead air was atypical of a late April day, and had seemed to cast a lethargic quiet over the pre-race proceedings. A thin pall of pewter cloud had begun to cast itself across the sun, which had become dull and quiet, as though the energy had been drained from it. A glow of warm light escaped over the edge of the gathering storm.

"Just keep Highlander going forward, Kye," Mr Sampfield had said, "He won't get jostled in such a small field and you can concentrate on getting him to jump well. They'll probably hunt round most of the way and make a race of it towards the end."

Kye was sweating as he waited at the start with the two other competitors, neither of whom he had seen before. He had no idea what tactics they would adopt in the race and could only trust that Mr Sampfield's prediction was correct. A trickle of perspiration ran down the back of his neck while his hands felt sticky inside his new riding gloves. Highlander shifted about beneath him, ignoring the other horses and trying to dip his head down to get a nibble of the grass beneath his feet. No-one spoke.

As the flag went down, Kye pushed Highlander Park forward, the other horses positioned one on either side of him. He heard the loudspeaker crackle to his right, as the commentator announced, "And they're off! It's a three horse race, but a very competitive one, with Kye McMahon riding Highlander Park in the Sampfield Grange colours, Luke Cunningham on his own young horse Merriott Marsh, and Gracie Samways on her father Anthony's Property Man. Merriott Marsh has taken quite a hold already, as they approach the first obstacle."

The first jump was positioned in front of the spectators' area, which was packed with enthusiastic people chattering and laughing as the horses reached the fence. Kye could see the familiar orange of the take off board and the neatly arranged spruce sloping up and away from him. Highlander jumped it accurately and without effort, just as if the two of them were working together at home.

Merriott Marsh with Luke Cunningham in the saddle soon pulled some way ahead of the other two horses. The small field rounded a shallow curve to the left and approached the second jump on a downhill slope. Just as the leading horse rose over the fence, there was a low growl of distant thunder and a few large spots of rain dropped onto Highlander's neatly plaited mane.

Much to Kye's relief, Highlander seemed totally focused on what he was doing, and ignored the deteriorating weather conditions. The two of them took the second jump cleanly and fast, and Kye's nerves began to subside. Unfortunately, Merriott Marsh was not so sanguine and appeared to be pulling ever harder against the contact. Luke Cunningham landed some two lengths ahead, the horse's head cocked awkwardly to one side as he fought his rider. Meanwhile, Kye could hear the even breath of Property Man behind him to his right.

"And Merriott Marsh is pulling ahead," the loudspeaker voice crackled, "Highlander Park is going well behind him and Property Man is up there with the pace."

The race comprised two circuits of the left handed track. As Kye had noted during his preparation for the race, the course went downwards into a dip in which there was a small stream, which had been turned into a water jump by the addition of a fence before it. The track then came gradually upwards around a long slow curve and followed along the route of a dry stone wall before turning sharply left onto a grassy slope by the lorry park, to return to the starting point. The winning post was positioned about fifty yards further on.

Even Sam's expensive field glasses could not keep Highlander Park in sight when the horse followed Merriott Marsh down the slope into the dip which held the water jump. As he lowered the glasses, an unfamiliar female voice spoke up beside him.

"Mr Sampfield Peveril?" asked the woman.

"Yes?" Sam responded, turning his head towards the speaker, who had positioned herself to his left by the parade ring. Gilbert and Sadie had already walked away down to the course itself, ready to see the runners pass them after completing the first circuit.

"Oh, good, I have got the right person," said Jessica Moretti, "My name is Jess. I'm a journalist. And a friend of Isabella Hall."
"Isabella Hall?" repeated Sam, looking around at the nearby spectators, "I wasn't aware that she was here today."

"Oh, she isn't," Jessica hastened to assure him, "In fact I don't know where she is and I'd love to get in touch with her again. Someone told me that she works for you, so I thought I would see if you could help me."

"I regret that I am unable to help you," Sam told her, firmly, unwilling to be drawn into any conversation about Isabella Hall or his supposed connection with her, "Mrs Hall was with me at Sampfield Grange for only a short time and has left. I have no idea where she is now. If you will excuse me, I am trying to follow one of my runners in this race."

"That's Highlander Park, isn't it?" Jessica persisted, having taken the precaution of reading the race card before approaching Sam, "I should love to do an interview with you about you and your horses. Perhaps for Go Pointing magazine, or Horse and Hound?"

"Well, if you wish," said Sam, desperate to get rid of this unwelcome interlocutor before Highlander Park re-appeared from the hidden section at the far side of the course, "You can make an appointment through my office manager, Bethany Morgan."

Nodding briefly to Jessica Moretti, Sam walked down the slope to join Sadie and Gilbert. Jessica watched him go, pursing her lips as she saw him join his companions. Jessica was quite used to being given the brush off by unwilling targets, but, if she was not mistaken, she had just been invited to call the Sampfield Grange establishment for a personal meeting with Isabella Hall's former employer. That was a good enough bit of work for the day, she decided, feeling glad that there was now no need for her to waste any more time pretending to enjoy this boring rural event.

As Sam reached the side of the course, Merriott Marsh and Luke Cunningham had passed the top of the hill at far corner and were silhouetted against the line of the dry stone wall. More large drops of rain were falling, and a few umbrellas were hastily being unfurled by members of the crowd. The sun was now completely obscured from view and the light had become dull whilst a slight breeze had started to whisk around the crowded spectators.

"That Cunningham horse is pulling like the devil," Gilbert observed, with satisfaction, "Bugger should run out of steam soon with any luck."

Highlander Park was now about four lengths behind Merriott Marsh. Watching once again through the field glasses, Sam could see Kye looking well balanced and relaxed in the saddle, and hoped that his new jockey would have the self-control to continue to be patient and await his chance to pass Merriott Marsh when the leader eventually began to tire. The third horse, Property Man, was still hard on Highlander's heels, as the small field progressed along the left hand side of the course towards the sharp turn which would bring them back towards the eagerly watching crowd.

As the three horses successfully negotiated the last obstacle before the sharp bend, a commotion suddenly broke out amongst the spectators standing on the inner side of the course opposite the Sampfield Grange trio.

"Come back here immediately, Oscar!" shouted a loud male voice in commanding military tones.

"Look there, someone's dog has got onto the course," Gilbert pointed out, entirely unnecessarily, as a chocolate coloured spaniel shot out of the crowd and turned towards the approaching horses, ears flying out horizontally alongside his silky head, the remains of a leather lead trailing behind him.

Oscar, unfortunately, seemed entirely oblivious to his owner's shouted orders and continued to run in the wrong direction along the centre of the track.

"And we have a canine escapee!" announced the commentator on the loudspeaker, "His owner needs to get him off the course, please, at once."

The three horses had by now reached the part of the course which ran towards and alongside the area where the increasingly wet spectators were gathered. The rain was quickly getting heavier and coats were being shrugged on and folded hats pulled from pockets, as the watchers attempted to keep dry whilst simultaneously following the unfolding drama created by the errant spaniel.

As Merriott Marsh, still yanking at the bit, pounded towards him, Oscar belatedly seemed to realise his imminent peril. He let out a sharp squeaky bark of fear and darted away sideways right across the horse's path. The antics of the disobedient dog seemed to be the last straw as far as the already overwrought Merriott Marsh was concerned and he jinked violently to one side.

Luke Cunningham did his heroic best to stay on board, but was instead deposited unceremoniously onto the turf almost immediately in front of the fascinated spectators. Merriott Marsh himself, relieved of his unwanted jockey, hurtled onwards towards the next jump, which had been the first in the initial circuit, and cleared it with aplomb, leaving the furious Luke Cunningham thumping the ground with his fist in angry frustration. Oscar, meanwhile, had disappeared into the crowd opposite and could be seen running across the cabbage field in the centre of the course followed by his futilely yelling owner.

Much to Sam's relief, Highlander Park had been far enough away from the unfortunate incident to be unaffected by it. Kye brought his mount to the next jump in good order and cleared it effortlessly followed almost at once by Property Man.

Kye had not seen exactly what had caused Merriott Marsh to unseat his jockey so unexpectedly, but he did have a clear view of the now riderless horse running ahead of him along the course. As the track curved round to the left, the horse lost its bearings and continued to run straight on towards an open field, where it soon came to a confused halt. A couple of alert orange-jacketed stewards quickly moved in to catch the sweating creature before it could career back onto the track.

"Come on, Landy, we're in with a chance here," Kye quietly told Highlander Park, who twitched one of his wet ears in response.

As the remaining two horses ran downwards towards the water jump, the threatening thunderstorm began in earnest. A sharp jagged streak of bright lightning split the sky to Kye's right, followed by the loud rumbling bang of the accompanying thunder.

Kye had no idea how Highlander Park was likely to react to a thunderstorm, but he patted the horse's smooth brown neck in the hope of reassuring him.

"We're just out for our usual morning ride," Kye whispered, as much to himself as to the horse, "Nothing to be scared of."

Sam's view of Kye through his field glasses was obscured as much by the falling rain as by the downward undulation of the terrain on the far side of the course. As they waited for Highlander to re-emerge into view, Sadie suddenly spoke.

"That woman who was talking to you just now, Mr Sampfield," Sadie began, "I've seen her before. She was at Punchestown."

"Really?" Sam responded, not having realised that Sadie had been watching him, "She told me she was a journalist. She's going a long way to get her stories if she was at Punchestown too."

"She said she was a friend of Stevie Stone," Sadie added, her gaze still fixed on the far side of the course.

"Stevie Stone?" repeated Sam, "She told me it was Isabella Hall who was a friend of hers."

"Well, she can't know Isabella Hall very well," Sadie said, puzzled, "At Punchestown, she was asking me who all the people were who were watching Tabikat at Cheltenham. She didn't even recognise her."

"Hmm," said Sam, "Maybe this is her way of getting to talk to people she doesn't know. I suppose these journalists have to have some way of starting up a conversation."

As Sadie nodded in response, Gilbert suddenly exclaimed, "The Samways horse has gone!"

Sam hastily put the dripping field glasses up to his eyes. Sure enough, Highlander Park and Kye were galloping unaccompanied alongside the long dry stone wall.

"Property Man seems to have come to grief somewhere in the back straight," crackled the loudspeaker, "I'm told that he ran out at the water jump. So Highlander Park is now the last runner standing."

"Come on Kye," shouted Sadie, "All you have to do now is get Landy round."

And so Kye did. Highlander Park himself seemed quite unaware that he was now the only horse left in the contest, and continued to gallop and jump as determinedly as if he still had a large field of competitors at his heels. As the thunder continued to grumble in the distance, Kye brought Highlander across the finish line in splendid isolation, attracting a damp and subdued cheer from the remaining crowd.

"And Highlander Park is the only horse to finish," announced the loudspeaker voice, somewhat superfluously, "Well done to Kye McMahon and the Sampfield Grange team."

Leaving Sam and Gilbert to follow behind her, Sadie ran eagerly forward to grab Highlander Park's sodden bridle, calling up to a breathless Kye,

"Well done Kye, that's your first win! Mr Sampfield will be pleased. And Landy ran a great race for you too, didn't you Landy?"

"It wasn't much of a competition," Kye told her, guardedly, as Sadie fussed over the wet horse, "I was the only finisher."

"That's just the point, Kye," Sadie told him firmly, rain running down her upturned face, "You finished, the others didn't. You had to keep Landy calm during that thunder and lightning. You know how he can behave sometimes. Property Man must have been scared by it. Miss Samways is a top rider. It's not like her to have a horse run out at a jump."

"Thanks Sadie," said Kye, pleased to hear Sadie so enthusiastic once again.

"Look, here come Mr Sampfield and Mr Peveril now to congratulate you," Sadie continued, "I'm sure they'll say the same, won't they, Landy?"

But as Sam made his way towards the victorious young jockey and his steaming mount, he was thinking of something else entirely. That journalist woman was clearly looking for Isabella Hall. She'd tried Punchestown racecourse and now she had come all the way to a point to point course in the middle of the English countryside. She was going to a lot of trouble. Perhaps she wasn't a journalist at all.

One thing was clear. Frank Stanley needed to be told about the woman who had called herself Jess.

8

At about the same time as Gilbert Peveril was lining up on Ranger Station at the start of the fourth race at Ashfordleigh Downs, Merlin ap Rhys was easing his black BMW sports car into the Saturday afternoon Esher traffic. Merlin had been riding during each of the two days of the prestigious Sandown Park meeting, the last big event of the National Hunt season. As soon as his last race, in which his horse had been unplaced, was completed, he had left the smart Surrey racecourse promptly to make his way home and concentrate on getting his life back into its usual well organised routine.

Merlin had deliberately put all thoughts of his personal problems out of his mind during the two days of the Sandown Park race meeting. Unexpectedly, however, he had been reminded of those problems when he had looked at the entrants for a two mile Novices' Hurdle, in which he was due to ride on the Friday. One of them was a horse called Penalty Kick, the protégée of a Lambourn trainer. Merlin had seen the horse run a few weeks earlier at Cheltenham. But this time, the owner's name, which he had not noticed on the previous occasion, had struck a sudden familiar chord. It was S Alvarez.

As he had left the weighing room to go to the parade ring, Merlin had made sure that he had walked alongside Penalty Kick's jockey.

"That 'orse you're ridin', Mark," Merlin had said to him, "Is the owner that Argie footballer, or is it just someone else with the same name?"

"It's him all right," the other jockey had replied, "Not that I ever see him. His wife comes to see the horse run sometimes. She's the one who's interested in the racing, not him. Abby, her name is. Nice lady."

"She 'ere today?" had asked Merlin, suddenly alert.

"Don't keep up with the gossip, do you, Merlin?" Mark had said, with a laugh, "Randy Santi's taken her off to Barbados, trying to patch up his marriage. Been cheating on her - with her sister, no less. Two for the price of one, lucky swine. Abby says she'll forgive him if he gives the sister up."

Once Merlin had joined the M4 and passed Heathrow Airport, he pressed the telephone icon on the steering wheel and selected Bryn's number from the list on the display panel in front of him.

After leaving his old mobile phone with Bryn in Chepstow on Thursday morning, Merlin had acquired a new state of the art device along with an entirely new phone number. His first call had been to his agent, Jackson Argyrides.

"This is my new number, Jacko," he had told him, "I lost my phone in Ireland."

"What you 'ave to change de number for?" Jackson had asked, crossly, "You can get 'em moved over, you know, Merlin."

"Too many people know the old one," Merlin had told him, smoothly, "I want to keep this one for business."

"OK," had grumbled Jackson, unconvinced, "You 'ave all your bookings for tomorrow and Saturday, so call me Sunday and then we talk about next week."

The second call Merlin had made had been to Sadie. He had not expected her to answer, which was just as well, because she did not. He had left a short message telling her his new number, adding at the end,

"Call me, *cariad.*"

But, so far, Sadie hadn't.

Merlin had followed this call up with text messages to family and close friends, including Bryn, and then had put the problem of the compromised phone into the back of his mind for 48 hours.

Merlin and Bryn were cousins, the sons of two sisters. Their chosen careers in life had quickly obscured any obvious resemblance between them. Whereas Merlin's occupation of riding racehorses had made him physically and mentally tough, strong and confident, Bryn was quiet, skinny, shy, and lacking in social skills. There was however, one area in which Bryn excelled, and that was wildlife photography. His passion had been born from the bird watching outings on which he had accompanied his father as a child. Whilst the teenaged Merlin had been mucking out local stables and eventually leaving South Wales for an apprenticeship in a racing yard in neighbouring Gloucestershire, Bryn had been spending many still and silent hours awaiting the perfect shot of a bird of prey riding the thermals in the skies above the valleys or another of a long beaked wader stepping elegantly in the wetlands along the coast near Newport. Bryn's beautifully crafted portraits of woodland birds and small animals in the South Wales countryside had won photographic competition prizes and some had been featured in wildlife and geographic magazines.

Bryn's natural compositional skills had been enhanced by the completion of a photography course at Coleg Gwent, where he had acquired knowledge of the digital photography which had replaced the old fashioned film camera skills he had learned from his father. The course had enabled Bryn to improve the range of his own artistic work – although he never travelled beyond the borders of Wales – as well as experimenting with the moving image through video. The course tutor had been sufficiently impressed with Bryn's abilities to offer him a job in his own photography business, which he ran from a camera shop in Chepstow. So, Bryn had been there ever since, and his hard work and sharp brain had ensured that there was soon very little he did not know about digital camera equipment, video recording and editing, and cinematic production.

Outwardly, Merlin and Bryn appeared to have little in common. But they shared a number of valuable characteristics: excellent observational powers, the ability to learn quickly, and a capacity for endless patience when it came to achieving any task in hand. They were also good friends.

When Merlin had left the camera shop on Thursday morning, he had told Bryn that he wanted to know everything there was to know about the video scenes shown on the mobile phone. Bryn had watched the embarrassing recording without comment, only saying at the end, "Is that your new girlfriend then, Merlin? She looks pretty 'ot to me. So what's the problem then? She married or somethin'?"

Merlin had not been sure which question to answer, and had eventually explained to Bryn that his girlfriend was indeed hot, but that she was not the woman in the recording.

"So, 'oo did the camerawork for this then?" Bryn had asked, apparently disinterested in the implications of Merlin's explanation.

"That's what I'm tryin' to find out," Merlin had stated, flatly.

Bryn answered Merlin's call almost as soon as the ring tone had made itself heard on the speaker in Merlin's car.

"'ello Bryn. You got anything for me?" Merlin asked, without preamble.

"I 'ave, Merlin, I 'ave - quite a lot, in fact," replied Bryn, his voice sounding not dissimilar to Merlin's own.

"*Siarad cymraeg i mi, Bryn,*" Merlin told his cousin quickly.

Merlin and Bryn had both spoken Welsh as children, but the many years of interacting with non-Welsh speakers had broken the habit, and they now usually found it easier to converse in English. Welsh had become a language reserved for discussions which other listeners were not intended to understand. This, Merlin decided, was such a discussion.

Bryn forbore to mention that there were no Welsh words for most modern technical terms and duly responded in Welsh, the words *fideo* and *ffon* being impossible to disguise,

"The video is not meant for viewing on a mobile phone, Merlin. It's a professional job."

"Go on," instructed Merlin, continuing to speak Welsh.

"If I am not greatly mistaken," Bryn went on, using as much Welsh as was practical, as he warmed to the technical theme of his discourse, "It has been shot on a top of the range 4K camcorder with 4096 x 2160 resolution, a 50 Hz frame rate and 4 channel 16/24 bit audio. That's why the sound and picture are so good. It's professional kit, Merlin, costs thousands."

"That's the camera you're describin', isn't it?" Merlin clarified, still in Welsh, as he manoeuvred the speeding BMW into the outside lane of the motorway, "So what's it look like then?"

"Well, it'll be a black chunky thing, with a lens in front," replied Bryn, "It's a camcorder, Merlin. You know what they look like. You must 'ave seen plenty of them at your racecourses."

"Yes, I 'ave, but I didn' see one in the room at the Adelphi," Merlin answered, sharply, "So 'ow easy is it to hide then?"

"Lookin' at the angles," Bryn went on, irritatingly practical, "I'd say it was on the other side of the room, maybe in a wardrobe, or in a bathroom opposite the bed. That's where the camera operator would be standin'. In the dark, so you couldn' see them. Or another option would be to set up the camera on a fixed rig and run it by remote control. I bet it was quite dark in that room, wasn' it? And I doubt you were lookin' around you much any'ow."

Merlin felt slightly sick. A secret professional recording, carefully set up in advance – by the so-called Lara? By someone else? Who? He took a deep breath.

"Let me get this right, Bryn," he said, "This recordin' is made to a standard to be shown in a cinema, is that it?"

"That's about the size of it, Merlin," Bryn told him, "And there's more. It's been altered."

"Altered? What's been altered?" asked Merlin, wondering whether it might be a good idea to pull in at a motorway service area to get his head together. The information emerging from Bryn's investigations was beginning to unnerve him.

"Well, it's the woman," Bryn told him, "'er face. It's been changed."

"Can people do that kind of thing?" Merlin asked, realising at once that this was a redundant question, as very clearly an unknown person had done exactly that, "'ow?"

"Well, when people make videos," Byrn explained, as if speaking to a child, "They don' just do it and get it right all in one take. It would take a genius to be able to do that. So they work on it afterwards with editin' software. Usually, they just cut out bits they don' want, you know, the borin' bits between the action or things which don' look good, generally tighten it up, like, so it makes better viewing. And you can add titles, captions, overlays, music, extra sound effects, improve the contrast, make the weather look better, that sort of thing. We do it all the time for people's wedding videos."

"So, what's been done 'ere, then?" asked Merlin.

"I can't tell exactly," Bryn told him, "I need to work out what software they used, first, but what I can see is that the woman 'as been made to look different. Not much change – that'd be too obvious – but her face 'as been made rounder and 'er nose a different shape. Something about the mouth, too. It's a pretty careful job, Merlin. Pro stuff. It would 'ave taken a while."

A sudden memory started to nag at the back of Merlin's mind. What had he said to himself when he first saw the video? That he remembered the woman looking better than she did in the recording? But why would any woman want to make herself look less attractive? Surely airbrushing, or its digital equivalent, was used for the purpose of making someone look better? Unless what she really wanted was to look like someone else.

"I need to think about this," Merlin told Bryn, "Is there anything you can do to, you know, sort of unscramble what 'as been done? So we can see what she looked like before?"

"I'll give it a try," Bryn promised him.

"And Bryn," Merlin added, "See if you can get some pictures of a woman called Abigail Alvarez. She's a footballer's wife."

"OK," said Bryn, slowly.

"See you at the shop in an 'our and a 'alf," said Merlin, and cut the connection before Bryn could ask him anything else

Long before the hour and a half had passed, Merlin was pretty sure he knew what conclusions he was going to reach once he and Bryn had reviewed the changes made to the recording. The woman called Lara had set Merlin up. She had got him, admittedly with little difficulty, to have sex with her in a bedroom in the Adelphi. Then, someone had edited the video to make it look as if it was Abigail Alvarez who was enjoying herself in the bed with Merlin.

Merlin knew nothing about Abigail Alvarez except what his jockey colleague had told him the previous day, which accorded with the lurid headline on the front of the gossip magazine which he had seen in Ireland. Had Abigail Alvarez or her husband been sent a copy of the doctored video? Did she even know who Merlin was?

Merlin decided that he needed to find Lara and make her answer a few questions.

9

Isabella Hall watched the tall man approach along the footway at the side of the harbour. He walked unhurriedly but his step seemed nevertheless to have a sense of purpose. At this distance, Isabella could not make out his features, but she already knew them well. He had thick, dark hair streaked with grey, hidden under the light straw hat, and there were blue eyes behind the dark sunglasses. His pace was even and he looked straight ahead as he moved along the quayside.

Military types just couldn't help but give themselves away, thought Isabella. She noted that he was carrying a brown leather bag slung over one shoulder of his white, open necked shirt. It looked like a camera case, but she was willing to bet that it wasn't. He had the appearance of a spectator at a cricket match. But there were no cricket matches being played in Mallorca.

Myriad patches of sharp sunlight glittered fiercely on the rippled surface of the blue water. Scores of white yachts lay moored in neat parallel lines at right angles to the harbour wall where the port's three fishing vessels would soon return with their daily catch. The metal rigging of the numerous yachts clinked quietly and persistently against their masts as the calm water rocked them gently. Across the harbour, the Club de Vela was holding its daily children's sailing class, the little single sailed boats dipping and swinging around a tight course of inflatable yellow buoys, whilst a blue clad instructor floated in an open boat in the centre, issuing directions. A large white ocean-going yacht slid gently past them under low power, scarcely disturbing the lightweight course markers.

Although it was as yet only May, the port of Faratxa was busy with groups of strolling tourists who quickly headed for the shaded cafes as the heat of the cloudless afternoon bounced off the concrete pavements. The café tables offered an extensive view of the upmarket little port, with its stubby red painted lighthouse perched on a stone jetty projecting across the harbour entrance.

Another lighthouse stood further out, high on a pineclad promontory which stretched into the sea.

A series of small hills surrounded the port. Once scrubby and bare, they were mostly covered with tan and white houses, their terraces open to the outside world. Dark green shrubs, stiff conifers and bright floral displays filled the gaps between the carefully maintained properties.

Isabella was watching the activities of the well-heeled port from the upstairs window of one of the harbourside dwellings. These narrow buildings with their sloping half-pipe tiled roofs formed a colourful terrace along the southern wall of the harbour. The ground floors were mostly given over to shops and restaurants, from which white-aproned waiters walked with trays, back and forth across the narrow street, to bring food and drinks to the chattering customers occupying the outdoor tables and chairs. Awnings and parasols protected the holidaymakers from the hot sun.

The buildings were painted in a variety of hues. Blue, grey and orange all featured. The windows of their upper rooms were protected by tall, slatted wooden shutters picked out in contrasting colours. Some had iron railed balconies with magenta and white bougainvillea and scarlet geraniums spilling over the edges. Steep narrow streets ran upwards between the houses, most of them containing more smart shops, bars and eateries. The sunny and picturesque harbour scene featured prominently on the postcards for sale in the souvenir shops.

Isabella wondered by what means Frank Stanley had arrived in Faratxa carrying just one small bag. Perhaps he had come from Palma in the red and yellow bus which stopped on the wider road by which the harbour came to an end. Here there was a dry dock, where the full size of some of the enormous craft could be appreciated once their hulls were clear of the water. Or maybe one of the white taxis with their single orange stripe had brought him. Or perhaps he had come in on one of the private boats which slipped regularly into the port. Also possible was the little black helicopter which had been buzzing about earlier in the day, or one of a couple of light aircraft which had droned past, their occupants no doubt appreciating the clear view of Faratxa from above.

More importantly, thought Isabella, why had he come? She had expected to be left alone now, but clearly the promises which had been made had already been broken. A surge of annoyance coupled with a prickle of fear ran through her already tensing body. She sat upright on the cushioned wicker chair and closed her eyes, breathing deeply and slowly. Images of the wet, mist-shrouded lanes around Sampfield Grange appeared in her mind. She pictured Sadie and Kye and the work riders bringing the Sampfield Grange horses clattering down the track alongside the dingy chauffeur's flat which had been her home for several months. She saw the beautiful Tabikat storming grimly up the hill at the Cheltenham Festival, Merlin in purple and gold silks urging him forward. She remembered too that Tabikat had since then won the Punchestown Gold Cup and that she had not been there to see it.

When she reluctantly opened her eyes, the figure of Frank Stanley had disappeared. It took her a moment to realise that he had reached the restaurant on the ground floor below her and was quietly talking to the elderly Mallorcan proprietors. Of course he would know Joan and Pilar, she thought resignedly. After all, they were there to keep an eye on her. And on anyone who might be interested in her.

Frank Stanley had not wanted to be in Faratxa any more than Isabella Hall had wanted to see him there. But in the seven weeks since he had sent her off on a private charter flight to Palma de Mallorca, there had been some unexpected and unwelcome developments. Whether these affected George Harvey too, he did not know, but he had another use for George. He needed to see them both.

The murmuring voices in the restaurant below sometimes irritated Isabella. The wealthy little port in which she was now located may have been idyllic, but the small apartment was as claustrophobic and limiting as the chauffeur's flat at Sampfield Grange had been. Granted she could still go out on regular bike rides in common with the many other cyclists who chose to tackle the various routes around the attractive Spanish island, but otherwise she felt like a prisoner. At least at Sampfield Grange she had had a job to do. But here there was nothing.

Isabella had noticed that other escapees from the climes of northern Europe had opened bijou little shops in the town. Perhaps she would do something similar one day, if ever the apron strings were loosened. There must be an end to it sometime.

Putting down with a bang the book she was hardly reading, Isabella crossed the red tiled floor to the wooden door at the other side of the room and snatched it open, just as Frank Stanley arrived on the small landing outside.

"Jailer coming to visit the prisoner?" she asked him quickly, without offering a greeting.

Frank Stanley frowned, but said merely, "Hello Isabella. I have asked Joan to bring us tea. Would you prefer something stronger?"

"Do I need it?" Isabella asked him, walking back into the room and taking a seat on the small sofa which faced a glass topped coffee table in the centre of the room. There was a circular fan in the ceiling above the table, switched off for now.

"I have no idea," Frank responded, taking a seat opposite her, "Pilar says George is out sailing."

"Good job I didn't join him, isn't it?" Isabella retorted, "Otherwise nether of us would have been here to see you. Which one of us do you want?"

Before Frank could answer, Joan, the bespectacled and stocky owner of the Agua Blau restaurant on the ground floor, came through the open door with a tray. As well as two metal-framed glass tumblers full of golden tea, it included a saucer with lemon slices and a small bowl of sugar. There was also a bottle of Laphroaig whisky and three small glasses. Joan made no offer to pour the whisky and left the tray on the coffee table, closing the door behind him.

Isabella looked at Frank Stanley, questioningly.

"This looks serious, Frank," she said, pointing at the whisky bottle.

"Maybe, Isabella," replied Frank, "Someone is still asking questions about Susan Stonehouse."

"But we expected that, didn't we?" Isabella said, picking up one of the framed glasses of tea, "After all, someone needed to explain why her name was listed in the racecard as Tabikat's owner. I thought the official line was that it was an mistake made by an inexperienced member of staff at Sampfield Grange, someone who doesn't work there any more."

"Yes, indeed," replied Frank, also reaching for his tea, "But these enquiries are being made despite those explanations, and we are not sure why. The person asking the questions is – on the face of it at least - a grubber for a social media scandal distributor called Hornblower Online. In the likely event that you have never heard of it, it specialises in digging out and publishing scurrilous rubbish about celebrities – soap opera stars, footballers, those sorts of people. Susan Stonehouse hardly falls into that category."

"Unless they thought using the name of Susan Stonehouse was part of some sort of gambling or money laundering scam?" Isabella said thoughtfully, "And you know that Konstantin Paloka accused Peter Stonehouse of arranging to kill him. Perhaps someone has picked up that loose end and is giving it a pull to see if anything unravels."

"That's possible, I suppose," conceded Frank, sounding unconvinced, "But this individual has been approaching Stevie, who told me about it, and was also seen speaking to one of Sam's yard staff, Sadie Shinkins, at the Punchestown Festival. Not sure what was said there, but, shortly after, there was apparently a call to Sampfield Grange from someone asking for Isabella Hall. And now there has been a request from a hitherto unheard of equestrian feature writer to interview Sam for Go Pointing magazine."

"So it's not just Susan Stonehouse, it's Isabella Hall they're asking about, too?" asked Isabella, sitting up in her chair, "But how would a scandal rag have got hold of the name of Isabella Hall? No-one outside Sampfield Grange has really had any contact with me."

"You were in public view in the parade ring at the Gold Cup," Frank reminded her, "But I agree that that does not explain how they got your name. And we have no evidence that the Palokas, or anyone connected with them, knew your name either."

"So what is Mr Sampfield – sorry, I can't think of him by any other title – going to do about the interview with the equestrian feature writer?" went on Isabella, shuddering visibly at the repeated mention of the Paloka name, "Surely the point to point season is about to finish, anyway, isn't it?"

"Yes, which is why we don't like the sound of the request," stated Frank, declining for the moment to answer Isabella's first question, "But that is only one of the issues I came here to discuss."

"So what else has happened?" Isabella asked, a note of alarm entering her voice.

Before Frank could reply, slow footsteps were heard on the tiled stairs outside the little sitting room and the door handle turned.

"Well, good afternoon, Frank," said the tall, grey-haired man who stood in the doorway, a walking stick in his left hand, "I wondered how long it would be before we saw you again. Isabella and I were just getting to enjoy hiding in plain sight amongst the European tourists."

Frank looked at George Harvey's narrow face with its high-bridged nose and hooded eyes. His face was flushed with colour, evidently from the sailing trip. In fact, Frank thought, both George and Isabella looked much stronger and healthier than the last time he had seen them. The sailing and the cycling, not to mention the Mallorcan food, were clearly doing beneficial work. Isabella's face had lost its tight pallor and her hair had grown longer and been coloured and cut into a more attractive style. Notwithstanding the walking stick, George was standing more firmly on his damaged leg, and his smile seemed less strained then before.

"You're looking well, George," he said, standing up to shake George's outstretched right hand, as George supported some of his weight on the stick, "You both are."

"What's this all about?" asked George, nodding at the whisky on the table, "Have you got bad news for us?"

George's tone was jocular, but Frank could sense the unease behind the question. Motioning George to sit down, Frank quickly repeated the information he had already given Isabella. George listened without speaking, although he exchanged more than one glance with Isabella, who sat silently looking toward the open window through which the sociable sounds of the restaurant below could be heard.

"But that is not why I'm here," Frank concluded, "We're monitoring that situation and there is nothing for either of you to do or to worry about at the moment. If things change, I will make sure that we continue to look after you both. Joan and Pilar have been made aware of the position. I have come here for another reason."

George picked up the whisky bottle and poured measures of the golden brown liquid into two of the waiting glasses. He looked questioningly at Isabella, who shook her head slightly and continued to drink the almost cold tea.

Frank opened the brown leather bag and took out two iPads. He handed one to each of his expectant companions.

"If you open those up," he said, shortly, " You'll find a report on them. The access code is Rialto, capital R, with the rest of the word in lower case. I want you to read it. Then we can talk."

So saying, Frank got up from his seat and left the room. Isabella could hear his footfall descending the stairs. She typed in the password and the file opened on the little screen.

It was the report of an Air Accidents Investigation Branch enquiry into a fatal accident.

10

AAIB Investigation

ACCIDENT

Aircraft Type	Ardua Altior 10
No and Type of Engines	1 Fellowes FE 66 piston engine
Year of Manufacture	New
Date and Time (UTC)	27 October at 1404 hrs
Location	Old Warnock Airfield, Somerset
Type of Flight	Private
Persons on Board	Crew – 1 Passengers – 0
Injuries	Crew - 1 (Fatal) Passengers – NA
Nature of Damage	Aircraft destroyed
Commander's Licence	Private Pilot's Licence
Commander's Age	35 years
Commander's Flying Experience	520 hours (50 on type) Last 90 days – 10 hours Last 28 days – 5 hours
Information Source	AAIB Field Investigation

Synopsis

The aircraft was on final approach for a landing on runway 07 at Old Warnock Airfield, Somerset, after an uneventful flight from Gloucestershire Airport. The weather at Old Warnock was bright and sunny following the clearance of earlier fog. After the aircraft turned onto final approach, it pitched downwards and descended in a steep nose down attitude and struck the ground. The pilot was fatally injured. The aircraft was destroyed.

History of the Flight

The pilot arrived at Gloucestershire Airport (EGBJ) where the aircraft is based at approximately 1100 UTC.

Witnesses in the briefing room recalled the pilot studying the weather reports on his iPad and announcing "the fog is lifting quickly". When asked by another pilot what he was planning to do that morning, the pilot replied that he was intending "to use the Altior's autoland system at a new airfield". The pilot said that he had purposely selected a quiet airfield which did not have an ATC, AFIS or AG, so that he could conduct his planned manoeuvres unimpeded by circuit compliance and traffic separation requirements.

The pilot booked out from EGBJ at 1236 UTC, giving his destination as "Old Warnock (no ICAO code)" and, after lifting 60 litres of fuel, departed from EGBJ at 1302 UTC. By this time, the weather was good with over 10km visibility.

The flight proceeded uneventfully. The aircraft climbed to an altitude of 3000 feet amsl. The pilot was working Gloucester Approach 128.55 until 1316 UTC after which he transferred to Bristol LARS 125.65 for a Basic Service and was allocated squawk code 5076. He reported at 1345 UTC that he would transfer to the Safetycom frequency 135.475.

An aircraft enthusiast located at the West side of the field was using a handheld radio tuned to 135.475. He observed the aircraft approaching from the North. He heard the pilot broadcast

Altior 10 making a left base join for a landing at Old Warnock, runway zero seven

The aircraft had just completed the left turn from base leg to final approach when the witness saw it suddenly lose altitude and dive nose first into the ground. Although he and others immediately called the emergency services and ran to the scene, the pilot had been fatally injured.

Old Warnock

Old Warnock airfield is located on private land in North Somerset near the village of Warnock. The airfield is situated in uncontrolled airspace and is unlicensed and unstaffed. It is used principally by microlights, gyroplanes, and model aircraft and drone flyers.

It has a single paved surface runway oriented 07/25, 595 x 35 metres.

Meteorology

The weather was dry but with widespread early fog. The fog cleared slowly in the South West of England, although it persisted elsewhere. It was mild with temperatures reaching 20°C in some parts of the region.

Records retrieved from the pilot's home computer showed that he accessed TAFs for EGBJ and Bristol (EGGD) at 0930 UTC. The TAFs current at that time were

EGBJ 270925Z 2709/2718 VRB03KT 0100 FG VV-\n BCMG 2710/2713 9999

EGGD 270915Z 2709/2718 12005KT 0700 BR BCMG 2710/2613 9999

At the time of the pilot's departure from EGBJ at 1302 UTC, the METARs for both EGBJ and EGGD showed visibility in excess of 10 km with a light wind mainly from the North East.

The ATIS current at EGBJ at 1302 UTC was as follows:

This is Gloucester Information Lima. Time 1300. Runway in use 09 right hand circuit. Wind Variable at 3 knots. Visibility 10 kilometres or more. Cloud Few at 4500 feet. Temperature 14 degrees centigrade. Dew point 12 degrees centigrade. QNH 1028. QFE 1025. On first contact read back altimeter setting in use. Noise abatement requirements apply. Departing aircraft contact Tower 122.90. Arriving aircraft contact Approach 128.55. Acknowledge receipt of information Lima.

Recorded Information

RTF recordings relating to the flight were obtained from EGBJ and EGGD. There was no record of any broadcasts on the Safetycom frequency but a witness at the airfield was able to supply some information from memory (see History of the Flight above).

The flight plan and communications configuration input by the pilot before leaving EGBJ into the aircraft's Astrak Mark 1 GPS unit (see Aircraft Information below) were held in its database and recovered from the aircraft subsequent to the accident. Evidence indicated that it had been controlling the aircraft until shortly before the impact with the ground. The unit has a colour screen which shows the position of the aircraft on a moving map display which includes topographic features, airfields and waypoints. On final approach to a runway, the point at which the autopilot software transfers control to the autoland software, a broken line extending from the runway centreline is displayed.

The Astrak unit contained a flight plan from EGBJ to Old Warnock. Radar evidence shows that this plan was followed at least until 1345 UTC when the pilot transferred to the Safetycom frequency and resumed the VFR squawk 7000. After 1400 UTC there were no further radar returns for the aircraft.

Examination of the unit by the manufacturer showed that the autopilot had been engaged following take off at EGBJ and had subsequently flown the flight plan which had been entered by the pilot until the aircraft reached Old Warnock and made its turn onto final approach at a height of 500 feet agl. The Astrak autopilot had at this point transferred control automatically to the auto landing system software.

Aircraft Information

The Ardua Altior 10 is a 'glass cockpit' aircraft and is equipped with an Astrak Mark 1 autopilot and fibre optic 'fly by wire' flight control system. The aircraft is also fitted with a conventional Attitude Indicator (AI), Directional Indicator (DI), Airspeed Indicator (ASI), Altimeter, and magnetic compass for redundancy.

The aircraft is of composite construction, powered by a Fellowes FE 66 piston engine and is fitted with a two-bladed constant speed propeller. It has four seats and is unpressurised. It has a fixed undercarriage.

The aircraft has a maximum take off weight of 1361kg and a maximum cruise speed of 170 KIAS. The published power off stall speed at maximum take off weight, with flaps and gear retracted, is 67 KIAS. Usable fuel tank capacity is 212 litres.

The Astrak Mark 1 is a combined autopilot and autoland system operated from the primary flight display. The control surfaces – elevator, elevator trim, ailerons, and rudder - are operated by fibre optic 'wire' connections. The Astrak software will fly the route input by the pilot prior to take off and will land the aircraft at the selected location. At present, the Astrak software does not offer automated take off functionality.

The operation of the Astrak Mark 1 system is described in detail in the flight manual. The manual contains the following instruction: *Do not attempt to hand fly the aircraft when either the autopilot or autolanding functions are engaged, as this may result in a mistrim and/or excessive control forces. Whilst the fly by wire system is designed to eliminate such problems, the control surfaces are nevertheless moveable to some extent by pilot input.*

The aircraft was built by Ardua Industrie S.p.A, Milan, Italy, and is maintained in the UK by an Ente Nazionale per l'Aviazione Civile

(ENAC) approved maintenance organisation. The Astrak Mark 1 system was developed for Ardua in the UK by Astrak Avionics, Cheltenham.

The aircraft had logged just under 400 hours and had no deferred defects. It had not previously suffered any damage.

Accident Site and Initial Wreckage Examination

The wreckage was found in a field one mile to the South West of the runway. The aircraft had struck the ground in a nose down attitude with a high rate of descent and low forward speed. The fuselage was orientated towards 070° M consistent with an approach to the North Easterly runway. The pattern of the damage to the underside of the wings indicates that the aircraft's original flight path was less steep than its nose down attitude, suggesting a sudden dive. Wing and tail attachments had failed. The propeller had detached and both blades were broken. Flaps were at 50%. The fuel tank had ruptured and was empty.

Weight and Balance

The pilot occupied the front seat and there were no passengers. There was one small flight bag found in the wreckage of the aircraft. The aircraft would have been comfortably within its published weight and balance limits.

Detailed Wreckage Examination

Damage to the flying controls was consistent with an impact with the ground. There was no evidence of pre-impact failures or control restrictions.

The powerplant showed no disconnections, apart from some overload failures caused by impact. There was no evidence of pre-impact mechanical failure or excessive heat in the engine.

The detachment and breakages to the propeller were consistent with an impact with the ground whilst the propeller was rotating.

The Astrak Mark 1 system was too badly damaged to test but the memory chip remained intact. Analysis of the data showed that the aircraft was under the control of the autoland system and had been correctly set up with an approach speed of 80 KIAS and 50% Flap. The autoland system had stopped working on impact and recoverable data in the memory was current up until an estimated 10 seconds prior to that.

Medical and Pathological Information

A post-mortem examination of the pilot revealed no evidence of any pre-existing medical condition which could have caused or been contributory to the accident. The pathologist concluded that the pilot was alive at the time of the accident and in contact with the flying controls. Toxicological results indicated no evidence of alcohol or drugs or carbon monoxide poisoning. The pilot died from multiple injuries sustained in the impact of the aircraft with the ground.

Pilot's History

The pilot had a PPL (Aeroplanes) obtained eight years ago with an IMC Rating which he had obtained shortly afterwards. He flew regularly and acquired the Altior 10 one year prior to the accident. His logbook showed that he had 50 hours already logged on the aircraft and that he had used the autoland functionality on ten previous occasions at EGBJ and Oxford (EGTK). According to his logbook the pilot had not previously visited Old Warnock.

Instructors who had flown with the pilot described him as conscientious and competent. They assessed his ability to cope with multi-tasking and unusual conditions as being higher than average and commented favourably on his familiarity with, and interest in, the aircraft's innovative technology.

Analysis and Conclusions

The aircraft struck the ground in a steep nose down attitude whilst correctly configured and under the control of the autoland system on final approach to the runway at Old Warnock airfield. There was no evidence of any prior mechanical or structural fault with the aircraft itself.

The data recovered from the Astrak Mark 1 flight control system showed that the autopilot was operating normally and had flown the pre-entered route without incident. The autoland functionality had positioned and configured the aircraft correctly for landing, although the last recorded data from the system was estimated at about 10 seconds prior to the impact, suggesting that the autoland system had been disengaged or disabled during the approach.

The pilot appears to have been conscious and physically able to take control of the aircraft during the approach. It is unclear whether the pilot purposely disconnected the autoland system in favour of making a hand-flown landing or whether the autoland system became non-functional for some unknown reason. The former appears unlikely, given the stated purpose of the pilot's visit to Old Warnock. In the event of the latter, the configuration and speed of the aircraft would not of itself have caused the aircraft to adopt an extreme nose down attitude – it would have continued to glide towards the runway. Some intervention by the pilot or a serious malfunction with the autoland system would have been required to bring about the fatal collision with the ground.

*

Extract from The Daily Mail, 12 May

Horror Plane Crash Stuns Onlookers
Model aircraft and drone flyers at Old Warnock airfield in Somerset watched in horror as a state of the art Italian Altior 10 plane dived into the ground in front of them, killing the pilot. An Air Accident report revealed that the horror crash happened in October last year as the 35 year old pilot desperately tried to land the plane. Twisted wreckage was strewn across nearby fields. The reason for the crash is not known but could have been caused by the automated Astrak landing system going haywire. Automated landing systems are commonly used on commercial flights all over the world.

Extract from The Times, 12 May

Fatal Crash Claims Pilot's Life

An enquiry into a fatal accident involving an Italian made Altior 10 light aircraft at Old Warnock airfield has concluded that pilot intervention or a serious malfunction with the Astrak Mark 1 autoland system may have caused the aircraft to nosedive into the ground whilst approaching the runway for landing. The Altior 10 is manufactured by Ardua Industrie S.p.A of Milan and the Astrak Mark 1 flight control system was developed and built by Astrak Avionics in Cheltenham. The Astrak Mark 1 system is a fibre optic fly by wire system which is unique to the Altior 10 aircraft. Although the pilot, who died from multiple injuries sustained in the impact with the ground, was experienced and familiar with the Astrak system, the accident raises serious questions as to whether such systems can be safely used by general aviation pilots as opposed to professionals.

11

Isabella Hall and George Harvey had just finished reading the Air Accidents Investigation Branch report and the associated news items when Frank Stanley quietly returned to the shady upstairs room with its North facing balcony window. He was sitting once again on one of the green cushioned wicker chairs with a small glass of whisky in his hand.

In the two hours since Frank had arrived at the quaint Faratxa apartment, the relentless sun had moved further on its course towards the seaward end of the harbour and was ready to fall below the tree-covered promontory guarding the route out to the open water beyond. Early evening drinkers had begun to congregate in the bars of the harbourside street below the balcony and their convivial multi-lingual conversations floated upwards through the open shutters, giving the apartment room the feeling of a holiday atmosphere.

"So what's this about, Frank?" asked Isabella, impatiently, "That report is utter rubbish. There was no accident at Old Warnock airfield last October. Something like that would have given Lewis and Kelly enough material for weeks of gossip and speculation. Even sensible people would have known and talked about it. And the airfield would have been closed for weeks too. It wasn't, as you well know."

"Nevertheless," Frank Stanley responded, placing his glass carefully onto the coffee table, "That report appeared in the Monthly Bulletin issued by the AAIB earlier this month. And, as you see, the mainstream press picked it up and featured it, as they always do with suitably interesting material when these bulletins come out."

"So this is a genuine AAIB report?" George Harvey asked.

"I didn't say that," returned Frank, "I merely stated that it had appeared in the May Monthly Bulletin on the AAIB website."

"So are you saying that it's fake?" asked Isabella, "That would explain a few things, then. I'm familiar with the Altior 10. It's a very smart little aircraft, with a glass cockpit and an autopilot and navigation system operated from the flight display screens. But it's not a fly by wire aircraft. However smart it looks, the control surfaces are all still operated by the pilot using normal mechanical systems. It's too light to need hydraulics and it's got a fixed undercarriage. I don't think there are any single engine light aircraft which have a fly by wire system. It would probably cost a fortune to make and to buy, even if they did exist."

"Anything else?' asked Frank.

"Well, I think the reports usually give the registration of the aircraft," said Isabella slowly, "And making an automated landing at an unlicensed airfield with no navigation aids would be a tall order even for something with advanced technology on board. Some visual piloting would have to be involved, either from on board the aircraft or remotely."

"What would you say," asked Frank, "if I told you that similar accident reports have appeared in official air accident publications in two other European countries, all involving an Altior 10 with a fibre optic fly by wire system?"

"All fake?" George intervened.

"All fake," stated Frank, and fell silent.

"So what you are saying," Isabella filled in, "Is that someone has gone to a lot of trouble to invent an air accident to a non-existent aircraft, or more than one accident by the sound of it, and to insert fake reports about them into genuine official air accident publications?"

"That's what it looks like," replied Frank.

"Three questions for you, then, Frank," said George, immediately, "How has this been done, why, and by whom?"

"And a fourth," added Isabella, pointedly, "Why have you come all the way here to Faratxa to tell us about it?"

"I can't answer all those questions," Frank responded, "But I'll tell you what I know. And then you will understand why I'm here."

So, as Isabella and George sat in expectant silence, Frank went on,

"You are correct about the report being a fake. As you have rightly said, Isabella, there was no air accident, fatal or otherwise, at Old Warnock airfield in October last year. If there had been, it would inevitably have been known about and reported in the media, not to mention the local area, at the time. As it was, there was no indication of any such accident until several months later, when an apparent accident investigation had reached its conclusions, and had published these in a report on the Air Accidents Investigation Bureau website.

"The AAIB publishes a monthly bulletin on the second Thursday of every month. The bulletin is presented as a single pdf document containing a number of reports. Most of the reports concern relatively minor accidents and potentially dangerous incidents to both commercial and general aviation aircraft in UK airspace. Many are self-reported by the pilot involved and do not require an investigation by the AAIB, nor, indeed, would one be possible in most cases. Field investigations are undertaken only when the accident is fatal or results in serious injury or consequential danger to the pilot, passengers or both.

"For very serious accidents, especially those with wider reaching implications, an investigation report would be published separately from the monthly bulletin. But accidents, even fatal ones, to a small private aircraft such as the Altior and its pilot, would be included in the monthly bulletin. Depending on the nature of the accident, the investigations can take some time, so the investigation reports usually appear some months after the accident itself occurred. In the case of this fake report, the accident apparently happened in October and the report appeared seven months later, in May.

"As I have said, a new bulletin is published on the AAIB website on a regular schedule each month. The mainstream press is aware of this schedule and will routinely scan the bulletins as they are published for anything which they believe will interest their readers. This is what led to the creation of the reports in The Daily Mail and The Times, extracts from which were included in your briefing.

"A range of knowledgeable people also take an interest in the reports published on the AAIB website – pilots, aviation enthusiasts, the specialist aviation press, those involved with the aircraft industry, to name but an obvious few. Because of this, any error or fakery would be quickly discovered, and that is exactly what happened in this case.

"The problem, though, is that the discovery came too late to prevent the contents of the fake report getting into the public domain. The Times and the Daily Mail both published a correction the following day. But far fewer people will have noticed the correction than read the original news item. Worse still, the automatic news bots used by online news media found the report as soon as it was published and the incorrect information went viral within an hour of the appearance of the report. There was no interest in a correction subsequently published by the AAIB on its site, so the fake information permanently entered the plethora of digital news items circulating around the globe. An online search on Ardua Industrie will now give the fatal accident at Old Warnock as its top hit. Articles and news items from both the AAIB and Ardua identifying the report as a hoax appear much lower on the results list.

"The AAIB report is not the first instance of an Ardua Altior 10 aircraft being the subject of a fake accident report. In April a news report of a non-existent accident to an Altior 10 appeared on the website of an Italian news radio station, apparently placed there as a result of information from the Agenzia Nationale per la Sicurezza delle Ferrovie, the ANSF, which is the Italian equivalent of the UK AAIB. The ANSF, when approached, knew nothing about the report and the item was removed, but, again, too late to stop it gaining some foothold in the minds of the Italian public. Shortly afterwards, a report was inserted onto the site of the Bureau d'Enquetes et d'Analyses pour la Securite de l'Aviation Civile, the BEA, in France. This also described an accident, apparently in Auxerre, to an Altior 10, another accident which never happened. In neither of these cases was the accident described as fatal, but in both instances there was an implication that there had been a failure of control on landing which had caused an impact with the ground. And both aircraft were said to have been fitted with the Astrak Mark 1 system.

"You have rightly said, Isabella, that no light aircraft is currently on the market equipped with a fly by wire system. Autopilots of various levels of sophistication are common, of course, as are glass cockpits, in light aircraft, but no form of autoland system is currently licensed for use in any small general aviation aircraft. Neither the Altior 10 nor any other aircraft is equipped with a combination system of the sort described in the AAIB report. As you said, the Altior 10 does have a glass cockpit with an autopilot which is operated by the pilot from the primary flight display. But its control surfaces are certainly not fly by wire operated. They are conventional cable controls moved by inputs from the pilot.

"Of the three fake reports which have so far appeared, the one on the AAIB website is certainly the most sophisticated. Although anyone with even basic knowledge of light aircraft and of the structure of AAIB reports would recognise it as a fake – as indeed the majority of the educated audience for the reports immediately did – it contains enough apparently authoritative information and background information to appear genuine at first glance.

"Your first question, George, was about how this had been done. That is probably the simplest question to answer. Straightforward hacking of the Italian radio station site, the French BEA website, and the AAIB pdf document was the basic method used. In the case of the AAIB report, the hacker simply removed the genuine pdf document and replaced it with another document which was identical in all respects except that it had the fake report inserted at an appropriate place amongst the real reports.

"Your second question was about why someone had done this. There are a number of possible reasons. The least sinister of these would be that it is some kind of practical joke, or something akin to trolling, designed to damage the reputation of Ardua Industrie or Astrak Avionics, or both. Such reports are bound to make investors or customers nervous and to be damaging to these businesses. The other, less likely, possibility is that it may be an attempt to damage the credibility of the AAIB and its equivalents in Italy and France

"A second reason, perhaps associated with the first, is that some sort of blackmail is planned. Pay up, or we publish more of these reports, that kind of thing. So far, though, no demand for money, or any other form of payment or favour, has been made to either Ardua or Astrak. Or at least, the companies have not told the authorities, if anything has in fact been received.

"A third reason is that this is some kind of message. What the message is and to whom it could be directed is something I'll come back to in a minute.

"You asked, George, who had done this. If we knew that, of course, we would not be sitting here discussing it now. But we do have some clues. Firstly, the person is clearly proficient in English, French and Italian, or has the assistance of other people who speak these languages. Secondly, he or she has some familiarity with aviation, particularly in the UK. Although the flaws, or more accurately, the omissions, in the fake AAIB report are easy to spot, there is great deal which is accurate. The weather reports, for instance, are genuine, although not for the date given in the text. The information about the airfields – frequencies, procedures, runways, and so on – is all correct. Where the report falls down is the lack of detail on the engineering aspects of such an investigation. These are glossed over, and a conclusion reached without a full description or discussion of the physical evidence. A genuine report would contain all this information. Our guess, therefore, is that the person, or maybe people, concerned is a pilot, an aviation enthusiast or someone involved with general aviation in some capacity, say, an aviation operations manager, air traffic controller, model aircraft flyer, or something like that. In other words, this is a person who knows enough about the aviation world to concoct these stories and make them sound superficially convincing.

"What is less clear is to what extent the perpetrator knows that the information in the story can easily be identified as fake. On the one hand, the person could be someone so relatively incompetent or naïve, a school student perhaps, as to think that the stories will be believed. Such a person's only interest would probably be in feeling powerful by making the authorities look foolish. On the other hand, the stories could have been concocted in the full knowledge that they would be quickly debunked, albeit after the false information had already passed on into the murky waters of digital news. If this second option is the correct one, then we have someone here who is trying to draw him or her self to our attention in a very specific way.

"You may wonder why I have so quickly passed over the option that this could simply be some sort of prank by a youngster or by someone obsessed with pretending they working in the world of aviation. Believe me, there are plenty of those types of characters. They lurk on forums and websites aimed at pilots, perhaps setting up false profiles for themselves and submitting posts and questions through which they aim to fool other members, and probably themselves, into thinking they are aviation professionals. This hacker could certainly be one of those people, were it not for two factors.

"You asked why I had come all the way to Faratxa to tell you both about this. The answer to that question lies in the two factors which make us believe that this individual, or individuals, is more than just a harmless online ego tripper.

"The first factor is that the route through which the hacks have been perpetrated has been traced. It does not lead back to some teenager's bedroom. It leads back to something you, George, know all about. It is the computer in what used to be a canalside wine museum in Frossiac."

Having listened to Frank's narrative without interruption or comment, Isabella and George both immediately reacted to Frank's revelation with audible gasps.

"Let me get this straight," George asked, his consternation evident in his voice, "Someone is using Maurice Vacher's old office computer to do this? Or..."

"Go on, George," prompted Frank.

"The computer in Frossiac is just acting as the host," continued George, slowly, "Which means that the origin of the hack is elsewhere - somewhere to which the Frossiac computer has a connection. But surely that route can't still be open. I should have thought they would have disabled it straightaway to protect their systems."

"Think about it George," Frank told him, "The trap you planted in Frossiac was designed to be sprung when someone typed the name Susan Stonehouse into the wine museum computer. The track back to Egzon's systems had been created by Egzon himself when he found the trail which you had intended him to follow in order to reach the Frossiac computer. Your ninja bomb then ran back through the route, destroyed Egzon's IT set up, and, as we found out later, Egzon himself. Then the route was deliberately left open in order to trap Aleksander and his people into thinking they were on the track of Susan Stonehouse. What if the route is still open now?"

"But surely," said George, "Egzon would have had understudies, minions who could have recreated the Paloka systems. They would have found the doorway to the trail and disabled it."

"You would have thought so," Frank said, "But for one thing. No-one would have known what it was for. After all, Egzon had created it himself. I doubt any of the minions, as you call them, would have been trusted with the campaign against Susan Stonehouse. My guess is that Egzon did that personally and I would stake my life on it that he also personally made the searches which led him to the Frossiac computer. When the attack happened, he died without having been able to tell anyone what he had done."

"But the person who traced Susan Stonehouse afterwards must have used it," objected George.

"I am sure they did," Frank said, "But there has been a lot of falling out in the Paloka empire. Once Egzon and Aleksander were out of the way, the vile set up started to implode. In fighting. Power grabbing. That sort of thing. We helped it on its way, of course. The drug dealing, arms trading, identity theft, people trafficking, child pornography, all that evil stuff is still going on to some extent. But the control is fragmented now and the Paloka empire no longer exists in the form it did. Egzon's systems are mostly still in place, but it is clear that no-one has the knowledge to use them in the way Egzon did. One wormhole leading to a computer in the South of France could be anything. Just one of many elements of Egzon's tangled tentacles in the dark web."

"But you said this aviation hacker is using the Frossiac route," objected George, "So he or she clearly knows about it."

"That's not the point," said Frank, "The point is, do they know that we know about it? That it was created by us and not by Egzon? In other words, are they using it because they think it is a convenient cover for their hacking activities, or because they want to draw their presence to our attention?"

"Why would they want to do that?" Isabella spoke up for the first time, "Surely they are not still looking for Susan Stonehouse."

"No, they aren't," said Frank, "I mentioned a second factor, and that is the location of the fake UK accident at Old Warnock airfield. We think they are telling us that they know what is there."

"And what's that?" asked Isabella, a note of fear creeping into her voice.

"Katz:i," said Frank.

12

From his vantage point on at the top of the hills above Sampfield Grange, Sam pensively regarded the familiar view of the smooth and distant sea, a neatly laid out silk scarf beyond the hedgerow patterned countryside which rolled out unevenly below him. The usually patient Caladesi Island snorted and shifted softly, occasionally shaking his handsome brown head to tell his rider that it was time that the two of them returned to the yard where breakfast would be waiting.

The easterly glow of the soft October sun effortlessly illuminated the motionless rural scene. Sam could make out the buzz of unseen traffic on the roads below, the chatter of distant birds, the cries of scattered sheep, the occasional call of a human voice and the answering bark of a dog. Otherwise, the last of the Summer countryside seemed to have stopped dead in its lazy tracks, half asleep, unwilling to give way to the approaching winter. The surrounding trees were still undecided, thick tinges of fired gold edging some of their leaves, the rest of the foliage still stubbornly green. Sam had passed bushes laden with fat blackberries as he and the rest of the morning ride had made their way upwards along the track taking them away from the Sampfield Grange yard.

Sam usually welcomed the approach of Autumn. It was the time of year when all the activities which made up his carefully ordered life were about to commence in earnest once again. Summer was an arid season when the horses and the people who worked with them went on their holidays and the unchanging routine of the Sampfield Grange yard wound down and almost stopped.

Sam had often found himself at a loose end in the Summer. Granted, he could attend as many prestigious flat race meetings as he wished, there being no shortage of invitations from friends and racing colleagues, but these were not events in which he had a personal stake. Traditional country pursuits came to a virtual halt in the heated weeks of August and many of his neighbours took themselves off to eat Mediterranean fare in cottages, castles and villas in the South of France, Italy and further afield. Sam generally disliked hot weather and had politely declined numerous offers from family connections, Gilbert Peveril and his wife Pippa in particular, to join them on such overseas excursions.

But this Summer had been different. The absence of Sadie from the Sampfield Grange yard, an informative few days staying with Eoghan Foley in Ireland, a greater than usual involvement in Summer jump racing occasioned by the need to extend Kye's competitive riding experience, and the determination of his childhood friend, Lady Helen Garratt, to involve him in her project to set up a centre for inner city youngsters to gain experience with racehorses had all claimed his time and attention. And that had led to the fuss about Old Warnock airfield.

Sam could see the airfield now. It lay to his right about five miles away alongside the rather unattractive village of Warnock in a flat and open area beyond the narrow stream which wandered along the westerly border of the Sampfield estate. A single hard surfaced runway surrounded by grass and overlooked by a few uninteresting buildings all showed up clearly in the mild morning sunshine. If Sam had ever thought about Old Warnock airfield, he had assumed it was part of the Warnock estate, belonging to the farm of the same name, a wartime white elephant left to take its chance in the empty countryside, of no interest to anyone other than the local youngsters looking for somewhere to hang around undisturbed by adults.

It had been Helen who had brought the airfield to his attention, assuming that Sam would be in a position to help her. The open land, with its nearby grazing, quiet bridleways and empty buildings had seemed a suitable location on which to establish her equestrian facility for retired racehorses. But her attempts to purchase or rent the land had run into unexpected difficulties.

"I don't know what the problem is," Helen had told Sam over the telephone, "My lawyer can't find out a thing about it. Mr Penney, the farmer at Warnock Farm, says that the land for the airfield was requisitioned by the Government during the War and his grandfather and father never got it back. They were compensated so they weren't too bothered. But no-one seems to know who owns it now."

"But surely the Land Registry has a current owner listed for the property?" Sam had asked.

"Apparently not," Helen had told him, sounding cross, "The property is listed as *Bona Vacantia*, which apparently means that it is ownerless and so by law passes into the ownership of the Crown, so, in effect, the Treasury. This usually happens apparently when someone dies intestate and there are no known kin, or else if it belongs to a company which has been dissolved."

"Can you not make an offer to purchase it from the Crown?" had asked Sam, not seeing the problem.

"You would have thought so," Helen had replied, sighing, "But there is a set of obstacles worthy of the cross country course at Badminton to negotiate, and every way we turn, the process seems to get more complicated. It seems to be up to the purchaser to make all the enquiries and present all the proofs that the previous owner is dead, or has gone out of business if it was a company that owned it, and has left the land unclaimed and unencumbered. And even then there are all sorts of disclaimers and caveats about possible third party rights over the land. Getting the information has been almost impossible. My lawyers are suggesting I should look elsewhere for a suitable site. But, honestly, Sam, this is so ideal, with you close by and plenty of room for everything we want to do."

Sam had not been sure that "everything we want to do" had been quite the correct description of his role in Helen's project. As far as he recalled, he had offered to help with finance and advice, but Helen had been clearly determined that he should do more than this.

"Can you find anything out, Sam, darling?" had asked Helen, adopting what she had clearly hoped was her most persuasive tone, "You're a neighbouring landowner. Maybe your estate people can get more information. Local knowledge and all that."

Eventually Sam had agreed to see what his Land Agent, Trevor Wills, could discover about Old Warnock airfield. In common with many of the employees of the Sampfields, the Wills family had served as Land Agents for three generations. Internet technology had in recent years diminished the burden of the work to the extent that the present Mr Wills was able to undertake other profitable employment for himself in addition to looking after the affairs of the Sampfield Grange estate. But the Sampfield family was still his foremost concern.

Even the experienced Trevor Wills, after making various enquiries in the local area, had been able to make little more progress than that which Helen had already reported to Sam.

"The land was definitely requisitioned by the Government during the War," Trevor had confirmed to Sam, "Which was when the airfield was established. It stayed in Government ownership after the War was over and the Penney family at Warnock Farm were paid for it. The interesting thing is that it never came up for sale once it stopped being used as an active airfield. As far as I can make out, it has not officially been declared as disused. I went up there and spoke to the microlight people and model aircraft flyers. They got their permission to fly there through the local council. So I checked with my contact there and she says there's an order in place which permits occasional recreational use but not the erection of any permanent structure or the establishment of any business. But that is a local planning restriction relating to environmental concerns, rather than anything specified by any owner, and that could be appealed should anyone have an appropriate proposal for the site which addressed the environmental issues."

"And what are they?" Sam had asked.

"Noise issues, potential for traffic congestion, pollution, lack of adequate infrastructure, that kind of thing," Trevor had told him, "Nothing which a developer could not easily address. But that doesn't seem to be the obstacle. It is to do with lack of available proof of recent ownership and associated rights over the use of the land. The Treasury won't allow anything to be done whilst that is unresolved. And there appears to be no way of getting any clarity without going to considerable expense."

Sam had thanked Trevor for his efforts and had decided to keep the unhelpful information to himself until such time as Helen contacted him again. To his relief, she had not yet done so, having spent much of the summer abroad with her husband, the musician Sir John Garratt, and their family. But Sam had no doubt that he would hear from her soon. Helen was nothing if not persistent.

Yielding to Caladesi Island's increasingly irritable shuffling and headshaking, Sam turned the restless horse in the direction of the track back towards home. The quiet time at the top of the hill had been intended to help him get his thoughts in order. Decisions needed to be made about races for Highlander Park and Curlew Landings, not to mention the future staffing of the yard during the next three months. Amelia Dicks had shown no sign of returning from her trip to Australia and her father was keen to retain Sadie's services.

Sadie, it appeared, was doing well at the Dicks establishment. At her request, Ranulph Dicks had helped her to apply for a BHA qualification certificate to enable her to ride his pointers in races. Sam had been surprised when Ranulph had spoken to him about this proposal.

"I support it, of course," Sam had told Ranulph, "Sadie is an excellent horsewoman. But she has never shown any interest in race riding before. She always told me that she preferred riding work and hunting."

"Well, it was her idea," Ranulph had told him, "She said she thought I might need a jockey with Amelia being away."

Sam had since wondered whether it was Merlin ap Rhys who had encouraged Sadie in this new ambition. He had not seen Merlin since the meeting at Cheltenham in April when Merlin had won his race on Fan Court. Merlin had been riding for Dorset trainer, Justin Venn, and, more recently, for some Northern trainers, people Sam did not know. Sam hoped that Merlin would still be available to ride Curlew Landings later in the month, not to mention the exceptional Tabikat, that is, if Tabikat were ever to come back into Sam's care. Curlew was no longer a novice and a campaign needed to be mapped out for him for this season. As for Tabikat, his future seemed to lie once again with Brendan Meaghan in County Meath.

The thorny blackberry bushes reached out across the well worn track as Caladesi Island picked his way along the familiar route. The sound of youthful voices from the yard below floated up on the rising warm air towards horse and rider. Sam recognised the Lancashire tones of Jackie Taylor, the recent, and very welcome, addition to the Sampfield Grange staff. Jackie had come to Sampfield Grange from Sir Andrew Cunningham's establishment, having been rather cautiously recommended by Kye.

"It's up to yez, Mr Sampfield," Kye had said, "But with Sadie gone, we could use the help, and I've known Jackie for a while."

Sam might not have been quite so receptive to the suggestion had he known in what capacity Kye had become acquainted with Jackie, but said he would consider Kye's proposal and duly contacted Sir Andrew Cunningham for a reference for the girl.

"Doing your own stable staff management these days, Sam?" Sir Andrew had chafed him, "That head lass of yours has gone to Dicks's place, I hear?"

"Unfortunately so," Sam had replied, "But she's due back in the New Year, so we're soldiering on here without her for now. The young lad I have looking after things whilst she is away is good, but he's young and lacks experience."

"He's the one who rode your horse to win that ridiculous race against our Merriott Marsh, is he not?" Sir Andrew had asked, "Useful young chap, I should say. Gilbert not mind being jocked off, then?"

"I suspect Gil was rather relieved, actually, Drew," Sam had told him, with a laugh, "I think young Highlander was beginning to get the better of him. We had a bit of a farce in a bumper at Newbury last season."

Sir Andrew had laughed in turn and had said he would ask his yard manager to call Sam with a reference for Jackie. The yard manager had confirmed Jackie to be a hard worker, good with the horses, a bit lacking in experience at racing yard level, but nothing that time and familiarity would not mend. So Jackie had duly been hired, to the scarcely concealed annoyance of Lewis and Kelly, the Sampfield Grange house staff, who expected to be consulted about all staffing decisions.

Kelly had immediately called Sadie on her mobile phone. She had been surprised to learn that Mr Sampfield had consulted Sadie before making the decision.

"But we don't know her," Kelly had objected, crossly, "She's not from round here. She's a Northerner, like Kye."

"I know her," Sadie had told her sister, "She looks after some of the Cunningham horses. I've met her at points when I've been riding for the Dickses. Luke thinks she's very promising."

"So it's Luke now, is it?" Kelly had said to Lewis later, "Sounds like Sadie might be too posh for us when she comes back here after Christmas. Hobnobbing with the bosses and all that."

Notwithstanding this unpromising start, Jackie herself had so far been a success, not only at helping Kye to keep his bed warm, but also at ensuring that the shared cottage was tidier than it had been since Sadie had departed.

As Caladesi Island clattered to his customary stopping point in the yard, the dark haired Jackie, who had been awaiting their return, came forward and reached out to take the horse by the bridle.

"Go in for breakfast, Jackie," Sam told her, "I'll deal with Cal."

Flashing him a bright smile, Jackie walked gratefully away in the direction of the house. As Sam dismounted the relieved horse, he saw Bethany emerge from the yard office, a sheet of paper in her hand.

"Good morning, Mr Sampfield," Bethany said hastily, before Sam could walk the long-suffering Caladesi Island into his stable, "There are a number of messages for you. People wanting you to call them back this morning."

"I'll come in to the office when Cal's settled," Sam told her, wondering what could be so urgent that the telephone calls had to be returned that same morning. He fervently hoped that it was not Helen wanting to discuss more worries about her pet project.

The four callers who all wanted to claim Sam's time that morning turned out to be Trevor Wills, Brendan Meaghan, Jessica Moretti, and a person neither Bethany nor Sam had heard of before, who had given her name as Mrs Meredith Crosland.

"I'll call them from the house after breakfast," Sam told Bethany, privately deciding to ignore the call from Jessica Moretti, whose name he recognised as likely to be that of the journalist who had spoken to him at Ashfordleigh Downs, "Did this Mrs Crosland say what she wanted to speak to me about? Could you not deal with her yourself?"

"I did try, Mr Sampfield," replied Bethany, bristling slightly, "But Mrs Crosland said it was a personal matter. She told me that Mr Foley in Ireland had recommended that she speak to you."

Sam nodded, intrigued by this information. He could not conceive of any reason why Tabikat's breeder should suggest that someone should contact Sampfield Grange. Taking the piece of paper on which Bethany had written the numbers in the clear handwriting on which her employer always insisted, Sam walked briskly along the path towards the house.

But Sam had little chance either to make the telephone calls or even to eat his breakfast in his accustomed peace that morning. As he approached the main house, which managed to look both imposing and comfortable in the October sunlight, Lewis, who had clearly been looking out for his employer, emerged from the boot room door.

"Mr Sampfield, a visitor has arrived for you," Lewis said, importantly, "He says he's your cousin. I've put him in the Music Room."

As Sam took in this unexpected piece of information, Lewis added, unable to keep his newest piece of gossip to himself,

"And I thought you might be interested, Mr Sampfield. Isabella Hall is back. Kelly saw her getting out of a car at the Charlton Arms."

But what Lewis did not dare to add was that Frank Stanley had been in the car with her.

13

Sam's initial reaction on entering the Music Room was that the boy looked exhausted. He was slumped in one of the green upholstered wing chairs by the unlit wood burner. A large and battered khaki rucksack lay on its side on the boarded floor to the side of the chair. The young man's eyes were closed and his chaotic blond hair had flopped across his forehead. He was tanned and fit looking, but skinny along with it, as though he had not eaten for some time. A rumpled sweatshirt above scruffy jeans and desert boots completed the picture.

Sam could not decide whether or not his guest was asleep.

"Ryan Urquhart?" he said, experimentally.

The boy in the chair opened his eyes immediately and sprang to his feet.

"Sorry, sir, just dozin' off there," he said quickly, in a strongly Australian accented voice still thick with sleep.

"There's no need to call me sir," Sam told him, "You're my cousin Teddy's son. I'm not sure in what exact family relation that puts the two of us, but I think we're perhaps second cousins, or something like that."

"Yeah, guess that's right," said the young man, visibly taking control of himself, "Pleased to meet you. Ryan Urquhart come to visit, as you can see."

Notwithstanding the stronger tone of voice in which Ryan was now speaking, he seemed to Sam to be unsteady on his feet. The hand which he held out trembled slightly.

"And I am pleased to meet you too," Sam told him, shaking the proffered hand, "Your father said you might be coming here. But you look exhausted. Have you eaten?"

"Hitched all the way from Heathrow overnight," Ryan replied, "Went wrong a few times, but in the end someone dropped me by a pub down the road here and I walked up. Just a bit stuffed. No breakfast yet."

"Very well," said Sam, "I haven't had breakfast either, so let me deal with that first. I don't want your father complaining that I haven't been looking after you properly."

Ryan laughed uncertainly, but obediently picked up his rucksack and followed Sam into the kitchen. The assembled work riders together with Kye and Jackie were gathered around the square pine table, tucking into their food. Kelly and Lewis hovered in the background, hardly able to contain their curiosity about the dishevelled traveller whose arrival had been so mysteriously signalled in a late night telephone call several months earlier.

"This is Ryan, from Mrs Sampfield's family in Australia," Sam said shortly, "I am sure you can all introduce yourselves. Kelly, make sure Ryan gets some breakfast and then find him somewhere to sleep. You and I can talk later when you're rested, Ryan."

Ryan simply nodded and sat down suddenly in the nearest chair, eyeing the food on the table hungrily.

"I'll shortly be making a number of telephone calls from the study," Sam told Lewis, "But I'll eat in the breakfast room as usual first."

When Sam finally reached his study after a relatively hurried breakfast, he already had another task to add to his list. Bethany had called through from the office to say that Merlin ap Rhys had left a message, asking whether it would be convenient to drop in to Sampfield Grange on his way back from Exeter races later that afternoon. Bethany had told Merlin that Mr Sampfield would be at home and available to see him.

Finishing the remainder of the coffee which he had brought through to the study with him, Sam first called Trevor Wills.

"Good morning, Mr Sampfield," Trevor greeted him politely, "I have some news about Old Warnock airfield which I thought might interest you. It seems that it is coming back into use. My contact at the local council tells me that an aviation business had been given permission to operate there. Apparently the instruction to the council came through a Government department, the Ministry of Defence she thinks. So it looks as if the Government still has a use for the place, after all."

"Helen isn't going to be pleased," thought Sam to himself, whilst telling Trevor, "Thanks for that information, Trevor. I appreciate your help. I trust that doesn't mean that there will be a lot of aircraft flying about the area."

"Well, the noise restrictions still apply," Trevor Wills told him, "Even the Government will have to explain what they intend to do to ensure there is no nuisance caused to local residents."

The next name on the handwritten list was that of Jessica Moretti. Sam took a pen and drew a line through the words. His intention to consult Frank before dealing with this so-called journalist any further was still unfulfilled.

Debating whether to speak next to Brendan Meaghan or the mysterious Mrs Crosland, Sam was saved from making a decision by the desk phone which shrilled intermittently to announce an internal call. Picking it up, he heard Bethany's voice.

"Mrs Crosland is calling again, Mr Sampfield. She's very insistent about speaking to you. Can I put her through to you?"

Reflecting that Mrs Crosland sounded rather like one of Helen's friends, Sam warily agreed to speak to her. Mrs Crosland herself wasted no time in getting to the point.

"Good morning, Mr Sampfield Peveril," she started, "I have a horse that I am wanting to send to you for training. Eoghan Foley in Ireland suggested I approach you. I understand you trained Tabikat for the Cheltenham Gold Cup this year."

"Good morning to you, Mrs Crosland," Sam butted in, hoping to stem this torrent of demanding information coming at him down the phone line, "It is very kind of Mr Foley to recommend me to you, but I don't train horses for other people. Tabikat was an exception."

"That's not a problem," Mrs Crosland continued, quickly brushing aside the objection, "Mr Foley appeared more than happy with what you had done with Tabikat. I am sure we can come to some agreement. I'll give you some information about my horse, shall I?"

Sam could tell that Mrs Crosland intended to provide the information whether or not he agreed to hear it, so he said, carefully, trying not to sound discourteous, "Very well, Mrs Crosland, but do please bear in mind what I have just told you. It is only because of your connection with Mr Foley that I am willing to discuss this with you."

"Very good," responded Mrs Crosland, as though Sam had not spoken, "The horse is called Katseye. He's a five year old gelding by Night Vision out of Mr Foley's Little Kitty Cat. He was bought by my ex husband for our daughter to go pointing. He'd won a couple of point to point races in Ireland and Gabriella did quite well with him here in England too. I'd like to see him in some proper races now. Gabby has gone to University and doesn't have the time. In any case, he needs a professional to bring him on at this stage."

As Mrs Crosland paused for breath, Sam took the opportunity to speak.

"Mrs Crosland," he said, "If I understand correctly, your horse Katseye is a half brother to Tabikat?"

"Yes, that's what I said," replied Mrs Crosland, not quite accurately, "Mr Foley and I think he could be as good as Tabikat. He's four years younger, of course, so just starting on his career really. I'd send him to Brendan Meaghan, but I want him trained in England so we can see him easily. You don't publish your training fees but I am happy to pay the going rate. We did look at Mr Dicks's fees as a guide."

Despite himself, Sam was intrigued. The opportunity to train Tabikat's half brother was not to be dismissed without some thought. He tried to remember what he knew about the sire, Night Vision, but nothing came immediately to mind.

"I'll need to think about this, Mrs Crosland," he told her carefully, playing for time, "May I call you back tomorrow?"

"I'll call you, Mr Sampfield Peveril," stated Mrs Crosland firmly, "About the same time, if that is convenient for you? And my name, by the way, is Meredith."

And before Sam could answer or say anything more, Mrs Crosland had rung off.

Feeling, with some justification, as if he had been steamrollered, Sam sat back in his leather studded chair and took a deep breath. Looking again at the piece of paper lying on the desk, he was reminded that Brendan Meaghan, whose name had been mentioned by Mrs Crosland, had also asked him to call. Perhaps, Sam thought, Brendan could tell him something about Katseye.

Brendan Meaghan appeared to be in a hurry when Sam got through to him a few minutes later.

"Look, you just caught me," Brendan said, apparently speaking on a mobile phone in the middle of a busy yard. Sam could hear horses moving about in the background, accompanied by the Irish accented voices of their handlers, and the sound of the engine of a horsebox being manoeuvred into position, "I'll not keep you. It's about Tabikat. The owners want to aim him at the Cheltenham Gold Cup again, so I need to make a plan for him. They want you involved again when he's in England."

Sam was more pleased with this information than he could express.

"That's excellent news, Brendan," he said, "Merlin ap Rhys is coming to see me later today. I assume the owners will want him to ride the horse again?"

"They do, to be sure," Brendan replied, "He won at Punchestown for them, so they'll not be changing anything. Declan will call you with our ideas."

"Before you go, Brendan," Sam interjected quickly, sensing that Brendan was about to cut the connection, "I've just been speaking to a Mrs Meredith Crosland. Well, she did most of the speaking. She's wants me to train her horse, Katseye, Tabikat's half-brother. Do you know the horse?"

Sam could tell that he had Brendan's full attention now.

"Well, now," Brendan said, "That is a surprise to me, and a welcome one. I wondered what had happened to Katseye when he went to England. I told Eoghan that it was a total waste of the horse's talent, that Englishman buying it for his daughter to ride in amateur events. The horse is a potential top chaser in my judgement. You'll be a lucky man if you get to train him, so you will, Sam. The sire, Night Vision, has produced some leading hurdlers and chasers here in Ireland. And the dam, Little Kitty Cat, she's no pedigree, as you know, but she was a real talent in the years that I trained her here."

"It sounds as if you think I should leap at the opportunity," said Sam, genuinely enthused by what he had head.

"Indeed you should," replied Brendan firmly, then reverting to his earlier manner, added, "Declan will be in touch. Good day to you now, Sam."

As Sam stood up, wanting to get outdoors for a while, if only by walking down to the yard where he could instruct Bethany to conduct some research on Night Vision's career, he became aware of Lewis waiting at the doorway.

"Mr Sampfield," said Lewis, immediately, "Kelly would like to know which room to make up for Mr Urquhart."

Sam looked blank. The recent conversations and their implications had caused him temporarily to forget the presence of his young Australian cousin in the house.

"Er .. where is Ryan now, Lewis?" he asked, not really interested in the minutiae of Kelly's housekeeping arrangements.

"Kye and Jackie took him down to the yard to see the horses, Mr Sampfield," Lewis told him.

"I'll go down there myself and talk to him," Sam said, "Tell Kelly to make up whichever room is convenient."

Arriving in the still sunny yard, Sam was welcomed into the office by Bethany, who informed him that Jessica Moretti had called again.

"Shall I make an appointment for her to see you?" Bethany pleaded, "She's a journalist. She sounds very nice. She says she's a friend of Isabella Hall who worked here when I was away."

"Leave it with me for now," Sam told Bethany shortly, "In the meantime, I have another job for you."

Whilst Bethany was working on her online search for information about Night Vision and Katseye, Sam found Kye and Jackie carefully measuring out feeds from the contents of the various heavy lidded bins in the storeroom. The diet for each horse was set out on an old fashioned blackboard hung above the door.

"Sir Andrew had a computer with all this stuff on," Sam heard Jackie telling Kye as he approached the storeroom door.

The two young stable staff were so engrossed in their task that they both jumped when Sam spoke up from behind them

"I'm looking for Ryan," Sam stated without preamble.

"Ryan's in the cottage, Mr Sampfield," Kye replied, brushing the dust from the feeds off his hands, "He was dead on his feet. He just lay down and sparked out in Sadie's old room. Do yez want me to wake him?"

"No, leave him to sleep," Sam replied, "Tell him to come up to the house when he's ready."

"I will, Mr Sampfield," said Kye, "Is Ryan going to be working with us in the yard? He seems to know a lot about horses and race riding."

"Well, that's up to him, I suppose," said Sam, not really knowing how to respond to this unanticipated question from Kye, "He's a family guest. I have no idea how long he plans to be here."

As his employer walked away towards the big house, Kye turned to Jackie.

"This is a real piece of shit, Jackie. Ryan's Mr Sampfield's cousin. He's not one of us. What if he's come here to take over from Mr Sampfield? Mr Sampfield's not got anyone else to take this place on when he can't run it himself any more. Maybe the family wants Ryan to be his heir or something."

Kye would not have been any less concerned had he known that Kelly and Lewis were just coming to exactly the same conclusion in the Sampfield Grange kitchen.

14

Sam had never visited Chepstow racecourse before and quickly concluded that this was not the best day on which to appreciate it. The usually soft Welsh air was heavy with imminent rain while hump backed grey clouds massed themselves over the long hill at the far side of the elongated oval course. A row of dark trees decorated the low skyline. The late October sun seemed to have gone at last on its winter holiday.

Sam had watched the Welsh National and some of the other jump races run at Chepstow racecourse only on a television screen, and a quick walk around the circuit with Merlin and Ryan had quickly convinced him that its undulations and slopes would be a challenge for Curlew Landings. The going at the course today was officially described as good to soft, but, if the threatening deluge were to arrive before racing started, it would certainly become softer. This would not suit Curlew at all.

The entry of Curlew Landings into a two mile handicap Hurdle had been Merlin's idea. Merlin had arrived, as promised, at Sampfield Grange late on the afternoon of Ryan's unexpected appearance earlier in the month, nonchalantly parking his black BMW sports car by the entrance to the stable yard. Ryan himself had by this time woken up, and, notwithstanding Kye's suggestion that he should go up to the house to speak to Mr Sampfield, had instead insisted on helping Kye and Jackie with their regular chores.

"Plenty of time to see him later," Ryan had said dismissively, "I like it better down here with the horses."

Merlin had sauntered into the yard to find the three young staff filling the numerous water buckets and haynets ready for the evening.

"'Ello there, Kye," Merlin had greeted them, "You 'ave some new 'elp 'ere, I see."

Kye had quickly introduced Jackie and then Ryan, telling Merlin only that Ryan was Mr Sampfield's cousin from Australia.

"An' I'm Merlin ap Rhys," Merlin stated in return, "I ride Curlew Landin's for Mr Sampfield. And Tabikat too, when 'e's 'ere."

Kye's sharp eyes had observed that Ryan's casual demeanour had changed suddenly on hearing Merlin's description of his role.

"You a jumps jockey, then, mate?" Ryan had asked.

"Yes, an' I am 'ere to see Mr Sampfield with some plans for Curlew Landin's this season," Merlin told him, walking off towards the box where the said Curlew was looking suspiciously over the half door.

"I got some great plans for you, I 'ave," Merlin told the horse, patting his neck.

Curlew nodded his head vigorously up and down as if to say that he approved.

"Plans for races?" had asked Ryan, who had followed Merlin across the yard, "Can I lob in? I'm trying to gen up on British racing."

"If Mr Sampfield doesn' mind," had said Merlin, airily, "Come on then."

"That doesn't sound good," Kye had said to Jackie, as Merlin had disappeared towards the house with Ryan in tow, "He's wanting a say in the racing decisions already."

Although Sam had had no objections to Ryan's presence at his discussion with Merlin, his surprise at what Merlin had come to Sampfield Grange to propose had made Sam wish that the two of them had been alone together. Lewis had brought a tray with tea and homemade cake into the drawing room. Ryan had sat slightly apart from Sam and Merlin, choosing an upright chair rather than one of the capacious sofas.

"I'm just an earwigger," he had told a mystified Sam by way of explanation.

"I haven't seen you since that day you won on Fan Court for Ranulph Dicks," Sam had said to Merlin, "And I owe you congratulations on the win on Tabikat at Punchestown. I was talking to Brendan this morning and he said the owners are aiming him at Cheltenham again. They want you to ride him."

Merlin had put his cup of milkless tea down on the low table.

"Brilliant news, Mr Sampfield," he had exclaimed, "When's Tabikat comin' 'ere?"

Sam had explained that he was about to discuss a plan for Tabikat with the Meaghans and had promised to keep Merlin informed.

"Now, what did you want to see me about, Merlin?" Sam had asked.

Merlin had leaned forward on the sofa and paused for breath before launching into his proposal.

"You know I've been ridin' for Justin Venn recently?" he had started, "Well Mr Venn was askin' me about Curlew. 'E's 'ad 'is eye on 'im for a while. Thinks 'e's a Champion 'urdle contender."

"The Champion Hurdle?" had exclaimed Sam, taken aback by this piece of news from Merlin, "At the Festival? That's a bit ambitious surely? You know Curlew didn't do well up the hill at the finish when we ran him at Cheltenham."

"That's what I said, Mr Sampfield," Merlin had responded, "Mr Venn didn' seem to think that was a problem. 'e said Curlew's a year older and stronger this season. And 'e asked if we were thinkin' of usin' 'is speed over a shorter distance. But 'e did say it wasn' 'is business to tell us what to do. But that's what 'e thought."

"He's right, it isn't his business," Sam had responded, "But he's a very successful trainer and we'd be wrong just to dismiss his opinion. What do you think yourself Merlin?"

"I've got an idea," Merlin had replied at once.

And it was Merlin's idea which had led to their presence at Chepstow races on this dismal Autumn day.

Merlin's proposal had been a simple one. If Mr Venn were right about Curlew's potential at Cheltenham, the best way to trial it would be to run Curlew over the shorter distance of two miles at a course which had some features in common with the famous Gloucestershire venue, that is, a left handed track with undulating ground. An uphill section at the end would be useful too, Merlin had said. Short of going straight to Cheltenham racecourse itself, there was nothing within reasonable travelling distance which fitted the bill better than Merlin's local course at Chepstow. Better still, there was a suitable two mile handicap Hurdle in two weeks' time for which Curlew's newly acquired mark would make him eligible. And if Curlew were to take to the new challenge, they could run him next in the Greatwood Hurdle at Cheltenham in November. And if either the Chepstow or the Cheltenham run did not work out, then there were still the alternative options of sending Curlew either novice chasing or looking for other handicap Hurdle races for him on flatter courses. That way, they would be keeping all Curlew's irons in the fire, Merlin had said, ultimately persuasively.

On the day of the Chepstow race, Sam had driven alone as usual in his black Audi to the course, following the M48 across the older of the two spectacular bridges across the River Severn. The venerable bridge itself was visible from the racecourse, the upper part of its structure swathed in shifting low cloud. Kye and Ryan had followed shortly behind in the Sampfield Grange horsebox containing the newly fit Curlew Landings.

In the two weeks since he had been at Sampfield Grange, Ryan had proven to be a real asset, Sam reflected as he waited for the horsebox to reach the sloping racecourse car park. Once Merlin had left Sampfield Grange, Ryan had suddenly spoken up in a strangely authoritative tone.

"I'd like to be in on this project," he had told Sam, "I can get that horse fit for the race, no drama. Kye's shown me all your horses and that one's a real beaut. If you'll let me, I'll shack up in that little outhouse with Kye and Jackie and work for you in the yard."

"Well, that's a very kind offer, Ryan," Sam had said doubtfully, "But I do need to see you ride first. Your father said you were a good horseman, but riding out on a cattle station is a bit different than getting a racehorse fit for a competitive event."

"Fair enough, Mr Sampfield," Ryan had said, "Just sounds like an ace way of me paying my way."

"Ryan, you don't need to pay your way, as you put it," Sam had replied. "You're a member of my family. And that means you don't have to address me as Mr Sampfield either. My name is James."

"If it's all the same to you," Ryan had replied firmly, "If I'm bunking with the others, I don't want them thinking I'm big-noting myself. Calling you Mr Sampfield like they do is fair grouse with me. And this posh house is a bit OTT for a cane toad like me."

Sam had not been not entirely sure he had followed Ryan's slang laden explanation, but had eventually agreed that Ryan could move into Sadie's empty room in the cottage just as if he were a regular member of the stable staff. Sam had had to hope that Teddy would not find out about the arrangement.

Sam had not been disappointed in Ryan. Even the suspicious Kye had had to admit that Ryan's riding skills were excellent.

"Pretty much born on a horse," Ryan had said dismissively, when Kye had commented on his confident schooling of Curlew over the practice hurdles. "Don't you just love 'em? Specially this one. He's ace, fair dinkum, or I don't know what way's up."

The effect of Ryan's hard work with Curlew Landings was clearly evident as Kye led the sleek and gleaming creature around the Chepstow parade ring. Merlin had called at Sampfield Grange on the previous day to work with him and had been openly enthusiastic about Ryan's positive effect on Curlew's attitude and race readiness.

"We're in with a chance, I know we are," Merlin had told Sam, as he had slid into his parked car, "See you tomorrow, Mr Sampfield."

As Sam stood in the centre of the compact parade ring, a tense Ryan at his side, he quickly tried to appraise the other horses in Curlew Landings' race. Curlew was one of the youngest horses, and had not run over the two mile distance before, so, unsurprisingly, his potential in relation to that of the other eight horses was unknown. Sam was not acquainted, except by reputation, with any of the other trainers standing with their connections alongside the increasingly gloomy Welsh race course. Although the race was being televised, no commentator attempted to interview Sam, nor was the familiar figure of online tipster Stevie Stone anywhere to be seen. Even Curlew's former owner, Toby Halstock, who had followed the horse's progress at both Newbury and Cheltenham, was absent. Sampfield Grange and the Chepstow racegoers had Curlew to themselves.

As Kye legged a confident looking Merlin up into Curlew's saddle, the threatened deluge of rain was still holding off. Once the race was over, it could rain as much as it wanted, thought Sam, as an unusually silent Ryan shifted restlessly from one foot to the other, his gaze following Merlin and Curlew.

As horse and jockey moved smartly towards the parade ring exit ready to canter onto the course, Merlin leaned down towards Kye, and asked suddenly,

"You seen much of Sadie recently, Kye? She's ridin' in points for Mr Dicks, I 'ear."

Kye chose the words of his reply carefully. It had been an open secret for months, both at Sampfield Grange and at the Dicks yard, that Sadie and Merlin were no longer spending time in each other's company. But Sadie had not said anything, even to her usual confidante, Kelly, about the relationship being at end, and had simply stonewalled with a shrug any direct questions about Merlin's whereabouts.

"Yeah, and she's doing very well," Kye replied, briefly.

"I knew she would," Merlin said, "She's a good ...."

But Merlin's words were lost to Kye as he released his hold on Curlew Landings' bridle, and the horse bounded eagerly forward onto the racecourse.

The two mile start was situated a short distance down the home straight to the left of the parade ring, which meant that Sam and Ryan were easily able to see the nine horses gathering for the race without the assistance of either field glasses or the big screen. The racecourse commentator mentioned Curlew as being a strong contender, dropped back in trip this season, and ridden by local jockey Merlin ap Rhys, a reference which earned a cheer from the also mostly local crowd.

As the starter brought down his yellow flag and the orange starting tape flew back, Merlin sent Curlew straight to the front as usual, and the horse's nodding head was the first to pass the Sampfield Grange trio congregated anxiously in the centre of the parade ring. The horses, closely grouped, pounded their way down into the dip to the right of the spectators gathered in the stands, as a few large drops of rain plopped onto the ground. Rounding the left hand bend, the field faced a stiff climb upwards towards the ridge which formed the far side of the course. Curlew seemed to be holding his own, but the pace was as yet relatively steady for the short racing distance involved and the picture could change very quickly, Sam knew.

The well packed field continued to progress smoothly towards the far end of the course, while Sam became increasingly conscious of Ryan moving about by his side. Ryan, it seemed, was riding every step of the race with Merlin and Curlew. He seemed oblivious to Sam and Kye as he muttered and swore under his breath, eventually jumping up and down on the spot as Curlew and Merlin passed the parade ring once again, still at the front and ready to go out on the final circuit.

"Give 'em hell, Merlin!" Ryan yelled, as if he had his life savings riding on the horse, "You bloody show 'em, Curlew!"

Whether it was Ryan's raucous encouragement which made the difference, no-one ever knew, but by the end of the second circuit, when the clouds had begun to drench the racecourse in gallons of pent up grey rain, Merlin and Curlew appeared once again on their left, still at the head of affairs, the rest of the field strung out like a procession behind them. As horse and rider passed the finishing post, Merlin was the only jockey whose face and clothing were not liberally splattered with Welsh mud. Curlew Landings had won in some style. The gamble had succeeded.

There were not many people available to watch the hasty prize giving in the little stand by the parade ring. Those hardy spectators who had stayed to watch the drenched horses cross the finishing line had quickly rushed back into the shelter of the cold stands and the warmer bar, whilst the placed horses and their connections were keen only to depart from the parade ring as soon as they could. Merlin, after a brief word with Sam following the award of the prizes, dashed off to the jockeys' changing room, leaving Kye and Ryan to make haste to get a scarcely troubled Curlew Landings back under shelter and ready for transport home in the horsebox.

"We'll talk about this when we're home," Sam called to them, clutching his soaking wet hat, as the two younger men fastened the ramp of the lorry whilst Curlew Landings munched nonchalantly from a haynet inside.

"Enjoy that, did yez?" Kye asked Ryan, as the horsebox nosed its way in the direction of the now almost invisible Old Severn Bridge, the wipers working at full speed to clear the water from the windscreen.

"Bonzer, mate," was Ryan's only comment, as he peered out of the window through the streaming rain.

"Yez planning on staying here all season?" Kye could not resist asking, "Helping Mr Sampfield with Curlew's training?"

"Can't, Kye, mate," Ryan told him, "I'm here on a visitor visa, that's six months max in the UK, then I'm out."

"That's OK, then," Kye replied, having done a quick calculation in his head, "Yez'll still be here for the Cheltenham Festival in March. If yez want to stay the whole six months, that is."

"No moolah, mate," Ryan told him, shortly, "Not allowed to work here and I can't be living off the boss all that time."

Kye merely grunted sympathetically in response, but his mind was racing. The Sampfields and the Urquharts were very wealthy. The idea that Ryan had no money seemed unbelievable. Kye remembered Lewis and Kelly telling him that Ryan's father had said something about Ryan having gone off the rails. Had his rich family disowned him? Was that why Mr Sampfield had not wanted him staying in the house, even after Kelly had made up a room for him there? The Sampfield Grange staff had suspected that Ryan's objective was to make himself useful to Mr Sampfield so he could start a career in the UK. But Ryan could not do that on a visitor's visa, from what he had just said.

"Can people work in jump racing in Australia?" asked Kye after a while, not really sure what he was trying to find out, "Does your family own racehorses?"

"Hard to do that there, Kye," Ryan told him, gloomily, "Jumps racing's mostly banned now in Oz. Animal rights people don't like it. Only happens in Victoria and South Australia now."

Kye's knowledge of the horseracing politics of Australia was non-existent, so this comment meant little to him. Fortunately, Ryan changed the subject to the recent performance of Curlew Landings, asking Kye for more information about Cheltenham racecourse and the Greatwood Hurdle race for which Curlew appeared to be destined.

When the horsebox finally reached Sampfield Grange and Kye prepared to take it up the narrow lane into the yard, their progress was halted by another box which was already in the yard and blocking the entrance to the garage. Mr Sampfield's Audi was parked alongside the unfamiliar grey and green lorry, which appeared from its livery to be a hire vehicle from a racehorse transport company. Kye could see Mr Sampfield speaking to the driver, who was holding out a brown folder towards him.

As Kye and Ryan watched from their vantage point in the cab, they saw the small figure of Jackie leading a large jet black horse down the ramp at the back of the parked lorry. The horse walked grandly down to ground level, sauntering along as if it owned the yard, then stopping dead to look slowly around at its new kingdom. It turned an imperious gaze towards Kye and Ryan as they sat in the Sampfield Grange lorry and shook its handsome head, snorting loudly as if trying to clear away the effects of its travels. Two small white stars were visible on its charcoal forehead.

It was not just the imperious looking horse which attracted Kye's attention. Standing with Mr Sampfield next to the lorry were two women, both of whom Kye thought he recognised. One was Lady Helen Garratt and the other was former Sampfield Grange employee, Isabella Hall. But as the two women walked away from the lorry to speak to Jackie, Kye realised his mistake.

The second woman must be the unknown Mrs Crosland, the owner of Katseye.

15

The cycle hire station in Frossiac was one of several such establishments which had opened along the old towpath of the Canal du Midi during the hot and busy months of the now departed summer. The innovative tourist venture had been a moderate success and the owners of the franchise were expecting to build on this encouraging start in the following year. The concept was simple and had been used with great success in major cities around the world. The bikes were hired and dropped off at any of the stations along the popular route, with repairs and replacements provided free of charge as part of the rental agreement. The machines could be moved up and down the canal to meet variations in supply and demand at the different outlets using the services of the many boats which plied the water during the tourist season. Even at the beginning of November there still remained a diminishing number of hardier customers for the new service.

The tall, grey haired man who was approaching the other side of the footbridge spanning the canal was not one of those customers, Guy knew. The canal itself lay dark and motionless beneath the wooden steps of the blue metal bridge, no longer subject to the damaging washes from the wakes created by poorly crewed holiday hire boats. Now the turgid water was drifting into its gloomy winter sleep, the slowly sinking leaves from the plane trees decorating its surface with dingy gold and decaying red.

The pedestrian on the Minervois bank was no stranger to Guy. George Harvey had not been seen for almost eight months in Frossiac, and much had changed since then. George had arrived unannounced, and, as before, his renewed residence had been signalled only by the appearance of a car with a Carcassonne number plate outside the most distant of the lakeside apartments. The reeded lake was glassy now, its unbroken surface reflecting the progress of the moving figure along the footpath towards the bridge. A few waterfowl glided quietly over the water forming geometric patterns in their tiny wakes.

Guy pulled his black fleece jacket more firmly around his body and rose from the folding picnic chair on which he had been sitting. Guy had questions to ask of Monsieur Georges Harvey.

George's progress over the bridge was considerably quicker than on the first occasion on which Guy had seen him in Frossiac. George still carried a stick to support his left leg, which swung stiffly as he ascended the steps, but this time he wore a tailored wool jacket and carried no computer case over his shoulder. To Guy, he appeared fitter and stronger, and, as George drew nearer, Guy could see that the older man's skin now had the healthy tan associated with outdoor life.

Guy remained silent as George reached the top of the arc of the elegant bridge and stopped, as if to take in the view.

"*Bonjour Guy!*" George called down to the figure standing on the Corbieres bank in front of the rack of brightly coloured bicycles, "*Est-ce que tu me reviens?*"

"*Mais oui, Monsieur,*" responded Guy, gritting his teeth, "But please, come down and speak with me in English. I am here alone, as you see."

As George made his way down the wooden steps, making only sporadic use of his stick, Guy unfolded a second chair and placed it next to his own.

"Please be seated, Georges," he said, pointing towards the red and white striped chair, "I was not expecting to see you again in Frossiac. Is Madame 'Arvai with you?"

"Regrettably not," George told him, sitting in the proffered seat, "She has other things to occupy her. And my visit here will be short. I came only to attend to something which I left behind here in Frossiac. But, tell me, Guy, what has become of the wine museum? You have bicycles here now, I see. And your brother, Maurice? Is he not here today? And your wives and children, are they all well? May I buy a drink for you later today in your restaurant?"

Guy's intention of asking some searching questions of George Harvey were somewhat undermined by the torrent of polite questions which George had just put to him. *Bien sur*, he had no proof that the mysterious Englishman was in any way responsible for the problems which had beset the Vacher family earlier in the year, problems which had led to the closure of the wine museum and Maurice's arrest along with that of other members of the local wine co-operative. George had been gone from Frossiac before these events had happened.

"You have not heard of our problems, then?" Guy said, experimentally, wondering whether George would reveal any knowledge which could confirm his suspicions.

"Well, I can see that the wine museum is no longer operational," George replied, propping his stick against the nearest bicycle and turning to look at Guy.

"Maurice is in prison," Guy said, baldly.

George raised his eyebrows.

"Tell me what happened, Guy," he said quietly, "It seems that it is your turn this time to relate a story to me."

Guy's account of the events which had led to the arrest of Maurice Vacher and several other members of the wine co-operative headed by Jean-Philippe Armand was brief.

"You will recall, Georges," Guy said, "That Marcel Lambert, our police officer, was in the museum one day when you were here, I think?"

"I do recall," replied George, slowly, "That there was a young man, a suspected drug dealer I believe, who had come here to the museum. I helped Monsieur Lambert to stop the man. I tripped him with my stick. But Maurice was not here that day. And nor were you."

"That is correct," agreed Guy, "I was away in Beziers, speaking to the owner of this bicycle hire franchise which I was then thinking we might add to the services offered here in Frossiac. Maurice had been asked to attend the tax office to explain some irregularities in the tax affairs of the business. But unfortunately, it appears that things were more serious than a simple tax problem."

George only half listened to Guy's halting explanation, most of which, in truth, he already knew. Indeed, the French police had offered the wine museum as a location for George's work in France on the basis that they were about close down the criminal operation in which the wine museum was involved. The wine co-operative, for which the museum was an outlet, had been one of a number of rural fronts for a money laundering operation run by a drug trafficking and gambling syndicate based in Marseilles. Guy was insistent that Maurice had not understood the full implications of the activities in which he had become involved, seeing it merely as an opportunity to reduce or avoid certain taxes which would have been due in relation to the profits from the museum. Jean-Philippe Armand, according to Guy, had been the person responsible for the local management of the complex scam, in which the proceeds of drug dealing and crime were turned into apparently legitimately acquired wine collections, whilst his brother Maurice and others had been innocent dupes. The authorities, in the initial form of the Traitement du Renseignement et Action Contre les Circuits Financiers Clandestins, and thereafter the Public Prosecutor, had, though, taken a different view, with the result that Maurice and a number of others were now serving custodial sentences, albeit for shorter periods than that of the ringleaders of the operation.

"And what of Claudine and the children?" asked George.

"They live now in Toulouse close to Claudine's parents," Guy told him, "So Monique and I remain here in Frossiac to run the bar and restaurant and also this cycling business."

George nodded and was silent for a while, as if trying to decide what to say next. Guy saved him the trouble.

"And what of you, Georges?" he asked, "Did you complete your story about the murder in England, the story which was not a story, but told of real events? What became of those people? I regret, I do not remember their names."

George shifted in his seat.

"The story has moved forward," he said, "But I cannot say that it is yet complete. You will remember, I suppose, that my friend Peter Stonehouse died from his injuries and that his wife Susan killed herself after being harassed by the Paloka family? The head of the Paloka family, Konstantin, had been murdered in prison and his sons held Susan Stonehouse responsible for his death and had vowed to be revenged on her. Well, the sons are both deceased now. Egzon died at his home in Tirana, of a heart attack or a stroke, or something of that sort. His brother Aleksander was found dead in England, apparently the victim of a road accident or killed by a drug dealer, or some combination of both things. The Paloka family criminal empire is being broken up by the police in a number of countries, probably including here in France. They were very dangerous people. As you know, I carried a gun to protect me in the event that they discovered that I was writing the story of Susan Stonehouse and thought that I could lead them to her. I now no longer need to carry a weapon with me."

George pulled apart the two sides of his jacket to emphasise the point.

"Then it appears to me that your story is at an end," Guy said, after some thought, "What else is there yet to happen?"

"The story is not at an end for the daughters of Peter and Susan Stonehouse," George reminded him, "Rather like the family of your brother, Maurice, their lives have been blighted by the criminal acts of others. You say Maurice was duped by Jean-Philippe into becoming involved in a serious criminal act which he did not fully understand. Peter Stonehouse likewise was drawn into an attempt to confront a drug dealer, Jerzy Gorecki, who had sold his sister the contaminated cocaine which caused her death. Peter did not know that Konstantin Paloka would choose that very same day on

143

which to have his people murder Mr Gorecki at the meeting which Peter had set up. Paloka's intention was to put the blame on Peter Stonehouse for Gorecki's murder. But his vile plan failed because Susan Stonehouse witnessed the crime and was brave enough to give her testimony in court. Peter paid for that meeting with his life, and Susan too in the end. At least your brother will leave prison in a few years' time and his wife and children will see him again. But Peter and Susan Stonehouse's daughters have been given a life sentence."

George had spoken the last few sentences rather vehemently and had emphasised his words by standing and pacing awkwardly up and down by the footbridge landing. A small breeze had sprung up, causing the reflective tags attached to some of the bicycles leaning against the wine museum wall to waver and flicker in the slowly dying light.

"Please, Georges," exclaimed Guy, jumping to his feet, "I had forgotten that the people in this unfortunate family were your good friends. You are right. We have all been the victims of the greed and wickedness of other people. Let me close my business for the day and we will go and see Monique and share a beer, maybe watch some football."

As Guy started to wheel the bicycles one by one into the dark interior of the former wine museum, George relaxed a little. The first step, that of regaining Guy's confidence, had been accomplished. He followed Guy into what had now become a bicycle storage area and quickly saw what he was looking for. The former wine museum computer was still in its same location. It looked like the same machine. It had not been replaced.

"Is that the same computer which was here previously?" he asked Guy, "Did the . . er .. financial investigators not take it away with them?"

"No," replied Guy, occupied with stacking the bicycles against the now empty wooden wine racks, "They came and took copies of things which I suppose were recorded on it, but they did not take the machine itself. This was good for me, as I did not need to buy a computer for the new business. But it is useless in any event at the moment."

"Useless in what way?" asked George, although he already knew the answer.

"It stopped working this morning," Guy told him, sounding exasperated, "Someone will come to fix it tomorrow, they say. In the old days, I would have asked Thierry to come to repair it, but, he too is now in prison."

"Shall I look at it for you?" asked George, almost holding his breath as he posed the question, "You know that I am a software developer. I use computers all the time. The fault may be something simple. Have you tried re-booting it?"

Guy shrugged.

"Please go ahead," he said.

Rather to Guy's surprise, George soon had the office computer up and running once again.

"Nothing serious," George announced, "It seemed to have dropped its connection to the network for some reason. Always try turning it off and turning it on again, that's the first rule. Now let me help you with the rest of the bikes."

George did not add that in the process of turning the computer off and on again, he had not only rectified the deliberately engineered fault which had affected all the cycle hire franchise computers that day, but had also installed a powerful and well hidden piece of spyware. This little device would do nothing at all unless and until someone accessed Egzon Paloka's old online route from Tirana. The expertly hidden cyberspy would then investigate and report on its findings.

"I am looking forward to meeting Monique again, Guy," said George, as the two men made their newly companionable way along the towpath towards the ancient stone bridge which carried the narrow road across the canal. A single car passed over the bridge as they approached, but otherwise the scene was deserted.

After some initial hesitation, Monique professed herself to be pleased to see Monsieur 'Arvai once again, particularly after George had made courteous enquiries after her health and that of the family and had listened once again to the tale of the dreadful miscarriage of justice to which her brother in law had been subject. The little bar and restaurant were empty, and the three of them sat together around a circular wooden topped table alongside one of the narrow windows set into the thick stone wall of the building, as the afternoon light began to deteriorate into an early evening gloom. A football match was being played on the silent television monitor attached to the ceiling in one corner of the room.

"I was hearing of you only recently, Georges," Monique told him, as she brought a second bottle of beer for each of them from the refrigerator, "An English lady was here who said that you had recommended to her the holiday apartments in Frossiac."

"Really?" responded George, trying to conceal his alarm, "Did she give you her name?"

"Yes, she has left a card," Monique told him, "It is behind the bar. I will give it to you. She wished to know if I was acquainted with you. She said she too was working on writing the story of the unfortunate Stone'ouse family and hoped you could help her with her work."

George held out his hand for the card which Monique brought out from its location tucked beneath the till on the bar counter. But he already knew the name which he would see.

Jessica Moretti.

16

"Merlin, my man!"

The gruff male shout reached Merlin ap Rhys's ears from the side of the North entrance to Cheltenham racecourse. As he turned to look towards the speaker, Merlin found himself grabbed in a hearty embrace accompanied by a hard thump on his back.

"Not seen you since that night in the Adelphi!" the portly man yelled in Merlin's ear, "Yer all right then, are yer, mate? I've made a bit of money on yer winners this year, thanks a lot."

Once released from the other man's sweaty grasp, Merlin recognised the speaker as the owner of The King's Sorcerer, the horse he had ridden in the Grand National at Aintree earlier in the year.

"'ello, Mr Weston," he responded, as politely as he could, "Glad to see you're enjoyin' life."

"It's Neil to you. And I'll enjoy it even more if yer give me some winners today," rejoined Neil Weston, grandly, "Speakin' of which, what d'yer think of that little treat we arranged for you at the Adelphi?"

Merlin froze.

"Little treat?" he asked, carefully.

"Yeah, that girl we booked for yer," went on Neil Weston, "Don't tell me yer didn't enjoy it. One of our lot's been with 'er before. Good girl, she is. Bit of a posh sort, pricey too, but gives yer a good time, guaranteed."

"Oh, er, right," replied Merlin, trying to regain his composure, "I didn' realise it was you 'ad organised her for me. Yeah, I 'ad a good time with her, thanks, Mr Wes .. er .. Neil."

"Well, my son, what about my winners for today, then?" Neil Weston insisted.

Merlin hurriedly marshalled his thoughts sufficiently to tell the overweight builder that Merlin's own rides that day, Fan Court and Curlew Landings, were both in with a good chance of winning, and that he should have a look at newcomer Katseye as a prospect for the future. As Neil shook Merlin's hand and started to move away, Merlin suddenly realised that his opportunity had arrived at last, and in the most unexpected way. All that summer he had been taking rides at Northern racecourses in the hope of coming across Lara or someone who knew her, but with no success.

"Er, Neil," Merlin said, detaining the other man with a grip on his forearm of a strength normally used for restraining overkeen racehorses, "That Lara. I'm goin' to Liverpool soon. I'd like to see 'er again. You don' 'appen to 'ave 'er contact details, do you?"

Neil Weston laughed, rather patronisingly, Merlin thought.

"I thought yer'd like 'er, Merlin," he said, "Yeah, I've got 'er details somewhere. Give me me arm back, son, and I'll take a look."

After a search through a worn and bulging leather wallet, which was produced from the sagging jacket pocket of what had once been a smart suit, Neil Weston pulled out and handed to Merlin a creased pink business card. In silver letters, was the single word Lara accompanied by a silver silhouette of a female figure leaning provocatively over a bar stool. Beneath the picture was a mobile phone number.

"Great, thanks, Neil," said Merlin, taking the card quickly, "Good luck this afternoon."

Walking along the chilly, and still relatively quiet, concourse of the racecourse towards the jockey's changing room, Merlin could not believe what had just happened. It had not occurred to him that the loud Essex builder and his mates had set up his encounter with the elusive Lara. Indeed it had not even occurred to Merlin that Lara might be a professional sex worker available for hire. Now that the truth had been revealed, Merlin felt like kicking himself. No-one but a professional would be likely to have the contacts to enable her to set up cameras to film people having sex in hotels. The only reason she had not asked him for money was because she had already been paid in advance by Neil Weston.

Notwithstanding the length of time which had passed since that April night in Liverpool, and the subsequent receipt of the video recording and associated still shots on his old mobile phone, Merlin had not heard another word from whomever had sent them. And, despite much puzzling, he was still no nearer to arriving at a plausible explanation as to why the face of Lara had been changed to resemble that of Abigail Alvarez. He had not even come across the Argentinian footballer's wife herself, as the horse owned by her husband had not been run at any race meeting at which Merlin had had rides. Until today, that was.

So, if Merlin were being blackmailed, the blackmailer had yet to play his or her hand. But now, Merlin thought grimly, he could at least try to find out what was going on before whoever it was went any further. He put the pink card into front pocket of the small rucksack which was slung over his left shoulder and resolved to put Lara out of his mind at least until racing was over for the day.

As Merlin sauntered past the Cheltenham parade ring, Sam was sitting rather tensely in his black Audi sports car in the car park higher up the hill. The November weather was not conducive to getting out of the vehicle whilst he awaited the arrival of the Sampfield Grange horsebox which contained Curlew Landings and Highlander Park. A chilly wind was blowing from the North West, bearing flecks of rain pulled from the grey clouds which were shifting irritably through the skies above the racecourse grandstand. Sam had passed numerous people dressed in winter running gear as his comfortable car had cruised effortlessly up the Evesham Road which cut through Pittville Park.

The sweeping, white railed entrance to the damp racecourse was still quiet, with only a small number of early racegoers loitering around to watch the horses, the star turns for the coming day, being unloaded. Sam knew that Katseye too was on his way to

Cheltenham, transported along with two horses from the Dicks yard. Sampfield Grange did not currently own a horsebox large enough for more than two horses.

Ryan Urquhart was travelling in the lorry with Kye, whilst Jackie had gone with Katseye to join the Dicks staff for the journey. Jackie, to Sam's surprise, had turned out to be a qualified HGV driver, and would be driving the Sampfield Grange box on its return journey from the racecourse, but there had seemed little sense in taking two boxes from Sampfield Grange when Ranulph Dicks had a spare berth in his lorry. And everyone knew, too, although no-one voiced it aloud, that if Kye were to be injured in his race, there would be no driver for a second vehicle.

Sam had, wrongly as it turned out, assumed that Ryan would have had the qualifications to drive large vehicles containing livestock on the cattle station in Queensland, and had suggested that Ryan be insured to drive the second box. Ryan, however, had quickly quashed this proposal, saying that he was a terrible driver and would not feel happy driving an unfamiliar vehicle on English roads. Given Ryan's casually confident approach towards everything else he had been asked to do, Sam had been rather surprised by his refusal. This had led Kelly and Lewis, still eager to know what rails Ryan had apparently gone off, to speculate that Ryan had been subject to some kind of motoring conviction.

"Drunk driving, do you think?" Kelly had whispered to Kye after Ryan had left the kitchen after breakfast.

Kye had privately thought it unlikely that anyone driving whilst drunk in the sparsely populated outback of Queensland would be noticed, let alone caught and convicted, but he kept his thoughts to himself. He was becoming increasingly uncomfortable about Ryan.

Notwithstanding his refusal to drive the horse transport, Ryan's presence was a godsend today to the Sampfield Grange yard and its naturally reclusive trainer. Sam's ambitions had until the recent past been limited to point to point racing and the occasional entry in Graded and Listed races at the smaller racecourses. The arrival of the talented Curlew Landings, followed later by the classy

Tabikat, had unexpectedly propelled the Sampfield Grange yard into the previous National Hunt season's limelight. Now, in the early stages of the new season, the previously quiet yard had three runners at Cheltenham races on one day. In the absence of Sadie, Ryan's help with the horses was more than welcome.

Curlew Landings would be running in the Greatwood Hurdle race, in accordance with Merlin's suggested plan. But to Sam's surprise, the newcomer Katseye had already held an entry in the two mile Supreme Trial Novices Hurdle at the same meeting, a commitment which Mrs Crosland, in the face of Sam's doubts, had insisted should be fulfilled.

"Mr Meaghan and Mr Foley both think he is quite capable of doing well," she had told Sam firmly over the telephone.

Poring laboriously over Katseye's racing form in the point to points in Ireland, Sam had to agree with his colleagues' reported assessment. The horse, ridden by a Miss F Foley, had won two races and been placed in two more. His misgivings arose from the fact that Katseye appeared not to have raced at all since he had been bought by the absent Mr Crosland. Although Mrs Crosland had told Sam that the horse had been procured for their daughter to ride in point to point races, Bethany had been able to find no record of any such entries in England. The horse had not been seen at a racecourse of any description for many months. It seemed to Sam to be a tough prospect to bring the animal straight into what would be a very competitive affair on one of Cheltenham's prestigious race days when everyone was on the look out for prospective Festival contenders.

Merlin, on one of his visits to work with Curlew Landings, had offered to ride out on Katseye and had been openly enthusiastic about his potential.

"I don' know why someone would buy 'im just to go pointin'" Merlin had told Sam, as they let the horses take a breather from their work on the panoramic top gallop above Sampfield Grange, "'E's pretty quick over 'is obstacles an' accurate too. Like is 'alf brother and with the potential to be good over any distance, I'd

151

say. Wasted just keepin' runnin' in amateur events, 'e'd be. Takes a bit of a grip, mind, but 'e's a youngster yet."

The other youngster, Highlander Park, travelling with Curlew in the Sampfield Grange vehicle, was entered in a conditional jockeys' race with Kye in the saddle. It had been Ryan who had encouraged Kye to ask his employer to use the day as a racing opportunity for Highlander, as he could conveniently accompany his stablemates who were going to Cheltenham.

"That race is just the ticket, Kye," Ryan had enthused, pointing out the selected race in the published schedule which he appeared to have researched on Kelly's kitchen iPad, "Landy goes well for you and we'll all be there – Mr Sampfield, Merlin, Jackie, me - to barrack for the two of you. That Mrs Crosland too, if she rocks up to see Katseye."

Sam privately thought that Highlander and Kye might be rather overfaced in the race concerned, given that the other jockeys were mostly nearer than Kye to riding out their claims, but had eventually agreed with the strangely insistent Ryan that Kye deserved a chance to show what the combination could do.

"Kye's a great little jock," Ryan told Sam, "I reckon he can knock the spots off of the lot of them. Just needs his chance."

As Sam carefully reviewed and re-reviewed his plans for the day, his mobile phone rang. The display on the car dashboard told him that Lady Helen Garratt was calling him.

Sam had been saved the trouble of imparting to Helen the news about Old Warnock airfield, as it appeared that her solicitor had been notified directly by the local council that the airfield was to be brought back into aviation use. She had called in at Sampfield Grange on the day of Katseye's arrival for the purpose of telling Sam. Sam, feeling a little guilty, had had to pretend that he had not been already aware of the recent development.

"Hello, Sam," the voice of Helen started now, without preamble, "Are you at Cheltenham yet?"

"In the car park, waiting for the horses," Sam told her.

"We're just setting out," Helen told him, "I'm calling to wish you luck today. We've a big group up in our box, and we'll all be cheering like mad for your horses. It's so exciting, Sam. You will walk up and meet everyone, won't you? Gilbert and Pippa are coming, you know. And that sweet Mr Halstock who used to own Curlew Landings."

Sam promised that he would do his best to visit the Garratt box during the day. Spotting the Sampfield Grange lorry at last appearing at the racecourse entrance, he quickly ended the call. Helen's enthusiastic support was only making him more nervous than he was already.

The last time Kye had been in the lorry park at Cheltenham racecourse had been on Gold Cup Day six months earlier. A tight knot nagged in his stomach as he manoeuvred the large vehicle into the nearest suitable space. The events which had unfolded in the racecourse car park on that day had certainly released him, temporarily at least, from the control of his brother Bronz and his drug dealing activities, but the price which Kye had paid had been that of helping the bizzies, something which had gone against all his instincts. Kye remained unsure whether Bronz and his associates suspected that Kye had co-operated with the police that day, and he had had to hope that they would not find out. Kye did not like being a grass. Nor did he like the implications that the role he had played might have for his future wellbeing.

There was no time for Kye to worry about his brother now. The horses needed to be unloaded and prepared for their races. And Kye could already see the smart red horsebox from the Dicks yard coming round the roundabout by the entrance to the racecourse car park.

Racing was due to start that day at 12.45. The miserable weather was showing no sign of improvement, and the massing cloud continued to send small and vicious spatters of rain across the large and tidily mown parade ring. Numerous warmly clad spectators clustered on the steppings and the galleries which led around and onto the impressive Princess Royal Stand, their dull coloured waterproof clothing contrasting with the warm gold of the stonework.

The first of the Sampfield Grange horses to run was Katseye. Whilst the exultant connections of the winner of the first race were being presented with their prizes, a soberly dressed and very nervous Jackie started to lead the impressive black gelding towards the parade ring. As horse and groom stepped away from the compact pre-parade area, they were carefully watched by a murmuring crowd which had gathered on the damp concourse above them.

Katseye had been groomed and turned out by Jackie to within an inch of his young life, and his demeanour showed that he knew it. The horse stalked grandly beside his diminutive young groom, gleaming with confidence and power, catching the eye of every spectator who saw him. Sam and Mrs Crosland, who followed behind, seemed to be part of the humble cortege of some ancient and powerful emperor. Even Merlin, when he joined them shortly afterwards in the parade ring, wearing the unfamiliar silver and black colours of Mrs Crosland, confessed himself impressed.

"'e looks a real picture, Mrs Crosland," Merlin told the owner, who, dressed in a well cut black coat decorated with a diagonal row of silver buttons, seemed more subdued than usual, "This your first time watchin' 'im in a pro race, is it?"

Sam had seen little of Mrs Crosland since the day over two weeks ago when he had returned from Chepstow races to find her standing with Helen by the hired horsebox at the entrance to Sampfield Grange. Mrs Crosland was the type of owner who made Sam glad that he rarely trained horses for other people. Not that she was impolite or in any way unpleasant, but he had the feeling that she, or more likely someone advising her, had her own plans for the horse and that he was merely the means by which they would be carried out. Notwithstanding her confident delivery of her instructions to him, it had become increasingly obvious to Sam that Mrs Crosland was not an experienced horsewoman. There was something nagging in the back of his mind, a feeling that he

154

had met Mrs Crosland somewhere before, but the run up to today's race meeting had been too busy for Sam to have had the time to try to get to the bottom of this latest mystery to disrupt his previously quiet life.

Watching the magnificent black horse jig-jogging towards the parade ring exit with Merlin perched on his back, Sam heard a familiar voice speak up from behind him,

"Well, Mr S-P, I've not seen you for a while," announced Stevie Stone, brightly, "And I've come to say a big hello to Meredith too."

Much to Sam's surprise, Stevie, her multi-coloured hair held together in a long plait down the back of her quilted pink jacket, flung her arms around Mrs Crosland, who hugged her enthusiastically in return.

"I didn't know you two were friends," Sam said, reflecting that Mrs Crosland must be at least twenty years older than Stevie Stone.

"It's complicated," Stevie told him, "But we've known each other forever, haven't we, Meredith? And," she added, in Mrs Crosland's direction, "Tabby Cat is going to interview you for the Smart Girls, once Katseye has shown everyone just how good he is. Tabby Cat and Jayce think he's in with a chance of a place, especially now the ground's gone softer. No reason why Smart Girls can't be owners too, you know!"

Sam smiled at the description of middle aged Mrs Crosland as a smart girl. He was relieved, though, that Stevie Stone had not proposed to interview him. Sam had managed to avoid the attentions of the TV presenter who had been roaming the ring during the race preliminaries. He would have had absolutely no idea what to say about his newly acquired equine charge.

Sam looked towards the big screen which showed the horses going down the walkway and onto the course. The chattering crowds were dispersing, moving determinedly towards the viewing areas. The monochrome combination of Katseye and Merlin was depicted on the screen, the horse bounding confidently down to the two mile start, whilst the racecourse commentator continued to identify the remaining runners as each of them left the horsewalk.

As Sam turned back towards his companions, he noticed a red jacketed figure standing in the Press area by the weighing room. He realised with an unpleasant jolt that this was the unwelcome journalist who had spoken to him at the point to point meeting at Ashfordleigh Downs all those months ago, and quickly tried to avoid her eye.

But she was not looking at him. She was looking at Stevie Stone and Meredith Crosland.

17

The two mile Supreme Trial Novices' Hurdle seemed to be over almost as soon as it had begun. The six young horses had the damp wind blowing behind them in the early part of the race and the packing field swept effortlessly up the hill towards the spectator filled stands. Sam, intently watching the big screen alongside Stevie Stone and Meredith Crosland in the almost deserted parade ring, saw the athletic black shape of Katseye, located in the middle of the small field, leaping confidently over the first two of the eight hurdles. The horse measured the obstacles with accuracy, as though making absolutely sure not to touch a single one of them.

Once the little group had reached the grandstand for the first time and was swiftly ascending the left-curving slope, Sam could more easily see what he had already guessed from viewing the first part of the contest. Katseye was pulling hard. Sam had never seen the horse run in a race, and, mindful of Merlin's comment that Katseye was capable of taking 'a bit of a grip', he had suggested that the horse be kept covered up as far as would be possible in such a small field. The last thing they wanted was for the gelding to pull his way to the front and for his speed to become uncontrollable. But it seemed that even Merlin's iron grip, as used on Neil Weston's arm earlier in the day, might prove insufficient.

The talented youngsters and their riders remained a compact fast moving group as they reached the far side of the Old course. The racecourse commentator excitedly informed the crowd that all six horses were still in with chance when they rounded the last bend of the course and attacked the upward climb to the finish. Sounds of encouragement began to swell and grow from the grandstands as the runners approached, reaching a crescendo as the finishing post drew nearer.

Stevie Stone and Meredith Crosland had remained nervously silent while the race progressed but now began to shout their own encouragement to Katseye and Merlin. Katseye had by now towed himself into the lead, but two of the other contenders were still close on his heels, which meant that in the last half furlong of the race, Merlin had to push Katseye onward for the first time so as to prevent the two chasing horses from getting past. Unfortunately, however, although Katseye continued to gallop on consistently, Merlin was unable to prevent one of the other runners overhauling them just before the line.

"I'm not sure the horse is fully race fit yet," was Sam's immediate explanation to the two women who stood, looking a little disappointed, beside him, "It's a while since he ran," he added pointedly, wondering whether this would bring forward any comment from Mrs Crosland, "So this was always going to be quite a challenge for him."

Merlin, on his return to the parade ring, with Jackie leading Katseye, shook his head and said much the same. But Sam, looking at the gelding, who in truth scarcely seemed troubled by his recent exertions, began to wonder whether this assessment was only part of the story. He had a gut feeling that the powerful horse might be better suited to a longer distance.

Merlin was booked to ride Fan Court for Ranulph Dicks in the following race, and parted from them quickly, telling Sam that he would talk to him again before the Greatwood Hurdle. Stevie seemed keen to find a suitable location in which to arrange for Tabby Cat to interview Meredith Crosland, but Sam was determined that this time Stevie should not leave before answering a question from him.

"That young woman up there," Sam said, indicating the red coated figure in the Press area, who seemed now to be speaking urgently to someone on a mobile phone, "I saw you talking to her when I was here a few months ago. My former yard manager, Sadie Shinkins, said that she was at Punchestown too. She asked Sadie some questions about Tabikat and mentioned that she knew you. And then she approached me for an interview at a point to point meeting a little while ago, this time asking after our old employee Isabella Hall who was with you on Gold Cup Day. Now she's been calling Sampfield Grange. Tell me now, is she a proper journalist, someone I should speak to?"

"Oo-er," replied Stevie, laughing, "I do know her and, yes, she is a proper journalist, if there is such a thing. She's a scandalmonger, running after celebs, trying to find nasty stories about drugs and extra-marital affairs, that sort of stuff. Not sure why she's after you, Mr S-P. Maybe you've got guilty secrets to hide? But seriously, I think she's probably come here today for the next race, when Randy Santi's got a runner. She's been collecting dirt about him and his sex life for ages now."

"Randy Santi?" asked Sam, trying to make sense of the strange answer.

"You're obviously not a football fan, are you, Mr S-P?" Stevie said, more seriously, "Santiago Alvarez is an expensively purchased Premier League footballer, whose performance in bed is more interesting to some people than his performance on the pitch. His horse, Penalty Kick, is running in the next race. He's recently got back together with his wife Abigail after having a fling with her sister. Abby will be here today and Jessica Moretti's gimlet eye will be right on them to see if they're all lovey dovey or stand six feet apart in the parade ring."

"Ah, I see," said Sam, deciding that Jessica Moretti was not the sort of journalist to whom anyone would voluntarily speak, "So you're saying that I should not give her an interview?"

"Why not?" asked Stevie, "It'll do her good to speak to someone decent for once. You can tell her about Katseye and Meredith here. Jess will be only too glad to think she's got one over on Tabby Cat with some inside information about Katseye's training."

With that, Stevie and Meredith walked away, leaving Sam unsure exactly what advice Stevie had given him. He remembered that Frank Stanley had been similarly unhelpful when Sam had spoken to him earlier in the month.

"Up to you, old man," Frank had said, sounding disinterested, "If she says she knows Stevie Stone, then maybe she's just trying to copy her success in the racing world. Professional backstabbing and all that. And as for Isabella Hall, she could have got her name from any of your suppliers."

When Sam eventually left the parade ring to follow Jackie and Katseye along the rubber surfaced track up the hill to the stables, the horses for the third race were being readied to move out of the pre-parade area. Sadie Shinkins' charge, Fan Court, was one of the most fancied runners, and many of the spectators who had crowded onto the wet and unsheltered viewing area had come especially to take a look at him.

The November meeting at Cheltenham racecourse was the first occasion since the morning on which she had left his home in Chepstow that Sadie had been obliged to come face to face with Merlin ap Rhys. Although Merlin had been to the Dicks yard on three occasions since that unhappy April day, Sadie had been successful in avoiding any interaction with him. But there would be no opportunity to avoid him today. Merlin was riding Fan Court and Sadie would be leading the horse up in the parade ring.

Sadie's strategy of ignoring Merlin and hoping that he might come back to her of his own volition had been spectacularly unsuccessful, Sadie had sadly admitted to herself. At a signal from Ranulph Dicks, she began to walk Fan Court towards the parade ring, which was already ringed with expectant racegoers, now mostly hunched together along the rails under open umbrellas. Others preferred to stay in the galleries above the parade ring, watching from the slight shelter provided by the buildings, which unhelpfully faced almost into the direction of today's wind.

Turning Fan Court to the left to join the parade ring path, Sadie could feel her heart thumping in her chest. Fan Court was blissfully unaware of his handler's agitation and walked serenely along the track, looking neither left nor right, whilst the seven other runners progressively joined the circular procession.

Had Sadie had a little more insight into the individual motivations of her fellow human beings, as opposed to her horses, she would have realised at once that men such as Merlin had little interest in being part of any group. Merlin revelled in being different. Being

160

excluded from established groups bothered him not at all. Hostility from others merely boosted his competitive instinct and determination to defeat them. If someone pushed him away, asking to be allowed to return would be the very last thing he would do.

In one respect, though, Sadie's approach had hit its mark. Merlin loved being the focus of attention and adulation, and he had certainly been the centre of Sadie's adoration. Now that that adoration had been withdrawn, Merlin missed the experience. He missed the exciting sex too, but he could get that elsewhere, or so he had thought. Somehow, mused Merlin, as he emerged from the weighing room and spotted Sadie leading Fan Court around the parade ring, making contact with old and new bedfellows had not proved as much fun as he had expected. Now that he could not have Sadie, he found that he wanted her more than ever. And some of his recent conquests had seemed to sense that they were second best and had proved less than enthusiastic about continuing their relations with him.

But Merlin had something more to concern him than his defunct relationship with Sadie. Scanning the parade ring as he approached Ranulph Dicks and the Todds, who were sheltering beneath a large golf umbrella in Fan Court's purple and green colours, he tried to spot Penalty Kick's connections. He could see the horse itself, a big iron grey gelding, walking around the parade ring immediately behind the dark Fan Court. Merlin watched Penalty Kick's jockey, Mark McConnell, as he approached a group of three people standing in the very centre of the lawn.

"Gotcha!" thought Merlin, quickly scrutinising Penalty Kick's supporters. They consisted of a Lambourn trainer who was familiar to Merlin, a tall athletic looking man with black curly hair and olive skin, and – yes, he breathed, it was definitely her – the small blonde haired, smartly dressed figure of Abigail Alvarez. The group was absorbed in conversation, only looking up when their jockey joined them. None of them even glanced in Merlin's direction.

"I've got to make 'er look at me, some'ow," Merlin said to himself, under his breath, forcing a smile onto his face as he approached Ranulph Dicks and Fan Court's owners, "Then I can soon tell if she knows 'oo I am."

Having replied glibly and automatically to the comments of the fussing Mrs Todd, Merlin was soon being legged up onto Fan Court by Ranulph Dicks who had had little to say to him. Merlin had ridden the horse a number of times already and needed no instructions. As Fan Court made his way down the horsewalk, Merlin could see the bobbing blonde ponytail of Sadie down below his left knee.

"Sadie, *cariad*, why didn' you call me?" he asked, suddenly, unable to stop the words coming out. "I don' understand you runnin' off like that without a word."

Merlin thought at first that Sadie was intending to ignore the question, but, without turning, she replied in a hard voice which he did not recognise,

'You know why I went, Merlin. Don't pretend."

Merlin could see that they were rapidly coming to the end of the curved part of the horsewalk and the point at which Sadie would release the eager Fan Court into the chute which ran parallel to the stands in front of the massed and damp spectators. He had only a few seconds in which to act.

"Meet me after the Greatwood 'urdle, Sadie," he urged, quickly, "I'll try to explain."

Sadie released Fan Court's rein and did not reply. The horse cantered smoothly forward along the upward slope. Merlin's brief chance with Sadie had gone, for now at least.

As the record later showed, Fan Court won the sodden steeplechase, his first race over fences, in some style. Having gone off favourite, he jumped and galloped fast and flawlessly, challenged only by Penalty Kick, the one horse still anywhere near him at the final fence, and streaked up the hill leaving the rest of the field trailing in his wake. As a result of the win, the jubilant Merlin and Fan Court were the last combination to leave the racecourse, following a brief, triumphal interview at the top of the hill with one of the day's TV presenters.

An excited Sadie had come to meet them, ready to bring Fan Court back into the parade ring and to lead him into the first place position in the winner's enclosure. Merlin was busy acknowledging the cheers and shouts of the spectators as horse, rider and groom progressed along the horsewalk, Fan Court blowing hot breath through his nostrils and tossing his handsome head with its striking white blaze. It was impossible for Merlin to speak to Sadie in the face of such tumult, particularly as she was patting Fan Court's neck and talking enthusiastically to the victorious horse. Once in the parade ring, they were surrounded by Ranulph Dicks and the Todds, together with another member of the Dicks staff who helped Sadie put a sweatsheet over the horse and douse him in water, as if enough were not already now falling from the darkening skies.

As Merlin pulled the small saddle and its coloured cloth from Fan Court's steaming back, Sadie moved unexpectedly to stand beside him. Merlin was about to repeat his request for a meeting when a commotion suddenly arose on the other side of the horse, where Penalty Kick and his connections were standing by the second place post.

"No' good enough!" Merlin heard a loud male voice say, "I expect 'im to win. I no' 'appy with the second best. You 'ave to 'it 'im, make 'im work 'arder."

The unfortunate grey gelding did not understand the criticism, evidently directed towards its trainer and jockey, but was certainly alarmed by the aggressive tone of the speaker's voice. Penalty Kick skittered sideways, knocking one of the yellow water buckets out of the hands of the groom who had been standing by ready to pour it over the sweating animal. Water sloshed to the ground, running around the expensively shod feet of Penalty Kick's owners, who jumped back with cries of annoyance.

Merlin and Sadie automatically stepped away from Fan Court's side, a precaution in case he too took fright and pushed them over. The incident was finished in seconds, but the effect had been to bring the connections of Fan Court to stand immediately alongside those of Penalty Kick. Merlin found himself looking directly into the face of Abigail Alvarez.

"Are you all right, ma'am?" he asked her, as she and her furious husband brushed droplets of water from their overpriced clothes, whilst Mark McConnell and Penalty Kick's trainer, standing behind them, tried their best not to laugh.

"Yes, I am, thank you for asking," replied Abigail Alvarez politely, whilst her male companion turned to vent his fury on the unlucky young groom, "Congratulations on your win. Come on, Santi, leave these people to their work. Let's go indoors now."

With that, she turned away from Merlin and walked away, her irritable footballer husband in tow, both of them watched avidly by the Premier League fans in the crowd. There had not been one flicker of recognition in her eyes. It was quite clear that she had no idea who Merlin was.

But if Abigail Alvarez had not recognised Merlin, someone had recognised Abigail Alvarez. As Merlin hoisted the saddle higher in his arms and turned to speak to Sadie, he saw that all colour had drained from Sadie's face. With a shock as cold as the bucket of spilt water, he belatedly realised why.

"You cheating bastard, Merlin," was all Sadie said.

18

Whilst Fan Court and Merlin were winning their two mile Chase, Kye and Ryan had been preparing an unexpectedly jittery Curlew Landings for his attempt at the Greatwood Hurdle. As Kye was to be riding in the race immediately following, it had been agreed, in the face of some reluctance on Ryan's part, that Ryan would lead Curlew up in the parade ring.

"Yez the one that got him fit for the race," Kye had told Ryan when Ryan had tried to decline the proposal, "I get the problem with the lorry driving, but this yez can do with yez eyes closed. It's just walking round leading Curlew until the bell rings and then Merlin comes and gets on. Then yez go and collect Curlew afterwards and take him back to where Merlin says. It's no problem, Ryan."

This conversation had taken place earlier in the week preceding the wet November Sunday at Cheltenham, and had necessitated obtaining suitable clothing for Ryan to wear. It had not escaped the notice of everyone at Sampfield Grange that Ryan had arrived with very few possessions, all of which were contained in the single tattered rucksack which he had brought with him on the day of his arrival. Sam's assumption that further luggage would be delivered later had quickly been dispelled and he had soon perceived that his Australian cousin's reportedly wayward son had little more with him than the clothes which he was wearing.

"Speak to Bethany," Sam had told Ryan, when it had initially been agreed that Ryan should assist in the yard, "I can't have you riding out on my horses wearing that outfit. It's not warm or waterproof enough for this climate apart from anything else. And the footwear is certainly not acceptable. Give Bethany your size details and she can order something using the office computer."

Sam had never in his life used a computer to order anything and had little idea of the processes involved, so he had then left the matter entirely in Ryan's hands. Bethany had duly ordered the clothing and footwear which Ryan had specified for her. In the absence of any offer from Ryan to meet the cost of the purchases, or to provide a credit card to which to charge them, she had simply used the Sampfield Grange account. Kitting Ryan out in something suitable for the Cheltenham parade ring had since required further purchases.

During the month which Ryan had now spent at Sampfield Grange, frustrated curiosity about him on the part of Kelly and Lewis had reached fever pitch. Kye and Jackie, who spent more time with Ryan than did the household staff, had been pumped remorsely by them for any titbits of information which they might have gleaned during their working day concerning Mr Sampfield's mysterious young relative. Kye had not been able to avoid reporting back what Ryan had told him on the journey home from Chepstow, information which had since been pored over and speculated about endlessly. Lewis had checked on the internet, using the kitchen iPad, the information about the temporary visa, and had discovered it to be true. As for the lack of money, they all knew that Mr Sampfield had paid for Ryan's new clothing, but then, as Jackie, rather unexpectedly, had pointed out, Mr Sampfield was benefitting from Ryan's unpaid help with the horses and surely it was only reasonable that he should make sure that Ryan had proper clothes to work in.

For their part, Kelly and Lewis were not prepared to risk asking Ryan direct questions for fear of causing some offence which might be reported back to Mr Sampfield. And so the uncontrolled speculation had continued without reaching any sensible conclusion.

Ryan had continued to work meticulously with Curlew Landings in the week leading up to the Greatwood Hurdle and Sam was confident that between them, they had done as much as possible to prepare the horse for his ambitious run. Ryan had followed Sam's training directions carefully, offering few comments other than voicing his agreement with what was proposed. On the day before the race, after horse and rider had completed a final piece of light work, the morning ride had made its way down the muddy track from the gallops, and Sam had had to confess himself impressed.

"You've done a first rate job with Curlew, Ryan," he had announced from his position on Caldesi Island's broad back, as the string of horses picked their way through the scattered puddles which were reflecting the ragged pieces of the lumpy cloud decorating the blue sky above them, "Anyone would think you had been training horses all your life. Your father vouched for you as a good horseman, but this has been most professional on your part. I was expecting something a bit more - if you'll pardon the expression - rough and ready from you."

Kye, riding just ahead of Mr Sampfield on Highlander Park, had pricked up his ears at the content of the conversation. Maybe now he would find out something about Ryan, he had thought.

"No offence taken, Mr Sampfield," Ryan had replied, promptly, "We're not all jackaroos in Queensland. There's a lot of top quality horse sport there, y'know."

"Indeed I do know," Sam had responded, quickly, "My mother, your Great Aunt Raldi used to be a top event rider, so I guess you must share her talents. Tell me, how was she when you left home, Ryan? Well?"

"Great Aunt Raldi?" repeated Ryan, seemingly reluctant to respond to the question, "Couldn't really say. Fine, I guess. Didn't see much of her, sorry, Mr Sampfield."

Ryan's unwillingness to engage with Mr Sampfield on a personal level had continued to intrigue the perceptive Kye. When asked by Jackie why he did not call Mr Sampfield by his first name, Ryan had simply explained that it was hard to think of Mr Sampfield as a member of his family or to feel comfortable living in the unfamiliar environment of an English country house. Notwithstanding the family connection, he had said, Mr Sampfield was a stranger to him. Ryan felt happier in his self appointed role as one of the yard staff.

Kye had thought privately that there was a much simpler reason for Ryan's determination to keep Mr Sampfield at arm's length. Talking about the horses, the conversation between the two of them flowed easily enough, but any other topic usually elicited short and offhand answers from the younger man. Bearing in mind that the distant Mr Urquhart had apparently described his younger son as having 'gone off the rails', Kye could understand Ryan's wish to avoid the risk of being asked questions about personal issues. Presumably Ryan had left home to escape the difficulties which had arisen between him and his father and would not want the same issues to be resurrected by his father's cousin on the other side of the world. In reaching this sensible conclusion, Kye had been partly correct, but, as he was later to discover, there was more to be learned about the evasive Ryan Urquhart.

Jackie had remained with Katseye since the completion of the second race, but was now free to help Ryan take Curlew Landings, who continued to jiggle irritably and to pull against the lead rein, down to the pre-parade area, where Sam was waiting to meet them. The cold wind and rain had abated slightly but dark clouds still massed threateningly above an unusually drab looking Cleeve Hill as it stood guard over the far side of the course. Curlew seemed unhappy with his damp and busy surroundings, glaring at a couple of pedestrians who were waiting to cross the track where it passed the wide Hall of Fame entrance to the racecourse buildings, and walking obstinately crabwise in the spattering rain along the black rubber surfaced path.

At the same time as Ryan and Jackie were escorting Curlew towards his ambitious and carefully planned attempt at the Greatwood Hurdle race, Isabella Hall was sitting in a comfortable armchair in the compact living room of a small stone cottage near the village of Warnock. The large flat screen TV which dominated the space was showing the afternoon's racing from Cheltenham.

Isabella had watched the fortunes of Katseye with some trepidation and had expressed her relief at his safe completion of the race to her younger companion, who was now standing behind the patterned armchair offering Isabella a freshly made mug of tea.

"I know he's talented, but making him come straight into that race after all this time was quite a big ask," Isabella had said, letting out her breath as Katseye had crossed the finishing line at the top of the hill.

TK Stonehouse had not agreed.

"Katseye could have won," she had said firmly, pushing her shoulder length brown hair away from her oval face, "But Jayce and Tabby Cat did say that he was one to watch for the future. I suppose this proves they were right at least."

Now, as Isabella tentatively sipped the hot tea, she observed Ryan leading the still unsettled Curlew Landings around the wet parade ring.

"Curlew's on his toes," Isabella remarked, "And I don't recognise the new lad. Must be Sadie's replacement."

"It's not your little drug dealer friend, Kye, then?" TK commented.

"No," said Isabella, "I'm trusting he's back on the path of the righteous. He'd better be. He's riding Highlander Park in the next race."

TK snorted.

"You're too nice," was all she said, "He very nearly buggered up our plans with Tabikat from what Frank said."

"Well, he didn't, and it's water under the bridge now," Isabella told her, firmly, "Look, here's His arrogant Majesty the wizard coming to mount up. With any luck, Curlew will chuck him off, the mood the horse seems to be in."

TK came to sit on the arm of Isabella's chair and watched as Ryan vaulted Merlin ap Rhys up into Curlew's small saddle. Curlew skirted crossly to one side whilst Merlin continued to sit with his feet out of the irons, legs dangling either side of Curlew's body, his right hand patting the horse's neck.

"You don't like him much, do you?" TK said, her tone signalling a statement rather than a question.

"I don't like the way he treats Sadie," Isabella told her, "Sadie loves it, of course. No man has ever taken so much trouble to keep her coming back into his bed. But it's all for his own gratification. Poor Sadie's too honest to see him for what he is."

"That was her leading out Fan Court in the last race, wasn't it?" TK countered, "They didn't look too friendly then, especially at the end."

"No they didn't, you're right," conceded Isabella, thoughtfully, "Maybe Sadie's come to her senses."

"Or maybe he's not quite as bad as you make out," TK laughed, amused at Isabella's vehement denunciation of the character of the Welsh jockey.

The TV camera was showing a panoramic shot of the wet parade ring, as the horses filed out of the exit into the horsewalk. Notwithstanding the unpleasant weather, eager crowds surged around the white plastic gates, keen to get a closer glimpse of the horses they had selected.

"A minute of your time, Mr Sampfield Peveril?" a newly recruited female TV presenter asked politely, pushing a microphone beneath Sam's nose, "Are you feeling confident about Curlew Landings' chances today? He's down in trip and up three pounds today after the win at Chepstow, isn't he?"

Whilst the electronic image of Sam outlined his thoughts on Curlew's chances for the benefit of the TV viewers, TK was studying the people standing alongside the trainer in the parade ring.

"Who are the fossils with your old boss, then?" she asked Isabella, bluntly.

"The stocky one is Gilbert Peveril, Mr Sampfield's cousin," said Isabella, slowly, "He used to ride Highlander Park in point to point races. I think the woman next to him with the umbrella must be his wife, Philippa, if I remember her name rightly. The man in the tweeds is, I guess, Curlew's former owner, Toby Halstock, and the tall woman in the waxed hat and trenchcoat is Lady Helen Garratt, Mr Sampfield's friend."

"Think I preferred the blond boy," TK said, laughing, "That lot look like a pensioners' outing – rich, posh pensioners, of course."

"Curlew's going off fourth favourite at 9 to 1," Isabella interrupted her, ignoring the disrespectful comment, "And he's been coming in steadily in the betting. Jayce and Tabby Cat have tipped him for a place and Stevie said she'd try for a vlog piece with Mr Sampfield, if Curlew does well."

"You're really into this, aren't you?" TK said, more seriously.

"I did work with these people for six months," Isabella reminded her, "And Curlew's a lovely horse."

"I have to go," TK told her, "We've got a lot on this evening, so I'll see you tomorrow, if you want to risk coming past on the bike. Er.. George should be back from France soon too, I think?"

"Tomorrow afternoon," Isabella told her, "Don't worry, I've still got the handgun and the panic button. I shouldn't need either any more, but Frank insisted. That nosy girl from Stevie's old school is hardly likely to find me here anyway."

"Don't be too sure," TK said, warningly, "She's been poking about in Frossiac, George said. That must mean that her news bots have picked up on those online searches for Susan Stonehouse which that Maurice Vacher did from there. Pretty serious nosiness if she's going all that way in person. Maybe she's more than just a dirt digger for the gutter press."

"Whatever she is, Frank's got her covered," stated Isabella, firmly.

As the front door of the cottage slammed itself shut behind the departing TK, the fourteen horses running in the Greatwood Hurdle were busily milling about near the two mile start. The rain had become more persistent and round blobs spattered over the lens of the camera, which was swaying on its windblown platform high above the racecourse. Isabella could see Curlew Landings being walked carefully around the edge of the group. Merlin had taken his feet out of the irons again.

At last, the starter climbed the steps of his little rostrum and brought down his yellow flag. The massed field set off like a cavalry charge towards the first of the eight hurdles. Two of the original entrants had been withdrawn on the basis of unsuitable ground and Isabella thought it likely that not all of those now running would still be there at the finish. The sort of ground on which the horses were about to run would be unlikely to be repeated in the much drier conditions usually prevailing at the Cheltenham Festival in March.

By the time the horses had reached the far side of the Old course, the field was already beginning to separate. At least three runners were struggling to keep up the strong pace set by the leaders, one of whom was Curlew Landings. Now that the race was under way, Curlew seemed to have settled into his challenge and was lobbing along determinedly under Merlin's firm guidance.

Isabella gasped as one of the leading horses fell heavily at the third hurdle from the finish, struggling breathlessly to its feet and trotting quickly off to the side of the track. Frustratingly, the unlucky faller had been going well at the time, although he was not among Curlew Landings' main opposition. The chief threats were in the form of the two joint favourites, Southern Cross and Rabbit Punch, both of which were hammering along slightly in advance of Curlew and Merlin. Up by Curlew's fast moving side was the third favourite horse, The Squire's Tale.

"Southern Cross and Rabbit Punch are leading over the second last together, but there are others still in with chances!" cried the commentator as the end of the race drew closer and the labouring horses approached the turbulent spectator stands, "Curlew

Landings and The Squire's Tale are coming through behind them to challenge up the hill. Southern Cross has belted the last but it hasn't slowed him down and he's being driven out to the finish. Rabbit Punch and Curlew Landings are hard on his heels and still making ground."

The clamour of the thousands of racegoers bellowing and cheering alongside the final hill rolled downwards to meet Merlin as he kicked and pushed and yelled at Curlew Landings to get up the steep slope. Isabella could see that Curlew was hating every minute of it. The rain and wind were blasting squarely over Merlin's green and red clad back as they swept up the hill with the other two leading horses, The Squire's Tale still trying to make ground behind them. Curlew's usually alert ears were flattened back against his handsome head as he stretched his neck forwards in response to Merlin's furious activity on his back.

"And Southern Cross has won the Greatwood Hurdle!" shouted the commentator, to tumultuous applause, "It's gone to the judge in a photo for second between Curlew Landings and Rabbit Punch. And the fourth horse is The Squire's Tale."

Isabella was not interested in the televised interview with the muddy and triumphant jockey of the winner. Instead she watched the blond boy, as TK had called him, come out of the horsewalk with a huge grin on his face to seize Curlew Landings by the left rein and to call something, presumably congratulatory, up to Merlin. Once the TV cameras had followed the winner down the horsewalk to his celebratory appearance before the enthusiastic spectators massing onto the steppings above the winners' enclosure, she was pleased to hear Curlew Landings announced as the second placed horse.

Watching Merlin, Mr Sampfield, the Peverils and Toby Halstock surrounding the sweating and exhausted looking Curlew, as the new lad doused the horse in water, Isabella noticed a second new Sampfield Grange groom pushing a bucket under Curlew's grateful white nose.

"Why that's …. what's she doing there?" Isabella said aloud.

19

By the time the horses competing in the Conditional Jockeys' race were being brought into the parade ring, the ominous dark clouds had given up trying to contain their watery load and persistent heavy rain was drumming relentlessly down onto the racecourse. Only Gilbert Peveril had elected to remain with Sam in the parade ring, their companions having quickly retreated to the warmth and comfort of the Garratt box in the grandstand.

"Who's your new lad, James?" asked Gilbert, peering from under his dripping brown fedora hat as a well-soaked Ryan led Highlander Park along the path under the deluge. Eleven more horses were joining the wet procession one by one, to be viewed by a diminishing number of the more hardy racegoers.

"My cousin Teddy's son from Mother's family in Australia," Sam told him, "He's staying with me for a while, helping in the yard whilst Sadie is at Ranulph Dicks's place. Ryan Urquhart."

"Hrrmphh," snorted Gilbert, "The boy won't be used to this kind of weather in November. Summer in Australia now, isn't it?"

"I suppose it must be," replied Sam, suddenly thinking that the global difference in the seasons would at least explain Ryan's lack of winter clothing on his arrival, "But Highlander Park should like the conditions, at least. You've ridden the horse through some mud in his time, Gil."

Kye, clad in the Sampfield Grange colours previously sported by Merlin, could see the two well dressed cousins standing expectantly in the middle of the parade ring. Kye's stomach was churning. The eleven fellow conditional jockeys who had joined him in the changing room had all seemed loud and confident, their relaxed manner only reminding Kye of his limited experience at this challenging level of race riding. He began to wish that Ryan had not been so determined to persuade Mr Sampfield to allow Kye to ride Highlander Park today.

"You ought to be stoked, mate," Ryan had said confidently to him earlier, as they trudged around the course together, "You're taking seven pounds off Landy's back and word is that he loves bad ground. No-one's expecting you two to rock up winners today, anyway. Just get out there and give it a blast."

Jackie too had expressed her confidence in Kye. Sadie had found time to come over to speak to him whilst she was preparing Fan Court for his journey home with Katseye in the Dicks lorry. Highlander Park himself seemed to be approaching the race in a tranquil mood, having apparently entirely forgotten his uppity and disobedient performance during the previous season at Newbury racecourse.

"Landy likes the rain," Sadie told him, "And now he doesn't have to cart Mr Peveril around any more either."

Kye circled Highlander Park carefully around the edge of the sodden equine group. The rain was dripping from the peak of the coloured cover over his riding helmet and Highlander's neatly plaited mane streamed rivulets of rainwater down the horse's firm neck. Kye's gloves felt clammy and wet, whilst cold water was seeping under the edges of his back protector and running down his sides. His boots felt slippery against Highlander's coat.

Waiting for the starter to call the riders forward, Kye tried to review the multiplicity of advice and instructions which he had received before the race. Ryan, in particular, having gone to the trouble to walk as much of the course with Kye as they had had time for after their arrival, had given a constant stream of commentary as they had moved along the track.

"This is a tricky section, you could get boxed in by the rail here, keep the horse wide, don't let the gap close ahead of you, Highlander's not used to big fields, he'll get bumped, try to keep him calm through that, don't waste too much energy on this slope, there's a long run still, give him some daylight over the hurdles ...."

Ryan's advice had soon become a long babble of detail which Kye felt he would be unable to retain, let alone carry out. Much simpler had been Mr Sampfield's instructions.

"Go out and enjoy it, Kye. This is all about getting some experience - for both of you. Just focus on giving Highlander a good ride."

With the attention of all the connections of Sampfield Grange fixed upon them, Kye and Highlander approached the starter at a calm walk. Sam and Gilbert stood stoically in the pouring rain in the parade ring, Ryan hovered tensely by the horsewalk, Stevie Stone and Mrs Crosland looked from the window in the Owners and Trainers bar, while Lady Helen Garratt and her party kept watch from their warm and comfortable viewing box. Jackie and Sadie had walked together down the hill from the stables to a position from which they could see the big screen in the parade ring. Someone had kindly lent Jackie an umbrella, and they were now huddled gratefully beneath it.

Merlin, emerging at that moment from the jockey's changing room, wearing a black waterproof hiking jacket, saw the two young women standing together by the weighing room. It took him a moment to recall the reason for their interest in this particular race but, having remembered, his quick mind suggested to him that he could use the situation to his advantage. Sadie could hardly flounce off in the presence of the other young woman, whom he recognised as the new talent at the Sampfield Grange yard. Unluckily for Merlin, his plan was immediately frustrated by the appearance of a red trousered young man who approached Sadie and Jackie with the apparent offer of an additional umbrella. As Merlin watched, Sadie moved with the newcomer under the second umbrella whilst Jackie helpfully shifted further away to stand on her own.

Merlin's eyes widened as he saw Sadie greet the man with the open and welcoming smile which she had previously bestowed on Merlin. A comment by the young man produced a laugh from Sadie and she did not seem to object when the newcomer put his arm around her waist to draw her further under the inadequate shelter.

"And 'oo the 'ell is that little bastard?" Merlin swore angrily to himself, pushing up the collar of his waterproof jacket, deciding to stay where he was and to watch the race on the screen. If nothing else, it would give him time to think about his next move.

The Conditional Jockeys' race was a muddy affair. Many of the horses struggled in the rapidly worsening ground, and the field was soon very strung out around the course. The runners quickly divided into those who liked bad ground and those who did not. Highlander Park was among the former group. Notwithstanding the large size of the field, there was little opportunity for bumping and barging and Kye found that he had a mostly clear run. Ryan's dire prediction of being boxed in against the rails did not materialise either. Remembering Mr Sampfield's instructions, Kye tried to enjoy the ride and, to his surprise, he found that he did enjoy it, calling out encouragingly to Highlander Park, who responded by galloping gamely through the mud with all the enthusiasm of a hunter out in the countryside, and bringing him home in a creditable fifth place.

One of the few people who had not watched Kye's introduction to bad weather riding at Cheltenham was Jessica Moretti. She was not interested in Kye. But she was interested in Sadie Shinkins, Merlin ap Rhys and Abigail Alvarez.

Jessica had indeed, as Stevie had told Sam, come to keep watch that day on Santiago and Abigail Alvarez. She had made sure to position herself by the winner's enclosure when the grey Penalty Kick was brought back to stand in the second place position after the two mile Novices' Chase. There were official photographers around the course who would capture the infamous couple on camera, but Jessica had had a mobile phone in her hand with the microphone switched on. Although the phone looked no different than those carried by the many spectators who surrounded her, this one had an enhanced lens, and, more importantly, a highly sensitive microphone. Pretending to take personal selfies, Jessica could hold out the phone in the direction of her quarry and pick up what they were saying.

Santiago Alvarez's bad tempered criticism of Penalty Kick's jockey had been duly recorded, as had the incident in which the ill-mannered footballer and his unfortunate wife had been forced to jump away from the spilled bucket of cold water. 'Santi Gets an Early Bath', the Red Tops were to announce gleefully the following day. But Merlin's polite enquiry after Abigail Alvarez's wellbeing had been picked up only by Jessica's microphone. And so had Sadie's subsequent comment to Merlin.

"Cheating bastard, eh?" had thought Jessica, eyeing Merlin with new interest. Jessica had at once recognised Sadie as the stable groom so eager to see Merlin in the winners' enclosure after the Punchestown Gold Cup. The angry comment from Sadie had clearly related to some spat between them, a spat which looked as if it involved Abigail Alvarez. Had Abby been cheating on her husband with this sharp looking jockey? That was news which would really show Abby in a deliciously bad light after her saintly behaviour towards her errant spouse and her treacherous sister.

Jessica decided that she needed to learn more from the jockey's spurned girlfriend. Or even from the jockey himself.

Pushing her wet black hair back under a flimsy red hood, Jessica could see Merlin ap Rhys still standing by the weighing room entrance as the Conditional Jockeys' race came to an end. Feeling in his pockets apparently for his car keys, Merlin called a farewell to someone inside the glass fronted building, and walked off towards the nearby exit. Jessica suddenly realised that she would have to move quickly to intercept this newly interesting man whilst she had the chance.

Hurriedly climbing the steppings, she soon found that Merlin's speed of progress was too fast for her, and that he had already walked halfway up the hill towards the car park. But something had stopped him, it seemed. Two people standing beneath an umbrella had apparently attracted his attention and he had gone over to speak to them. Coming closer, Jessica now saw that one of the couple was the angry stable girl from the parade ring and that the other was a young farmer type she thought she remembered seeing at the tedious country races at Ashfordleigh Downs.

Reading the body language of others was one of Jessica's specialities, honed sharp over many years of dubious practice. She watched the jockey shaking the young farmer's hand and nodding, apparently politely, to the blonde girl, who stood silently whilst he took his leave towards the car park. As Jessica followed Merlin's progress out through the gates, she saw him pause to take a mobile phone from his pocket and to produce a small rose pink card from which he appeared to read a number and to stab it into the phone.

"Pink?" thought Jessica, "A woman, then? And one whose number he doesn't keep in his phone. Might not be Abby, but well worth a bit of digging."

Only the most dedicated of the day's racegoers, and those with a direct interest in the closing event, had decided to remain for the last race. Kye, returning to the horsebox park clad in dry clothing, hoped that Highlander Park and Curlew Landings were in the lorry and all ready to travel. He looked round in the gathering gloom for Ryan.

Ryan had been the first to congratulate Kye on his ride. Running up the horsewalk to grab the mud-covered Highlander Park, he had shouted up to Kye, "Bonzer ride, Kye, mate! Real pro!"

Kye was not sure he had actually followed any of the advice Ryan had so liberally dispensed, but he had grinned breathlessly down at his work colleague and accepted the praise nevertheless.

Approaching the Sampfield Grange box, Kye could not stop himself from glancing carefully around for any sign of his brother, or, more likely, anyone who might be associated with him. Bronz himself was, he knew, in prison and would certainly be made to wear an electronic tag on his release. The chances of Bronz coming in person to Cheltenham racecourse were therefore non-existent, but there was nothing to stop Bronz sending someone else to find out just what role Kye had played in having Bronz arrested. And Kye had no idea what had happened to the hard faced fellow dealer, Sheryl.

But no-one approached Kye on that miserable day except Jackie, who was waiting by the lorry.

"Well done, Kye," Jackie told him, planting a kiss on his cheek, "Ryan's gone on with Katseye and the Dicks people. I'm going to drive us and the horses home. You've done enough for one day."

With that, Jackie climbed into the cab of the box and motioned Kye towards the passenger seat.

"Where'd you learn to drive one of these, then?" Kye asked, as Jackie manoeuvred the large vehicle out through the racecourse gates and towards the busy roundabout. It was almost dark now, and the gleam of headlights reflected blurrily up from the road surface. Pedestrians darted amongst the queuing traffic, eager to get under shelter somewhere.

"In the Army," Jackie said, shortly, much to Kye's surprise.

Relieved of the need to drive the lorry himself, Kye soon relaxed and began to doze in the warm cab. The swoosh of the windscreen wipers and the sound of the tyres lifting water from the dark surface of the M5 were hypnotic and he was only vaguely aware of the passage of time as the lorry and its precious equine cargo progressed South towards Sampfield Grange.

He was roughly awakened by Jackie shaking his arm.

"Look Kye, what's that?" Jackie said, her anxiety sounding in her voice.

Kye peered blearily through the rain streaked windscreen.

"It looks like a fire," he said, uncertainly, "Somewhere over Warnock way, I think."

Twenty minutes later, as Jackie brought the horsebox to a standstill in the Sampfield Grange yard, they saw Kelly running out of the house to meet them. Although it was still pouring with rain, she wore no coat and held one of the numerous large umbrellas normally kept in the boot room. Her face was ashen in the headlights of the lorry.

"What's up Kelly?" asked Kye, jumping down from the cab, wide awake now.

"Kye and Jackie, thank God!" Kelly exclaimed, "There's been the most terrible accident at Old Warnock airfield. An aeroplane has crashed and they say there are people in it. There's a huge fire. You can see it from here. Lewis has gone up there to see if he can help."

As Highlander Park and Curlew Landings were unloaded from the box, Kye and Jackie could see the glow of the fire in the distance and smell the burning that was borne on the wet wind towards them.

20

Almost four hundred miles to the West of Old Warnock airfield, the cold front and associated low pressure which had brought the penetrating deluge of grey rain to Cheltenham races had long since passed on its easterly way and no longer disturbed the evening peace of Enda's Farm. The downpour which had saturated the bowl of green hills, which gave the town of Gleannglas its name, had been succeeded by a damp and cold breeze which shaped the few remaining clouds into moonlit shards and allowed the points of bright stars to shine out between them.

Few guests stayed at Enda's Farm in November. Only hardy walkers and those looking for the cheaper prices usually offered in the winter season were interested in braving the potential for frequent soakings and the need to live almost permanently in waterproof clothing and stout boots. Eoghan, Caitlin and Niamh had said goodbye earlier in the day to a young Dutch couple who had praised everything about the establishment, except the weather, and who had been more than keen to drive off down the long descent of the farm lane in their hired car with a view to sampling the distant fleshpots of Dublin.

The departure of their only guests had left the three owners of the rural establishment free to spend the already darkening afternoon as they wished. Eoghan and Caitlin were happy to ride out in all weathers with the tougher guests who enjoyed their pony trekking excursions, but there was no requirement to do that today. Niamh, Caitlin's older sister and the widow of Eoghan's brother, Enda Foley, after whom the secluded holiday centre, which had once been a working farm, was named, did not share their passion for horses and the outdoor world, and confined her activities to an administrative role in the business.

Niamh Foley had never remarried following the violent death of her husband Enda at the hands of his uncle, Callan Sullivan, almost thirty years ago. Her brother in law, Eoghan, his career as a jockey almost simultaneously ended by a horrific fall at Navan racecourse, which had left him with a shattered knee, had returned to shoulder the responsibility of running his brother's farm, as well as helping Niamh to provide for the four small children who had so tragically lost their father. Soon after, Caitlin had also come back to live at the farm. She had been away for almost ten years, no-one knew where. Caitlin herself had said nothing and her firm and dignified silence on the subject of her recent life had forestalled any questions from either Eoghan or Niamh, mainly for fear that Caitlin might decide to leave again.

In the years which had passed since those traumatic days, Eoghan, who had been Caitlin's childhood friend and now became her lover and the father of their three sons, had never pressed her for information. Their new relationship as adults, together with the need to earn a living, had quickly propelled them into a new and challenging world, in which their joint present and future inevitably eclipsed the fading memories of their recent separate pasts. Occasional reminders had sometimes slipped through the progressively closing shutters, once after the first of their children was born, when Eoghan had heard Caitlin singing to the baby in an unknown language, and again when a traveller had approached Caitlin on the hills above the farm, a dark haired man who had addressed her as Catalina. Caitlin's conversations with some of the foreign guests who stayed at Enda's Farm had betrayed her knowledge of languages and places of which Eoghan knew nothing, and she had surprised him one day by picking out rippling flamenco chords on a guitar proffered by one of the visitors.

These memories had soon become buried and obscured, and, after nearly thirty years, Caitlin's unexplained time away from her family and from Gleannglas had become a distant fact of history, no longer important to either of them. The memories of their early teenage years had instead become more vivid as they had built their shared life in the familiar environment in which they had existed as children before the real world had crashed its way in.

The departure of the damp Dutch guests and the lack of urgent work to claim his attention had meant that Eoghan had had the time to watch the televised coverage of the afternoon's racing from

Cheltenham in England. Eoghan and Caitlin had been at Cheltenham on Gold Cup Day in March earlier that year, watching Tabikat, the magnificent horse which they had bred on Enda's Farm, run into third place. Today, they had seen another of their horses, Katseye, a younger half brother to Tabikat, run in a two mile Novices Hurdle.

Eoghan had sat unmoving on the battered sofa in the family living room, watching every step of Katseye's performance in the two mile race. On the arm of the sofa had perched Caitlin, with Niamh and her youngest daughter, Feanna, seated on the remaining cushion and arm respectively. Feanna was the only one of Niamh and Enda's children still resident at Enda's Farm.

Feanna, a black haired and deceptively strong woman, was a talented amateur rider. She was the Miss F Foley listed in the race records studied by Sam which showed that she had ridden the imperious Katseye to his two victories and two places in Irish point to point races. Other riders had been openly surprised to see 'such a slight person', as one had described her, on the back of a horse which the same individual had rudely referred to as being 'built like a brick shithouse'. As another rider had soon pointed out, the horse was far too well bred to justify such a disrespectful description, and it also quickly had become clear that Miss F Foley, when she had taken the classy animal out onto the course, was very far from being over horsed.

Feanna had been a toddler when her father had been killed, and remembered nothing of him, although of all his children she was the one who resembled him most, with her deep, dark eyes and restless spirit. Nowadays, she worked with Eoghan and his oldest son, also called Enda, to run the breeding and equestrian side of the family business.

Eoghan and Feanna, unlike Mrs Crosland, had been more than pleased with the performance of Katseye. They had not thought that Katseye would sweep up the hill in the imperious manner that his current owner had apparently expected. His entry in the competitive race had been forced on them by circumstances, the opinion of Eoghan having been that the horse was not yet ready to race in such challenging company, not to mention being potentially unsuited to the short distance. Second place had therefore been seen by them as a highly creditable achievement, especially as the horse had appeared relatively fresh at the end.

"He'll do," Eoghan had said, "But we need those people in England to keep him right."

"Do you think I should go there myself?" had asked Feanna, not for the first time. The beautiful Katseye had been her particular project and she had been sorry when he had been sold to the English businessman to be ridden by his daughter, who appeared now to have no interest in him.

"Not yet," Eoghan had told her, "These things take their own time. What they have in mind for this one is anybody's guess. Tabikat will be back there soon enough too, and perhaps then we will be able to understand their plans."

Niamh had looked up at the mention of Tabikat.

"To be sure, Tabikat was in good order when I saw him at Punchestown in April," she had said, "And Brendan thinks he has a good chance of winning the Gold Cup at Cheltenham next time. I suppose the horse is now to be allowed to run in Aoife and Efe's colours? It would be a welcome thing to have some of their employees from their business to join us there, as they did at Punchestown."

Niamh always referred to Levy Brothers International, the Bahrain based property development and international commodities trading bank, owned by her son in law Ephraim Levy, as though it were a local grocery shop in Gleannglas. She simply assumed that the young people who were given a day out to see Tabikat's races as a reward for some recent business achievement were personally known to her daughter and son in law, and would greet them by introducing herself as 'Niamh Foley, Efe's mother in law'. Niamh had never quite understood the reason for the solicitous deference which this description of herself seemed always to engender in the employees whom she met.

"Well, I believe Danny and TK have no further need of Tabikat's help," Eoghan had told her, "So the young Welshman will now be riding in the Levy Brothers colours in the future."

"And those of Mrs Crosland," had put in Feanna, pointedly, while the horses for the next race had started to enter the ring, and Katseye had been led by Jackie out of the range of the television camera. Feanna had kept her eyes on Katseye until he had disappeared from sight, after which she had jumped from the arm of the sofa, saying she had work to do before it got dark.

Caitlin had watched her niece pass by the small window beyond which the slowly clearing grey sky was visible, and had said to Eoghan, "She should be allowed to go with the horse, Genie. You and young Enda can manage without her at this time of the year."

Eoghan had followed his partner's gaze towards the window, and had nodded slowly. Niamh had let out a sigh, but said nothing. They had turned their attention once again to the rest of the races to be shown on the television and Katseye had been discussed no further.

Eoghan, shrugging on an old grey fleece jacket, stepped out from the house into the gathering damp darkness of the chilly evening with the intention of speaking to his son Enda about the welfare of their horses, when a distant movement caught his eye. A green car was slowly making its way up the farm lane towards the gate. The rising moon, floating conveniently free of the tattered clouds at that moment, enabled Eoghan to recognise the vehicle as a taxi from the local town.

Caitlin, clad in a long waxed waterproof coat and a woollen hat, had followed Eoghan out into the yard. Spotting the approaching car, she stopped by his side, saying, "We are surely not expecting guests? Who is coming here at this time of the evening? And without even a phone call?"

A long buried memory tugged at Eoghan's mind, a memory of an Autumn evening a little over sixteen years ago. On that occasion, the approaching vehicle had been a brown horsebox containing a pregnant mare called Maire, later to be known as Kat's Gift, whose foal Little Kitty Cat had become the dam of the successful Tabikat and Katseye. In his heart, Eoghan had always suspected that there would be a day of reckoning associated with the unexpected gift to them of the mare which had founded his horse breeding business. Instinct suddenly warned him that that day could have finally arrived.

Caitlin too seemed to be aware that something unsettling was about to happen, and moved closer to Eoghan's side, taking his hand as they both waited in silence for the approaching vehicle to reach the wooden gate. Ghosts wrapped themselves around the farm buildings as if ready to whisper to those within that old promises were not to be forgotten and old debts must always be repaid in the end. Unnoticed, Niamh slipped out from the door behind them, her brightly coloured quilted jacket contrasting with the dull garments worn by her sister. The three of them faced the gate as the car drew near and stopped.

The man who slowly clambered out looked feeble, bent forward over his stomach, his breath coming in gasps as he struggled from the back seat of the taxi. He wore an ancient tweed jacket and cap over threadbare corduroy trousers and a pair of brown laced boots which had evidently seen much hard usage. Paying the taxi driver from a handful of coins pulled from a sagging pocket, the newcomer turned towards the gate and looked into the expectant faces of his reception party.

"Genie, I need your help," he said in a rasping voice which was nevertheless familiar to Eoghan and Caitlin, if not to Niamh.

"You said that once before, Oisin," Eoghan told the man, moving forward to open the metal farm gate, as the taxi turned around and disappeared down the track, its headlamps illuminating the line of tidy fencing on either side, "What is it that I can do for you this time? I see on this occasion that you have no mare with you."

"No," agreed Oisin Cassidy, putting a shaking hand on the open gate as if to support himself, "But it is the mare I have come to see you about. Do you have her here still?"

187

"I do indeed," replied Eoghan, cautiously, "But she is very old now and you surely cannot be wanting her back after all this time? I doubt she will last another year."

"And the foal?" persisted Oisin, ignoring Eoghan's question.

"The foal is a mare of fifteen years of age," Eoghan told him, "She is here too under our care but her breeding career is long finished now."

Oisin nodded and his grip on the gate tightened slightly. A moving shadow behind Eoghan seemed momentarily to catch Oisin's attention, and Eoghan realised that his son Enda and niece Feanna, alerted by the arrival of the car, had also come out into the yard. The crescent moon illuminated the little group, the four older people in the centre and the two younger ones behind them, standing tense in the darkening farmyard, Niamh's jacket the only splash of colour brightening the gloom.

"I told them," said Oisin, suddenly, his words emerging in a gasping rush, "I told them that I had sold the mare to Brendan Meaghan."

As the words left his mouth, Oisin's knees buckled beneath him and it was only the quick reaction of young Enda, who moved forward to support him, which saved Oisin from collapsing completely onto the stone surface of the yard.

"Bring him into the house, Enda," Caitlin told her son, and Enda picked the older man up as if he were a child and carried him into the living room where Oisin was placed on the ancient sofa from which the family had been watching the racing earlier that day.

"When did you last eat, Mr Cassidy?" asked Niamh, kindly, as Oisin lay breathlessly on the sofa, the thinness of his frame pitifully evident, "Shall I bring you something?"

Oisin shook his balding head, from which his threadbare cap had been dislodged as Enda had carried him into the house. Feanna had picked it up and placed it on a table by the door.

"I cannot eat," he said, "I have a cancer in my stomach. There is nothing to be done now."

"Why are you here then, Oisin?" asked Eoghan, taken aback by this revelation, "Should you not be in the hospital? Shall we get some help for you?"

"I need to tell you the truth of what happened, Genie," responded Oisin, whilst everyone in the room stared at the sick man, who seemed almost scared of what he was about to say, "I cannot go to my grave with this in my soul."

A silence followed, in which Oisin turned his head to look at Niamh, who had shrunk back against the wall by a small window overlooking the farmyard.

"Callan Sullivan killed your husband Enda Foley because Enda did not repay his debts," Oisin stated, flatly.

"I know that," replied Niamh, quietly, returning Oisin's gaze.

"And you, Genie, you too should be dead," went on Oisin, his voice low, looking now at Eoghan, "They sent a sniper for you that day at Navan. He was to shoot you through the head. But your horse fell and the bullet went wide. You have lived a charmed life, indeed you have, Genie."

Eoghan struggled to keep his voice steady as the memory of that terrible day which had ended his career as a jockey snapped back fresh and sharp into his mind.

"And what is your part in this, Oisin?" he asked.

"Callan Sullivan kept my horse dealing business alive when it came to me from my father," Oisin went on, speaking with some effort, "My father had been in debt to him for many years. And so it was that I helped Callan Sullivan with his business and he helped me with mine."

"Indeed? And just what did you do, Mr Cassidy?" asked Niamh, suddenly, in a hard voice.

"Callan Sullivan's money went into my business and came out again. It looked like money for horses, but it was money for guns, guns and other things, things for killing people," said Oisin, hesitantly, the rasping in his voice becoming more noticeable, "I told myself that the people it killed were far away, I did not know them, they were up by the border, in Belfast, in London, places in England. But it was wrong, Genie. There were children killed, you know, and women, not only the British soldiers. But I did not stand up against Callan Sullivan. In the end, your brother Enda Foley did."

"Enda had no choice," said Eoghan, shaking his head, "I refused to stop the horses and my brother Enda suffered the consequences. I should have done what Enda asked...."

As Eoghan's response tailed off, Niamh spoke again.

"I have told you before, Eoghan, that my husband Enda created his own trouble with Uncle Callan," she said, "You were not to blame. You knew nothing of what Enda had been doing. He sold his soul to the devil and tried to sell yours too. You were right to refuse."

Feanna, seeing her mother's stricken and determined face as she spoke of Feanna's dead father, moved towards Niamh and gripped her hand.

Notwithstanding his evident distress, Oisin seemed determined to continue his narrative, but his voice was beginning to fade. Eoghan leaned closer to hear what he was saying. Caitlin remained standing, staring at the dark glass of the window, saying nothing. Young Enda and Feanna were still, trying to comprehend the disjointed story being told by the unexpected visitor.

"When Callan Sullivan was arrested and was sent away to prison, I thanked God that I was free," Oisin went on, haltingly, "But then, Genie, you were home again here in Gleannglas with your career gone and your leg no good. I saw how you made your business here at the farm, with Mrs Foley and your own missus to help, looking after your family, making a new family of your own. I wanted to help you. You deserved it. You were a good friend to me when we were at Mallows together as lads. I offered you to take a share in my own business, you will remember?"

Eoghan nodded.

"Thank God, Genie, that you did not take it," Oisin continued, his feeble voice rising in pitch, "For men such as Callan Sullivan have influence even from behind prison bars and walls. His followers found me again, right enough. But the chain was broken and for many years they had no part for me to play. Without that part, I had to run an honest business, and at that I was no good. But I had to make things right with you, Genie. So I came that day sixteen years ago with Maire for you. I should not have done that, Genie. I soon learned that I had brought trouble to you. So I told them I had sold her to Brendan Meaghan. I told them that Brendan had said he would hide her for them."

"Hide her?" repeated Eoghan, "And who are these people who wanted to hide the mare? You told me that day, Oisin, that you had bought her from someone who could not afford to keep her."

Oisin's chin had by now sunk onto his chest and he started to cough. Eoghan's son Enda went into the nearby kitchen and returned with a mug of water which he held to Oisin's open lips. Oisin took a few sips but declined to take hold of the mug.

The pause allowed Niamh to take charge.

"We will find you a bed for the night, Mr Cassidy, and you will tell us what more it is you have to say in the morning."

Oisin seemed almost to be asleep, so it was decided to leave him on the sofa covered with a warm blanket whilst the Foley family tried their best to make sense of the unfinished story which had been told to them.

When he eventually went to bed that night, Eoghan found that his injured knee throbbed for the first time in many years, and that he dreamed of Niamh's coloured jacket, except that it was being worn by his dead brother Enda, and the bright colours had turned to blood. Eoghan could see the mare Kat's Gift standing in the distance on the racecourse behind Enda, but she was not the elderly horse she had now become, but was young and in foal, and Enda too was a young man like Eoghan's own son. But as Eoghan reached out to take the mare's bridle, Uncle Callan appeared as if from the earth between them and dragged the terrified horse away, leaving Eoghan collapsed on the ground, with Caitlin holding his head on her chest as he wept. Eoghan woke with a start from the nightmare to find Caitlin sitting in a chair by the bed, her fingers interlaced on her lap, her greying dark hair loose around her shoulders, her green eyes fixed on something unseen in the distance.

When Eoghan entered the living room that morning, he found Oisin Cassidy dead on the floor by the sofa. Oisin was lying in a pool of black blood which he appeared to have vomited up from his diseased stomach during the night. His right arm was reaching out as if towards the greasy tweed cap which Feanna had left on the side table. Following Eoghan into the room, Caitlin called out urgently to their son to send for an ambulance to come to the farm, although they all knew that a doctor could do nothing.

"What was Oisin thinking, coming here to tell me these stories from the past?" Eoghan asked Caitlin in despair, "He should have been in the hospital not running around killing himself like this."

"Oisin Cassidy wanted to tell you what happened," said Caitlin, as they and Niamh waited together in the living room for the ambulance to reach the farm, the younger members of the family having resumed their normal work in seeing to the horses, "And to explain his own part in it."

Caitin was silent for a few seconds. In the distance, the ambulance was climbing the farm lane towards them.

"And I must do the same," said Caitlin.

21

Caitlin Kennelly, at that time only sixteen years old, her back towards the strengthening morning sun, rode into the cool breeze which was lifting the grasses on the hills behind the Foleys' sleeping farm. Since the terrible events of yesterday, when Tarragon had been buried and Eoghan had left to return to Mallows, something deep inside Caitlin's bright soul had begun to ache with a pain she had never thought possible. It was as if a well locked box had suddenly sprung open inside her chest, its carefully packed contents bursting out uncontrollably, so that it snatched the breath from her lungs and made her gasp with the shock of it.

Perhaps sensing the emotional burden being carried by her young rider, Branna, Caitlin's sturdy Connemara pony, quietly followed their well trodden route to the special stream from which she and her now dead equine companion Tarragon had often drunk the clean, cold water. Standing with the patient Irish ponies in those happy times had been two young teenagers, a girl and a boy, thrown together by circumstances and their shared love of the horses, and now separated by the promises made on behalf of the boy by his older brother. The last precious tie which had held the oblivious youngsters together had now disappeared with the death of the older pony, the loyal Tarragon who had first brought them together on the farm track leading down into the town.

Caitlin had never experienced true loneliness before. Bereavement was more familiar, her mother having died when she was three years old, but she had scarcely understood what was happening then, and her older sister Niamh and her father had been there to comfort and care for her. But now Niamh was married to Enda Foley and had two children of her own, and her widowed father had his own friends and life at the Gleannglas racecourse where he worked. Eoghan, Enda's younger brother, and Caitlin's only human friend, had gone to Mallows stud and racing yard as an apprentice, returning home once a month to ride Tarragon once again. But now Tarragon was dead and Caitlin knew that Eoghan would come home no more.

Everyone else had a life and a future, but Caitlin had nothing of her own, except the pony Branna. Left largely to her own devices from a young age, Caitlin reasoned that it was now up to her to seek her own future. So she had departed from the farm, leaving only a short note to tell her sister not to worry about her, and had set forth into the beckoning summer world beyond the awakening hills.

The familiar route provided a goal at least, and, in the absence of other instructions, Branna took Caitlin unerringly towards it. The travellers and their horses were encamped on the other side of the hill. There was a route along the higher part of the slopes which led to the North and thence to the coast, and eventually, to the mighty River Shannon.

Since Eoghan had been away at Mallows, Caitlin, when she was not helping her sister at the farm, had ridden out in the hills on Branna as often as she could. On the longer summer days, they had made trips ever further away from the farm surroundings, and Caitlin had been able to see that the world in which she lived was limited and contained. There were other people and other communities beyond the circle of the Gleannglas hills and she hoped that one day she could meet them and maybe even be part of them. The freedoms of her childhood had now been reduced, albeit with the benefit of an apparently secure home and happy family, to life on the remote Foley farm, where the presence of Uncle Callan had overshadowed them all.

Caitlin was not sure what it was about Uncle Callan, the brother of the dead mother of Eoghan and Enda, which unnerved her. Callan Sullivan drove a jaunting cart in the town of Gleannglas and was a respected citizen with a wife and three daughters. Nonetheless, his occasional presence at the Foley farm had seemed to Caitlin to cast a shadow over the household, sending Enda into a black mood, which caused him to stand alone in the fields, staring at the sky, his fists clenched, whilst Niamh watched him helplessly from the living room window. Uncle Callan always greeted, and then ignored, Caitlin, Niamh and the children, addressing himself only to Enda in private on his infrequent visits. But the depressive effect of his presence, although infrequent, would hang like a dead weight over the young family for days afterwards.

Some months earlier, on one of Caitlin's increasingly frequent excursions into the comfort of the hills, she had been surprised to see coming towards her on the earthen track a young girl of about her own age who was riding a stocky piebald cob. On that day, Caitlin had been riding Branna, although often she had taken Tarragon instead, now that Eoghan had been no longer able to ride his precious pony on a daily basis. The strange girl had said nothing to Caitlin, silently turning her black and white pony around to fall in step with Branna, matching her pace. The two riders had proceeded side by side across a grassy hillside decorated with the grey shadows of the puffed up spring clouds which floated across the sun-flooded blue of the sky.

After a few silent minutes, Caitlin had said uncertainly to her new companion, "I am Caitlin, and this is Branna. We live at the Foley farm down the hill."

The other rider had responded eagerly, an unfamiliar sharp edge to her voice, and a strange accentuation in her speech which Caitlin had never heard before.

"I know that," the girl had said, "You and I are cousins. My name is Mirela and this is Luca."

The piebald pony had nodded his head as his name was mentioned. Branna had emitted a little whinny, as if greeting him.

Caitlin had turned her head so as to look at the newcomer more carefully. Mirela had stared calmly back at her. She had bright red hair, like Niamh's, and deep black eyes. But whereas Niamh had fair skin, Mirela's was darker even than Caitlin's brown outdoor tan. She wore gold hoop earrings similar to Caitlin's own.

"How can we be cousins?" had asked Caitlin, puzzled.

"Our grandmothers were sisters," Mirela had replied, as the horses had continued to pick their sociable way along the overgrown track which was beginning to slope downwards towards the other side of the hill. The isolated Foley farmhouse was now hidden from sight, "Your pa at the racecourse down there by the town and my pa are cousins. That makes us cousins too."

Caitlin had drawn Branna to a reluctant halt on the path.

"I have to go home now," she had said, "But can we meet here again tomorrow? I did not know I had a cousin. We can be friends now."

In this way had begun a series of regular meetings between the two girls. Mirela, it seemed, had an older brother, but, as Mirela had crossly informed Caitlin, he spent all his time with the other young men in their travelling group. There was no girl among the younger generation of travellers who was the right age to be Mirela's friend. So, Luca had become her constant companion, in fact her only companion, until Mirela had spotted Caitlin making her lonely way around the hilltop tracks and had found out who she was. Caitlin was able to tell Mirela in return that her own stepbrother now had no time for her, as he was away learning to be a jockey.

"Enda and Uncle Callan made him go," Caitlin had said, recounting the gist of a heated conversation which she had partly overheard through the living room door, "Uncle Callan said Eoghan had to repay Enda's debts."

"Are jockeys rich men then?" had asked Mirela, as they stood by the special stream with the drinking ponies.

"I suppose they might be," Caitlin had replied, doubtfully, trying to imagine Eoghan as a wealthy man with a big house in the town and the owner of as many horses as he could ever want to buy. Her own father had been a jockey once, she knew, and he was certainly not rich.

Niamh, when Caitlin had cautiously asked her about the girl who had said she was their cousin, was suspicious, saying she knew nothing of any cousins, and advising Caitlin to be careful. But, their father Diarmuid, when questioned by Caitlin on one of her increasingly rare visits to the Gleannglas racecourse, confirmed the information, shaking his grizzled head as if in exasperation at being reminded of his cousin, Mirela's father.

"We were brought up together near Monamor, Eirnin and I," Diarmuid had told Caitlin, "We were much of an age. But he had restless feet, to be sure. He wanted to see the world and what was in it, and not to stay here at home to become a horseman like me. I have heard nothing of him for many years. My memory tells me that married a Roma, a girl from far away that he found on his travels and so her family became his family. I cannot at all recollect her name now. Something like a flower, I believe it was."

When asked, Mirela had confirmed that her mother's name was Florica.

"Would you like to meet her?" Mirela had asked, "And Arnaldo my brother?"

Now, on the first day of the great sorrow following the burial of Tarragon and the apparently permanent departure of Eoghan from the Foley farm, Branna, herself bereft of her equine companion, picked her customary and unerring way towards Mirela, Caitlin's friend and cousin.

The four families which made up the group of travellers were making ready to depart on that bright August day, and so they took Caitlin and Branna with them. Unknown to her sister Niamh, preoccupied as she was with her concerns for Enda and for their two little children, Caitlin had been a welcome member of Mirela's family for many months now. Her early morning appearance was accepted as a normal part of the day, and soon Caitlin had melded seamlessly into their fluid existence as they moved South over the hills towards the town of Monamor.

Whilst Enda and Niamh were searching in vain in the local area for Caitlin, Caitlin herself was travelling ever further away, sitting on the back of Branna as if in a dream, alongside the coloured vans of the travellers.

They reached Monamor on the second day. A big summer festival was about to commence in the town. The weather was still warm and the streets were brightly decorated and full with sunlight. The family of which Caitlin's father had been part during his childhood lived close to the town, and it was on their smallholding that the travellers stopped and the horses were turned out to graze. Mirela's father, Eirnin, a tall grey-headed and still restless man, had kept his roots in the area, and, as Caitlin soon discovered, visited his family every year, as if for a holiday. Caitlin was introduced to them as the daughter of Diarmuid Kennelly, now living in Gleannglas, and from that moment no-one seemed to question her presence in the family group.

The Monamor festival was an entirely new experience for Caitlin. The streets of the little stone-built town were thronged with laughing and noisy people, many of whom seemed to be visitors to the area, and spoke with unfamiliar accents and even, amongst themselves, in foreign languages. Walking cautiously along the bunting-hung main street, as the crowds pushed and shouted good naturedly around them, Caitlin and Mirela watched them swarming around the numerous market stalls. The stalls sold everything from a soft brown substance, which Mirela said was called fudge, to more familiar foodstuffs such as bread, albeit moulded into complicated shapes, an astonishing range of round cheeses, and trays of extravagantly decorated cakes and pies. Other stalls sold brightly coloured jewellery, locally made clothing for both adults and children, and beautifully crafted bags and toys. Mirela seemed to know many of the stallholders, and introduced Caitlin gaily to each of them as 'my cousin Catalina'.

Caitlin had no money, but Mirela bought them both a slice of the gooey, sweet fudge, which the two girls ate from the white wrapper whilst looking in awe at a show in which smart and beautifully dressed young women walked up and down on a raised platform. Caitlin learned that the women were models and that the clothes had been designed and produced by dressmakers from places all across the South of Ireland. In the side streets, they watched jugglers and musicians, who collected money from the spectators in red and green hats at the end of their performances.

As it grew dark, the crowds migrated to the many pubs and bars, from which the sounds of singing and musical instruments could be heard. Spectacular and loud fireworks were let off in a green area at the end of the main street, the brilliant explosions illuminating the ring of craggy hills which surrounded the town. A noisy circus and funfair were encamped outside the town, and Mirela and Caitlin crept among the vans which were parked behind the exciting looking mechanical rides and shrieked with laughter at the terrified faces of the riders, all of whom seemed nevertheless to enjoy their experience. There were animals at the circus too, including beautiful white horses which cantered around a ring in the multi coloured circus tent, which Mirela said was called the Big Top, changing direction in obedience to barely perceptible instructions from their handler. Caitlin thought that she might like to be a horse trainer in a circus.

Caitlin had been in noisy and drunken crowds before at Gleannglas racecourse, but there everyone had been present with the single objective of watching or participating in the racing. The variety and colour, the noise and exuberance, of the Monamor Fair took Caitlin's breath away and filled her with excitement and optimism. The angry gash in her heart caused by absence of Tarragon and Eoghan began to hurt a little bit less.

The presence of Mirela played a significant role in Caitlin's renewed wellbeing. Caitlin's childhood had been a lonely one, brightened only by the now departed Eoghan, and she embraced the new friendship with gratitude and relief. Mirela, for her part, clearly enjoyed the experience of introducing her new cousin to the wonders of Monamor Fair and to the many people who were so well known to her family. Caitlin soon became used to being known as Catalina, the assumption of the new name being another step, as she saw it, to cutting the ties of her past. She pushed to the back of her mind any thought that her father and sister might be concerned for her welfare and perhaps even searching for her.

The Monamor Fair lasted three days, three days which passed too quickly for Caitlin. It ended with a spectacular street parade, more fireworks and the crowning of one of the beautiful young women as the August Queen, after which she was able to sit in a gilded chair on a platform in the town square. People came to pay homage to her, leaving flowers and gifts of money at the foot of the throne, gifts which later were donated to the local hospital by the August Queen herself.

On the fourth day, Caitlin's new world fell apart.

"You'll be going home to your father now," Eirnin said to her as the two girls sat on a rug by one of the travellers' vans on the family smallholding, idly watching Mirela and Luca and the other horses as they cropped the grass in the neighbouring paddock, "Tomorrow we are to be leaving for Cork. Will your father be coming to bring you home or shall you take the pony yourself?"

To Caitlin, Eirnin's mode of speech was like her father's, but with a little of the accent of his wife Florica mixed into it. As Caitlin was later to learn, Eirnin rarely spoke in his native tongue except when in Ireland, and not always even then. Florica spoke in her own language to Mirela, Eirnin and the other travellers, a sharp and gritty language which Caitlin did not understand. Mirela seemed happy to speak in either language, changing from one to another depending on to whom she was talking.

Caitlin was unable to reply for a moment.

"I have no home now," she eventually said, "I want to stay with Mirela."

Florica had come up behind Eirnin and seemed to have followed the conversation in spite of the language difference.

"You are not of an age for us to take you away from your family," Eirnin said firmly, "*Gardai* will surely come to take you home and we are not happy to attract their notice. To stay with Mirela for this holiday is enough. I will make a telephone call now to your father at the Gleannglas racecourse, or perhaps to your sister or her husband if they have a telephone in their home."

Caitlin felt the blood drain from her face and a sick feeling suffused her stomach. Mirela gripped her arm and looked silently at her father. Florica, standing behind, said something to Eirnin.

Eirnin cleared his throat, and began speaking haltingly as if unused to delivering long speeches in Caitlin's own tongue.

"If your father will give his permission, perhaps you may come with us," he said, "But you and he will need to know that we are going to Cork to board a boat that will take us to France. In France, we have work. The grape harvest is in the South. We will all work in the vineyards there. And then we travel further, to Spain, to Sevilla, which is Mirela's mother's home. We will not be near Gleannglas again for many months. It will be May when we return."

Caitlin stared with round eyes at her father's cousin, dumbfounded by this information. The idea that Mirela's family spent their time in other countries had never occurred to her. She had only a hazy idea where France and Spain were situated, and had never heard of Sevilla. She did not even understand what sort of work harvesting grapes might involve.

"I would like you to speak to my father," she stated, after a pause, "But not to my sister or to Enda. They will make me come home."

The conversation with Caitlin's father, Diarmuid, took place face to face later that day. Diarmuid drove in a truck over to Monamor, which was in reality only a short journey by road from Gleannglas, and a deal was struck. Caitlin would remain with the travellers until the following May when they returned to Cork on the ferry from Roscoff. Diarmuid, recognising that Caitlin had clearly inherited the restless gene which ran in Eirnin's blood, concluded that if she were to travel away from Gleannglas, he would rather she did so in the company of family. Notwithstanding Eirnin's unconventional lifestyle, Diarmuid trusted his itinerant cousin and knew that Caitlin would be treated as one of Eirnin's own children.

Diarmuid's only significant objection was a practical one. Caitlin had no passport. Eirnin waved this problem aside.

"We will easily see to that," he said, "I have documents that she can use. Girls of Florica's family who are married and no longer travel with us have passports they do not need. So they leave them with us. Caitlin can use one of them. The photographs are not good and the officials treat us all with contempt when we travel. None of them will notice anything."

Gripping her father's hand as he was about to leave, Caitlin kissed him on the cheek and whispered her thanks. Diarmuid was already wondering whether he had done the right thing by his younger daughter, but his mind had been made up by a genuine concern at what might become of her if he refused her the opportunity of a new life with people who at least were part of his family. It seemed to him the least of various possible evils which could befall her. Had he been a more worldly man, he would have realised that travelling on a false passport was a criminal offence, and that the loss of her own identity would put the teenage Caitlin entirely at the mercy of the traveller community, dependent on them for her return to her native land. But these possibilities did not occur to Diarmuid.

Caitlin asked only two things of her father. The first was that he should ensure that Branna was being properly looked after when she was left behind in Monamar. The second was that he should not tell Niamh and Enda where she had gone, only that she was safe with members of her father's family. She did not mention Eoghan.

"Well now, Enda has been searching for you this last week," Diarmuid told her, "But I will do as you ask."

When given this information by Diarmuid, Niamh guessed the truth, but Enda had not heard the story of the newly found cousin amongst the travellers and accepted the information with relief.

And so it was that Caitlin, for official purposes, became Catalina Lopez Garcia and remained so for three years. Leaving the coloured vans and horses with the family in Monamar, the group of travellers, or *gitanos,* as they became known on their journey, departed from Cork by ferry the following day. The destination was Roscoff in France, where they were joined by more travellers and continued their journey to the South housed in a collection of battered caravans towed by decrepit looking pickup trucks and ancient cars. The passport of Catalina Lopez Garcia did its intended work in ensuring that Caitlin remained part of the extended family company, the French customs officer scarcely glancing at it as he waved the party quickly onwards through the port barriers.

All the families in the now enlarged travelling group were related to each other in some way or another, so the presence of Catalina was accepted without comment once Eirnin had announced that she was the daughter of his cousin, and under the guardianship of his wife and himself. The disciplinary code within the group was strict, and, although some of the dark and rough young men eyed the incoming female lasciviously, they knew better than to approach her without the permission of her adoptive father and then only in the presence of his family. Although Caitlin did not know it, there quickly grew up an unspoken assumption amongst the travellers, perhaps fostered by Florica for Caitlin's protection, that cousin Catalina had been brought with them as a prospective bride for Mirela's older brother Arnaldo, and was therefore beyond the aspirations of anyone else.

The ragged band of travelling families steadily moved South, heading towards the vineyards of Bordeaux and beyond, aiming, as was their regular custom, to join the annual influx into the area of workers for the grape harvest. Investment in mechanical harvesting methods had yet to become worthwhile in an era when plentiful cheap itinerant manual labour was available and the industry depended almost entirely on the mobilisation of a temporary army of human grape pickers. Caitlin's knowledge of European geography and viniculture was non-existent, and she observed only that the weather became ever hotter and the roads dustier as their comfortless journey continued.

Caitlin soon realised that she could no longer readily understand the speech of those around her. Mirela's family now spoke exclusively in a language which Caitlin much later learned was a Romani version of Spanish, called Calo, and many of the people they met on the road and in the sweltering and insect filled vineyards, spoke French. Dozing in the heat of the battered pickup truck which was carrying them towards her new existence as a seasonal agricultural worker, Caitlin longed desperately for the company of her pony, Branna. She eventually sought refuge in her own imagination and memories, conjuring up fanciful pictures of Eoghan working at Mallows or riding in a race at Gleannglas racecourse, with her two little nieces cheering him to victory. Then she would wake with a start, the fumes of the badly maintained vehicle lodged in her nose and lungs, scratching at the insect bites on her arms and legs, and finding Mirela's head leaning on her shoulder.

Eirnin and Florica were kind to Caitlin, but they were rough people, accustomed to being outcasts within a society which despised them whilst still being willing to make use of them when it suited. In the disciplined vineyards, with their extensive terraces covering the undulating hills of South Western France, the vines themselves arranged in long rows neatly supported by wooden posts and lines of metal wire, Mirela and Arnaldo worked immediately alongside the bemused Caitlin. They showed her how to move along the line of vines in convoy with her fellow harvesters, where exactly to cut through the stems so as not to damage the grapes, how to tell which grapes might have rotted and must be discarded, and, most importantly, how to conserve her energy by developing a rhythm to her actions. Caitlin had never seen or tasted a grape before, but soon learned to tell when the fruit were ripe through the look and feel of their skin. The back breaking work, with its constant bending, stretching and lifting, together with the relentless heat, made her feel sick and dizzy, even though she drank clean water as often as possible and wore a protective hat and gloves. At those times, the other family members silently took on her work until she could join them again, and soon Caitlin was able to hold her own, and to contribute as many of the shallow boxes of picked fruit as the other girls of her age. In her exhaustion, she slept too heavily at night to dream of faraway Mallows and Gleannglas, and could not at first join in the singing and dancing which the more hardened pickers enjoyed together in the evening.

As the exhausting and sweaty days turned into weeks, the backbreaking work of the harvest at last became a thing of the past. Caitlin had by now became hardier and stronger, her skin darkened by the sun, and the insect bites and the heat worried her less. She had begun to learn the language of her new family and to become part of their life and ways. Eoghan and the Mallows horses were banished to a lost and different world.

It was raining when the scruffy convoy of vans and trucks left France and continued their southward migration into Spain. Although the power was leaving the sun, as the Northern hemisphere tilted away from its star, the rain bore little resemblance to the colder and cleaner rains now falling in Ireland. Caitlin had greeted the arrival of the rain and cooler temperatures with some relief, having thought that perhaps seasons did not exist in this harsh new world into which she had so recklessly stepped. She had, though, no reason to regret the change. Her friendship with the lively Mirela, and, increasingly, with the more withdrawn Arnaldo, whose initial reticence towards Caitlin had by now worn off, more than compensated for the discomforts of her present lifestyle. She wished only that Branna and Luca were with them. But there were no horses with the convoy of vans.

When Caitlin asked about the ponies, Mirela laughed happily and said that they were safe in Monamar, enjoying a good rest, which would suit lazy Luca very well, and that they would soon have plenty to do when the family returned there in May. But, she told Caitlin, there would be lots of horses to be seen at their destination for the winter, a city called Sevilla, a historic capital in the province of Andalucia in the far South. In Sevilla, her father expected to do business, she said, which would help them survive the winter once the money from the grape harvesting had been spent. Caitlin, who had no notion of the hardship associated with a hand to mouth existence, simply nodded, and asked no more. All her wages from the vineyard had been handed directly to Eirnin.

The Sevillan winter during which Caitlin reached her seventeenth birthday was the first of three in which she was just one unremarkable member of the indigenous *gitano* community in which her young companions Mirela and Arnaldo had been brought up. Her grasp of Calo soon became fluent and, when the disreputable convoy of vehicles eventually rolled into the *barrio* of Triana in the city of Sevilla, she looked no different than any of the other members of the extended family group. Her black hair was long and thick and her old hooped gold earrings had been replaced with larger and flashier ones. Mirela had curled her hair using scrumpled sheets of newspaper held into rolls by metal clips which dug into Caitlin's skull while she slept. She and Mirela shared a bed in the back of one of the tatty vans together with the bugs and fleas which had also made it their home.

Whilst Caitlin had been conscious that her travelling companions were separated from the rest of the society in which they moved, the four months which she had spent with them had been largely on the move, with little opportunity to mingle with the resident population in the places through which they had passed. Caitlin's temporary guardians, Eirnin and Florica, had discouraged the girls from venturing beyond the encampment of vehicles when they had stopped, and the other vineyard workers had mainly been itinerants such as themselves. It was in Sevilla that Caitlin first experienced something unpleasant and different. In an area which had been their own home for centuries, Caitlin learned that the *gitanos* were no longer welcome.

Triana, at first sight, seemed to be a lively and attractive area of the grandiose old city. Bright coloured traditional buildings housed artisans and musicians and well-stocked food markets appeared regularly in the picturesque streets. But the Sevillan authorities, mindful that the city's famous *flamenco* tradition acted as a magnet for a revived tourist trade, were keen to retain the cultural attractions of the traditional *barrio* but not the people who had originally created them. The scruffy old family *corrales* and the well-known associations with dealing in *cocaina* had made the *gitanos* disliked and feared as violent criminals, with the result that plans were being made to move the community of which Caitlin became a member out to the Southern edge of the city where the tourists could not see them.

Standing on the picturesque *Puente de Triana* with Mirela one day, Caitlin was on the receiving end of thrown stones and incomprehensible abuse shouted towards them by aggressive teenage boys, who fled when Arnaldo appeared by their side and shouted equally incomprehensible abuse back at the *payitos,* as Arnaldo called them contemptuously.

December and January in Sevilla were relatively cold months with occasional chilly showers, but to Caitlin, used to a freezing and rain drenched Irish winter, the cooling city with its fading sun felt like heaven. Best of all to Caitlin was the *corral* on the western outskirts of the town where some of the *gitanos'* ponies and donkeys were kept. Eirnin was occupied with business of his own, managed from the dilapidated Triana residence which housed the extended family of Florica, whilst Florica herself appeared immersed in local concerns. The three youngsters frequently escaped, when they were not needed at home, to the small, bare and dusty piece of land where the animals were tethered, overseen by two squat and taciturn men who seemed to take little interest in them. The equines themselves were well mannered and quiet, sometimes being used to pull loaded carts into the town, but were mostly left to their own devices as they munched on the meagre supplies of hay which were regularly thrown down for them.

Caitlin and Mirela paid the ponies and donkeys more attention than they had received in many a month, riding them around bareback in the limited space, brushing their coats and plaiting their manes and tails. The two men nominally in charge of them took little interest in the girls' activities, and seemed to spend much of their time occupied with refurbishing and painting a traditional van which Mirela said would be pulled by one of the ponies in a parade in April when a big festival would take place in the city centre.

Arnaldo did not deign to join in with the horse-related activities which kept the two girls so occupied, but would sometimes demonstrate his riding skills on one of the faster ponies which Mirela told Caitlin had once performed in a circus. Arnaldo could ride the pony at speed around the piece of open ground in front of the workshop where the silent men were working, and would slide under the animal's belly, whilst picking up items put on the ground by the applauding girls. His black curls almost brushed up the dust whilst the pounding hooves missed his head only by inches. Even the ugly artisans would stop their work to watch him, shouting *ole!* and *vamos!* as each trick became more daring. For the rest of the time Arnaldo would help with the work on the painted van, once carrying some heavy wooden boxes which were delivered to the site and stowing them carefully at the back of the warehouse under bales of hay.

If Caitlin had been wiser in the wicked ways of the world, she might have wondered what the boxes contained and questioned why they needed to be hidden. But, fortunately for her own safety, she said nothing. Instead, she asked Arnaldo if he would teach her to do daring feats on the circus pony, a request which he rather patronisingly refused, saying that such tricks were not to be attempted by girls. In the face of Caitlin's persistence, bolstered by some support from an enthusiastic Mirela, Arnaldo eventually agreed to help Caitlin learn to canter the pony around the small arena whilst she stood upright on its back. Caitlin proved a willing pupil, loving the feel of the horse's haunches moving beneath her bare feet, her now long and thickened hair streaming out behind her, her trailing skirt tucked up into a leather belt, as she adjusted her weight, and bent and straightened her knees to remain in balance. But, Arnaldo soon noticed that the two grubby workmen had stopped making their slow repairs to the decorated van and were looking at Caitlin's bare legs instead. He abruptly stopped the impromptu lesson, telling both girls it was time to return home. Caitlin had fortunately had too much fun to notice the unwanted attention she had attracted from the disreputable men.

Sevilla's *Feria de Abril* gave Caitlin her first experience of bullfighting. The weeks leading up to the *Feria* were filled by the creation of traditional costumes for both the male and female members of the family. Caitlin had little knowledge of dressmaking, but knew how to use a needle, and was soon immersed in the excitement of creating her own *traje de gitana* from an outfit given to her by Florica and in learning how to flare the skirt in the proper *flamenco* style. The family of which Caitlin had so quickly become part spent the slowly lightening evenings practising dances in readiness for the *Feria*, dances which they would later perform for onlookers at street fairs in Ireland, to which they were due to return once the *Feria* was over. The dresses and the *trajes cortos* worn by the men were valuable working garments and were carefully stored and cared for when they were not being worn.

Caitlin found that she had much to discover about the music and the dances, but she learned quickly under the tutelage of Mirela and her mother Florica. Although the guitars and violins which accompanied the dancing were usually played by the men, Caitlin asked to be allowed to try her hand at recreating the thrumming and rippling chords which the players caused to explode from the body of the instruments and to generate associated stamping and clapping from the dancers. Under Florica's supervision, a serious faced young man sat by Caitlin for some time, showing her how to run the backs of the fingers of her right hand ever more quickly over the taut strings whilst forming the distinctive chord shapes on the fret board with her left. When Caitlin's fingers became so raw and painful that she could not continue to play any longer, her youthful tutor stood and bowed formally both to her and also to Mirela, who had sat with Caitlin during the impromptu lesson, before walking away.

"Yanko is going to be my husband," Mirela whispered in Caitlin's ear, following the young man with her eyes as he rejoined the other musicians, "He will soon be one of our best *flamenco* guitarists. And then, Catalina, you can be married to Arnaldo, and we all can sing and dance together. Arnaldo is a very good dancer. He dances with our mother, as my father has never learned the *flamenco*. Our mother was once a champion. People came here to Triana especially to watch her dance. Arnaldo has inherited her talents."

Mirela's words shook Caitlin like the jolt of a cart running over a rut in the road. And, in the way of such unwelcome jolts, it rudely woke the passenger who had been slumbering on the journey - the passenger who had been carried along the road, oblivious to where the driver was heading, not seeing what was going on around her or what the other passengers were doing and saying.

But before she could ask any questions of Mirela, the guitars and violins and drum struck up again and the opportunity was lost.

Mirela was certainly right about Arnaldo's skills as a dancer, thought Caitlin, as she watched her friend's brother through newly opened eyes that evening. Watching Arnaldo dance with his mother, she studied his taut frame, his shoulders pulled back, his chest forward, arms curved behind him. The short jacket which he wore had been embroidered with gold threads by Mirela, and his black trousers clung to his buttocks and legs, emphasising the muscles which rippled visibly as he stamped and curled his way around his dance partner. Florica's dancing was breathtaking, elegant loops and curves created by her still slender arms, rattling castanets at her fingers, her black and red dress swirling around her as she spread a black fan imperiously towards Arnaldo. At the end of the dance, the watchers, whose numbers had grown during the course of the evening, and who were ranged around the walls of the dingy yard, applauded and shouted enthusiastically. Caitlin could see many of the younger women looking admiringly at Arnaldo, as he bowed to them, his black hat in his hand, and she felt confused to think that this fierce young man was to be her husband. Caitlin did not want to marry anyone.

The bullfights lasted for a whole week at the *Feria*. The street parades preceded them, such parades as Caitlin had never in her wildest dreams imagined. The painted van pulled by the pony into Triana from the family's dusty yard was almost hidden from sight amongst the myriad numbers of smart carriages which entered the city and drove around in the area reserved for the *Feria* itself. The beautiful working costumes which had been so carefully sewn by Mirela's family were all but invisible amongst the similar traditional costumes worn by nearly everyone in the packed and thronging crowds, many of them much grander and lavishly decorated, and generously adorned with shawls, fans and jewellery. The ladies in the elegant carriages drawn by plumed and shining horses looked to Caitlin like princesses. When she mentioned her thoughts to Mirela, Mirela agreed seriously that they probably were princesses, or at least grand members of the nobility.

The bullfights took place in the extravagantly coloured and ornate *Plaça de Toros*. Although the days when Florica's family had included famous *picadores* and *matadores* had long gone, some of her relatives were still employed in supporting roles at the bull ring, mostly caring for the horses ridden by the *picadores,* whose job it was to prepare the way for the *matador* to take on the fighting bull in the ring. Obtaining seats at the bullfights was almost impossible, but Florica's connections secured her family members access to some of the cheaper seats, located in the full sun. Now that it was April, the sun was high and hot once again and a cloudless sky glared blue and unforgiving overhead. Mirela and Caitlin, chaperoned as usual by Arnaldo, were crammed into their narrow space amongst the sweating crowds, their hair tied back under wide brimmed hats, their warm faces hardly cooled by their flapping fans.

Caitlin had been intrigued by the concept of someone fighting a bull. In rural Ireland, bulls were farm creatures, usually oversized and grumpy, kept under control by a metal ring put through the nose, and always best avoided, except by the cows, when put out in the fields. Any competitive activity which took place involving them would be at the agricultural shows where the farmers vied to demonstrate the excellence of their bull's conformation and pedigree, and the quality of the calves it had sired. Caitlin had not imagined that these large and generally dull animals could be kept for fighting either amongst themselves or with a man.

The prestige of the bullfights at the *Feria* in Sevilla was such that famous *matadores* were attracted to face the bulls there. Mirela and Arnaldo knew the names of all the most admired fighters, who at that time had the status which would later come to be associated with international footballers and rock stars. Caitlin was delighted to discover that these men were dressed in the same *trajes cortos* as Arnaldo was wearing, but even more extravagant and garishly coloured. The huge area with its grand coloured stonework and a curving line of decorative arches, which shaded the rich people in the expensive seats, towered over the participants in the stylised fights which took place on the sand of the arena. Caitlin loved the horses with their bright decorated costumes, designed to protect their bellies from the sharp horns of the bull. The goring and twisting horns, said Arnaldo, could split a horse open and kill it, a not infrequent occurrence before horse protection had been made compulsory at bullfights.

The view from the cheap seats was not good enough for Caitlin to see the details of the first of the six fights that day. Taller people sitting in front of her obscured her view, and the figures involved in the gripping tableaux were far away. But even she could see the style and art involved in the performance of each *matador*. The goaded bull, sharp spears piercing its bloodied neck, pushed in by assistant fighters who Arnaldo said were called *banderillos*, was a fierce black creature, completely unlike the bulls of the Irish countryside. It charged angrily at the small costumed figure of the lead *torero*, the *matador*, who elegantly stepped and twisted away from its flashing horns, flourishing a red lined black cape. Each time it seemed as if the bull would catch the daring man and hurl him into the air, but somehow this did not happen, and eventually the bull tired and was defeated. Caitlin did not enjoy seeing the bull die, but the elaborate ritual of the fight was an intoxicating spectacle, as the crowds screamed and cheered and groaned around her, calling out in the language which she could now understand.

The fighting movements of the adored *matador*, who was now standing and bowing to receive the adulation of the ecstatic spectators, were just like those of Arnaldo's dance, she thought.

"Arnaldo," Caitlin called out over the shrieking hubbub of the people around them, "Would you like to be a *matador*?"

Caitlin could not hear Arnaldo's reply, but his brown eyes looked directly into hers and a grin spread across his handsome, sweat streaked face as he nodded vigorously.

Perhaps it would not be so bad to be married to Arnaldo after all, thought Caitlin.

22

The sunny August Friday marked Caitlin's fourth visit to Monamor fair. She had already decided that it would also be her last visit. Almost exactly three years ago, she had left her home at nearby Gleannglas and embarked on an adventurous journey which she had not planned. During that time, her friend Mirela had been travelling with her and the two girls had enjoyed almost three years of companionship. But at the end of the third winter in Sevilla, Mirela had been married, amid rapturous family celebrations, to talented *flamenco* guitarist Yanko, and so this year Mirela had not returned with the travellers to Ireland. Caitlin missed her desperately.

At the end of her first Winter and Spring in Sevilla, Caitlin had made the return journey to Ireland in Mirela's lively company. The dilapidated procession of vans and trucks had departed the city early one promising May morning when the wearisome heat had been already trying to penetrate the stout defences of the streets and buildings. The only change to the group which arrived the previous Autumn had been that the painted van which had participated in the *Feria* parade had been brought along with them, strapped onto a trailer pulled by one of the rusty pickup trucks. The lavish costumes which the girls had worn at the April event had also been taken, carefully packed into large trunks and stored in one of the trucks. Caitlin had been excited to learn that she and Mirela would be dancing at country fairs in Ireland and England over the summer, performing alongside the famous Florica and her son Arnaldo.

With no harvest to interrupt their return, that first journey to Roscoff from Sevilla had been accomplished over a few sweaty and uncomfortable days. Caitlin had grown used to the heat and had been surprised to find herself shivering as they had boarded the ferry which would take them to Cork. After that, they would travel on to Monamor, and there at last she would see Branna again.

Soft rain had started to fall from a blank grey sky as the ferry had docked in Cork. The girls had disembarked on foot, pulling their padded jackets around them, new garments which had been unexpectedly given to them by Florica 'to keep them warm' when they had boarded the ferry. The passport of Catalina Lopez Garcia had once again worked its deception on the immigration officials and the two girls had waited on the quayside for the rest of their party. Once the convoy of tatty vehicles had been driven out from the belly of the ship, the pair had climbed into their place in the back of one of the vans, still talking excitedly about what they would do when they were able to ride out on Branna and Luca once again.

"Will they remember us?" had laughed Caitlin, although she had been privately sure that the sturdy ponies had excellent memories and would recognise them immediately.

"You must remember to speak to them in your own language," Mirela had replied, "Not the language of Triana any more. Luca and Branna will not understand you and will think you are a stranger."

So engrossed had been the girls in their plans that they had not noticed that after a short time the convoy of vehicles had come to a halt, and hushed male voices had been speaking roughly outside. They had been able to hear Eirnin's voice amongst them, apparently giving instructions, instructions which seemed to relate to the decorated van perched on the back of the trailer. Replies had come from a number of other voices, all speaking in the local language.

Caitlin had wanted to peer out from their position in the truck to see what was going on, but Mirela had pulled her back.

"Do not let them see you," she had instructed, firmly, "You know that we are not allowed to watch the men's business."

Caitlin had been about to shrug off her friend's sudden grasp when something unexpected had stopped her. She had not been sure, but one of the voices had sounded familiar. It had sounded like Enda Foley's voice. Caitlin had certainly not wanted anyone at the

Foley farm to know that she was with the travellers' convoy. She had feared that she might be forced to return home and to resume her former restricted existence, not to mention being called on to explain where she had been for the last nine months. So, she had obeyed Mirela's urgent direction and had instead strained her ears to listen to what was going on outside.

Although Caitlin had become unused to listening to her own language, she had soon been able to make out most of what the men were saying. They had appeared to be moving something heavy from the painted van on the trailer. There had been instructions by one of the gruffer voices to make haste, whilst another, younger, voice had confirmed that a tractor was coming up alongside. Thuds and scraping sounds had followed this comment, until someone had eventually said that everything was in place. Then Caitlin had heard Eirnin's voice once again as he had seemed to be walking alongside the vehicle in which she and Mirela had been sitting. Eirnin had been in conversation with another man whose voice Caitlin had also recognised. It had not been Enda this time. It had taken Caitlin only a few seconds to realise that the new voice had belonged to Uncle Callan.

Caitlin's hand had flown to her mouth and she had had to stop herself from screaming. No sooner had she returned to the shores of Ireland and already Uncle Callan had been back in her life, and not for any pleasant reason, she had been sure. Caitlin had seen Mirela looking at her sharply, wondering what had caused the colour to drain so suddenly from the face of her friend.

"Is Callan Sullivan a friend of your father?" Caitlin had asked, under her breath. But Mirela had shaken her head in confusion. She had never heard of Callan Sullivan.

The half heard voices of Enda and Uncle Callan had catapulted Caitlin back into the real world that Summer, and had made her begin to realise that the travellers convoy of which she was part was not the innocent band of itinerant workers which it had seemed. Her emerging suspicions had intensified when Florica had silently taken back the quilted jackets which she and Mirela had worn on the ferry from Roscoff. Caitlin had never seen the

215

garments again until the following May, when they had again been given to the girls to wear for the sea voyage. On neither occasion had Florica been genuinely concerned about their warmth. It was clear that they had become smugglers of whatever was stitched into the jackets. They were unwitting and unwilling smugglers, but smugglers nonetheless, and would be charged as criminals if they were caught.

Mirela's urgent injunction not to ask about the men's business had been borne of experience, Caitlin had eventually grasped. Wanting more time to work out what was happening and so to understand it better, she had resolved to keep her emerging worries to herself and to try to enjoy that first Summer travelling around Ireland in the renewed company of her beloved Branna.

Branna had indeed not forgotten her, and Caitlin had tried hard to focus her love and attention of the bay Connemara pony and to blank out the spectre of Uncle Callan. But the thoughts which had been awakened in her clever mind would not be banished. The hidden boxes in the ramshackle stable in Sevilla had been in the decorated van, she was sure. Uncle Callan and other men had come to take them away using a tractor. Was it Enda's tractor? Did her sister know? What did the boxes contain? What was in the padded lining of the warm jackets which Florica had made them wear? Was it the *cocaina* about which the *payitos* had taunted them on the bridge in Triana? Or something else? And was Arnaldo, the young man she was supposed to marry, part of the 'men's business' to which Mirela had referred?

In the two years which had followed, Caitlin had, through these questions and the observations which had led her to ask them, slowly come to understand the nature of the activities in which she was playing a part. The questions had formed and crystallised over many months, as more and more of the life of her new family had been revealed to her. Caitlin had also learned that her compliance with what was happening was taken for granted, not least because she was travelling on a false passport held by Eirnin, a criminal act in itself, and that any money she earned was always taken by him too. Worse still, as Eirnin was apparently engaged in business involving Enda and Uncle Callan, there was no one she could tell

216

about what she had learned and nowhere for her to go if she was minded to leave. Caitlin could not be sure that her own father was not also involved in the 'men's business'. If he were involved, then he could not help her either. Even if he were not involved, she might be endangering him by telling him what she now knew.

In this way, Caitlin had gradually concluded that she had no choice but to make the best of her present situation, which was in truth very far from being unbearable, and to look for her chance to break away. The August morning at Monamor Fair could be about to provide her with that opportunity. The tarot card reader had told her about the Wheel of Fortune and she had been looking for it everywhere ever since.

Mirela's marriage to the musician Yanko in Triana had brought about significant change to Caitlin's situation. At the age of nineteen and no longer able to travel as a sister to Mirela, it had quickly become evident to Caitlin that her future life with the traveller family depended on her marriage to Arnaldo. Her choice was stark. Either she married Arnaldo, or she returned to the Foley farm. As Arnaldo's wife, she would remain at the behest of the traveller group and continue to be involved in what she now knew were criminal activities. If she returned to her former home, Uncle Callan and Enda, who seemed to be involved in some of the same activities for reasons which Caitlin could not guess, would once again be in charge of her life. Her only other option was to go to live with her father at the racecourse, but not knowing whether he too was under Callan Sullivan's malign influence.

Caitlin would have liked to talk to Arnaldo about his family's expectations of him. Loyalty and discipline amongst the community was absolute and she knew that Arnaldo would not have even dreamed of doing anything which went against his parents' wishes. If Eirnin and Florica had decided that Arnaldo should marry cousin Catalina, then Arnaldo would do so, notwithstanding the fact that there were other young women amongst the Triana families who would have been glad to be selected to be Arnaldo's wife.

217

There were, however, two practical obstacles to the marriage between Arnaldo and Caitlin. These had been set out in some detail by Florica during a discussion to which she had summoned Caitlin following Mirela's wedding. The first was that, as Caitlin was travelling on a false passport, using that false identity in a marriage ceremony would make the union invalid. Steeped in Catholic tradition, Eirnin and Florica could not contemplate their son being effectively living with a woman to whom he was not married and their grandchildren rendered bastards as a result. This first problem, though, could relatively easily be resolved by solemnising the marriage in Ireland, where Caitlin could use her own identity.

The version of the marriage plan created a second obstacle, which was that Caitlin was under the age of twenty one, and the requirements of Irish law at that time were that she would need her father's permission to marry. It appeared that the marriage would not necessarily be made invalid merely because the required consent was not given, but Florica had no doubt that the priest would ask why the father was not present at the wedding to give his permission, particularly where a traveller family was involved. So, it was agreed that Diarmuid's permission would be sought by Eirnin during that summer in Ireland and that the wedding of Arnaldo and Caitlin would take place at Eirnin's family home in Monamor at the time of the August Fair.

Without Mirela, Caitlin's third summer travelling in Ireland had been a lonely experience, but it had given her an opportunity to make her own plan. Her only confidante had been Branna, who Caitlin rode along the Irish roads and lanes in the wake of the travellers' vans, which still included the painted van which had originally come from Sevilla that first Spring.

Arnaldo had sometimes come to ride beside Caitlin. The engaged couple had not been allowed to be alone together, but, as they had been riding in full view of the rest of the travelling party, no chaperone had been needed and they had had a rare opportunity to talk without being overheard. Arnaldo had been still expected to spend his time with the men when they were encamped or performing at the fairs, but on the road rules of etiquette had been less rigid.

Since their engagement, Arnaldo had become more reticent with Caitlin than when she had been treated as his sister. Caitlin had known better than to speak on anything other than neutral subjects, but she had been curious to know whether Arnaldo was marrying her only from a sense of duty to his parents, when he could have had his pick of any of the girls in Triana.

"I asked for a tarot card reading when we were at the fair in Ennisgarriff," Caitlin had ventured, as their ponies had nodded their way along a deserted road beneath a summer sky fluffed with white clouds.

"And what did you learn?" had asked Arnaldo, slightly contemptuously, "Such things are for gullible women and children."

"Your mother believes in the cards," Caitlin had replied, hotly, "She says that they can open your mind to things which are hidden from others."

"What things are hidden from your mind, then, Catalina?" had asked Arnaldo, "You very well know you will have a handsome husband and soon there will also be handsome sons and beautiful daughters."

Caitlin had laughed, saying, "You are very vain, Arnaldo" and Arnaldo had cantered away, waving his grubby, brimmed hat and laughing in response.

But the memory of the tarot reading had unsettled Caitlin and it was that feeling of unease which had prompted her to mention it to Arnaldo. She had entered the stuffy little booth on the village green where the Ennisgarriff Summer Fair had been in progress, thinking only to pass the time, and to amuse herself with something which would help her to forget the absence of Mirela's company. The middle aged woman who had sat in the tent, swathed in a black and red shawl decorated with gold tassels provided the sort of tawdry fairground attraction at which she and Mirela would have scoffed at one time. But Caitlin had been struggling to understand and make a plan for her uncertain future, and, remembering Florica's words, had wondered suddenly if this person could reveal things to her. Caitlin had felt as if her own wishes and intentions remained hidden even from herself.

The tarot reader had sat in a darkened tent, which was lit, in spite of an intermittent sun pushing bravely between the passing showers outside, by two guttering tin oil lamps reminiscent of some of the Moorish artefacts which Caitlin had seen in Sevilla. Caitlin had watched tarot readers before and had admired the precision with which they had laid down and then interpreted the cards. To Caitlin there had seemed to be something almost scientific about it, although she had been told that the specific interpretation was dependent on the reader's intuition and feelings, and that different readers would set the cards out differently.

"You are one of Florica's dancers," the woman in the tent had stated, as Caitlin had sat down, offering a coin which had been given to her by a member of the public who had been watching their show, and which she had managed to conceal from Florica's sharp gaze, "She intends you for her handsome son."

Caitlin had already begun to regret her decision to request the reading, and had started to get up from the hard chair on which she had been seated. The woman had waved her back into her place.

"Do not go, my dear," she had said, firmly, "I will give you a fair reading, not one which is for the *payos*, who only want to hear of good fortune and weddings. You seem to me to be a young woman with an interest in learning."

As Caitlin had sat down again, the strange woman had taken her hand and had closed her eyes for a few seconds. The reader's hand on hers had felt cool and smooth, and had been adorned by golden painted fingernails and henna tattoos, making Caitlin's own small hand feel rough and work hardened in comparison.

"You are very young," had said the woman, opening her eyes again and looking Caitlin full in the face.

The tarot reader had had before her two packs of rectangular cards, each tied with a black ribbon. Taking the slimmer of the two packs, she had undone the ribbon and had shuffled the cards slowly. Gathering them back together neatly in her patterned hand, she had taken the top card, and laid it face down on the worn brown cloth spread over the circular table. The back of the card had been purple with a pattern of small gold stars arranged in a regular design.

"I have chosen this card for you, my dear," the woman had told Caitlin, "Turn it over."

Caitlin had done as she was instructed. The card had shown an enthroned female figure, her robes adorned with a white cross and a yellow crescent moon at her feet.

"The High Priestess," had said the reader, " She represents secrets and a future as yet impenetrable. Silence, wisdom, patience – these are qualities you possess and which you will surely need as you seek that future."

The woman had placed three more cards from the same pack just above the High Priestess, arranged in a line along the table, their faces hidden from view.

"We begin from the past which has brought you here and the future to which you are preparing to go," the reader had stated, turning over the first card and placing it face up. It had shown a stylised picture of a buttery moon in a pale sky with two dogs beneath it. Then the next two cards had been turned, and had shown a white robed angel pouring liquid into a goblet and an orange wheel adorned with strange symbols and surrounded by winged animals.

"The Moon here symbolises your past," the woman had begun, after looking at the three cards for a while, "The Moon hides enemies and is full of danger and deception. The card of

221

Temperance shows that you have endured your situation in life with patience and fortitude but have little to show for your efforts. You are searching for a way forward but you have not yet found it. This depends on the Wheel of Fortune, the third card, which shows that chance will play a part in your future."

Caitlin had held her breath as three more cards had been placed on the table, forming a second line below the first. Turning the three fresh cards over, the woman had revealed the pictures, saying,

"This will help us to see more. They show the chief of the influences which will shape your life."

Caitlin had looked at the pictures. They had consisted of two naked people, a male and a female, with an angel hovering above them; an angel blowing a trumpet above more naked figures arising from coffins; and, upside down, a jauntily dressed young man sauntering along in the sun.

"These are the Lovers," the reader had observed, slowly, "So you will experience love. The Lovers are beneath The Moon, so your love will reach into the past and will be affected by its dangers and deceptions. But here is Judgement. There will be a change and a new outcome and it will arise from your fortitude, but you will have to remain patient. The Fool here is reversed and tells of youth, folly and ignorance, perhaps on the part of a future lover, or perhaps on your part too. In any event, love will come to you through Fortune, as you can see from the cards."

"I am engaged to marry Florica's son Arnaldo," had said Caitlin quickly, "Are the pictures about him?"

"These cards cannot tell us that," the woman had responded, speaking rather hesitantly, "But let us see if we can discover any more. The Wheel of Fortune rules your future but the minor cards may give us some guidance. Or they may tell us only the same things again."

So saying, she had taken the second, larger, pack of cards and had removed the ribbon. Eight cards had then been laid out in two rows of four. Caitlin had looked in puzzlement at the array of designs and figures on the new cards as they had been turned over. The woman had muttered and fussed over them for some time, saying eventually, and with more authority,

"The King of Swords is the first card and is reversed here. This is an evil and powerful man and the Judgement will come upon him. Those bringing forth the Judgement will include the Knight of Wands whose card lies alongside him here. This card too is reversed, so there will be discord, perhaps a marriage which will be frustrated. Beneath these two appears the Eight of Swords, reversed again, and the Page of Cups. The Page is a young man who will render service, unforeseen and unexpected service, to the woman whose situation is signified by the Eight of Swords, here, who is unquiet and in difficulty. These four cards are the influences of the present which will reach into the future."

Moving her attention to the four cards to the right of the group, the woman had continued, her voice sounded increasingly confident,

"These cards may be telling us something of what the Wheel of Fortune could bring. The Three of Swords represents delay and the Two of Cups beneath speaks of love, passion and friendship. Alongside the Three of Swords is the Six of Cups. Although telling of your future, this is a card of the past, of memories and childhood. Its appearance here above the final card, the Ace of Pentacles, a most favourable card, says that this card of the past will be the source of your future happiness and contentment. There is much waiting and endurance shown in your future, my dear, although you will have help to overcome it and so you will find in the end what you are seeking."

As Caitlin walked down the sunny Monamor street, wearing one of Mirela's old red dresses, her dark hair loosely tied back with a green scarf, she thought of the tarot reading from earlier that Summer and wished fervently that the Wheel of Fortune would now start to revolve in her direction.

From behind, an arm went gently and proprietorially around her slim waist.

Caitlin turned with a start and found herself looking up into the smiling face of a young man. Standing several inches taller than Caitlin, his fair hair reflected the light of the sky, and laughter creased the edges of his bright blue eyes. The August sun had caught his pale skin and Caitlin could see the beginnings of sunburn on his cheeks and forehead. He had a wide mouth, with white, even teeth showing in a bright grin which was directed towards the confused Caitlin.

"You looked nice," the young man said, simply, his arm still around her waist, "Shall I walk with you?"

"The Page of Cups," thought Caitlin, and, to her great surprise, fell instantly in love with him.

A mere two weeks later, Caitlin was sharing a cramped room in a County Meath racing yard with two other stable lasses and had been accepted as young Niall Carter's established girlfriend.

Escaping the clutches of Eirnin's family had been less difficult that Caitlin had anticipated. When appealed to by Caitlin for his help on that Fortune blessed day, Diarmuid had proved surprisingly firm in refusing to give his consent to her marriage to Arnaldo. Diarmuid had simply told his cousin that he missed his younger daughter and needed her and the pony Branna back at home with him at Gleannglas racecourse. Eirnin, although frustrated, was not willing to dispute the authority of Caitlin's father in such an important matter and so Caitlin and the pony had returned home with Diarmuid.

Caitlin had not seen Arnaldo following the meeting between their respective fathers but she had felt sure that he would not regret the loss of his prospective wife and that a girl brought up in the travelling community would suit him better as a wife. She had tried to banish any thought that Arnaldo might have felt humiliated by her father's outright refusal to countenance the marriage between the two of them. And now her overwhelming fascination with Niall Carter occupied Caitlin's every waking thought.

The relationship between Caitlin and Niall had progressed like an unstoppable fire in a tinder-dry forest. In those first moments after they had met, Caitlin had spoken only to ask her Page of Cups his name. The tarot reader might, if she had been there, have reminded Caitlin of the other young man shown in the cards of her reading, the one sauntering in the sun, the card upside down, the image that the reader had called The Fool reversed.

"I'm Niall," the young man had told her, the cheeky smile still crinkling his face, "And who are you, beautiful little lady?"

"I'm Cat... uh, Katy," Caitlin had stammered. She had been about to give her now accustomed name of Catalina, but had quickly decided against it.

"Catakaty?" had asked Niall, laughing, "What sort of a name is that?"

"You can call me Kat," Caitlin had told him, quickly deciding that if she were to shake off the shackles of her past, it would be an appropriate time to give herself a new identity.

"Pleased to meet you, Lady Kat," Niall had said, with a mock bow, and Caitlin was so overcome that she could hardly breathe. No-one had ever treated her like that before, even in fun. She had never been the centre of anyone's admiring attention.

Niall Carter was the eldest son of Fergal Carter, a racehorse trainer with a relatively successful yard located near Navan racecourse. Niall had been in Monamor that day by chance, having been sent to collect a horse which his father had bought on an earlier visit, but for which at the time there had been no available transport. The purchased horse had not yet arrived for the agreed pick up, so Niall had been kicking his restless heels at the Monamar Fair, that is, until he had spotted the attractive Caitlin.

In the few hours which Caitlin and Niall had spent together walking in the streets and surrounding countryside of Monamor, the new horse all but forgotten, they had created a breathlessly conceived and, to them, eminently feasible plan. This had required Fergal Carter to employ Caitlin as a stable lass and bring her to her live in with the other staff at the yard in County Meath. Even Branna was invited to join the party, as a new and reliable pony would definitely be needed for Niall's two little sisters to ride.

The Wheel of Fortune seemed to have turned at last in Caitlin's direction, because it appeared that Fergal Carter was known to her father from their days together as jockeys. Following a rather more measured intervention by Niall's mother Bryany, a formal offer of employment as a stable hand, with associated accommodation at the Carter training establishment, was issued to Caitlin in her real name. Diarmuid had signed the papers as soon as they had arrived. By mutual agreement, neither he nor Caitlin had mentioned to the Carters Caitlin's recent existence as a traveller, merely saying that she had been staying abroad with relatives and now needed to find a job at home in Ireland.

At Caitlin's request, Diarmuid had also agreed to say nothing to Niamh and Enda of the new direction in Caitlin's already complicated life. Having belatedly realised the dangers of his earlier plans for Caitlin with Eirnin's family, Diarmuid had been glad to have the opportunity to set matters right, as he was sure he was now doing. Having Niamh or Enda interfere with his latest decision was not desirable, although in truth, Niamh, had she known, would have welcomed Caitlin's return to live and work in a familiar and well regulated environment.

Caitlin, or Kat, as she had now become, took to life in the Carter racing yard as a duck to water. She had no fear of the powerful and beautiful racehorses, having been brought up amongst them during her childhood, and was quick to learn the yard's own methods of handling and caring for them. Her rough and ready equestrian skills were soon honed by her regular work riding the racehorses through the soft morning light of County Meath. She was quick to recognise that the other stable girls were envious of her relationship with Niall, whose good looks and sunny disposition, not to mention his natural talent as a jockey, had previously made his company much sought after by the more youthful female staff.

Fergal and Bryany had initially been dubious about the sudden employment of Kat, but her calming influence over their previously rather irrepressible son soon caused them to warm to her. Rather than providing a distraction from his work as an apprentice jockey, Kat had seemed to give him a new stability, listening to his comments about the horses and giving him her carefully considered opinions about his riding skills in return.

"Diarmuid Kennelly's daughter is a small gem," Fergal commented wryly to his wife, as he saw the two young people laughing together one morning in the dull warmth of the cobbled stable yard whilst Caitlin plaited the black tail of one of their runners that day.

"A shame the same could not be said about Diarmuid himself," Fergal's wife observed pointedly in response, "But it is far in the past now and his poor wife herself a long time dead. If we can help her child, then that is some benefit at least."

Caitlin's career at the Carter yard lasted for six years, during which Niall rode out his claim and became a successful professional jockey whilst Caitlin herself became the Carters' head lass. The pressure on the two of them to marry, so that they could eventually take over the running of the Carter yard, was intense. Niall would have married Caitlin without a second thought, but it was Niall's blithe approach to such a serious, and, at the time, irrevocable step in his life which made Caitlin cautious. Much as she loved her Page of Cups, she strongly suspected that marriage would not prevent Niall from putting his arm around another girl one sunny August day. Indeed, she was to see him do just that on numerous occasions during the years which she worked at the Carter yard.

Caitlin quickly perceived that she had a choice between marrying a young man whom she loved, but suspected was likely to be unfaithful to her in the future, or remaining his partner on an informal basis, notwithstanding the whispering and scandal which she knew would be attached to the latter arrangement. Niall himself cruised onward through his life and advancing career with a cheerfully dismissive attitude to the dilemma, telling his concerned mother that any decision to marry would be made by Kat. So Caitlin made her own choice and decided to enjoy her happy situation whilst it lasted. Apart from anything else, she was becoming a highly experienced horsewoman and knew that she could take her skills elsewhere when the time came.

In Caitlin's fifth year at the Carter establishment, she almost came face to face with Eoghan.

The weather at Fairyhouse racecourse that day was unremittingly cold and wet. Heavy dark clouds pressed threateningly on the flat countryside, the distant hills made invisible by the lowering murk. The horses walking round the parade ring in the early December gloom were unbothered by the conditions, but the stable staff leading them up felt differently. They were well wrapped up in thick jackets, gloves and hats, some even with scarves covering the lower halves of their faces.

Caitlin was walking with a statuesque bay chaser called AC DC, a horse which was likely to revel in the heavy conditions out on the course. Niall was away for the weekend in England, riding another Carter trained horse in the Hennessy Cognac Gold Cup Chase at Newbury racecourse, and another jockey had been booked for AC DC that day at Fairyhouse. As Caitlin moved briskly around the parade ring, trying to ignore the rain falling onto the knitted hat into which her dark hair had been carefully wound up, she watched the jockeys come out into the parade ring to join their connections.

Caitlin had seen the race information. She knew that Eoghan would be amongst the jockeys riding in that race. She had been well aware of his successful career with the Meaghan yard, and, more recently, as an independent jockey, as Niall had frequently mentioned the prolific Genie Foley as one of his chief rivals.

"You or your father might know him, Kat," Niall had said to her, "I believe he comes from Gleannglas, or somewhere near there."

"Indeed I do know him," Caitlin had replied, carefully, "We were children there together. I remember him learning to ride. He went as an apprentice to Mallows and did not return to Gleannglas. I have not seen him for many years now."

Caitlin had no trouble recognising Eoghan that day if for no other reason than by the racing colours which he was wearing as he strode out to join the owner and trainer of the horse he was to ride. She stole a glance at him, as AC DC jigged along impatiently along behind her, rattling at his bit, eager to get on with the business of running.

Eoghan was no longer the pale and skinny teenage boy she remembered from the Foley farm. He had grown taller and his physical frame, like Niall's, had become strong and athletic. He walked with determination, his shoulders square, chatting to one of the other jockeys before they separated to join their respective groups of connections.

Caitlin caught a few of the words Eoghan exchanged with the owner, a heavily built man wearing a light brown raincoat and holding an umbrella.

"Pleased to see you again, Mr McShane," Eoghan said, "I hope Mrs McShane is well. And your daughter too."

Eoghan sounded confident and assured, thought Caitlin. She could not believe that it was she who had first taught him to ride. He did not once look in her direction. But then, he did not know she was there, Caitlin told herself, quickly suppressing a small stab of betrayal. Soon the jockeys mounted their rides and Eoghan was gone from her sight.

Without really intending to do it, Caitlin started to look out from that day for Eoghan's name in the racecards at the courses where the Carter yard had runners. Seeing Eoghan at Fairyhouse had awakened a rush of half forgotten memories in Caitlin's tightly guarded heart and her early years at Gleannglas racecourse and the Foley farm reappeared in the front of her mind in clear detail. She could not easily forget Eoghan's final departure eight years ago following the death of Tarragon and the raw emotion of that moment, carefully suppressed over the years, suddenly sprang up anew and caught at her throat. Did Eoghan even know that she had left the Foley farm at all? Did he care?

Both Niall Carter and Genie Foley had rides at the famous Cheltenham Festival the following March, although neither had the honour of winning the much coveted Gold Cup on the final day. Caitlin's relationship with Niall was by that time gradually slipping away, and she was sure that at least one of the two girls who accompanied the Carter horses to the English event was sharing Niall's bed whilst he was staying in the Regency town. Niall himself on his return was as sunny and attentive as ever towards her, telling her in detail about his rides and the people he had met, reminding her pointedly that it had been her decision not to accompany him there.

"You need to get yourself a passport, Kat," he told her, "And then you can come next time."

"I'll be at the Punchestown Festival with you," Caitlin replied, evading the question. There was nothing to stop her obtaining a legitimate passport in her real name, but the memory of Catalina Lopez Garcia, the unfriendly immigration officials, and the mysterious quilted jackets had given her an enduring aversion to travelling through seaports.

On a late winter Sunday during the following racing season, the morning sun was already shining brightly through the bedroom window of the small cottage which she shared with Niall. Niall himself was sleeping peacefully beside her, his smooth face a picture of childlike innocence, his lithe body spread-eagled across the bed, spiky fair hair pushed back from his forehead by the feather pillow. There was no racing that day, so, apart from the usual morning work riding, no horses needed to be made ready for travel or competition. There was only a meeting at Leopardstown racecourse later in the week, at which Niall was due to ride.

Caitlin heard the telephone shrill in the downstairs room of the stone built cottage. It was the extension line from the main house. Springing down the wooden staircase, she lifted the receiver.

"Morning, Kat," said the cheerful voice of one of Niall's younger brothers, "There is a lady on the line for you. She says she is your sister. She called you Caitlin, but it was definitely you she wanted."

Caitlin stood in silence as the call was transferred to the cottage telephone. Niamh had never telephoned her before. She had not been aware that Niamh knew where she was. Their father must have told her, she thought. Had something happened to one of the children, she wondered, or was their father himself ill?

But it was none of those things. After a perfunctory greeting, Niamh came straight to the point.

"Enda has asked Eoghan to stop a horse," she stated, starkly, "It is the time for Enda's debt to be repaid by Eoghan."

Trying to remain calm, Caitlin quickly asked,

"And what shall I do about it, Niamh? I suppose our father told you where I am. But Eoghan does not know I am here and working with the racehorses. I have never even spoken with him at any of the races."

"You need to warn him, Caitlin," Niamh told her, her voice low and urgent, "Or I believe Uncle Callan may try to harm him, and Enda too."

"What is the name of the horse?" asked Caitlin, not knowing what else to say.

"Singing Bamboo," Niamh replied, promptly, "He is running at Leopardstown races later this week."

"What's happening, Kat?" called Niall's voice from upstairs, "Come back to bed and tell whoever it is to go away."

In the event, Singing Bamboo did not win his race, having been brought down at the last by a loose horse which ran across the field and cannoned into him. His jockey Genie Foley was left sprawled on the ground as the remainder of the field, including Niall Carter's horse, thundered past. Even Singing Bamboo scrambled quickly to his feet and ran after them.

"Do you think Eoghan Foley fell deliberately?" Caitlin ventured to ask Niall, as she led his sweating horse back towards the parade ring and their first place spot.

Niall looked at Caitlin as if she were mad.

"Genie Foley?" he scoffed, "I doubt even he could have set that one up. But there's no way he would lose a race. Not for any money. I sometimes wish he would."

Caitlin heard no more from Niamh in the weeks which followed and began to wonder if Niamh had exaggerated the threat to Eoghan. She carefully followed Eoghan's rides, including those at the Cheltenham Festival, having decided that the danger in which Eoghan appeared to have been placed now warranted her presence. Somewhat to Niall's surprise, she had insisted on accompanying the Carters' horses this year on their journey via the ferry to Fishguard, having at last obtained a legitimate passport for herself. The stable girl who would have normally accompanied the Carter horses to Cheltenham stayed at home, even though Niall put up a spirited case to justify her presence. Caitlin judged that she already had enough concerns to occupy her without being distracted by philandering on Niall's part.

Nothing out of the ordinary had occurred with any of Eoghan Foley's rides, including the three at the Cheltenham Festival. Granted he had not won all the races in which he had competed, but there was no doubt that all his horses had been ridden to the best of their ability and someone would have had to be unusually suspicious to think otherwise. His latest ride in Ireland, a chaser called Lee Ho, had run to a convincing victory.

Following the Carter team's return from the Cheltenham Festival, Caitlin, coming in to the cottage unexpectedly early after settling the travelling horses back into their stalls and leaving other staff to do the rest of the work, found Niall lying in their bed with two naked stable girls draped over him. Two pairs of horrified female eyes stared at Caitlin as she stood motionless in the doorway of the bedroom, whilst the third pair, the bright blue eyes belonging to her Page of Cups, creased up in an only half guilty grin.

"Come and join in, Kat", was all he said, laughing out loud as his female companions rushed to gather up their underwear and then had to wait until Caitlin stood aside to let them out of the bedroom doorway, "This is like O'Reilly's Circus. And a great performance it is, too."

Niall's laughter and mock serious pleas for her to return followed Caitlin down the stairs, as she marched out of the cottage and through the stable yard entrance into the lane outside. A cold darkness was gathering, but Caitlin had ridden the horses many times along the familiar lane and now made her way forward on foot without hesitation. Behind her, she could hear angry shouts and loud shrieks from the yard, as lights were turned on and the faintly heard voice of Fergal Carter was calling out to ask what in God's name was going on.

Caitlin soon found herself on a small bridleway alongside Navan racecourse. The sounds of the disrupted peace of the Carter yard had now been lost in the gloom. Caitlin could hear herself sobbing, her breath coming in short gasps, as she hurried along the unlit path. Stopping suddenly dead in her tracks, she made an effort to control herself and to become calm. As she stood stock still in the dark night, the moon emerged from behind a lump of silver edged grey cloud and illuminated the silent scene with a cool and pale light.

A man was standing in front of Caitlin on the path. He had dark unruly hair onto which was crammed a brimmed hat. He wore a brown waistcoat over a yellow shirt and a dark scarf was tied around his throat. Beneath were black cord trousers stuffed into leather boots. He was looking straight at her.

"Catalina," he said, quietly.

Caitlin almost dropped to her knees in shock and the man jumped forward to steady her.

"*Hola, Arnaldo*," Caitlin whispered, as she stood and looked him in the face.

Two weeks later, Caitlin was crouched uncomfortably in the hedgerow which ran along the back straight of Navan racecourse. Beside her was Arnaldo. Neither spoke. They were watching the racecourse intently, but they were not amongst the spectators today.

Not far away to their left at the eastern end of the oval course was an open ditch, one of the nine fences positioned around the jumps course. Much to Caitlin's relief, the early April day was bright and breezy, the scattered white clouds not large enough to obscure the strong rays of the afternoon sun. But Caitlin shivered as she clutched the bag which she had brought with her, its contents representing a desperate bid to save the life of Eoghan Foley.

Arnaldo had told Caitlin that an anonymous sniper would be positioned on the road outside the perimeter of the course and directly by the side of the same open ditch. A decrepit travellers' van, which would soon apparently break down at that exact location, so as to provide a brief and quickly removed hiding place for the lone rifleman, would be waiting for it on the same road. The driver would then bring the killer to the travellers' camp where it would be Arnaldo's role to get him away before anyone had time to work out what had just happened.

The surprise which both Caitlin and Arnaldo had felt at meeting on the out of the way track a fortnight earlier had prevented the expression of any recriminations which either of them might have wanted to direct at the other. Instead, Caitlin had only been able to stutter, in the half forgotten Calo, a question as to why Arnaldo was in Ireland before the *Feria* had taken place, and Arnaldo had simply wanted to know why Caitlin was weeping alone on a deserted moonlit path in County Meath.

Seeing that Caitlin was shivering, not entirely from the evening cold, against which her stable work clothes offered more than adequate protection, Arnaldo had taken her back to the travellers' encampment, set up in a field about half a mile away. Not wishing to deceive a man who had for a short time been as a brother to her, Caitlin had haltingly summarised the events which had taken place in her life since that last summer in Monamar. She had concluded by explaining what her sister Niamh had told her about the threat to Eoghan's life and how she had been trying to protect him, but without knowing exactly what form the reported threat would take.

Arnaldo had listened without comment, curling his lip and looking away at the description of Caitlin's life with Niall Carter, and slamming his clenched fist onto the side of the van when Caitlin had described the scene from which she had just run away. But it was the threat to Eoghan's life which had caught Arnaldo's attention.

"You say this man is your stepbrother, Catalina?" Arnaldo had clarified, "He is not another of your lovers?"

Caitlin had shaken her head.

"No, Arnaldo," she had replied firmly, "I love Eoghan because we were children together. I first taught him to ride his pony, Tarragon, and now he is an admired and successful horseman. In those days, I used to call him the horseboy, *el caballerito*. But we were never lovers. We were too young for that. My sister says that the time has come for Eoghan to repay his brother Enda's debt to Callan Sullivan. I know, Arnaldo, that you know Enda Foley and Uncle Callan. Mirela and I heard your father speak to them on the road from the ferry at Cork. Uncle Callan is an evil man, Arnaldo. My sister is afraid of him."

"You sister has good reason to be afraid, Catalina," Arnaldo had told her, seriously, "The reason I am here is to help the man who has been paid to kill your stepbrother. Callan Sullivan said he was a traitor who could expose our work and have us arrested."

"Eoghan?" had exclaimed Caitlin, weakly, "Eoghan is supposed to be paying his brother Enda's debts by stopping horses from winning their races. I am certain that he has refused to do this and that this is the reason that Uncle Callan wants him dead. And his death will punish my sister's husband too."

Arnaldo had turned away for a few moments, apparently thinking hard. Eventually, he had said, "I have no love for Callan Sullivan, Catalina. He is a bad man. I cannot go against him, but I will help you save your stepbrother. This I do for you because you were my sister's friend and she loved you."

"And how is Mirela?" had asked Caitlin, humbly, "I have missed her."

"She is a mother to two children," Arnaldo had said, with an unexpected burst of laughter, "And I too have a wife and a son now."

"I am happy for you both," Caitlin had replied, and she had been sincere.

Shifting her position in the bushes, waiting for the first of the jump races on the Navan card that afternoon to begin, Caitlin had been overwhelmed by the speed at which events had moved since she had walked away from the Carter training yard. Housed overnight with a young *gitana* in one of the travellers' vans at the direction of Arnaldo, who now seemed to be the leader of the group, Caitlin had returned to the Carters the following day to collect her possessions and to tell them she was leaving.

In vain had Fergal and Bryany pleaded with her to stay. The two stable girls, they said, had been dismissed. Niall himself had been nowhere to be seen and Caitlin had not asked for him. Bryany, tears running down her cheeks, had attempted to apologise for her son's behaviour, but Caitlin had stopped her.

"Niall has made his own decisions," she had assured Bryany, "He is a free man. I am not his wife."

Now Caitlin watched as the ten chasers left the parade ring on the opposite side of the racecourse and cantered down to the start. Beside her crouched Arnaldo, silent and still.

Caitlin could see the top of the grubby traveller van on the road, as it suddenly stopped close to the location of the open ditch. The scene which she and Arnaldo had rehearsed seemed to unfold as if in a dream. She took the mirror from her bag. She had practised this move many times over, Arnaldo at her side, on the previous day, carefully watching the approach to the open ditch. If they could blind the gunman with the light, he would miss the shot.

What happened in the first race at Navan that afternoon made headlines in the racing papers, although not for the right reasons. Eoghan Foley was riding a big, long striding bay chaser called Langham Light, trained by local trainer Cormac Meaghan. Rounding the first bend in the lead on the second circuit and approaching an open ditch, Eoghan found himself blinded by a flashing light, as if from sun reflecting off a mirror. Worse, Langham Light was temporarily blinded or at least distracted by the sudden glare, and failed to take off at the fence. The horse crashed through the top of the birch and landed awkwardly on its side. Eoghan was catapulted from the saddle and landed with his full weight on his left knee. As he tried to roll away, another horse came over the fence and in its efforts to avoid the stricken Langham Light, stepped with full force on Eoghan's already injured knee and shattered the bones to pieces.

The sniper's bullet buried itself harmlessly in the ground in the centre of the course.

When the battered van carrying the gunman arrived two minutes later at the travellers' encampment, Arnaldo was there to meet him.

"You'll not be needing me any more," the faceless assassin announced in the harsh accent which Arnaldo had come to associate with the men of the North who were Callan Sullivan's friends, "That little bastard won't be riding any horses again."

237

As the gunman started to disassemble his weapon, Arnaldo reached out and stuck a knife between his ribs and straight through what passed for his heart.

Meanwhile, Caitlin lay rigid on the damp ground, watching the staff on the racecourse rushing to help the injured Eoghan and to put down the fatally injured Langham Light.

"What have I done?" she whispered to herself.

As clearly as if she was standing next to her, Caitlin heard the tarot reader's voice,

"You have saved his life, High Priestess. It is time to return home."

23

Sam watched Tabikat, his magnificent former charge, striding in his customary lordly fashion around the bitingly cold Newbury parade ring, the bespectacled Claire O'Dowd holding him lightly by the rein. The previous year's running of the Hennessy Gold Cup had been the occasion on which the beautifully turned out and talented chaser had first attracted his attention. Since then, Sam had had the frustratingly brief experience of training the horse himself and had been rewarded with third place in the Cheltenham Gold Cup earlier in the year. Much had happened in the time since he and Tabikat had first crossed paths at this same meeting one year ago, Sam reflected, as he followed the horse's elegantly measured paces along the oval track.

Once again, Sam was merely a spectator in the centre of the crowded Newbury parade ring that day. He was standing with Lady Helen Garratt, whose husband Sir John owned the powerful Alto Clef, one of the other fancied runners in the famous race. Stevie Stone, her signature multi-coloured hair spreading down her back, was roaming as usual around the parade ring with her iPad, gathering information for Tabby Cat to report on his vlog to his loyal following of Smart Girls, aided as always by racing tips from the invisible, and apparently permanently hung over, Essex lad Jayce. Sam had not yet spoken to Stevie. He was due to see her later.

Jayce had tipped Tabikat to win this year's big race, now sponsored by the bookmaker for which Stevie Stone had previously worked. It was the horse's first reappearance on any racecourse since his victory in the Punchestown Gold Cup seven months earlier. Alto Clef, the reigning Welsh National champion, was also Jayce's tip for an each way bet. The bookmakers had not entirely agreed with Jayce's selections, but the two horses were certainly amongst the favourites with most of them. The starting prices shown on the big screen had both of the horses at short odds, with Tabikat currently second favourite at 2/1 behind the Cheltenham Gold Cup winner Macalantern at Evens.

As had been agreed between Brendan Meaghan and Sam, with some reluctance on the latter's part, Tabikat remained at present with the Meaghan yard, and had been brought over from Ireland on the ferry the previous day. Merlin, in the light of his success with the horse, had retained the ride on Tabikat, probably, Sam thought, to the chagrin of Brendan Meaghan's son, Cormac. Cormac, though, had other rides that day, including one in the following race, an extended two mile Hurdle in which Sam's newcomer Katseye was due to run with Merlin on board. Jackie and Ryan had accompanied Katseye to the Newbury course, Kye having been awarded a break from travelling following a win two days earlier on Highlander Park in a Novices Hurdle race at Taunton. Kye would instead be watching the racing on the TV in the warm Sampfield Grange kitchen with Kelly and Lewis.

The fourteen jockeys were starting to emerge from the weighing room, their coloured jackets standing out against the background of dark coloured clothing worn by most of the spectators and connections on the wintry Berkshire day. Sam could see Merlin in the Levy Brothers' blue and gold, striding confidently towards Brendan Meaghan who was accompanied by a lady Sam recalled seeing alongside Brendan on the television coverage from Punchestown. Two smartly dressed younger people stood with them.

Sam wondered briefly who they all were. He remembered Brendan Meaghan telling him that those who came to watch Tabikat's races were usually people from the bank which owned Tabikat. There was certainly no sign of either TK Stonehouse or Daniel Levy, who had stood with Sam to watch Tabikat on Cheltenham Gold Cup day – nor was there any sign of Isabella Hall and George Harvey. Even Stevie Stone had now deserted the parade ring.

Alto Clef's jockey, dressed in the Garratts' gold and red quartered silks, shook hands with Sam as well as with Helen and John. In response to Helen's question, the tough looking young woman assured the owners that she was very much looking forward to the ride. Newbury, she said, was her favourite course. The confidently spoken jockey was quickly legged up by the horse's Lambourn trainer, who seemed to have little to say in the way of riding instructions, and the grey bulk of Alto Clef was soon bobbing his way along the horsewalk, just behind Merlin and the mahogany coloured Tabikat.

"You won't know whether to cheer for Tabikat or Alto Clef today, Sam," Helen remarked, mischievously, as the little party made its way back to the owners' viewing area in the Berkshire Stand, having decided to leave the rest of their lunch guests to watch the race from the balcony of the hospitality box elsewhere in the same building. "Perhaps we should be hoping for a dead heat."

"Not bloody likely," grunted Sir John, irritably, clamping his fedora hat more firmly onto his balding head, "After the amount I spend on that animal, I want him to win. I need the money."

As Sam sat in the Owners and Trainers seating area, his field glasses dangling from their leather strap across the front of his brown tweed jacket, he laboriously consulted the racecard and the racecourse viewing screen to evaluate which runners represented the main threats to Tabikat and Alto Clef. The bookmakers had old rivals Less Than Ross, Stormlighter and Harry Me Home amongst the shorter priced runners, but the large field contained some unfamiliar names. One of the newcomers which caught Sam's eye was a sturdily built liver chestnut gelding called The Page of Cups, trained in Ireland by Niall Carter. The field also included former winners of the Grand National and the Irish National, but these seemed to Sam to be horses whose most successful days were now in the past.

Lifting his field glasses, Sam watched the runners mustering at the start on the far side of the left handed course. Tabikat looked as calm and focused as ever, Merlin walking him round in the middle of the milling group. At last, the distant starter brought down the yellow flag, and the horses charged forward towards the first fence, where one of their number immediately fell, hampering two other runners, who were unexpectedly pushed into the rear. The remaining horses forged onwards past the tall row of trees which formed the backdrop to the back straight.

Sam was relieved to see that all the favoured runners had survived the upset at the first fence. The faller had risen to its feet and was forlornly pursuing the other horses as they swept around the first bend to meet the cross fence. The pace had begun to steady and the entire field, including the riderless horse, hurtled past the stands and over the water jump with no further incident. Sam saw Tabikat and Alto Clef lobbing comfortably along in the front half of the group, neither of their jockeys yet needing to make much effort.

By the time the runners reached the sixteenth fence on the far side of the course, eleven horses were still in the running. One horse had been pulled up and there had been a second faller. The loose horse had given up the chase and taken the opportunity to run back to the comfort of the stables. The main contenders were all still standing, but, coming into the home turn, the picture began to change. Tabikat and Macalantern cruised to the front, whilst the wearied field began to string out behind them, with Alto Clef and Less Than Ross still in close order behind the leaders. The Page of Cups was half a length behind them.

The crowd eagerly watching from the packed stands was becoming louder and more animated as the leaders approached the final four jumps. Some of the most energetic spectators viewing from the middle of the course had run over from the far side and were leaping about and waving their arms furiously as the runners approached. By contrast, several of the horses at the rear of the field were tiring, and three of them were quickly pulled up after the fourth from last fence.

As the remaining contenders took the third last, it was still impossible to guess who would win. Tabikat and Macalantern were neck and neck, both jockeys working like maniacs on their backs. Alto Clef's rider seemed to be lifting him over the jumps by sheer willpower, the weary horse responding gamely to her efforts. Less Than Ross was fading fast as he approached the second last, and barely crawled over the obstacle, allowing The Page of Cups to run on to challenge the front three.

Helen and her husband soon became animated, shouting loudly to encourage Alto Clef, whilst Sam sat silently, willing Tabikat to win, not least because it was Macalantern, the Cheltenham Gold Cup winner, who was challenging him. Sam could see the faces of both the jockeys, grimacing with determination as they pushed their mounts into the final fence.

"And its Tabikat and Macalantern together at the last!" yelled the disembodied voice of the racecourse commentator, "A great jump from Tabikat and he lands in front. And Tabikat's getting away faster from the fence. Macalantern is trying to come back at him."

The run in to the finishing line seemed to take forever, as if the horses were moving in slow motion. Macalantern was unable to overhaul Tabikat, who ploughed solidly across the line with his rival a length behind, Merlin waving his whip in the air in triumph. Hard on their weary heels came Alto Clef and The Page of Cups, vying for third place, which went to Alto Clef by a narrow margin.

Sam applauded Merlin and Tabikat as they walked back to the winners' enclosure following a breathless interview with a TV presenter who had approached them on the course brandishing a large coloured microphone. As Sam stood with a slightly disappointed Helen and John Garratt alongside a sweating Alto Clef in the third place spot, Helen whispered cheekily in his ear,

"You were secretly cheering for Tabikat then, weren't you Sam, darling?"

Sam was unable to deny that she was right, and smiled weakly in response.

"I should go and congratulate Brendan," he told Helen, "Then I will stay down here for Katseye in the next race."

As Sam approached Brendan Meaghan, who was standing with his three connections, Merlin having gone to weigh in, a curious incident took place. Niall Carter, the trainer of the fourth placed horse, had also come forward to speak to Brendan. Brendan appeared to be attempting to introduce Niall Carter to the older lady in his party.

"I have no wish to be introduced to this man," he heard the woman exclaim, as she abruptly turned her back towards Niall Carter's outstretched hand, to the evident surprise of the two young people who were accompanying her. Niall Carter laughed uncertainly and walked away, giving a brief farewell gesture to Brendan.

During the prize giving, Sam discovered the identity of the affronted Irish lady, the announcer having described her as "Mrs Niamh Foley, representing Levy Brothers International." This was Caitlin's sister, he remembered, once married to Eoghan Foley's deceased older brother. But why Mrs Foley should show such antipathy towards the amiable looking Niall Carter, Sam could not guess.

When the black Katseye strutted in all his grandeur into the parade ring, the gelding looked as if he had the extended two mile race already in the bag. Sam had wanted to take advantage of Katseye's status as a Novice to find races in which the horse could run against other less experienced competitors, but Mrs Crosland had been having none of it.

"Katseye must race at Newbury on Hennessy Gold Cup day," she had told Sam over the telephone, "I have someone interested in buying him and that is the only day the man can come."

Sam had felt rather aggrieved that Mrs Crosland seemed determined to pursue some erratic plan of her own in relation to the interesting horse, apparently not seeing fit to involve him in the process.

"I see," Sam had responded, rather coldly, "In that case, Mrs Crosland .. er, Meredith, I should say .. we will have no choice but to let Katseye take his chance in something more challenging."

Sam had agreed to meet Meredith Crosland in the centre of the parade ring before Katseye's race, where she would, she said, be accompanied by Stevie Stone and the prospective buyer, whose name she had not disclosed. Waiting for the party to arrive, Sam observed the reaction of the assembled spectators to the smartly turned out Katseye, many of whom seemed to be consulting their racecards to find out more about him. His brief form now included the second place in the classy race at Cheltenham, but, other than that, there was nothing to see other than the bold typed successes in the Irish point to point races. Beside him, Jackie walked demurely along, a diminutive figure alongside the powerful dark animal whose coat shone like polished jet. If nothing else, Katseye would win the best turned out prize, Sam thought.

Brendan Meaghan appeared unexpectedly at Sam's elbow.

"We're happy to see Katseye looking so well," Brendan said, his eyes following Katseye's imperious progress along the path, "Your staff have done a great job keeping him fit, to be sure. Mrs Foley and I will be watching eagerly from the stands."

Sam shook hands with Mrs Foley, slightly wary that he might provoke the same reaction as had been accorded by her to Niall Carter. But Mrs Foley was all smiles and enthusiasm.

"My youngest daughter, Feanna, used to ride Katseye in his point to point races," she informed Sam, proudly, "And she will be watching eagerly too, I daresay, but through the television in our living room. Be sure to tell your clever jockey to speak kindly to the horse in the final furlong. He would rather hear a female voice, but that can't be helped now."

And with this mysterious statement left hanging in the air, Niamh Foley and Brendan Meaghan walked purposefully off in the direction of the Berkshire Stand.

More horses were by now entering the parade ring, the field numbering eight declared entrants in total. Only one of the other runners had vied with Katseye in the recent two mile Supreme Novices Trial at Cheltenham and it was not the horse which had beaten him.

Sam did not notice Meredith Crosland until she tapped him sharply on the shoulder from behind. Sam turned hurriedly to see a group of three people, comprising Meredith Crosland herself, Stevie Stone, who seemed to be trying to remain in the background, and a smartly dressed dark-haired man of about Sam's own age.

"Good afternoon, James," Meredith Crosland began, without preamble, "This is my contact, Arturo Ardizzone, who has come to see Katseye run today."

Sam shook hands with the grey clad and black hatted stranger, who seemed to Sam very familiar, although he could not for the moment recall where he might have met him before.

"I am very pleased to meet you, Mr Ardizzone," he said, "Have you visited Newbury racecourse before?"

"No, this is my first visit," Arturo Ardizzone replied, in fluent and only slightly accented English, "But I 'ave visited Cheltenham on a number of occasions. I enjoy English racing. As I am sure that Meredith 'as told you, I wish to become an owner of steeplechasers in this country. She 'as suggested this 'orse Katseye to me. I already think 'e looks very impressive. Do you expect 'im to win today?"

"To be frank, Mr Ardizzone, I am not able to say," Sam responded, making sure that Meredith Crosland could hear him, "This is only the second race in which Katseye had competed at this level so we are still learning about him. My staff have got him fit and well, so the horse should certainly give a good account of himself. But, forgive me, I am assuming from your name that you are from Italy? Do you own racehorses there?"

"Certainly, I do," the other man replied, "I 'ave eleven 'orses in training at 'ome. I spend a lot of time in England on business, so I am 'oping to extend my activities to this country too. I plan also to visit Ireland."

"I assume you have a bloodstock agent?" Sam went on, before Meredith Crosland could intervene, "Will he or she be joining us?"

"My agent will be joining me on Monday," Mr Ardizzone informed Sam, "But I am 'ere on my own today to see this animal which has been recommended to me by Meredith. I believe he is of Irish breeding?"

Before Sam could give the Italian any more information, Merlin appeared at his side, now dressed in the black and silver colours of Mrs Crosland. Merlin shook hands with everyone, including Stevie Stone, who had remained silent throughout the discussion between Sam and the prospective buyer.

"I understand that this 'orse is the 'alf brother to the one on which you 'ave just won the Gold Cup," Mr Ardizzone said at once to Merlin, "I 'ope 'e will now be successful too."
When the bell rang to indicate that the jockeys should mount, Sam went forward to leg Merlin up and walked alongside the horse and jockey for a few paces, behind the quiet figure of Jackie.

"Very well done with Tabikat," he told Merlin, "And I'll need a word with you sometime about Curlew. In the meantime, see what else you can learn about this horse in his race. His breeder just told me he responds well to a kind female voice."

"So would I, if I 'ad 'alf a chance," thought Merlin, as Jackie released the rein on the classy creature and the horse turned left to canter along in front of the quickly filling spectators' viewing areas.

Walking back to rejoin his party in the centre of the parade ring, Sam suddenly remembered where he had seen Arturo Ardizzone before. The Italian had been speaking in a televised news interview in the aftermath of the fire at Old Warnock airfield.

Arturo Ardizzone was the owner of the company which had built the aircraft which had crashed.

24

The accident at Old Warnock airfield had come as an unpleasant shock to those living in the local area, not least because the apparent reopening of the defunct aerodrome had in fact produced very little change in the activity there. The regular model aircraft and drone flyers had been allowed, even encouraged, to continue to practise their hobby at the otherwise disused facility, whilst the two resident microlight owners had carried on with their local flying uninterrupted. A few small helicopters now visited the airfield, as well as the occasional light aircraft, but this too had been an infrequent but not unknown occurrence in the past.

The single change which the airfield users, as well as potential local objectors, had experienced was that the runway had been repaired and improved. A new surface had been laid, and various yellow and white lines and the runway numbers had been repainted. A large and secure concrete sided building had been erected on the North side of the site, which was assumed to be for the purpose of storing contractors' vehicles and airfield equipment and paraphernalia. No runway lights or approach guidance systems appeared to have been planned. This had allayed the concerns of nearby residents that the airfield might be being prepared to be brought into commercial usage, perhaps for a flying school or private business jets.

Trevor Wills, the Sampfield Grange land agent, had made further enquiries of his contact at the local Planning Office, and had been assured that no further application for commercial use had been made by the Government agency which appeared to own and operate the airfield. The initial planning consent given for use for 'aviation related business' appeared, so far at least, not to have involved any additional aircraft movements. So, after an initial flurry of worried indignation, the local community had settled back into its previously disinterested relationship with the airfield, whilst everything had seemed to continue much as it had done for many years.

And then, one wet November evening, an aircraft had crashed on the runway and burst into flames. The airfield, being small and unlicensed, had no fire fighting facility of its own, so the local fire service had been called into action. Fortunately, it appeared that a practice drill had been arranged only a week earlier, which meant that the fire service response had been fast and effective. But the amount of aviation fuel which had been spilt on the runway had caused the fire to burn fiercely for some time, lighting up the heavy clouds hovering over the airfield and casting a vapid glow over the village of Warnock and further abroad.

Lewis had not been the only person who had rushed up to the airfield to offer unspecified assistance. A number of nearby residents had also made themselves available to help, but the police officer guarding the main gate to the airfield had stopped them in their eager tracks.

"The Incident Commander has created an exclusion zone around the North side of the field," she had told the fascinated group of locals, their staring faces illuminated by the glow of the fire, "There are oxy-acetylene gas canisters stored on the site and the heat may cause them to explode. Stay back here, please. Do not put yourselves in danger."

As Lewis had waited, desperate to know more about what was going on, two ambulances with blue lights and sirens had been allowed through the gate and had been directed by another police officer to an area away from the exclusion zone. An emergency helicopter had hovered overhead, searchlights directed towards the ground. Press and TV cameras with accompanying reporters had begun to arrive. The scene at the airfield gate had gradually developed into a large party, even though Bonfire Night was past, at which everyone was asking everyone else what was happening, and nobody could give anyone an answer.

The accident appeared to have happened at the end of the gloomy afternoon, when it had become too dark for the model aircraft and drone enthusiasts or the microlight pilots to continue with their pastimes. The airfield had apparently been deserted when the doomed aircraft had come in to land. Why anyone should want to land at an empty airfield in the dark and rain was a mystery. The flight would have been a challenging one, and most amateur pilots would have avoided taking such a risk. Speculation that the aircraft had suffered an emergency had been rife amongst the chattering crowd, stoked further by the TV reporters who were trying their best to fill the time slots they had been given. With no real information to report, speculation and conjecture were all that had been available.

Sam had arrived back at Sampfield Grange at about seven o'clock that evening to find his household gathered in the kitchen watching Lewis and the other assembled neighbours being interviewed, to little useful purpose, by a reporter called Max Bennett. Sam had both seen and smelt the fire as he had neared home and had been relieved to discover that Sampfield Grange itself was not affected. Having established the basic facts of the incident, which was not difficult, as these were being repeated relentlessly on the TV coverage, Sam had left his staff to their own devices, concluding that a more considered summary of what had happened would probably be available in the morning.

In the daylight of the following morning's exercise rides, the Sampfield Grange work riders had been able to see from the top gallop the smoking wreck of a blackened aircraft on the distant runway at Old Warnock airfield. People appeared to be wandering about amongst the wreckage, but the fire engines and the ambulances had gone. A small blue helicopter had been parked close to the North side of the runway, the oxy-acetylene gas cylinders having presumably been moved or else cooled sufficiently so as no longer to be at risk of explosion. Two four wheel drive vehicles had been parked on the runway itself. A single police car had remained situated across the gate.

Sam, sitting on the patient Caladesi Island, had taken his field glasses with him but had been able to make out little more than that which had been visible to the naked eye. He had assumed, correctly as it turned out, that the people and vehicles present on the airfield were part of an accident investigation team. Putting the field glasses back into the capacious pocket of his waxed riding jacket, he had returned to the waiting string with his directions for the day's exercise. As far as Sam had been concerned, his Cheltenham runners, Katseye, Curlew Landings and Highlander Park, now enjoying a well-deserved rest, had been more in need of his attention than the incident at Old Warnock airfield.

Had Sam remained to look for longer through his well-used field glasses, he would have seen another vehicle, a military looking Land Rover Defender, arrive at the airfield, and would have no doubt been surprised to have recognised the three people who had emerged once the vehicle had stopped alongside the debris strewn runway. Sam would have observed Frank Stanley and George Harvey stepping forward to shake hands with two of the people already at the scene, and then TK Stonehouse, who had been the driver of the elderly vehicle, following behind them, speaking into a mobile phone and waving to the helicopter pilot as she did so.

Instead, the morning ride had returned on schedule to the Sampfield Grange yard, just as Ryan and Jackie had arrived with the small horsebox, which Jackie had driven to the Dicks yard to collect Katseye and Ryan, who had both stayed there overnight. Lewis, who had returned from the airfield late the previous evening with little to report, had been keen to discover whether Jackie had picked up any gossip from Sadie or any of the other staff at the Dickses. But the Dicks yard was further away from Old Warnock airfield than Sampfield Grange and no-one there had known anything more than had been reported on the TV news the previous evening.

When the yard staff and work riders had assembled around the kitchen table for breakfast, the local news section at the end of the breakfast programme, which was airing on the kitchen television, had been reporting on the aircraft crash incident once again. By this time, however, it had appeared that more information had been available to the TV news team.

"Following yesterday evening's aircraft crash at Old Warnock airfield in Somerset," the newsreader, her name helpfully captioned at the foot of the screen as Sophie Wilde, had begun, "An Air Accidents Investigation team is now at the airfield. It has emerged that the aircraft which crashed onto the runway in bad weather, and was subsequently destroyed by fire, was an Altior 10 single engine light aircraft manufactured by Ardua Industrie S.p.A in Milan, Italy. It is not clear at present how the aircraft came to be at the airfield, which until recently has remained little used since being decommissioned after the end of the Second World War. We have no reports as yet of fatalities or injuries as a result of the crash. The police have not given any statement at present, but we understand that a preliminary review of the initial findings will be issued shortly by the AAIB, to be posted on their website. We will of course bring this to you as soon as it is available."

That week, whilst the work of the Sampfield Grange yard had gone on as normal, an eager Lewis had assiduously checked the Air Accidents Investigation Branch website, until, on the Thursday, he had been rewarded by the appearance on the screen of the kitchen iPad of the entry he had been seeking.

"Look, Kells," Lewis had announced, triumphantly, "The plane crash report. It's here at last. We can share it with the others at lunchtime."

"That newsreader said that she would report it as soon as it was available, too," Kelly had enthused, coming to look over Lewis's shoulder, "So we can put the TV on then, too."

"But let's read it first," Lewis had told her, unable to contain his own curiosity for as long as the two hours still left until lunchtime. The other staff had been all down in the yard and Mr Sampfield had been in his study talking on the house telephone to his financial adviser in London.

The report which Lewis had so eagerly anticipated was disappointingly short.

*

AAIB Special Bulletin

Published	19 November
Date of occurrence	14 November
Aircraft category	General aviation – fixed wing
Report type	Special bulletin

Aircraft destroyed following impact with the runway.

ACCIDENT

Aircraft type	Ardua Altior 10
No & Type of Engines	1 Fellowes FE 66 piston engine
Year of Manufacture	New
Location	Old Warnock Airfield, Somerset
Type of Flight	Private
Persons on Board	N/A
Nature of Damage	Aircraft destroyed
Commander's Licence	N/A
Commander's Age	N/A
Commander's Flying Experience	N/A
Information Source	AAIB Field Investigation

The Investigation

The AAIB was notified of the accident at 1900 UTC on 14 November and immediately initiated an investigation. This Special Bulletin is published to provide preliminary information gathered from ground inspection, the aircraft avionics system, and other sources. The investigation is continuing and a final report will be published in due course.

Preliminary Information

The aircraft was on a private local flight in the vicinity of Old Warnock Airfield. Old Warnock Airfield is located on private land in North Somerset near the village of Warnock. The airfield is situated in uncontrolled airspace and is unlicensed and unstaffed.

It is used principally by microlights, gyroplanes, and model aircraft and drone flyers. It has a single paved runway oriented 07/25, 595 x 35 metres.

The weather at Old Warnock at the time of the accident was very poor. The cloud base was less than 1000 feet amsl with intermittent heavy rain. The wind was from the North West, estimated at about 15 knots.

The Ardua Altior 10 is a 'glass cockpit' aircraft and is equipped with an Astrak Mark 2 autopilot and a fibre optic 'fly by wire' flight control system. The Astrak Mark 2 is a combined autopilot and auto take off/landing system operated from the primary flight display. The Mark 2 system is a prototype designed to allow the aircraft to be flown without a human pilot, all parameters for the flight having been entered into the system prior to departure.

The aircraft was built by Ardua Industrie S.p.A, Milan, Italy. The Astrak Mark 2 system was developed for Ardua Industrie in the UK by Astrak Avionics, Cheltenham, using an original design produced by Katz:i d.o.o, a now defunct advanced technology company located in Rijeka, Croatia.

Accident Site

The aircraft struck the centre line of the runway in a nose down attitude. An intense fire developed shortly thereafter. Firefighting and other local emergency services attended the scene. The aircraft was destroyed.

Further Investigation

The aircraft wreckage has been removed to the AAIB facility at Farnborough and the investigation continues with the assistance of representatives of the States of the manufacturer of the aircraft and the original designer of the flight control system.

*

The initial outrage and associated demand for answers expressed by various commentators on the report, which hit the headlines, as intended, in time for the lunchtime news, that an aircraft with no pilot had been flying in the vicinity of Old Warnock airfield had been heightened further when Arturo Ardizzone, the owner of Ardua Industrie S.p.A had agreed to host a press conference at the hotel in London where he was staying. The event had aired live on the lunchtime news of various broadcast and online media, and had attracted an eager audience in the Sampfield Grange kitchen. Even Sam had been persuaded to turn on the large television in the drawing room, having completed his business with his financial adviser David Rose, and realised that he would probably not get any sensible work out of his staff until the eagerly awaited press conference had concluded.

Arturo Ardizzone, speaking excellent English, had been refreshingly brief and to the point. The aircraft, he said, had been equipped with the prototype Astrak Mark 2 system, and had taken off and landed successfully on more than one occasion. If necessary, he clarified, the aircraft could be operated from the ground, overriding the electronic system, meaning that a human pilot could be effectively in control of the aircraft, if this was required for safety reasons. In this respect, he pointed out, the aircraft was nothing more than a larger version of a drone, a piece of aerial technology with which people were already perfectly familiar.

The benefits of the electronic system were that it could be flown equally well in conditions of poor weather and visibility, as the software did not rely for collision avoidance on a human pilot responding to visual or aural information obtained from looking out of the aircraft window or from instruments and alarms within the cockpit. The system was designed to operate at low level in situations where no navigation aids or airfield approach systems were available to assist take off or landing. The test flight in the poor weather conditions was a normal part of the programme for the final approval of the upgrade to the software design.

The Astrak Mark 2 system, he had continued, differed from the Mark 1 system in that the upgraded system now included fully automated take off and land capability. The source software had been designed originally by his former subsidiary, Katz:i d.o.o, based in Croatia. The system itself had originally been called Katz:i, but the name had been changed when the contract had been transferred to Astrak Avionics in the UK.

Asked why the aircraft, notwithstanding all these assurances, had crashed into the ground rather than landing safely, Arturo Ardizzone had initially replied that the findings of the AAIB on the accident should be awaited. Persistent hostile questioning by one of the reporters had, though, eventually produced a crack in the façade which the Italian manufacturer had until then successfully maintained. The reporter had asked whether the original software had been produced 'on the cheap' by poorly qualified staff in an EU accession country which was just emerging into the world's technological business economy.

Ardua Industrie, Arturo Ardizzone had said, firmly, was a family owned company which took its responsibilities seriously. Buying into a Croatian technology company in order to provide jobs in Rijeka in the electronics industry had been undertaken with sound business objectives in mind. Pressed as to why the Croatian company had been closed down, he had said that this was a matter which he was not prepared to discuss, as legal proceedings were currently in train. Asked whether any of the redundant employees of the defunct company had been given jobs at Ardua Industrie or Astrak in order to continue the work, Mr Ardizzone had been scathing.

"It appeared that they were not to be trusted," he had snapped, "That is why we are pursuing legal action against them. Criminals and crooks."

Neither Lewis nor the reporters assembled at the press conference were to know that not only was the AAIB Special Bulletin a carefully concocted fake, but also that much of what Mr Ardizzone had had to say was entirely untrue.

But a young man sitting, fists clenched with rage, in front of a bank of computer screens in a basement room in the southern suburbs of Tirana could recognise fake news when he saw it. He was an expert. He had even been the original author of some of the sentences which had been so carefully copied word for word into this most recent AAIB report.

25

Merlin had made a booking with Lara's Services for Lara herself to meet him for an evening meal at the Hard Day's Night Hotel in the rejuvenated old business district not far from the historic Liverpool waterfront area. After the unwelcome experience at the Adelphi Hotel eight months earlier, Merlin had judged that another venue would be preferable. The name of this establishment, one of a number from which he had been asked to select, had seemed horribly appropriate in the present circumstances.

Arranging the long sought confrontation with Lara had been an unexpectedly business-like experience. The pink card which Merlin had been given by Neil Weston had proved to be little more than a starting point. Dialling the printed number whilst walking through the rain in the Cheltenham racecourse car park had produced an immediate response from a recorded purring female voice.

"Lara's Services are at *your* service," had murmured the speaker, "If you have an account number, enter it now. Or, just hold for more options."

Merlin had by then reached his black BMW and had shuffled quickly into the driver's seat, watched curiously from a distance by the gimlet eyed Jessica Moretti.

"For Lara's escort and personal services, enter 1," the husky voice had continued, "For Lara's erotic movies and images, enter 2. For Lara's chats before bed, enter 3. And for Lara's exotic toy emporium, enter 4. For anything else, Lara is not available right now."

Merlin had pressed 1 into the keypad of his mobile phone and had started the engine of his expensive car. As he had begun to drive out of the racecourse car park, another female voice had made itself heard through the car's internal speaker. This voice was quite different from the first. For a start, it was a real person.

"Lara's Services," had said the efficient sounding voice, "Have you booked with us before?"

"No, I 'aven't," Merlin had replied, manoeuvring his car quickly towards the exit, "I 'ave ..er .. been with Lara before, but someone else booked it for me."

"In that case," the female respondent had gone on, promptly, "You will need to set up an account with us before we can take your booking."

"OK, no problem," Merlin had replied, as he had watched for an opportunity to pull out onto the busy roundabout at the racecourse exit, "What do I do, then?"

"I will text a password to the number you are calling from," the business-like woman told him, "As well as the address of Lara's website. Go onto the site, enter the password, and the instructions for making and paying for your booking will be given to you there. Thank you for calling Lara's Services."

The line had gone dead before Merlin could say any more.

Sitting before his laptop at home in the little Chepstow cottage later that evening, Merlin had accessed the website address and entered the password which he had been sent. After providing credit card details to set up a personal account, a process which had at first made him slightly nervous, but had turned out in reality to be no different than that for any online retail service, he had been able to access a calendar through which to make a booking to see Lara herself.

A picture of Lara had popped up on the screen when he had selected her name from the four women who appeared to be employed by Lara's Services, so Merlin had at least felt confident that he had booked the correct person. Lara had appeared to be bookable for blocks of several hours, the minimum being four hours, including overnight. Various questions had been asked as to the services which would be used during the period for which Lara had been hired, including, Merlin had been interested to discover, whether a film recording should be made.

After some thought, he had opted for a four hour evening slot on the day of the forthcoming Becher Chase at Aintree, for drinks and dinner only, with no additional services added, and had been given several hotel restaurant venues in Liverpool from which to choose. The booking system had then informed him of two things, the first, that he was responsible for all restaurant and bar bills, and the second, that, as he was a new client, Lara would be accompanied on this occasion by a minder who would remain at a discreet distance throughout the evening. Finally, Merlin had been presented with an eye wateringly expensive summary of the cost of Lara's company for the evening, which would be charged to his credit card on his acceptance of the booking terms and conditions.

"In for a penny, in for a few 'undred pounds," thought Merlin grimly, selecting the Accept caption on the screen, "That bloody Neil Weston must 'ave spent a fortune on that night at the Adelphi."

On the afternoon of his meeting with the hitherto elusive Lara, Merlin had ridden for Justin Venn and another trainer at the Becher Chase meeting. His ride in the Becher Chase itself had been curtailed by a faller in his path, which had required some fancy footwork to avoid being brought down, and which had resulted in his mount having been put well out of contention in the keenly contested race.

"Like Katseye all over again," Merlin had thought crossly, as he had pulled the sweating and alarmed horse into a slow canter, knowing that there was little point in wasting energy in trying to chase the now distant field. With no chance even of place money, it would be foolish to risk a valuable horse further in an already lost race. There would be another day for them both.

Katseye, Merlin reflected, as he sat in the smart restaurant, had been similarly unlucky in running a week earlier at Newbury, although the cause had been quite different. The field for the race had comprised eight horses. No-one had wanted to go off in front to make the pace, which had then become unrealistically slow for a race of just over two miles in distance. Katseye had disliked being held, and had pulled and tugged crossly against the contact, so Merlin had eventually allowed him to go to the front once again, a position from which the horse had bowled along happily for a while, jumping the hurdles quickly and accurately. But towards the end of the race, the rest of the field having by then moved up to join them, a tussle for the lead over the last hurdle had resulted in a heavy bump from another horse which had jumped across them. Katseye was a big animal, and the collision had produced little physical effect, but he was also a fairly inexperienced racer, so the barging by the other horse had given him a shock. As a result, Katseye had slowed momentarily after the fence, evidently wondering what was happening to him, a hesitation which had allowed the other horse to press its advantage and run on to finish in first place. Although a Steward's Enquiry had followed, the places, to the annoyance of everyone connected with Katseye, had not been reversed.

Merlin had arrived early for the meeting with Lara, placing himself at the table which he had been told would be reserved in his name. After some thought, he had decided to treat the encounter as a business meeting, and had dressed in a smart grey suit over a cream shirt and a pale blue silk tie. The table was in a quiet corner but easily visible to anyone acting as Lara's minder whilst she was in the company of her unfamiliar client. Merlin wondered whether the minder would have accompanied them into the bedroom as well, but that was fortunately not relevant to his current plans.

Lara arrived promptly at the agreed time, walking across the restaurant towards Merlin with a smile. Merlin, standing up to receive her, at once remembered why he had found her so attractive. She wore a smooth green dress which clung to her slim figure, and a number of small items of gold jewellery. Her blonde hair was twisted into a loose knot above one ear, and decorated with gold thread. She was not tall, although stiletto heeled sandals added a little to her height. Merlin found it difficult to believe that she was a professional sex worker. She looked entirely respectable, like a trophy girlfriend for a successful businessman –

261

or a footballer, he thought suddenly, remembering the purpose of his meeting.

"Hello again, Merlin," Lara greeted him, sitting down on the chair opposite his, "It's lovely to be spending time with yez again. Thanks for inviting me."

Although it was a Saturday evening, and not long before Christmas, it was as yet early and only a few of the restaurant tables were taken. Groups of smartly dressed people were congregated around the bar and at the small tables near the windows. Merlin found himself suddenly regretting that his meeting with Lara was not a real date involving a genuine attraction on both sides, rather than a paid-for encounter which might well, after what he had to say to her, have an unpleasant outcome.

"Good to see you, too," Merlin responded, trying to sound as if he meant it, suddenly finding himself strangely unable to decide what to say. In the Adelphi Hotel, when he had not known Lara was a sex worker, he had not had any such difficulty.

Fortunately, Lara did not appear to notice his hesitation, and continued to chat pleasantly and politely with him, asking about the afternoon's racing, his opinions about Liverpool, and a number of other neutral topics. Merlin had to admire her professionalism, which was clearly designed to put uncomfortable, tongue-tied clients at their ease. He began to feel almost guilty about the questions with which he was about to confront her and decided to enjoy the meal first. He could return to the difficult business of the doctored video recording once they had eaten.

To Merlin's relief, Lara was happy to drink nothing more than the sparkling water which Merlin ordered for himself, and to be content with a meal with similarly restricted calories. Lara clearly also had a professional interest in keeping her body in good shape, Merlin realised uncomfortably.

Eventually, putting his knife and fork down on his plate, and draining his glass of water for the final time, Merlin decided he could wait no longer to ask the question to which he had been seeking an answer for the last eight months. He felt around in his jacket pocket for his old mobile phone, which had remained charged, but unused, since that time.

"What's this about then, Lara?" he asked, bluntly, handing her the phone, on which the video was playing with accompanying sound track clearly audible. Fortunately, although the restaurant was beginning to fill up, no other diners were near enough to overhear them.

Throughout the meal, Lara's pretty face had worn a pleasant and relaxed smile and her blue eyes had looked directly into Merlin's as she had made small talk with him. As she took in the contents of the video, Merlin saw her guard momentarily slip, before she returned the phone to him, the sound and picture cut off suddenly by the pressure of one of her small, manicured fingers.

"It's the video recording of our night at the Adelphi, Merlin," Lara began, smoothly, having recovered her equilibrium, "It's what Mr Weston ordered for yez. In fact I even have a DVD for yez too, but I didn't have an address to send it to. It's here in my bag. I was going to give it to yez this evening, so thanks for reminding me, Merlin."

"And does that one 'ave Abigail Alvarez's face on it too?" asked Merlin, trying to remain calm.

"I hope not, Merlin," replied Lara, carefully, clearly recognising that an explanation of some sort was going to be required, "And it should not be on yez phone either. I don't know what's gone wrong. My video guy seems to have made a mistake, that's all."

"'ow can someone alter someone's face on a video by mistake, Lara, if that's your real name?" asked Merlin, caustically, beginning to feel annoyed, "Don' treat me as if I'm stupid. This recordin' 'as cost me my relationship with my girlfriend."

"Yez didn't tell me yez had a girlfriend when we were at the Adelphi," Lara stated, pointedly, "Or I would have made sure that the recording didn't go direct to yez phone."

"I didn' know anyone was recordin' anythin' then," Merlin told her, crossly, waving away a hovering waiter who wanted to clear the plates and offer the dessert menu, "That bloody Neil Weston arranged all that without tellin' me. Said it was a surprise. Well it's certainly been that, all right."

"I'm sorry, Merlin," Lara told him, "Do you want to get yez girlfriend back, then? Is she still very angry?"

"Don' try to change the subject, Lara," Merlin snapped, "That's not the poin', is it? It's why your face 'as been changed to look like someone else's. Are you tryin' to blackmail me?"

"Blackmail? Certainly not," responded Lara, quickly and firmly, "That's something I would never do. More than my business would be worth."

"Well your .. video guy... clearly 'as a line in doin' this sort of stuff," Merlin said, firmly, "Why else would 'e change people's faces on videos? I don't know 'oo else 'as seen this. But anyone 'oo 'as seen it would think I'm screwin' this Abigail Alvarez. Why? I'd never even 'eard of the woman until I saw this and found out 'oo she was."

"Some clients like to have these edits made to the recordings," Lara replied, quietly, "Then they can pretend that they are with someone else and not with me."

Merlin tried to absorb the implications of this statement.

"So ..," he said slowly, "There's someone who likes to pretend they're doin' it with Abigail Alvarez, then?"

Lara nodded, saying nothing.

"And your video guy thought it was me?" Merlin went on slowly, "Why?"

"I'm not sure he thought it was yez," Lara said, "I think he just got his instructions mixed up."

"So the other guy, whoever 'e is, 'as probably just got video of 'imself in bed with you, then?" Merlin continued, "And 'as 'e complained?"

"He has," Lara said, "But until now I didn't know that yez were on the other end of the mix up. As I told yez, Merlin, the DVD hasn't been changed. Here it is, yez can watch it at home and check for yezself."

"No thanks," Merlin replied quickly, rejecting the offered package which Lara had pulled from her bag, "I don't wan' anything more to do with this. This 'ole thing 'as caused me enough trouble already. But what about the other guy? Why was 'e so keen to have it look like Abigail Alvarez was with 'im rather than you?"

Lara remained silent once again, looking at Merlin fixedly, her hands folded on the table in front of her.

"'e's 'ad the same problem as I 'ave," Merlin said slowly, "'e didn' want stuff on 'is phone showing 'im in bed with you, did 'e? 'e didn't wan' 'is girlfriend, or 'is wife or whoever, seein' it either, did 'e?"

Lara still said nothing.

"And so, 'e's asked for your face to be changed so you look like 'er!" Merlin announced, finally working the problem out, "Then anyone findin' it on 'is phone will think he was with 'er. Even if she finds it, 'e'll probably persuade her that it's a video 'e made 'imself without tellin' 'er. What an arse'ole."

"I can't comment on that," Lara observed, sharply, "All I can tell yez is that no-one is trying to blackmail you, Merlin. I'm sorry if yez have been worried."

"But," Merlin said, ignoring her, "What's to stop this video on my phone goin' to someone else? Someone 'oo could use it to blackmail Abigail Alvarez, makin' out she's 'aving an affair with me. That might suit that bastard of a 'usband of hers. Give 'im a 'old over 'er."

"That's just fantasy, Merlin," Lara told him, looking alarmed for the first time, "I promise I will make sure this version of the recording has been destroyed. It's just a mistake, Merlin, like I said."

Merlin stood up.

"I'm goin' to pay the bill, now, and then I'm leavin'," he said, "I don' shock that easy, but this is real shitty stuff, Lara. If I do 'ear of any dirt about Abigail Alvarez, then I'll know where it's come from."

"Please, Merlin ... " Lara began, but Merlin had already gone. The other diners occupying nearby tables clearly assumed that the well dressed young couple had had a row, and were working hard at pretending not to look at her.

After a few moments' thought, Lara gathered up the wrapped DVD from the dining table. As she did so, a tall and athletic looking woman in a short black evening dress came towards her and sat down in the chair which Merlin had vacated.

"That looked a bit heavy," the woman said, "You OK, Lara?"

"Yes, thanks," Lara sighed, no trace of the local accent now sounding in her voice, "Just a mix up over a video recording. He was pretty upset about it. Said his girlfriend had left him. Thought someone was trying to blackmail him."

"Guilty conscience," the other woman remarked, sourly, "Daresay he deserves it. They all do. But, we have another problem, Lara."

"What's that?" asked Lara, suddenly alert.

"You were being watched," Lara's minder told her, "Woman with black hair at the table by the bar. She's gone now. She was pretending to do selfies on a mobile phone, trying to get you and your client in the background."

"Do you know who she was?" asked Lara.

"Well, the barman has never seen her before, so I hacked her phone through her hotspot," the minder said, "Her name's Moretti, Jessica Moretti."

Lara thought for a moment.

"I think we had better tell Frank Stanley," she said.

26

Jessica Moretti could not believe her luck. The boring country racehorse trainer had agreed to give her a personal interview.

The Sampfield Grange office manager had called her two days ago, offering a meeting for today. Mr Sampfield, the woman had said, rather importantly Jessica thought, would be available that morning to speak to Ms Moretti, if the date and time were convenient to her. After such a long period of being stonewalled, this had been an unexpected surprise to Jessica, who had accepted immediately.

The proposed meeting had included the offer of watching the Sampfield Grange string being exercised on the gallops. Jessica had not been entirely enamoured of the prospect of watching horses running around on cold hillsides on a freezing December morning, but had had to admit to herself that a genuine equestrian journalist would not have found this to be a problem, and, indeed, would probably have welcomed it as a good source of inside information on the horses. Ever the professional, Jessica had made a heroic effort in the last two days to learn something about horse racing and training, including reading the vlogs directed by Stevie Stone at the Smart Girls, and browsing through current copies of the Racing Post, Go Pointing, and Horse and Hound. She had also tried to find out more about the reclusive James Sampfield Peveril himself, a task which had proved more difficult.

The research had all been very tedious, Jessica reflected, as she drove her red Fiat Barchetta along the unlit lanes which led from the M5 towards Sampfield Grange. A scarlet sun was gradually making itself visible through a scarf of grey cloud which lay along the tree-silhouetted horizon in front of her, sending a feeble pink and yellow glow into the sky above. The headlights of the little car picked out the ragged shapes of hedgerows, interspersed by wide barred farm gates on either side of the lane, and, once, a large tractor with glaring headlights swerved without warning out of a track to one side of the lane, apparently without seeing her. Jessica could feel mud being thrown up from its enormous wheels onto her precious car as she continued her unenjoyable journey. She longed for her familiar environment of North London, where the roads had streetlights and were clogged with predictable, if aggressive, cars, vans, and lycra-clad men on racing bicycles.

The stories which Jessica had been following over the past few months had run into a mire even deeper than that through which she was now driving. Randy Santi seemed to have returned to his best behaviour, taking his wife to the Caribbean for a holiday earlier in the year and then apparently remaining faithful to her since then. Jessica had almost tired of keeping tabs on them and on Abigail's sister, who appeared to have found another man to keep her occupied, when she had witnessed the unexpected incident at Cheltenham racecourse just over three weeks ago. The angry blonde stable girl had clearly suspected her Welsh jockey boyfriend of cheating on her with the saintly Abigail.

Switching her attention to the hitherto unknown new target, Merlin ap Rhys, Jessica had expected to be rewarded with evidence of liaisons between him and Abigail Alvarez. But his life had turned out to be a picture of dullness, travelling around the country riding horses for money, and then returning home to some godforsaken place in the depths of the Welsh countryside in the evening. The hacking of Merlin's sparsely used mobile phone by one of Hornblower's expert IT staff had produced little information other than a record of his work bookings and text messages exchanged with friends, family, his agent, and a few uninteresting women.

Jessica had thought her persistence had at last been rewarded when her hacker colleague had informed her that a meeting had been arranged by Merlin with a woman in Liverpool whose name appeared to be Lara. No number for anyone called Lara appeared in the phone's contacts list. Could this be a disguised name for Abigail Alvarez, Jessica had thought, with sudden hope.

But this too had proved to be a dead end. The woman who had spent the evening with the jockey was not Abigail Alvarez, although she did look a little like her. The angry stable girl must have made a mistake based on the resemblance between the two women, Jessica had concluded in frustration.

Jessica would have called a halt to her exploration of Merlin's activities at that point, had it not been for two things. The first was that Merlin and Lara appeared to have had some kind of argument which had resulted in Merlin leaving Lara alone in the restaurant. The second was that Jessica had discovered the following day that her mobile phone had been hacked and all pictures taken during that evening had inexplicably been out of focus. Asking her colleague at Hornblower Online to check her phone for spyware, she had, to her relief, been assured that none had been planted on the phone.

Jessica had not known what to make of these developments, but could not see how she could make any further useful progress. She had been in the dirt-dishing game for long enough to know that someone was bound to make a move sometime, and that she would eventually benefit from waiting patiently until they did. In the meantime, she had asked her hacker colleague to find out anything he could about the mysterious Lara.

The other story on which Jessica had been working, which she had calculated to be more likely to make her name than grubbing around in Santiago Alvarez's sordid sex life, was that connected with Susan Stonehouse. Jessica had once known Susan Stonehouse personally, through her connection with Susan's daughter, now known to the National Hunt racing world as Stevie Stone, tipster to the Smart Girls. Jessica remembered the Stonehouse family as having been spectacularly uninteresting, and had therefore been astounded at the dramatic events which had recently surrounded them, events which had resulted in the sudden deaths of both of Stevie's parents.

Given the amount of publicity which had surrounded the trial for murder of Konstantin Paloka, whose imprisonment for life had been brought about as a direct result of Susan Stonehouse's evidence against him, there had been remarkably little press coverage of her death. Indeed, she appeared to have been cremated and her ashes scattered alongside those of her recently dead husband before her suicide on the rails of Golders Green Underground Station had even been reported. The press coverage had made much of the death threats and cyber trolling to which Susan Stonehouse had been subjected, apparently by the Paloka family, speculating that this had driven her to take her own life.

Jessica had thought the story of the suicide very odd. Having met Susan Stonehouse on a number of occasions, Jessica had found it difficult to believe that she would have committed suicide at all, least of all in such a public manner, when her two daughters, presumably also devastated by their father's recent death, had been still alive to support and care for their mother. But what struck Jessica as most inexplicable was Susan's apparent choice of the platform at Golders Green Underground station from which to make her fatal jump. There were at least three Northern Line stations closer to the Stonehouse family home, from one of which Susan Stonehouse would surely normally have travelled to her work as an accountant on a regular basis. There was no reason for Susan to be at the more inconvenient Golders Green station at all.

Narrowly avoiding a horse and rider, both clad in bright reflective kit, ambling along in the dawn light on the wet lane leading past Old Warnock airfield, Jessica remembered how she had immediately asked Hornblower's IT team to set its newsbots off in search of information about Susan Stonehouse. But, other than the reports already in the public domain, the web crawlers had for many months found nothing. Jessica had almost forgotten about the venture, when, later that year in November, a text had reached her to say that there had been online activity relating to Susan Stonehouse in a remote part of France. The web searches were being conducted by someone in a small village that Jessica had never heard of, called Frossiac.

Jessica had not at first been able to justify the time and cost of a trip to some unknown corner of another country, so she had simply asked for the monitoring activity by the bots to continue. As a result, she had discovered that the searches relating to Susan Stonehouse had continued intermittently until earlier in the current year, after which they had stopped completely in mid January. After a pause, more activity had been detected, this time in even more distant Albania, which again had stopped at the beginning of March.

Taking advantage of a fortuitous invitation from a well heeled friend to join a hen party in Bordeaux for a fully paid girls' weekend, Jessica had travelled ahead of the rest of the group, hiring a car at Bordeaux airport and making the two hour drive from there to the unpromising canalside location of Frossiac. Making enquiries at a local bar, she had discovered from the garrulous owner that she indeed knew the person who had been researching the story of the Stonehouse family. Pressed further, the woman had told her that the Englishman's name was Georges 'Arvai. M 'Arvai had claimed to be a friend of the Stonehouse family but had left the village some weeks earlier, following a terrible incident in the wine museum after which a number of local people had been unjustly arrested. No-one knew if and when M 'Arvai would return. More in hope than expectation, Jessica had left her business card with the bartender and had returned, none the wiser, to her party in Bordeaux.

Notwithstanding the apparent existence of all this research work on Susan Stonehouse, nothing at all had been published anywhere in the world's press, either in print, online or on social media, until one day, her name had popped up prominently as the owner of a horse due to run in the Cheltenham Gold Cup. Even Jessica had heard of the Cheltenham Gold Cup. So she had gone along to watch not only the race, but the people who had turned up to support the horse. And that had in turn sent her, first, to another Gold Cup horse race in Ireland and eventually, eight months later, to this miserable country lane on this bitter December morning.

The main entrance to Sampfield Grange was, to Jessica's relief, wide and well lit by lamps standing on large stone gateposts. A short uphill slope led her into the stable yard, which appeared to be a hive of busy activity. Groups of warmly dressed young people were milling around, towing athletic looking horses by the reins in their wake around the stable yard.

As Jessica tentatively parked the Fiat by the fence, she suddenly felt unusually nervous. This world was like nothing she had ever experienced before. She knew very little about horses and how they were trained. Did all these young people work here? Were they employees or students? Did they live in the grand old house which was emerging from the dawn light on her right hand side? Where were these gallops which had been mentioned? And how was she going to get there?

As Jessica stood hesitating uncharacteristically by her car, a young woman with her dark hair fastened back in a short plait approached her.

"Hello, are you Ms Moretti?" asked the girl, her accent sounding anything but local. Mancunian, Jessica guessed.

"Yes, I'm Jess Moretti," replied Jessica, pulling herself together quickly, and trying to sound confident, "What's your name?"

"I'm Jackie," the girl told her, "Mr Sampfield asked me to look after you this morning."

"Is he here?" asked Jessica, looking quickly around the busy yard, "I can't see him anywhere."

"He'll be down later," Jackie replied, "His friend, Mr Stanley, is joining him today, so they'll follow us up once Mr Stanley arrives. That's Mr Sampfield's horse there. He's called Caladesi Island. And Mr Stanley is going to be on Ranger Station over there. They're all tacked up ready to go."

Jessica looked doubtfully at the two powerful bay hunters which were waiting quietly nearby, tied by thick coloured ropes to loops of twine which were hanging from iron rings set into the wall of one of the honey coloured stableyard buildings, striped rugs draped over their broad brown backs.

"Is Mr Stanley a racehorse trainer as well?" Jessica ventured, realising that she was expected to ask questions about horse training activities.

"No, he isn't," Jackie replied, "He's someone Mr Sampfield's known since they were both at school. He comes and rides with Mr Sampfield sometimes. But just for fun. And he goes to the races with him sometimes, especially the big meetings."

Jessica could not see that there was any fun to be had from getting up early on such a cold morning to ride horses. It suddenly occurred to her that the old school friend might be the tall man she had seen in the parade ring at the Cheltenham Gold Cup race, in other words, someone who had nothing to do with Susan Stonehouse at all.

Jessica had had the foresight to bring a pair of green Wellington boots and a blue quilted waterproof jacket and matching gloves. She was glad she had done so when Jackie indicated that the two of them were to walk up the muddy and hoof-pocked track which ascended the hillside behind the stable yard and the adjoining garage. Trudging up the slope and sucking in the cold, clean air, listening to Jackie's running commentary about the Sampfield Grange horses, Jessica began dimly to understand why some people enjoyed spending time in the country. A stunningly clear vista slowly began to open out on her left hand side, revealing itself little by little as they ascended the slope. Then, as she reached the top of the hill, breathing hard, Jessica realised with a sudden start of surprise that she could see the sea in the distance, grey and silky beyond a panorama of shadowy fields, some with white frost still decorating their Northern corners. As she stopped to recover her diminishing breath, which was coalescing into a cloudy mist in front of her flushed face, the weak sun continued to strengthen and to paint the hedges and meadows in new shades of varied sombre colours, whilst dispersed groups of farm buildings, and even an airfield, made themselves newly visible. Traffic noises throbbed quietly through the still air and invisible sheep could be heard bleating plaintively nearby.

Jessica's short-lived appreciation of her unfamiliar environment was cut short by the clatter of hooves and tack behind her. She and Jackie stood aside as five horses marched briskly past, their riders chatting amiably, and turned along the side of the ridge to their right. The cold grey skeletons of bare trees lined the skyline above them.

"That's Kye on Highlander Park and Ryan on Curlew Landings," Jackie told her, pointing at the two leading horses, "Then Honeymoon Causeway's the grey one and the last two are Palm Harbour and Indian Rocks. Their riders come in to help us out in the morning and after they finish school too. They're mostly at College or doing A levels. Come on, let's go on after them before we miss the exercise."

Jackie broke into a jog, following the equine group along the narrow pathway, so Jessica had no choice but to follow her in the cumbersome rubber boots as best she could. The horses had now started to trot and were quickly disappearing into the distance.

"Do we have to wait for Mr Sampfield Peveril?" asked Jessica, once she could speak again.

"No. Kye and Ryan will take their horses over the hurdles a couple of times," Jackie told her, quickly, "And the others will just do a general workout on the top slope."

"Are Kye and Ryan jockeys?" asked Jessica, casting about for an appropriate question.

"Kye's a conditional," Jackie replied, "Ryan's Mr Sampfield's cousin. He's Australian."

"And what about you, Jackie? Do you ride the horses as well?" Jessica went on.

"I do, usually," Jackie told her, "I ride Katseye. But he's got a schooling session with his race jockey later this morning, so that's why I'm free to talk to you instead. His jockey's called Merlin ap Rhys. He's one of the best jockeys around."

Jessica's stomach lurched. Merlin ap Rhys was not someone with whom she wanted to come face to face at the moment. She didn't think he had seen her in the Liverpool restaurant, but the hacking

275

of her phone that evening had made her suspicious that someone connected to Merlin had known that she had been watching him and his female companion. Jessica did not want to have to answer any awkward questions from Merlin until she was surer of her ground.

At that moment, the sound of more horses approaching from behind them caught Jessica's attention. Jessica realised that this must be Mr Sampfield Peveril and his friend. The two men on their big hunters were soon alongside them.

"Good morning to you, Miss Moretti," said Sam, politely, "I trust Jackie is looking after you well today?"

"Yes, she is, thank you," Jessica replied, "She's being very helpful."

"Very good," Sam responded in turn, "In that case, I will leave her to answer your questions, and we can speak together later."

The two powerful horses moved off smartly towards the row of jumps leaving Jessica no time to get other than a brief glimpse of the second man, who remained silent and made no attempt to introduce himself. The riders positioned the horses close to the line of hurdles, and Jessica realised that Mr Sampfield was now supervising the training session from the back of his impressive looking horse. The other horse stood alongside, its rider apparently viewing the proceedings with interest and making an occasional comment.

Jessica suddenly felt very foolish. Why was she wasting her time here? There was nothing to be seen other than dull, rural people going about their normal daily work. A genuine equestrian journalist would have probably found it interesting, but she was not an equestrian journalist. As she mentally kicked herself for the waste of her time, she became aware that Jackie was speaking to her.

"Will you be staying for breakfast, Ms Moretti? You can talk to Kye and Ryan and ask them some questions before you see Mr

Sampfield. And you can meet Katseye, if you like, before Merlin gets here."

"When is... er ... Merlin coming?" asked Jessica, nervously, wondering how on earth she was going to get out of being pressed to stay for the rest of the morning in this out of the way place which appeared to have nothing productive to offer her.

"Oh, not for a couple of hours at least," Jackie explained, "I expect Mrs Crosland, the owner, will be here then as well."

"Mrs Crosland?" asked Jessica, now recalling the woman she had seen embracing Stevie Stone on the horrible wet day at Cheltenham racecourse, "Is she a friend of Stevie Stone, the racing vlogger?"

"I don't know .." started Jackie.

"Or Isabella Hall?" Jessica cut in, becoming tired of subtlety, and determined to throw the dice one final time.

"Isabella Hall? You mean the person who used to work here?" Jackie replied, sounding surprised, "I wasn't here then. But Lewis and Kelly say Isabella was Mr Stanley's girlfriend. Nothing to do with the horses."

"And Lewis and Kelly are ..... ?" asked Jessica.

"The house staff," Jackie told her, "You can talk to them at breakfast. And all the work riders too. They're all dying to meet you."

Jessica had to admit to herself that she was now well out of her depth. Talking to rich landowners' servants and horsey teenagers was far outside her comfort zone. Even the confident Jessica doubted her ability to keep up the equestrian journalist persona over a meal where she was to be the centre of attention, especially when there was clearly nothing of interest to be discovered in this godforsaken country backwater.

To Jessica's intense relief, her mobile phone, stowed in the pocket of her bulky outdoor jacket, suddenly rang shrilly. Although she did not recognise the number, she stabbed gratefully at the green button, relieved to hear only a recorded junk message to which she could pretend to respond.

"Yes, yes, of course, I see," Jessica spoke urgently into the phone, as Jackie studiously continued to watch the exercise session over the hurdles.

"I'm sorry," Jessica told Jackie, quickly, shoving the phone back into her pocket, "Please give my apologies to Mr Sampfield Peveril, but I have to return to London immediately. I'll call and make a new appointment to see him."

So saying, Jessica turned and ran down the slope, slithering and sliding along the way in the unfamiliar Wellington boots. Jackie waited quietly until she could see the little red sports car moving along the lane below them and so was sure that Jessica had indeed departed. Then she walked quickly towards Mr Sampfield and his companion.

"She's gone, Mr Sampfield," Jackie told her employer, as he looked at her questioningly, "We scared her off all right."

"Thank God for that," said George Harvey from his precarious position on Ranger Station's broad back, "Now please get me off this horse before I fall off. I just hope Frank knows what he doing."

"If you do find out, perhaps you could ask him to share it with me," added James Sampfield Peveril, pointedly.

27

"So what was all that about then?" Kye asked Jackie, as he slid down from the brown back of the still chirpy Highlander Park.

"Just some journalist who wanted to interview Mr Sampfield," Jackie told him, taking Highlander by the bridle whilst Kye ran the metal stirrups up the leathers and began to remove the saddle, "But she got an urgent phone call and had to go before she could do the interview."

"Journalist?" intervened Ryan, unexpectedly, from his position atop Curlew Landings, who had been brought to a restless halt nearby, "Bloody stickybeaks. What did she want, then?"

"No idea," Jackie replied, "Like I said, she went off before she spoke to Mr Sampfield. I just told her about the horses and the staff here and what we were all doing."

"The staff?" Ryan persisted, to his colleagues' surprise, "What d'you tell her about me then?"

"Umm... I said you were Mr Sampfield's cousin Ryan from Australia and that you were riding Curlew Landings," Jackie told him, "What do you think I said? Did you want to be interviewed too?"

"Shit, no," Ryan said, dismissively, "Hate those bastards. They're bloody muckrakers."

As Ryan clattered off across the yard on Curlew Landings, Kye silently raised his eyebrows at Jackie, who simply shook her head and shrugged.

Mr Sampfield and his companion had returned ahead of the rest of the ride, so Caldesi Island and Ranger Station had been left with rugs over their backs, tied up in the yard awaiting the attention of the returning staff. Sending the work riders indoors for their breakfast along with a now silent Ryan, Kye asked Jackie,

"Here Jax, can yez just come and have a look at Cal's leg with me?" There was in fact nothing amiss with Caladesi Island's leg, but Kye wanted to ask Jackie a question.

"That bloke who was with Mr Sampfield..." he started.

"Mr Stanley you mean," Jackie interjected.

"That wasn't Mr Stanley," Kye told her, "I know what he looks like. Who told yez it was Mr Stanley?"

Jackie looked at him, suddenly wary.

"Well, who was it then?" she asked, quickly, evading Kye's question.

"Yez won't know him, but I think he was with Isabella Hall on Cheltenham Gold Cup day and another time at Cheltenham races before that," Kye told her, "Isabella called him George when I talked to her about him."

"Oh," said Jackie, more confidently, "That's all before my time, then."

"So where'd he go then?" asked Kye, "Is he with Mr Sampfield? What did he come here for?"

"Don't ask me," Jackie replied, "Mr Sampfield just told me to take the journalist woman up to the gallops, while he waited for Mr Stanley to arrive."

"So it was Mr Sampfield who told you it was Mr Stanley, then?" Kye insisted.

"You're getting me confused now, Kye," Jackie said, sounding rattled, "Probably I just assumed it was Mr Stanley. I know he's been here riding with Mr Sampfield before."

"Well, anyway," said Kye, "What's Mr Sampfield doing riding with this George, or whatever his name is?"

So engrossed was Kye in trying to solve the mystery that he did not notice a watery shadow falling across the ground beside the increasingly impatient Caladesi Island, as a tall figure moved up behind them.

"Don't worry, Jackie," said Frank Stanley, "George has left, and you two are now going to walk into the house with me and corroborate the position that I was out riding with Mr Sampfield this morning."

Jackie gave a small sigh of relief.

"Yes, sir," she said, as Kye looked questioningly from her face to that of Frank Stanley.

"Unfortunately, Kye, we still need to protect Isabella," Frank told Kye, firmly, "Just do as I ask, please. Support Jackie's account of events when we get into the house. And I need to speak to Mr Sampfield along the same lines. Jackie can provide an explanation for you later."

In accordance with this clearly delivered instruction, Lewis and Kelly soon saw that Mr Stanley, having apparently returned from his morning ride with Mr Sampfield, was being accompanied towards the metal studded door of the boot room by Kye and Jackie.

"Mr Sampfield's already gone through to breakfast, Mr Stanley," Kelly told him, politely, "Will you be joining him?"

"I will," Frank replied, shortly.

Turning quickly to thank Kye and Jackie for their assistance with his horse, he departed from the kitchen without further comment, leaving Jackie to explain to a disappointed Lewis that the journalist was not only unable to join them for breakfast but was unlikely to be back for some time, if at all.

Sam had little to say when Frank Stanley joined him in the breakfast room, simply looking questioningly him as he sat down on the opposite side of the polished table.

"Thanks for your help, as always, Sam, old man," Frank began, reaching for the silver coffee pot which stood between them.

"Is Jackie involved in this too?" Sam asked, wearily, "Because I'd appreciate it if she didn't simply disappear when she's finished doing whatever task it is that you have for her. She's a good worker and I need her."

"That's up to Jackie," Frank replied, pouring the black coffee into the gold patterned bone china cup, "But I'll tell her what you say, of course."

"The last time I saw George Harvey was with Isabella Hall at Cheltenham," Sam went on, "Which reminds me, Lewis claimed a while ago to have seen Isabella in the local area again, so I am assuming that she too is here with George. He's not much of a horseman, so why did you want him to ride with me? Something to do with that journalist, I suppose?"

"We need to establish a connection in her mind between you and George," Frank told him, "Rather than between George and the Stonehouse family. I don't think she knows George's name other than as a fellow researcher into the Stonehouse family story. She's never met him. So the idea was that she should be induced to think that the man she will have seen at Cheltenham was your friend Frank Stanley and that his presence in the parade ring was because you had invited him, not because he was connected with the owner of the horse. Whether this set of suggestions will cause her to make the inferences and reach the conclusions that we're aiming for, remains to be seen, but she does seem to have given up, for now at least. We have more cards to play against her, if not."

"I am not even going to ask what is going on," Sam continued, "Because I know you won't tell me. So do please eat your breakfast and tell me how long you will be staying today. I have Merlin ap Rhys coming here for a schooling session with Katseye later this

282

morning, at which you would be welcome to join us. Katseye's owner, Mrs Crosland, will be here too."

The topic of conversation turned to the Sampfield Grange horses, not least because Lewis had entered the room to enquire what Mr Stanley would like for breakfast. When Lewis had departed to fetch the order of scrambled eggs and bacon, together with more coffee, Frank changed the subject.

"Your young relative, Ryan," he said, to Sam's surprise, "What do you know about him?"

"Ryan?" repeated Sam, "Well, he's the son of my Australian cousin Teddy Urquhart. I understand that he's fallen out somewhat with his father – 'gone off the rails' was the expression Teddy used, as I recall - and has decided to travel the world for a while. His father suggested to him that he might come here. He's a good horseman and he's done a fine job for us with Curlew Landings, getting the horse fit for some big races."

"When did you last see Ryan before this year?" asked Frank, taking a piece of cold toast from the slatted silver rack by the coffee pot.

"I have never seen him at all until he arrived here in October," Sam replied, slowly, setting down his cup, "But Teddy told me he was coming. Is there a problem, Frank?"

A pause in the conversation was enforced by the return of Lewis bearing the scrambled eggs and bacon carefully laid out on a white plate with a gold rim and carried on a large tray. Once Lewis had left them alone again, and the two men were confident that they had heard his footsteps disappearing along the polished wooden floor of the hall, Frank continued.

"I'm not sure whether there's a problem or not, Sam. Jackie tells me that Ryan lives with her and Kye in the staff cottage and that he calls you Mr Sampfield, as if he were a member of your staff. She and Kye have been assuming that it is a ploy on his part to avoid your quizzing him about family issues. Not unreasonable, in the circumstances, I suppose. Do you have any idea what form his apparent 'going off the rails' has taken?"

"Unfortunately, I can't help you there," Sam responded, thoughtfully, "Teddy didn't tell me, and it was hardly the kind of topic which I could introduce with Ryan directly. I can try to find out more from Teddy or Tessa, Ryan's mother, when we next speak. But I really can't imagine what a young stranger from the outback of Australia could be doing which would be of relevance to you, Frank."

"Neither can I," Frank told him, "We are just being very cautious, given the interest Jessica Moretti has shown in activities at Sampfield Grange. Jackie, as you have now realised, is my eyes and ears on this matter, and she has simply done her job by reporting her concerns to me."

"I can see that I shall have to be careful what I say when she is around," mused Sam, not entirely happy with the news that Jackie was in communication with Frank Stanley about his staff, particularly one who was a member of his family.

"Jackie is only looking out for everyone's best interests," replied Frank, obliquely, "She has a job to do, as do I. Thank you for breakfast, Sam. I must leave now, so, regretfully, I will miss Katseye's schooling session. I will arrange to ride with you again soon – genuinely. I have enjoyed revisiting some of our old hacking routes again."

"You are always welcome at Sampfield Grange, as you know, Frank," replied Sam, shaking Frank's outstretched hand, "You could join me for some drag hunting, too, if you have the time."

Alerted by the opening of the breakfast room door, Lewis was quickly ready with Frank's coat and hat, which had been carefully placed on the hall stand earlier in the day by Jackie. Passing the neatly decorated Christmas tree in the main hall, Frank left the house by the heavy front door, which creaked on its long iron hinges, its outside face attractively adorned by Kelly with a large festive wreath.

Kye and Jackie watched silently from the stable yard as Frank Stanley climbed into his mud spattered four wheel drive vehicle and turned it quickly out through the gateposts to move down the lane towards the main road. Ryan had disappeared into the cottage and they were alone for the first time since before breakfast.

"So what's going on Jax?" asked Kye, in an unfriendly voice, "Yez working for Mr Stanley are yez? A bizzy are yez, then?"

"I'm here to keep an eye on you, Kye," Jackie said, ignoring his tone, "And you'd better get used to it. You think those drug dealers are going to leave you alone, after what you did? Maybe you fooled them into thinking you had a lucky escape that day, but then again maybe you didn't. Mr Stanley doesn't want them getting a hold over you again. And I'm not a bizzy. I work in personal protection. I'm a bodyguard."

"Why should Mr Stanley care about me?" snapped Kye, walking away, and calling back over his shoulder, "And I don't need a bodyguard either."

Jackie remained standing alone as Kye stamped off into the feed room. She had a soft spot for this lost young man to whom Frank Stanley and Isabella Hall had wanted to give a chance of a respectable career. After all, she herself had benefited from similar support. But she couldn't tell Kye that she now had more things on her mind than whether Bronz and Sheryl might try to get their hooks into him again, nor even whether he might say something to them, or anyone else, to betray the secrets of Isabella Hall.

What was really troubling her was why Ryan Urquhart was travelling on someone else's passport. Either that, or he was not Ryan Urquhart at all.

28

The early January weather had been uncharitable to Wales and the West of England. An area of low pressure in the North Atlantic had brought a mass of cold air sweeping down from the North West across the Welsh mountains and into central and southern parts of England. The Welsh National at Chepstow, which had been won for the second year in succession by Alto Clef, had luckily escaped the wintry deluge by a few days, whilst Cheltenham racecourse had been covered with several inches of snow only the day after the successful completion of its New Year's Day meeting. Race meetings at Hereford and Bangor-on-Dee had been abandoned and Wincanton racecourse was keeping its metaphorical fingers crossed for an improvement by the weekend.

Sampfield Grange lay comatose under a deep blanket of white snow. The fence posts alongside the entrance lane were capped with sparkling white mounds dripping like thick icing sugar in the bright sun which belatedly shone from an unclouded and pale blue sky. Alongside the wide and frost-laden entrance gates, the thinner tree branches had been bent earthward under the unaccustomed weight of their freezing load and were struggling slowly skyward again as their melting burden turned gradually into water.

The usual sounds of the orderly stable yard were muffled, not least because the staff had put on woollen hats and gloves, with protective scarves covering their mouths. Few of the young work riders had joined them that day. The lanes between Sampfield Grange and the conurbations of Charlton and Warnock were filled with deep snow underpinned by a layer of treacherous ice. Tractors taking feed and hay to the outdoor animals had churned up many of the pristine white surfaces, exposing the residual slush to the freezing air and allowing it to solidify into an impromptu and uneven skidpan for unwary motorists. Even had the youthful riders been able to travel, perhaps in a parental four by four, there was nowhere for the Sampfield Grange horses to be ridden, the gallops having been completely buried beneath a thick, cold carpet.

Sam stared restlessly from the wide drawing room window at the unusually attractive winter scene. The garden hedge glittered prettily in the sunlight as a lone robin hopped quickly across the lawn, leaving stick-like little footprints over the top layer of the shaded and still crisp section of snow. Beyond the boundary of the house garden, the uplands behind the half-buried back wall of the garage had taken on an alpine appearance, the surface of the snow covered track as yet unbroken by ugly footprints or other evidence of human or equine activity. The resident bulbs and corms were still tucked safely under the ground, ready to send out their new shoots in the ensuing weeks. Meanwhile, the regular line of trackside trees stood rigid like frozen sentinels, overseeing the magically changed scene, their windward sides evenly plastered with bright frozen snow. The cold and empty sky was silent, such local birds as had dared to venture forth having congregated in the Sampfield Grange kitchen garden, where Kelly had placed liberal food supplies on the wooden bird table and the steely cold circular surface of the snow clad sundial.

It was nine o'clock in the morning, and the movement of the world had come to a calm and empty halt. It was a good day on which to finalise the plans for the horses.

"I'm entering Curlew in the Kingwell Hurdle next," Sam told Merlin, using his mobile phone so as to avoid leaving his pleasant position at the ornamental Italian writing desk by the drawing room window, "He came out of the race on Boxing Day at Kempton Park very well and I can start Ryan working with him again once this spell of bad weather has ended."

Merlin, having no rides that day, had not planned to be up early, but longstanding habit had forced him into wakefulness, alone in his attic bedroom in Chepstow, as soon as the pale dawn had begun to assert itself in the East. He had brought a large mug of tea up from the kitchen and had been idly scanning the Racing Post on his iPad when Sam had called.

"Fair enough, Mr Sampfield," Merlin agreed, "'E was in pretty tough company in that race, so coming in second like 'e did was a good performance. I'm still confident for 'is chances in the Champion 'urdle, if 'e keeps sound."

"Fan Court's win in the Novices Chase was certainly worth watching too," Sam added, "It was an excellent notion of yours, Merlin, entering Curlew at Kempton Park on the same day as Fan Court. It was good to see Sadie there too and have her help with Curlew. Ranulph said he had decided to aim Fan Court at the Arkle Novices' Chase at the Cheltenham Festival now. That's two potential top rides in the diary for you already, Merlin. And there will probably be three soon, with Tabikat."

"Yes, what's the latest on Tabikat?" asked Merlin, mentally closing his ears to the unwelcome mention of Sadie's name. Apart from the necessary communication when leading Fan Court up in the parade ring and onto the course, Sadie had treated Merlin distantly and politely, as though they were casual acquaintances.

"Tabikat's still with the Meaghans," Sam replied, slightly defensively.

"Well, they did a great job winnin' the Chase at Leopardstown with Cormac Meaghan ridin' 'im just after Christmas. Shame I couldn't be there myself that day," Merlin went on, oblivious to Sam's tone, "The 'orse really seems to 'ave got the measure of Macalantern this season."

"The Meaghans are making the decisions rather than me, but I believe they have in mind the Festival Trials day at Cheltenham at the end of this month." Sam told him, firmly, "Then Tabikat comes to Sampfield Grange for the last few weeks before the Festival."

"And Katseye?" Merlin asked, "What are you doin' with 'im now? You thinkin' of 'avin a crack at one of the Novice 'urdles at the Festival? I think that 'orse 'as a lot more to come. We 'aven't got to the bottom of 'im yet, in my opinion. 'e may be better over a longer distance. And he's goin' to shape up well to go over fences in the future."

Sam, too, had been thinking along just those lines. Katseye's talent and quick progress had proved to be quite a revelation, although, considering the horse's bloodline on the sire's side, and the mysteriously hidden, but clearly classy, pedigree on the dam's side, perhaps this should not have been so unexpected a development. Night Vision, his well regarded sire, had had an impressive career both over hurdles and fences.

Katseye's previous successful performance in competitive Irish point to point races had also stood him in good stead. Following the frustrating incident in the race at Newbury at the beginning of the month, Sam had decided to run Katseye again at the same course at the meeting between Christmas and New Year, using the opportunity to experiment with a longer distance. After some thought, and following consultation with Eoghan Foley in Ireland, he had taken the gamble of entering the horse in the prestigious Challow Hurdle, knowing that he would come into the event as a rank outsider.

"I'm convinced that the form the horse has shown here so far is less than his true capability," Sam had told Eoghan Foley over the telephone when he had been considering the entry, "Winning those points in Ireland can't have been an easy ride for him."

"I will put my niece, Feanna, on the phone to you," Eoghan had responded, not having expressed any opinion one way or the other on the matter, "She is the one who has worked with the horse, and ridden him too, and she knows him better than anyone."

The quiet voice of Feanna, after she had introduced herself and listened carefully to what Sam had to say, had expressed confidence that Katseye was quite capable of performing well in top hurdling company either in the UK or in Ireland.

"He is a future superstar, to be sure, Mr Sampfield Peveril," Feanna had stated flatly, "It will do him the world of good to find himself with horses as good as he is. It will give him a proper challenge. Will Merlin ap Rhys be riding him again for you? My mother thought he did a good job, although she said his voice was far too loud."

"I'll tell Merlin to shout more quietly," Sam had responded, amused by the young woman's comment, "Although I am not sure he will take any notice. I suppose the horse has been used only to your voice when he's been racing. And his work rider here at home is female too."

"Katseye's a wonderful ride," Feanna had responded, wistfully, "Your work rider is a very lucky woman."

"You are always welcome to come here to ride Katseye whenever you want," Sam had assured her at once.

Katseye had indeed been one of the longest priced horses in the top class six runner race, and had defied the odds to run into a close third place only a length and a half behind the winner, an expensively purchased Lambourn trained horse. Spurred on by this success Sam had already provisionally entered Katseye in all three of the available Novices' Hurdle events at the Cheltenham Festival, deciding to leave it until nearer the time to decide which of them might prove the most suitable.

Stevie Stone had been in the parade ring at Newbury on the day of Katseye's race, Jayce and a chatty Tabby Cat having tipped Katseye to the Smart Girls as a good each way bet.

"Feanna did not want them to sell the horse," Stevie Stone had told Sam, by way of explanation, when Sam had taken the opportunity of Meredith Crosland's absence to ask Stevie about the Foleys' decision to sell what was clearly a top quality racehorse to a private home, "And she certainly does not want him to go to yet another owner. Perhaps you should offer to buy him yourself, Mr S-P."

Bringing his thoughts quickly back to the present conversation, Sam told Merlin of his plans to run Katseye on Festival Trials day at Cheltenham at the end of the month, in the same race in which Curlew Landings had competed the previous season.

"That's fine, Mr Sampfield," Merlin responded, "And will that Miss Foley you told me about be joining us there? She must be very 'appy to see her 'orse doin' so well."

Sam recognised that Merlin probably had reasons, other than their joint interest in the horse, for hoping to make the acquaintance of Feanna Foley, whose comments he had reported to Merlin at Newbury. It had become evident, both to Sam and to Ranulph Dicks, that Sadie no longer appeared to be interested in Merlin's company. On those occasions on which Sam had seen Sadie over the last two months, at local hunt meets and point to point meetings, she had invariably been accompanied by an attentive Luke Cunningham. Sadie, it appeared, had been doing well riding the Dicks horses but Sam wondered how things would develop once Amelia Dicks returned home in February. For his own part, he would be more than happy for Sadie to ride his own pointers once she was back at Sampfield Grange, but he wondered whether the horses of the Cunningham establishment, not to mention the son of the owner, might now prove more attractive to her.

Deciding to go down to the yard, Sam stood up from his position at the reading desk, not noticing that the cable of the tall lamp by his chair was trailing untidily across the polished boards of the floor. Catching his foot in the cable, he brought the elderly lamp down with a heavy crash onto the bookshelves at the side of the room, directly striking the heavy wooden shelf on which the useless and neatly dusted video cassettes were stacked. The plastic boxes in their cardboard sleeves cascaded chaotically from their storage space as the lamp struck them, sliding to the floor in scattered groups of twos and threes, some shooting across the polished floor beneath the furniture.

"Damn it!" swore Sam crossly, not quite under his breath, kneeling down to retrieve the dispersed objects.

Picking the bulky cassettes up, Sam started to pile them haphazardly onto the coffee table, intending to tell Kelly that they needed to be tidied away again into their usual orderly place on the shelf. The fallen lamp appeared to be unbroken, he noticed, but the thick parchment shade had been damaged and would need to be replaced. As he quickly stacked the cassettes, Sam could not help but pause as he noticed their labels. Even with the disadvantage of dyslexia, the words on them were so familiar that he had no difficulty in reading them. Memories of his mother's eventing triumphs, names of horses they had trained together, prizes awarded by his father to aspiring junior riders, an elderly dog which had died in his arms when he was a child, the construction work to replace the Victorian yard buildings with the present equine facilities, all jumped back into his mind like old photographs suddenly unearthed in all their original clarity.

Sam took a deep breath and sat down abruptly on the capacious sofa, staring at the pile of clumsy plastic tape cases in their cardboard shrouds. What on earth was the use of keeping all these important memories shut up in these cardboard packets? It would be interesting to see at least the best of them again, he thought, perhaps with Teddy and Tessa when they came to visit later in the year. Maybe even young Ryan would be interested in some of his family's history. But there was no machine available at Sampfield Grange on which to play these defunct cassettes in their obsolete format, the original video cassette player having been disposed of years ago when it had stopped working and could not be repaired. Perhaps it was possible even now to obtain a replacement. Sam decided that he would ask Lewis to find out.

Pushing the last of the fallen cassettes onto the heap on the coffee table, Sam noticed the corner of what looked like a piece of blue paper sticking out from the open side of one of the cardboard cases. Pulling it carefully out, Sam discovered that it was an envelope. He read with difficulty the words *To My Son James* written in black ink on the front. It was his mother's over-large and erratically formed handwriting.

Puzzled, Sam was about to open the mysterious envelope when the vibrant shrill of the house telephone echoed around the main hall outside the closed door. Sam stood and put the letter into his pocket, just as Lewis knocked to announce that Mrs Urquhart was calling from Australia.

"I'll speak to her from my study," Sam told the hovering Lewis, walking quickly across the hall.

Tessa Urquhart, in contrast to her husband, spoke at a normal volume and her first words were to assure Sam that his mother was well.

"Aunt Raldi's fine, James. She's away with the fairies, it has to be said, but she's loving helping us with the horses," Tessa told him, "Just like a kid with a new pony. The horses are right with her, too. Seem to know she's not the full quid any more. Don't you worry, James, she's as happy as a larrikin here and we all love having her back here in her old home."

Sensing from Sam's silence that he was not entirely happy to hear this news, which, in truth, painted a rosier picture of Raldi's state of health than was actually the case, Tessa pressed quickly onto other topics.

"Teddy and I were thinking of coming to the UK at the start of March," she went on, "To see the racing at Cheltenham. If you'll have us."

"Most certainly, it will be my pleasure," replied Sam, hastily gathering his thoughts together, "Young Ryan's still doing an excellent job for us here too, so he will be able to show you round the place and tell you all about our horses."

"That's good to know," Tessa said, after a pause, "We don't get to hear from him ourselves."

"Tell me, Tessa," Sam began, "Teddy said there had been some .. er .. difficulty with Ryan. Is it going to be uncomfortable for you to be here together?"

"No, probably a good thing for all of us," Tessa responded, stoutly, "He and Teddy need to talk. Teddy just couldn't hack Ry's news, that's all. Not the way Ry said it, anyway."

"News?" Sam asked.

"Yeah, Ry told Teddy he was gay," Tessa went on, "Teddy didn't handle it at all. Hit the bloody roof, in fact."

Sam was glad that he was sitting down. His stomach lurched upwards towards his ribs as he took in Tessa's words. Vomit rose in his throat and he had to swallow hard to stop himself retching.

"You still there, James?" Tessa asked.

"Yes, yes, of course, Tessa," Sam responded weakly, "I have a bit of a cold coming on at the moment. It must be all this bad weather we're having. Er .. has Teddy come to terms with Ryan's .. er .. news now?"

"Not sure," Tessa said, "It hit him like a bingle, you know, James. Ry didn't hold back. Just said it, right out. Then he went walkabout, as we say here."

Sam could afterwards remember very little of the subsequent conversation with Tessa during which the arrangements for her and Teddy's visit were discussed. Thumping through his head was the memory of his mother's words after she had found him and Frank as teenagers slumbering together one afternoon in a sunlit bedroom: no-one must know about your feelings for Frank, you have responsibilities to your family. His mother had said she would find him a suitable young woman, whilst Frank had been banished from Sampfield Grange, forever, as it had seemed then. No suitable young woman had ever been found, notwithstanding his mother's best efforts, and Sam had never seen Frank again until a little over a year ago when Frank had arrived so unexpectedly at Sampfield Grange on a fog-shrouded Autumn morning. Was this to be Ryan's fate too – a life of disappointed love and closely guarded secrets, not to mention losing the person most precious to him? Surely that was not necessary in this day and age? Was Teddy really so intolerant a parent?

As Sam sat staring silently out of the study window onto the snow-covered paddock, where the sheep were pulling at two half eaten bales of hay which had been put out for them, Lewis and Kelly were excitedly comparing notes in the Sampfield Grange kitchen.

Lewis had somehow failed to replace the receiver on the hall phone, and the conversation between Mr Sampfield and Mrs Urquhart had been audible to anyone standing nearby. And Lewis had, of course, been standing very nearby, ostensibly waiting to ask Mr Sampfield what should be done about the mess of cassettes and the damaged lamp which Lewis could see through the door of the drawing room.

"So that's what Mr Urquhart meant about Ryan going off the rails," whispered Kelly, her eyes like saucers, "Who'd have thought? He doesn't act gay. What do you think Mr Sampfield will do? Do you think he will be upset, like Mr Urquhart? Perhaps that's why Ryan doesn't want to stay in the house, in case Mr Sampfield finds out."

"Well, we can't tell Ryan that we know," Lewis chipped in, conspiratorially, "But let's ask Kye and Jackie whether they've noticed anything – you know – about him. He lives with them, after all."

Their interesting conversation was eventually interrupted by the appearance of Mr Sampfield himself in the kitchen on his way to the yard. Having described briefly to Kelly the accident to the lamp and the consequent scattering of the ancient video cassette collection, Sam turned to Lewis.

"I think it would be interesting for me to view some of those old recordings, Lewis,' he said, "Is it possible to obtain a machine on which to play them?"

"I think we could do better than that, Mr Sampfield," Lewis told him, confidently, "We can get them transferred onto a more modern medium, like a DVD, so you can watch them on our existing equipment."

"I see," said Sam, although not really understanding what Lewis meant, "Well, see what you can do, will you, Lewis? I'm going down to the yard to look in on the horses. There are plans to be made for them once this weather improves."

Sam would have been considerably more anxious about his plans for his horses had he known that, at that moment, Merlin ap Rhys was being questioned by the police on suspicion of involvement in the murder of a Liverpool sex worker called Lara Katz.

29

Unexpected development. Will call in later.

said the text message on George Harvey's mobile phone.

Standing with his back to the curved window overlooking the snow-covered village street, along which numerous children were slithering and sliding in the already dying sunlight, rarely used toboggans trailing behind them, George raised his eyebrows as he looked at his two companions.

"Something's happened, according to Frank," he told the other two occupants of the small and darkening room, "He'll be here later."

"Better make sure Lewis doesn't see him on the way, then," commented Isabella Hall, "Or that'll be all over the neighbourhood again. Do you need to discuss a change of plan? I'm just an observer on this one, but things don't seem to be working the way you wanted."

"Well, we don't know yet," TK Stonehouse interjected, from her usual perch on the arm of Isabella's chair.

"You said that nothing more's come through the Frossiac route since the accident," Isabella reminded her, "So, you don't know whether your man has even seen the accident report or listened to what Mr Ardizzone had to say at the press conference."

"Oh, believe me, he's seen it," George said, firmly, "It's been all over social media. Frank's people made sure of that."

"And what about the report of the death of Lara?" asked Isabella, "Has that gone public yet? That's a pretty big move in the plan if your assumptions about this whole business are correct."

"No, it isn't public yet," George told her, firmly, "Only the person who was threatening her has been given that information at the moment. I've no idea who that person is and whether it even affects our plans. Frank will tell us when he comes, I guess."

"Frank's got that scandalmonger woman from Stevie's old school off your case," TK pointed out, trying to change the subject, "So at least that's been a success. And we still have Meredith in reserve, if the obnoxious Jessica comes back again. We're going to have Meredith there anyway on Gold Cup day, just to be on the safe side."

Isabella sighed heavily, pushing the fringe of her now shoulder length hair away from her eyes. The drawn and haunted look which had characterised her face when she had worked at Sampfield Grange had all but gone, but traces of the stress could be seen in the occasional widening of her brown eyes and the slightly clipped tones in which she still sometimes spoke.

"I'm tired of all this hiding and pretence," Isabella announced, irritably, "Skulking about in disguise like a pantomime villain, driving miles away from here just to go for a bike ride or a run, attending that point to point meeting where Sadie was riding last month and having to make sure she didn't see me. If we really think this Jessica Moretti is off my case now, surely we could relax a bit? Even if Lewis and Kelly do find out I am in the area, surely they will think I have just resumed my fictitious love affair with Frank? Especially now Frank will be in the area more often."

"Let's see what Frank says," George replied, putting his hand on her shoulder, "But, for what it's worth, I agree. How did Sadie get on at the horse racing, anyway?"

"Well, she did very well, I thought, riding two of Ranulph Dicks's horses," Isabella mused, "And she was with a new man, not that arrogant Welsh wonder, Merlin ap Rhys, any more. It was someone a bit more up market, called Luke Cunningham – he's a point to point rider too. I recognised him from the time I went to Cuffborough races once. He's the son of Sir Andrew Cunningham, a friend of our Mr Sampfield, no less."

"And what about that drug dealer lad that Frank has had Jackie minding?" asked TK, still trying to steer the conversation away from Isabella's personal concerns, but remembering with quickly hidden discomfort that Kye, like the dead sex worker, had played his own role in the Liverpool vice scene.

"As far as I know," replied Isabella, "He's doing well as a conditional jockey. I've spotted him in a couple of races on TV. But he and Jackie have fallen out since Frank had to tell him who she really was a few weeks ago. And Frank and Jackie are both still not happy about that lad from Australia being at Sampfield Grange. That day you were riding at Sampfield Grange, George, when Frank called in here afterwards, he asked if I'd heard anything about the Australian relatives when I was there. But I hadn't. "

"We can ask Frank about all that too, when he gets here," George stated, "But if he's coming from Liverpool, he may be a while."

Frank Stanley, though, was not coming from Liverpool, but from Chepstow. Even so, it was dark by the time he arrived at the little stone cottage on the outskirts of the rural village of Warnock. TK and George had been to Old Warnock airfield and back in the time it had taken Frank to complete his journey, where little was happening for the simple and old fashioned reason that the runway was covered in snow and there was no equipment with which to clear it. The model aircraft flyers and the drone enthusiasts had remained at home, whilst the microlights and gyroplanes had stayed locked in the ancient wartime hangar.

Frank and Isabella were sitting opposite each other in the living room of the little cottage. An open bottle of Scotch whisky stood on the table between them, Isabella having on this occasion apparently agreed to share some of it with Frank.

"Well, what do you have to tell us," George asked Frank when they had all seated themselves around the table, TK having fetched herself a soft drink in preference to the whisky, "Which could not be said over the phone?"

"You are probably not going to believe this…." Frank began, slowly, "But the man who I was told was threatening Lara in the restaurant in Liverpool was none other than our Welsh jockey friend, Merlin ap Rhys."

Whatever news the three other occupants of the room had expected Frank to impart, this information was certainly not part of it. They remained silent as Frank related the story which Merlin ap Rhys had told the police who had come to his snow covered doorstep that morning.

Merlin had been annoyed to hear the loud and persistent banging at the street door, which had required him to descend from his comfortable billet in the attic room just when he had been about to call a local girlfriend to see if she fancied some fun with him, preferably indoors and out of the snow.

"All righ', I'm comin'," Merlin had shouted out crossly, as he had descended the wooden stairs in his bare feet, wearing only a pair of grey jogging bottoms, and had wrenched open the wooden door, "Why the 'ell are you makin' all this bloody racket?"

Even Merlin's muscle power had been insufficient to withstand the force of the pair of armed police officers who had pushed their way into the house, sending him flying backwards onto the tiled floor.

"What the fuck?" had yelled Merlin, as he had tried to get to his feet, "What the 'ell do you think you're doin'?"

"They're arresting you, Mr ap Rhys," had said a tall man clad in a black coat and brown fedora hat, who had been standing behind the two silent police officers, one of whom had been pointing a handgun at the recumbent and shocked Merlin, "Or at least they will do so if I tell them to."

"And 'oo the fucking' 'ell are you then?" had asked Merlin, defiantly. The demands of his chosen career meant that he was not as easily frightened as many people who found themselves in such a position might have been.

"Can we talk somewhere more suitable, please, Mr ap Rhys?" Frank Stanley had asked him, politely.

So, Merlin had led the three visitors into his living room and had learned that a Liverpool sex worker called Lara Katz had been found dead, probably murdered, the previous evening and that Merlin had been identified as a likely suspect.

"Me?" Merlin had exclaimed in bewilderment, "I was nowhere near Liverpool last night. I was 'ere. Racin' was all abandoned 'cause of the weather. 'oo said it was me, then?"

"We know that you know Miss Katz," Frank had told him, "Because you were seen and heard threatening her in a restaurant in Liverpool before Christmas. Why was that, Mr ap Rhys? Did someone pay you to do it?"

"Pay me?" had spluttered Merlin, beside himself with fury, "What do you think I am? I'm a bloody jockey, for God's sake! I'll tell you why I was angry with 'er. I thought she was bloody blackmailing me, and someone else, that's what."

"Blackmailing you? Tell me about that – the full story, from the beginning," Frank had requested him, carefully disguising his surprise at Merlin's answer. Frank had signalled to the two police officers to go out into the hall, whilst he and Merlin remained seated on the leather armchairs on either side of the unlit wood burner. Merlin had pulled on a faded blue T shirt which had been draped over the back of an upright chair in the corner.

And so Merlin had related the story: the receipt of the compromising pictures and video which had been sent to his phone, the discovery that they had been altered to show the face of a woman he had never met, his attempts to discover whether the woman Abigail Alvarez herself was involved in whatever was going on, his futile search for the elusive Lara, the eventual receipt of Lara's business card from Neil Weston, all leading to the meeting in the Hard Day's Night Hotel restaurant during which he had tried to get to the bottom of what was happening and had

301

been told about the apparent mix up with the alteration of the video recordings.

"And do you know what I found out?" Merlin had told Frank Stanley, his voice still unsteady with annoyance, "That woman, Abigail Alvarez, 'er 'usband, that footballer, was behind it all. Wanted the stuff sent to 'is phone with his wife's face on it. So that no-one could tell 'e'd really been with Lara. I suppose 'e was worried about phone 'ackin' and the gutter press getting 'old of it, I don' know. But my problem was that Lara's lot 'ad a fake video of me making it look like I was screwin' around with Santiago Alvarez's wife. That's why I was talkin' about blackmail. Maybe someone's been blackmailing that Abigail for all I know. This 'ole thing's cost me my relationship with my girlfriend, Sadie, too. She saw the video on my phone and walked out."

Merlin had paused for breath, but, before Frank could say any more, Merlin had asked, "What 'appened to that Lara, anyway? You said she was dead. Per'aps she was blackmailing someone else, someone 'oo didn't stop at just talkin' to 'er like I did."

"Did you know that you were being watched by a journalist at the Hard Day's Night Hotel, Mr ap Rhys?" asked Frank, ignoring Merlin's question.

"A journalist? No, I didn'," had spluttered Merlin, in response, "What was 'e doin' there? Looking for crap news, was 'e? Was it 'im who gave you my name?"

Frank Stanley had remained silent for some moments. Merlin, too, had by now run out of steam, and had sat with his head in his hands, shaking it from side to side as he looked at the floor.

"What a fuckin' mess," Merlin had muttered eventually.

"I am inclined to agree with you, Mr ap Rhys," had replied Frank Stanley, slowly.

"So what 'appens now?" had asked Merlin in a more normal voice, "I didn' 'ave nothin' to do with whatever 'appened to Lara. My sister Rhian an' 'er 'usband Thomas, they can tell you I was 'ere yesterday."

"I believe you, Mr ap Rhys," had said Frank Stanley, standing up, "What I am trying to decide now is whether I can trust you."

Frank Stanley's narrative stopped and he looked at the faces of his still stunned and attentive audience.

"Let me guess," Isabella spoke up, "This journalist who was following Merlin ap Rhys was our friend Jessica Moretti?"
"The very same," Frank replied, "Hoping for publishable scandal on Santiago and Abigail Alvarez by shadowing our friend Merlin. Jessica wasn't interested in Lara at all, although I imagine she might be now, if she found out that Mr Alvarez was one of Lara's clients."

"So what's the plan now with Lara?" asked George, "When is her death going to go public?"

"The Merseyside police will announce it in time for the evening news bulletins," Frank replied, firmly, "They will mention that all her clients, whose names and credit card details are known to the police from her company's records, will be contacted for questioning. They will also be asking for information about a man with whom she was seen arguing in the Hard Day's Night Hotel restaurant on a specific date in December."

"But I thought you just said that Merlin was not a suspect," Isabella objected.

"I did," Frank replied, "But we are the only people who know that. Anyone else taking an interest in the case will be very keen to find out who he is. And I don't just mean tabloid journalists and internet trolls."

"But you could be putting him in terrible danger," TK exclaimed, "What if our man finds out who he is?"

"That's the idea," Frank replied shortly.

"And Merlin's agreed to this?" asked George, astonished.

"With some conditions," Frank Stanley told them, "Firstly, that we expose Santiago Alvarez's dirty secret and secondly that we help him get back his former girlfriend, Sadie Shinkins, who I'm told works at Sampfield Grange. "

"I can't believe it," Isabella whispered, "Perhaps the selfish little so and so has some moral values after all."

"Merlin's a young man still and actually quite courageous, I should say," Frank said to her, curtly, "Just because his personal life may not meet with your approval doesn't mean his willingness to help us should be refused."

As Frank spoke, his mobile phone shrilled in his jacket pocket, stopping Isabella from making the curt reply which had risen to her lips. Lifting the phone to his ear, Frank listened for a few moments, whilst his companions watched him anxiously.

"Well," he said, as he pressed the button to end the call, "Lara's death may not have been necessary, after all. Someone has just launched a denial of service cyber attack on Ardua Industrie S.p.A. All of their systems are down."

"And what does the attacker want?" asked George, already knowing the answer.

"The Asrak Mark 2 source code," replied Frank, "As installed and fully commissioned in the Altior 10."

30

The flight deck screens had been dark, except for one. That screen had been lit with a lurid red light.

FUCK YOU EGZON it had said.

Egzon Paloka's ugly, bloated corpse had been removed by the time Dominik Katz had been given access to the windowless and foetid basement room in which the younger of the two Paloka brothers had spent the last months of his worthless life. Closeted in semi darkness, hunched in a reinforced chair before the bank of computer screens which had represented his earthbound flight deck, Egzon had spewed evil across the internet connected world, ostensibly for the material benefit of the Paloka criminal empire, but also to satisfy his own taste for online combat and destruction. Even at a time when his swollen body might have still been capable of it, Egzon would never have dared to engage in a physical fight. But in the virtual world, he had been a ruthless and highly skilled opponent.

His brother Aleksander, who had taken over the Palokas' vicious business empire following the death in prison of their father, Konstantin, had not cared for Egzon, but he had found Egzon's skills more than useful. Like his father before him, Aleksander had been motivated by the opportunities afforded by technology to further the illegal pursuit of power and riches. So, Egzon had continued his work with the dark web to create avenues through the ethernet to support the family's evil trade in depravity: pornography, paedophilia, online blackmail, drug dealing, arms trading, people trafficking and anything else through which they could exploit the weak, the vulnerable, the desperate, and the unsuspecting. This work had been, to Egzon, uninteresting, but the ever-escalating battle which he had watched being fought between cyber criminals such as himself and the various government agencies determined to defeat them had fascinated him. Here had been a true life conflict in which he could use his well honed skills to square up to the best minds in the world, and all without moving from his seat.

Egzon had particularly enjoyed the challenge of developing complex security devices, not only to protect the Paloka systems and prevent their detection by the forces ranged against him, but to attack with virtual weapons the systems of his opponents. Egzon, had he been a decent man, would have been one of the world experts in cyber security. But now Egzon was dead. It had appeared that one of his cyber opponents had succeeded in defeating him. The message from the successful attacker had been plain to see on the single working screen, and the shock had been more than Egzon's overstrained and diseased cardiovascular system could bear.

Aleksander had not missed his brother. There had been plenty of techno nerds within the Paloka empire eager to take Egzon's grubby place, and they had not hesitated to put themselves forward to their new boss. Aleksander had chosen two of them. One of them had been set to work on the re-creation and renewed protection of Egzon's former responsibilities for online crime whilst the other had been assigned responsibility for the specific task of discovering who had perpetrated the successful cyber attack against the Paloka empire. This second individual was now dead, as was Aleksander himself. Whatever had been discovered about the successful attacker had clearly enabled this still unknown figure, or the organisation which controlled him or her, to destroy Aleksander as well as his younger brother.

Dominik Katz was the former of the two individuals selected by Aleksander and he was still very much alive. In his first hours in his coveted new role, he had sat on Egzon's reinforced chair, apparently making an assessment of where and how he was going to start work, but in reality considering how best he could use the task he had been given as his impatiently awaited chance to pursue a long anticipated campaign of his own. Dominik had not needed to learn how Egzon's systems worked. He had been acquainted with Egzon and his work for a long time, and many of Egzon's defence systems had been designed with the assistance of Dominik Katz.

Dominik Katz, pale skinned and bespectacled, had once been an ordinary and law abiding young man. Along with the other members of his clever family, he had owned a technology company, Katz:i d.o.o., based in Rijeka in Croatia. Dominik himself had specialised in cyber security applications, designed not only to protect his own company's systems from external online attacks, but offered as part of the business itself, providing advisory services and expertise to other organisations. The original company had been set up by Dominik's father, Isak Katz, as a watch and clock making business. The proprietor's name and initial had later been reversed so as to reflect the image of the new and evolving technology business in the digital era. It had been Isak's father, Leonid, who had first brought his young family to Rijeka, his ancestors having fled the Russian pogroms. Hidden and protected by local Croatians during the Nazi Holocaust, the family had survived this latest and most merciless threat to their wish for a peaceful existence and had continued through the subsequent political upheavals to strive to be successful and hard working members of their adopted community.

The era of the internet and online trading had brought new threats to the Katz family's desire for a quiet existence. Physically fleeing from countries where threats and adversity were to be found was no longer enough. Persecution, abuse, theft and deception could now be perpetrated from afar against any business, group or individual. Dominik's quickly acquired expertise in cyber security and encryption had been a legitimate and profitable response to the rising threats faced by all businesses now relying on an online trading presence.

Isak Katz and his wife had produced two children. Dominik had been the elder and his sister Lara had followed a year later. Lara too had inherited her fair share of the family's sharp intelligence, not to mention ancestral Russian beauty, and, under Isak's tutelage, had become a junior chess prodigy, competing successfully all over Europe, as well as being an outstanding mathematician. At the age of seventeen she had left Rijeka to study mathematics at the University of Cambridge in England. And it was whilst Lara was in England that fortune had once again begun to turn against the remaining members of the Katz family.

The first step towards the destruction of Isak's hitherto successful business had been the signing of a contract with a company in Italy called Ardua Industrie S.p.A. The original agreement had been a simple one, to provide consultancy and software services for the security of Ardua's systems. The Ardua specification had been rigorous, as the company was engaged in the development of fly by wire avionics, some of which were likely to have military applications. Most specifically, in terms of what was required to be protected from cyber attacks, were the associated flight control systems which would incorporate Artificial Intelligence.

Moving further forward in their business relationship, the two companies had signed a subsequent contract, which had been much more complex and had involved the active contribution by Dominik himself to the work of Ardua Industrie. This work had led to the eventual development of a fibre optic fly by wire system which had become known as Katz:i. In return for Dominik's work, Ardua Industrie, a family owned company headed by the charismatic Arturo Ardizzone, had made a major investment in Katz:i d.o.o, enabling the previously small specialist company to expand the scope of its business into new and hitherto untapped areas and to become a significant employer in its home town.

The second step in the process had come about two years later, as a result of an economic downturn, which had been no-one's fault, but which Isak, now out of his depth in managing the expanded company, had failed to anticipate. Although Arturo Ardizzone had assisted in bailing out the overstretched enterprise, it had eventually collapsed, leaving hundreds of staff out of work and a large number of unpaid debts. Refused further help from his main investor and unable to raise finance elsewhere, Isak had accepted an offer from Arturo Ardizzone to buy the failed company out from bankruptcy and, having dealt with the debts, to make it part of the Ardua Industrie group. Isak and his wife had then slipped into a relieved retirement in a nearby picturesque seaside resort, whilst Dominik had become an employee of Ardua Industrie.

Far from being grateful for this solution to his family's latest problems, Dominik had bitterly resented his enchainment, as he saw it, to the business of Arturo Ardizzone. Had this man not approached his father's company in the first instance and allowed it to expand into something his cautious parent could not easily manage, then Dominik would have inherited a sound family business to develop in the way he, rather than an interloper, saw fit. As it was, Dominik was now working for someone else, a stranger, who stood to make a lot of money from the innovative aviation technology applications of which Dominik himself had been entirely, or so he convinced himself, the inventor.

Had Dominik's sister been in Rijeka, she might have stemmed the furious resentment which had begun to eat into Dominik's mind. Lara might have pointed out to him that he had been only one cog in the large machine which had developed the advanced avionics software for Ardua Industrie. Lara would have contradicted Dominik when he had insisted that the associated Artificial Intelligence developments were his sole work and that he, and he alone, actually owned the Ardua Industrie technological products. But Lara had been far away, now completing a PhD at the University of Liverpool, where she had been recruited to a research team headed by her former tutor at Cambridge.

With this reasoning in his enraged mind, Dominik had seen it as no more than his moral right when he had downloaded onto his own IT system the entire source code to all the Katz:i software and had left only a subtly corrupted version sitting within the Ardua Industrie computers. The subtle corruption had been lethal. As soon as one of Ardua staff had logged on for work the following morning, a powerful virus had immediately activated itself and destroyed most of the company's IT capability as well as the majority of the Katz:i application itself. When Dominik Katz had been contacted for help by one of the senior staff of the panicked IT Director, Dominik had been nowhere to be found. Dominik had vanished.

Once the full extent of the problem had been discovered, Arturo Ardizzone had been required to report it to the government authorities who had been his clients for the plundered software application. This had led to the transfer of the work to Astrak Avionics plc in Cheltenham in the UK. But Astrak's hands were tied. Without access to the Katz:i original source code, together with the discovery that what little code they could access was corrupt, there was a limit to what they could immediately do to help.

Whilst the CEO of Astrak Avionics was explaining this unpalatable fact to the authorities who had commissioned the work, Dominik had relocated himself to Tirana in Albania to become part of the criminal empire of the Paloka family. Egzon Paloka had long been one of his respected cyber adversaries and Dominik had had no difficulty obtaining a position in Egzon's malign operation, now using his expertise against the very systems which he had himself designed to protect the IT integrity of businesses around the world. Dominik had naturally done a good job for the Paloka family and his loyal service had quickly been recognised.

Working his way up the greasy pole of his corrupt new environment had required Dominik to ignore many things which shocked and appalled him. But his burning hatred of Arturo Ardizzone had convinced Dominik that anything he did was justified in order to achieve his objective of revenge. Dominik's assiduous monitoring of the activities of Ardua Industrie had soon informed him that Astrak Avionics had been engaged to recreate the Katz:i system under the Astrak name. Dominik had been sure that this would not be a simple task, but, having researched the new supplier, he had learned that Astrak was a company well capable of developing fly by wire software supported by Artificial Intelligence, not least because it was benefiting from consultancy services from a team from the University of Liverpool which included someone he knew very well.

That person was Dr Lara Katz, Dominik's sister. Dr Lara Katz represented Dominik's weak spot, because it was she who had provided expert advice to Katz:i d.o.o. to support the development work he himself had done. If anyone could help Astrak Avionics to recreate the destroyed software application, it was Lara. Lara's eidetic memory and associated perfect recall abilities would render useless his efforts to destroy and corrupt the advanced avionics software application. Astrak would not need to develop anything of its own. The Astrak developers could simply copy it from the information held in Lara's brain.

Dominik's fears on this score had, though, been quickly allayed when he had learned from an announcement on the Ardua Industrie website that Dr Lara Katz was not to be advising Astrak, as she had left the research group, her previous association with the failed company Katz:i d.o.o having, it was said, created an insurmountable conflict of interest. In vain had Dominik attempted to contact his sister, thinking that perhaps she would want to play a part in his own plans for a different future for the valuable software application as well as his planned revenge on Arturo Ardizzone.

But Lara too had vanished. Sending numerous electronic web spies out into the ether, Dominik had waited for one of them to unearth some trace of her in the virtual world. And eventually one terrible day, one of the spies had reported in, telling him that Lara Katz had been found.

When he had looked at the information he had been sent, Dominik had been sure that there had been a mistake. His sister had become a sex worker, it had appeared, albeit a rather classy one with her own online business. But there had been no doubt about it. Once he had successfully hacked into the expertly protected website, he had viewed a picture of her on the webpage of the company, unimaginatively called Lara's Services. It had been a few years since he had seen his clever sister, and in the picture she had looked older and somehow sadder, her face thinner and lavishly made up.

These were the depths to which Arturo Ardizzone had reduced his family, Dominik had raged silently, striking the desktop in his fury. He himself was working for a criminal empire whose disgusting activities he had done his best to ignore in the face of his own personal objectives, and now his sister had become a common prostitute.

So, as soon as Dominik had been finally sitting in Egzon's vacated seat, he had considered that he had free rein, perhaps even a moral right, to begin to exact retribution on Arturo Ardizzone.

Dominik's initial actions had been experimental. Ferreting through the tangled tunnels of Egzon's presence in the dark web, he had sought out routes through which he could start his work. A useful one had soon made itself visible, although Dominik could not readily see for what purpose Egzon might have previously used it. It appeared to be a safe route through legitimate business websites in Italy, eventually ending with a small and apparently unprotected personal computer in a small shop in a remote part of rural France. Dominik had decided to try the route out for size, and so, one April evening, he had placed a fake report of an accident to Ardua Industrie's best selling light aircraft, the Altior 10, which had been used in the initial test flights with the Katz:i system on board, on the website of an Italian news radio station in Italy and had waited to see what would happen. A few days later, for good measure, he had, through the same route, inserted a similar fake report onto the website of the Bureau d'Enquetes at d'Analyses pour la Securite de l'Aviation in France.

In the event, nothing much had happened, other than that the reports had been removed, but, Dominik had been gratified to see, not quickly enough to stop references to them appearing in the list of results produced by commercial online search engines on such topics as Ardua Industrie, Astrak Avionics, and Altior 10 aircraft. These references, many posted by well-intentioned environmentally concerned organisations, clearly implied that the accident was attributable to some fault with the aircraft's unique fibre optic fly by wire flight control system. None of the many Altior 10 aircraft in normal use by General Aviation pilots around the world was even equipped with the experimental system, but the general public and potential clients of Ardua Industrie did not know that.

Emboldened by this small success, Dominik had next attempted something more ambitious. Knowing that the Katz:i software was being redeveloped in England, and guessing correctly that the Altior 10 would continue to provide the flight test environment, he had decided that England was the next place to strike. According to the aviation charts, the nearest airfield to the town of Cheltenham, where Astrak Avionics plc was based, was Gloucestershire Airport. Using his knowledge of the nature and scope of the early test flights, Dominik had searched the charts for a suitable airfield on which to stage a fake and fatal accident to a fictitious aircraft. The chosen airfield had to be within 80 nautical miles of the apparent departure point of Gloucestershire Airport. The facility should not be in commercial use or equipped with any type of air traffic control or advisory service, nor with aviation navigation or landing aids. It should preferably offer the challenge of local airborne obstacles, such as drones and model aircraft, which the Artificial Intelligence in the software application would have to be able to detect and avoid. Dominik had identified and discarded three possible locations on the aviation chart, and had selected one after viewing each of them carefully using a satellite imaging application. The selected location had been called Old Warnock airfield, which was about 60 nautical miles to the South of Cheltenham.

The carefully researched fake report had appeared in May, the accident itself having been said to have taken place several months previously. As had happened in the cases of the earlier, less comprehensive efforts, this report had been quickly removed from the UK Air Accidents Investigation Board website, but, once again, not before it had done its damage by being reported in the press. But this report had been more of a challenge to the authorities in the UK. It had specifically mentioned the Astrak Avionics onboard system in a Mark 1 version. This report had been intended by Dominik to provoke a response.

The response had, though, been puzzling to Dominik. For several months, once again, nothing had happened. The disintegration of the Paloka empire following the death of Aleksander had occurred over the same period of time, and so had necessitated some care on Dominik's part to watch his back as the controller of the systems supporting the Paloka online activities, whilst inferior lieutenants fought amongst themselves to move into the criminal space which Aleksander had vacated.

Dominik's fake air accident report had, as before, been routed through Egzon's wormhole, the label he had mentally given to the little outlet through Frossiac. Eventually, at the end of the summer, Dominik had discovered that a watching device had been newly placed into the little French computer. Dominik had poked at the device for a while, fearing that some kind of sabotage was planned, but the little bug was harmless. It had appeared to have no purpose other than to let Dominik know that it was there.

Whoever had installed the listening device, Dominik had concluded, evidently knew that the French computer was the source of the fake reports. But did the person know the source of the virtual route through which the reports had reached the host computer? A suspicion had begun to take shape in his mind. If the cocaine-addled colleague who had been charged by Aleksander to discover the means by which Egzon's systems had been destroyed had been alive, Dominik would have shared his suspicions with him, but it was too late. The more he thought about it, the more Dominik was sure. The person who had placed the little sentinel on the computer was the same person who had attacked and destroyed Egzon. The apparently useless route to France may have been created by Egzon, but Egzon himself had used it only once. The second time it had been used had been by Egzon's opponent, and then it had been to send a lethal ninja bomb into the heart of the Paloka systems.

Whoever was looking at what Dominik was doing was the same person who had gone up against Egzon. And won. Now that same person was letting Dominik know that he or she knew all about Dominik too.

Whether the unknown opponent was connected with Astrak Avionics or Ardua Industrie, Dominik could not fathom. Undecided as to what to do next, he waited. His patience was rewarded by the appearance in the online news of what seemed at first to be a real accident to an Altior 10 aircraft at Old Warnock airfield, quickly followed by an initial published report. When he read the report, Dominik could see at once that it bore the hallmarks of a fake. His own phraseology from the May report had been copied and, most brazenly, the onboard flight software was now described as the Mark 2 version of Astrak's new system. So, his opponent was letting him know that the system was progressing in its re-development. What was more, it appeared that the report had been routed to the press by the opponent via Egzon's wormhole, as if the opponent were taunting Dominik.

Dominik had listened with cold and mind-numbing fury to the lies of Arturo Ardizzone broadcast at the ensuing press conference. Arturo Ardizzone had made it clear that he believed Katz:i d.o.o. were crooks who had swindled him, even referring to what Dominik knew was non-existent legal action.

Dominik understood now that he had a fight on his hands.

31

By the end of January, the questioning of Merlin ap Rhys by the police in relation to the murder of sex worker Lara Katz had become old news.

Providing information to the police to assist them in a murder enquiry was fortunately not amongst the offences which might justify a suspension of Merlin's license by the British Horseracing Authority. Notwithstanding the gossip and lurid speculation the incident had attracted from some quarters, Merlin's normal riding activities had continued uninterrupted by anything other than the weather and a minor injury during January. Sam's initial concern at the unwelcome possibility of Merlin being suspended had led him to contact the BHA directly for clarification, after he had tried and failed to grapple with the dense printed detail of the Rule Book. If Mr ap Rhys wished to use the paid services of an escort agency, Sam had been told, that was a matter entirely for Mr ap Rhys.

Less fortunate than Merlin had been Santiago Alvarez. The police had methodically contacted all the clients listed in Lara's excellently maintained computerised payment records. Santiago, like Merlin, had had an unassailable alibi for the date and time of Lara's death, as he had been playing in a televised match for his Premier Division club, and could not therefore be considered a suspect. Oddly, though, the fact that he had been questioned appeared to have somehow been leaked to the press. The PR department at his prestigious club, which had old fashioned roots and a strong family tradition, had been besieged with complaints and questions, whilst reporters and paparazzi had made camp outside the gated mock Tudor residence which the player shared with his wife Abigail. The football club itself had decided, reluctantly, to keep its expensively purchased star striker off the pitch for a few games, until the immediate furore associated with the murder had died down, and, with any luck, the murderer had been identified and arrested.

But instead the scandal had got worse. A hack reporter called Jessica Moretti had received from an anonymous source a DVD which had contained two recordings of a naked Santiago Alvarez having somewhat unconventional sex with a woman in a hot tub. The two recordings were identical, other than in one respect. In one of them, the face of the woman sharing the activity in the tub was Santiago's wife Abigail, and in the other the same woman's face was that of Lara Katz. It had not taken the technonerds at Hornblower Online long to establish that the recording showing Lara's face was the original and that it had been altered to make the woman appear to be Abigail.

The contents of the DVD, expertly put together by Merlin's cousin Bryn from an original supplied through Frank Stanley, had solved a mystery which had puzzled Jessica for a long time. Hornblower's persistent hacking of Santiago Alvarez's mobile phone and home computer had produced many recordings of Santi enjoying sex with his wife, but not a single one of him in consort with anyone else. The fact that the salacious material might have been doctored by Santiago Alvarez, or someone working on his behalf, to show his wife's face had not occurred even to the suspicious Jessica. She had not thought the louche footballer to have so much grey matter between his ears, and was furious at being so easily outwitted.

Vengeance on Jessica's part had been both quick and effective. In the face of the efforts of the Alvarez family lawyers, Hornblower Online had quickly published the damning material, and the social media outlets of the world and their associated trolls had taken it up with lascivious enthusiasm. Randy Santi had been internationally and publicly vilified, and was now being expensively divorced by his cruelly deceived wife. Disciplinary action was being taken by his employer for gross misconduct and for bringing the Premier League club into disrepute.

Although a one-way journey home to Argentina had potentially beckoned for Santiago, his club, with an eye to its future profits, had remained keen to retain his valuable goal scoring services, and had eventually decided to punish him only with a substantial fine and further period of suspension. Reprehensible though his behaviour towards his wife had been, there were many who sympathised with the player's desire to protect himself from illegal hacking by the gutter press of his mobile phone and home computer system. And, the person with whom he had committed the adultery appeared to have been a prostitute who had presumably been party to the deception and was now dead.

Merlin thought that the arrogant and duplicitous Santiago Alvarez had got off lightly. He felt sorry for the footballer's wife, and fervently hoped that her horse Penalty Kick would provide her with some racing fun during the grim time before the press found itself fresh victims to persecute. After the initial flurry of accusatory reporting, he himself had been largely left alone, thanks mainly to the fact that the now uninteresting story of Lara's Katz's unsolved murder had completely disappeared from the news media.

Someone else who thought that Santiago Alvarez had got off lightly was Jessica Moretti. Jessica could not get out of her mind the unexpected meeting which she had witnessed between Merlin ap Rhys and Lara Katz, a meeting which had ended in an argument. She was convinced that the full story of the relationship between Santiago Alvarez and Lara Katz had not yet been uncovered. Jessica had considered, and quickly discounted, the possibility that Lara had been providing a similar service to Merlin ap Rhys as she had to Santiago Alvarez. Merlin was unmarried and insufficiently famous, as far as outfits like Hornblower Online and its like were concerned, to be a target for hacking. Merlin's former girlfriend, though, had clearly seen something which had caused her to believe that Merlin was having an affair with Abigail Alvarez. Was there more to this video faking business than Santiago simply protecting his own reputation? Was he also trying to implicate his wife by creating fake recordings and pictures of her having sex with other men? This would certainly have enabled him to return with interest any accusations by her of adultery on his part, concluded Jessica. Was it Santi's insurance against Abigail discovering his infidelity? And had Merlin somehow found out that his face was being used to perpetrate this deception and confronted Lara about it in the restaurant that evening?

Jessica had resolved to keep an eye on Merlin. She felt in her bones that there was interesting material yet to be discovered.

Merlin had been booked to ride Katseye at Cheltenham's Festival Trials day. Brendan Meaghan had already confirmed that Merlin would keep the ride on Tabikat, who was being brought over to run in the Gold Cup Trial Chase at the same meeting, whilst Ranulph Dicks had decided that Merlin would continue to partner Fan Court in the two mile Novices Chase.

Merlin's planned visit to Sampfield Grange during January had been eagerly awaited by Lewis and Kelly. The relatively trivial gossip about Ryan turning out to be gay had been entirely eclipsed by the apparent involvement of the star jockey, who was Sadie's ex-boyfriend into the bargain, in a murder enquiry. Sadie was to remain working at the Dicks yard until the middle of February, and had been stubbornly unresponsive when her opinion on Merlin's involvement with the sordid case had been sought, but Kelly knew that her sister would be unable to avoid Merlin when he rode Mr Dicks's Fan Court at Cheltenham races at the end of the month. Merlin himself had been equally tight lipped during his schooling sessions with Curlew Landings and Katseye, as both Ryan and Kye had confirmed in the face of relentless interrogation of them by Lewis. Only Jackie had offered the more sympathetic comment that Merlin must be having a tough time and needed to be left alone to get on with his job.

Approaching the brick buildings of the Cheltenham racecourse stables, Sam was pleased to see the red haired figure of Declan Meaghan walking towards him. Sam had not yet met Declan face to face but recognised him from the television coverage of race meetings in Ireland.

Introducing himself and shaking the younger man's hand, Sam said enthusiastically,

"I'm very much looking forward to seeing Tabikat again. You have been having a lot of success with him recently, I know. How confident are you for today?"

"Tabikat's in good order, to be sure, Mr Sampfield," Declan told him, promptly, "And we're in with a good chance today. But, we have a different problem which I need to mention to you."

"Oh, and what's that?" Sam asked, slightly alarmed by Declan's tone of voice.

"The owners, the bankers, Mrs Foley's family," Declan began, his words tumbling out erratically, "They want you to take over again as Tabikat's trainer, as from today, that is. He's not just to come to you as a livery until the Festival like we agreed. It's a permanent arrangement."

"But why?" Sam managed to respond, "The owners haven't contacted me about this. Is this a final decision, Mr Meaghan? Did the owners explain their reasons?"

"It's Declan, and the reasons are ours not theirs," Declan continued, rather mysteriously, "My father has been receiving threats. Both he and the owners want the horse out of harm's way."

"Threats? What on earth do you mean?" asked Sam, shocked by this information.

"It's a long story," replied Declan, wearily, "And one for which you must ask my father or Genie Foley, as it is not mine to tell. My father is not here today, as you see, but he will be watching our horses on the television, to be sure."

Declan having declined to elaborate further on his strange announcement, Sam went to take a brief look at the handsome Tabikat, who was being readied for his later race by a sad looking Claire O'Dowd. Sam then went in search of Ranulph Dicks and Sadie. In the light of this news, he needed to speak to both of them, as well as to Merlin, once Fan Court's race was over.

The eight runners for the Novices' Chase were elegantly treading the path around the parade ring by the time Sam had made his way down the hill through the gathering crowds. The motionless sky above Cleeve Hill was leaden and forbidding, the warmth of the iconic rock face of Cleeve Cloud seeming to have faded away in the dull light. The vicious gales which had swirled across the West side of the country during the previous week had abated, to be replaced by a directionless lull which pressed down onto the landscape like a cold hand.

Sam could see a warmly clad Sadie leading a clearly revved-up Fan Court around the parade ring, Merlin walking forward towards the horse to be expertly legged up by Ranulph Dicks. The Todds were standing together on the centre lawn, Mrs Todd with her fur collar held around her throat by an expensively gloved hand, Mr Todd with a tartan scarf crossed around his throat and tucked beneath the lapels of his black overcoat. Stevie Stone was in the Press area talking into an iPad, a fur hat covering her long hair. Sam stood for a moment, taking in the scene. Threats to Brendan Meaghan, he thought, his mind racing. From whom?

Watching the horses being released into the horsewalk before making their way down to the start, Sam observed that Sadie and Merlin had had nothing to say to one another. Fan Court was clearly oblivious to any tension which might have existed between his two human attendants, and bounced out along the course with enthusiasm, Merlin poised lightly in the irons over his withers. Close behind them was the grey shape of Penalty Kick, whose presence in the parade ring had been the subject of some interest, the unsurprising absence of his beleaguered owners notwithstanding.

The pictures appearing on the big screen in the Cheltenham parade ring were also being shown in an interval between races at Taunton racecourse, at which Kye and Ryan had just arrived with Highlander Park in the small horsebox. With Jackie required to accompany Katseye at Cheltenham, as well as to drive both him and his half brother Tabikat home to Sampfield Grange, accompanied by one of the work riders, Sam had had no choice but to send the two young men together and to take the risk that Kye might be unfit to drive on the return journey. Ryan had remained staunchly reluctant to add his name to the insurance policy. The assumption eventually settled upon by his puzzled colleagues had been that Ryan had some form of driving conviction to which he was reluctant to confess.

Gilbert Peveril and his wife had agreed to represent Sam at the Taunton race meeting.

"Happy to do it, of course, James," Gilbert had said, when Sam had called him with the request, "But with all this work going into Curlew Landings and those Irish imports, as well as Highlander coming on now, and the other horses running in the points, isn't it about time you got some more help in, especially at the weekends? Your Australian cousin will be off again on his travels, no doubt, and that young Sadie might well decide to stay with Dicks, you know."

Kye had been relieved to be able to make his emerging riding career his principal focus in recent weeks. The revelation that Jackie had been asked by Frank Stanley to keep an eye on him had been an unwelcome one, particularly as he had previously considered himself to have been instrumental in recruiting her to the Sampfield Grange team. Deciding, not entirely reluctantly, that he could not give up sharing his bed with Jackie without arousing suspicion on the part of Lewis and Kelly, and probably Ryan too, he had eventually negotiated an uneasy truce with his bedfellow, as part of which she had assured him that nothing would be reported back to Mr Stanley without Kye's knowledge.

"I only agreed to do this minding job for him 'cause I really like you, Kye," Jackie had assured him when Kye had recovered a little from his original annoyance and had decided to speak to her again.

"What's yez connection with Mr Stanley then?" had asked Kye, crossly, "He got a hold over yez too, has he?"

"No, he hasn't," Jackie had replied, firmly, "But he got me the job with Sir Andrew when I came out of the Army. I'd nowhere else to go. My C O recommended me to him. Mr Stanley's been good to me. Gave me a chance when no-one else would. Like he's given you a chance, too."

Through this uneasy resumption of mutual trust, Jackie and Kye had managed to keep their respective secrets away from the ears of Lewis and Kelly, who had soon found sufficiently interesting alternative material in the form of Ryan and then Merlin.

The news that Ryan had come out as gay to his apparently disapproving father had surprised Kye. His observation of Ryan over the three months since Ryan's arrival had certainly led Kye to conclude that Ryan was hiding a secret. This particular secret would not, though, have been Kye's first guess. It certainly explained Ryan's reluctance to engage with his cousin Mr Sampfield on a personal level, as well as the fact that Ryan's conversations with his colleagues were almost exclusively on the topic of horses and race riding, about which Ryan was clearly very well informed. Ryan's real character and opinions had been well disguised by his gung ho manner and exaggerated Aussie Strine, which, Kye had also observed, sometimes slipped when Ryan was not concentrating. Perhaps he had just told his disapproving parents that he was gay for some ulterior motive of his own, thought Kye, although he could not begin to fathom what that motive could be.

"Look, there's Merlin going out on Fan Court," Kye said deliberately loudly to Ryan, who appeared to have been asleep throughout the uneventful drive down the M5 to Taunton. The large viewing screen by the racecourse finish line was clearly visible from the horse box park.

"I'll get the ramp down," offered Ryan, springing into energetic wakefulness and jumping down from the cab of the lorry, "I can see after Landy, if you want to go out and recce the course."

Whilst Ryan was releasing a perky Highlander Park from his mobile accommodation in the horsebox, Kye remained in the driver's seat, gathering his thoughts ahead of the race in which he was due to ride later that afternoon. Now a more experienced jockey, the nerves which had once plagued him before races were less severe, but he still needed to concentrate on staying calm. Kye had ridden at Taunton racecourse before and was familiar with the contours and dimensions of the course, which, like

Cheltenham, was overlooked by attractive upland countryside, in this case the picturesque Blackdown Hills. That was, though, the only similarity between the two racing venues. Taunton racecourse was flat and the horses travelled in the opposite direction to their route at Cheltenham, going right handed around a mostly oval course.

Gathering his own kit together, Kye noticed that Ryan had left his battered rucksack behind on the passenger seat. As Kye reached forward to pick it up, to his annoyance, the bag toppled off the seat into the foot well, its contents spilling untidily onto the floor.

"Shit!" swore Kye, grovelling down to gather the mess together.

Suddenly, amongst the jumble of personal items on the horsebox floor, Kye spotted a passport. Even Kye could see at once that was not an Australian passport, but a familiar burgundy coloured European one. It had the UK's royal coat of arms on the cover.

Before he could help himself, Kye had picked up the passport and opened it at the back page. There was Ryan's familiar face staring out at him. But the name on the passport was not Ryan Urquhart. It was Travis Byrne.

32

Sam had not seen Tabikat since the talented chaser had won the Gold Cup race at Newbury. Waiting expectantly with Declan Meaghan in the oval parade ring as the seven horses running in the Cotswold Chase paced their way around the rose coloured path, Sam felt as if he had gone back in time. Apart from Declan and himself, plus Merlin, who was walking over to join them clad in the blue and gold silks of Levy Brothers International, there were no smartly dressed connections standing in the centre of the parade ring to support the magnificent horse that day. Sam had been assured by Declan Meaghan that his father Brendan, still shown in the racecard as the horse's trainer, would be watching at home, and Sam had no doubt that the Foleys would be doing the same, but the absence of any other connections in person that day seemed to Sam a shame.

Tabikat, though, Sam reminded himself, was not short of a wider circle of supporters. Stevie Stone would be watching him race in between recording her popular vlogs, not least because Tabby Cat and Jayce had tipped Tabikat to win, even suggesting that the Smart Girls might risk a two horse forecast on the result, with Macalantern to finish in second place behind Tabikat. Lady Helen Garratt and her party would certainly be cheering for Tabikat from their box above the grandstand, since her own horse Alto Clef was not entered in this race. Sadie, who had come to the course with the Dicks staff, would be rooting for Tabikat to win, as would the rest of the Dicks team, who had helped him train Tabikat last year. Meredith Crosland, soon to join him for Katseye's race, would surely be interested in Tabikat's performance, given the relationship between the two Irish bred horses.

Most tellingly, all the bookmakers had Tabikat as favourite.

Sadie had been overjoyed when Sam had told her, as she had led the rug-covered and victorious Fan Court from the winner's enclosure, that Tabikat was to come permanently to Sampfield Grange.

"Amelia's back from Australia next week, Mr Sampfield," Sadie had enthused, as Fan Court had walked obediently up the lengthy black rubber-surfaced track towards the stables at the top of the hill, "So I can take over with Tabikat for you straightaway - assuming Claire's not coming with him, that is?"

Sam had assured Sadie that Sampfield Grange was to be in sole charge of Tabikat with immediate effect. Sadie was too happy at hearing the news to ask him for further details or an explanation.

Merlin also had been pleased with the information and even Ranulph Dicks had offered his congratulations, Sam having decided to say nothing to either of them about the reported threats to Brendan Meaghan. Sam intended to call Frank Stanley before he tackled either Brendan Meaghan or the Foleys about the worrying information. Given his recent experience with Tabikat and his complicated connections, Sam felt sure that Frank would somehow be involved in whatever was now going on.

Watching the horses congregating by the starting point further down the hill, Sam could not but agree with Declan Meaghan that Tabikat looked to be in excellent order. In the parade ring, the horse's coat had shone with health and he had walked confidently forward with Claire O'Dowd at his side, both of them looking as if Tabikat already had the race in the bag. Last year in the same race, the horse's first run at the challenging Cheltenham course, Tabikat had gone well in the gusty and damp conditions, finishing in fourth place. Everything pointed to a better performance now on his second attempt.

Amongst those competing against Tabikat today were old rivals Macalantern, Less Than Ross and Harry Me Home. An interesting addition to the field this year was Niall Carter's The Page of Cups, which had run well in the Gold Cup Chase at Newbury almost two months ago. The ground was still soft, thanks to the effect of the melting snow from earlier in the month, conditions which had been succeeded by damp and windy weather, which in turn had abated only in the preceding week. Many of the trainers had feared heavy going on the course, but bright sunshine in the last few days had secured an improvement.

An orderly start and a steady pace ensured that the first circuit of the race provided few clues to the eventual winner. Following the race through his field glasses as well as on the viewing screen, Sam could see that Tabikat was taking the jumps cleanly and without difficulty. Merlin was motionless in the irons, allowing the clever and perfectly balanced horse to make his own decisions as he approached each obstacle. As the tightly grouped field passed the crowded stands to turn along the ascending left curve which took them away from the finishing line, a few of the jockeys at last started to make their planned moves.

"There's been an injection of pace in the back straight and Macalantern is now moving clear of the field," called the commentator, glad to see something new to report, "The others are content to watch and no-one is going with him at the moment."

By the time the horses had reached the highest part of the far side of the course, the seven runners had become strung out, with Tabikat's chief rivals amongst the leaders. Merlin had resisted any temptation to challenge Macalantern for the front spot, ignoring the usual taunting comments of the horse's jockey, Aidan Scanlon, as he had started to pull his mount ahead of the others. Merlin was biding his time and had not moved a muscle. Tabikat continued to motor along smoothly, still without making any serious effort.

As the field turned for home and faced the final two obstacles, the rearmost member of the equine procession, evidently not coping well with the soft ground, and having climbed his way over the preceding fence, had been pulled up. His resigned jockey stood up in the irons to watch his rivals streaking away up the hill ahead.

"They come to the last and that's a terrific jump from Tabikat," cried out the commentator, as the thousands of hardy racegoers packed into the spectator areas roared and yelled their personal encouragement, "Tabikat's getting to Macalantern as they come up the hill. Macalantern can't hold on. Tabikat is closing fast....."

Sam all but held his breath as he watched the two powerful chasers, necks stretched out, their jockeys pushing and shoving and shouting on their backs, hurl themselves towards the finishing line. There was no doubt about it. Merlin had timed his run well. Tabikat would be the winner.

"And first to cross the line is Tabikat!" announced the commentator, excitedly, as many people in the crowd noisily congratulated themselves on their good choice of the favourite in the race, "Second is Macalantern. The Page of Cups finishes in third place. And the fourth horse is Less Than Ross."

The racecourse operator's contract with the TV company covering the race meeting required Merlin to wait with Tabikat beyond the finish line to be interviewed by one of the presentation team, a young woman newly recruited that year from one of the racing papers.

"Well done, Merlin. Were you confident you were going to win there? Talk us through the final stages of the race," the interviewer said, excitedly, as she walked up to Tabikat's side.

Merlin was only too happy to do just that, speaking into the large microphone held up to him on a stick, as he manoeuvred the steaming horse around in a small circle. A smiling Claire O'Dowd darted forward to grasp the rein and pat Tabikat exuberantly on the neck. Tabikat himself nodded his aristocratic head at the many admirers watching him through the means of the TV camera and continued to walk forward with his customary unruffled decorum.

Back in the well attended parade ring, a second TV presenter was approaching a beaming Declan Meaghan with a more conventional microphone.

"Well done, Declan," the bespectacled male presenter began, as other racing reporters began to cluster round them, holding mobile phones and notebooks, "That was some performance from Tabikat. Does he go to the Gold Cup now?"

"Thank you, Craig," responded Declan, quickly, "We've been very pleased with the horse at home. But you will need to ask his new trainer, James Sampfield Peveril here about the future plans."

The presenter looked initially confused, but quickly recovered his equilibrium as Declan stepped back to indicate that he should direct his questions to Sam. Sam, similarly caught off balance, was only able to say,

"We'll have to see how he comes out of the race. But, yes, the Gold Cup is definitely a possibility again this year."

The shrilling of Sam's mobile phone provided an excuse to avoid any further difficult questions, but Declan's intended job had been done. The entire racing world had been told on live television, to be quickly followed by the online and print news media, not to mention the Smart Girls vlog currently in preparation by the nearby Stevie Stone, that Tabikat would no longer be with the Meaghan yard in Ireland. Those who had made the threats would certainly, Declan knew, be amongst that audience.

The call which had come through so conveniently to Sam was from a highly pleased Gilbert at Taunton, informing his cousin that 'young Highlander' with 'that lad of yours up' had won their race. Kye was doing well, Sam reflected, but he knew that he would soon have to help the young jockey obtain more rides under Rules with other trainers. If Kye were to continue to rely solely on Sampfield Grange and Highlander Park, he would never have the opportunity to ride out his claim as a conditional jockey. Useful though it was to have Highlander's racing burden reduced, the present arrangement was unsustainable in the longer term. Even more pressing was the need for a new jockey eligible to ride Sam's pointers in amateur events. Kye himself could no longer be put up, now that he was set on the professional career ladder, and so Sam had been relying on Gilbert and the suitably licensed friends to supply the amateur riders he needed. Sam hoped that Sadie would in future ride for Sampfield Grange, when Amelia Dicks resumed riding for her father, but, other than Sadie, Sam currently had no other amateur jockeys regularly available to him.

A tortuous and exciting cross country race was being run prior to Katseye's event. Sam could see Jackie leading her grandly turned out charge down the long black track towards the pre parade ring. Sam also spotted Meredith Crosland, wearing her signature black coat with its diagonal line of buttons, walking purposefully in black boots alongside a warmly dressed Arturo Ardizzone. Sam took a deep breath. Dealing with one owner was enough of a new experience for him, but now there were potentially two of them.

"Good afternoon, James," Arturo Ardizzone greeted Sam, with a slight inclination of his fedora covered head, "I am very 'appy to see you again. And you are now to be training the winning 'orse Tabikat, I understand. That 'as made my decision very easy now. I 'ave told Meredith 'ere that I will undertake to buy Katseye from 'er and I 'ope you will agree to continue to train 'im for me."

"That is very good news, Mr Ardizzone," Sam responded, politely, not quite sure that he meant what he said, "But will you not want to see how Katseye performs in this race before making your decision?"

Ignoring the steely glare of Meredith Crosland as she heard Sam's unhelpful comment, the Italian laughed.

"I am entirely confident the 'orse will do well in 'is race," he said, firmly, "It is where 'e races next is what we need to discuss."

Arturo Ardizzone's confidence was not misplaced. Katseye and Merlin went out onto the course as third favourites and came back the winners. The bookmakers were soon quoting ante post odds for Katseye for all three of the Novices' Hurdle events at the forthcoming Cheltenham Festival.

"I will be in contact with you very soon," Arturo Ardizzone told Sam and Merlin, after they and outgoing owner Meredith Crosland had received their prizes from the representative of the race sponsor. Stevie Stone had come quickly over with her iPad, ready to interview Meredith for the Smart Girls vlog, and Sam hoped he would be able to take his leave quickly without giving offence.

"In the light of the sale of the horse," Sam began, politely, "I assume we shall not be meeting each other again .. er .. Meredith."

"On the contrary, James," Meredith Crosland all but interrupted him, "I shall certainly continue to take an interest in both Katseye and Tabikat. I shall be here on Gold Cup day with Stevie."

Driving down the gloomy and dismal M5 later that afternoon, Sam tried to put Mrs Crosland's intentions out of his mind. The horsebox containing Tabikat and Katseye had already motored on ahead with a happy Jackie in charge. Sam, travelling in the comfortable Audi, thought it was quite likely that he would catch them up before they reached Sampfield Grange and that he would quickly become involved in the unloading and settling in of the returning horses. He decided it would be expedient to call Frank Stanley from the privacy of the car.

"Congratulation on your two wins this afternoon," Frank said, answering the call immediately, "And I hear you have Tabikat back with you again, and a new owner for Katseye."

"Is there anything you don't know, Frank?" asked Sam, somewhat sarcastically, whilst nonetheless feeling gratified at Frank's interest.

"Well, it was all reported on the television," Frank pointed out, "And the news about Katseye was mentioned on Stevie Stone's vlog."

"In that case," Sam responded, slowing the car to match its speed to that of the diminishing line of red tail lights which signalled that the junction with the M4 was not far ahead, "Perhaps you can tell me what has been going on at the Meaghan yard."

There was a pause on the line, until Frank eventually spoke.

"You've got me there, Sam, old man," he said slowly, "You'll need to be more specific, I'm afraid."

Frank listened in silence as Sam outlined the scant information which Declan had given him.

"So are the threats to Brendan himself, or to the horse?" asked Frank.

"Declan didn't tell me," Sam responded, feeling a little foolish that he had not asked this obvious question himself.

"I'll look into it," Frank told him and ended the call with nothing more than a brief goodbye.

As Sam was concluding his conversation with Frank, the lorry driven by Kye with Highlander Park on board was entering the gates of Sampfield Grange. Both Kye and Ryan were jubilant at the victory in the Taunton race and Ryan had talked about little else on the journey home.

"Landy's going to go places, sure of it," Ryan had said, more than once, whilst outlining various options which he would have in mind for Highlander Park's future career, were he to be in charge of his training.

The need for concentration as he drove along the busy motorway had prevented Kye from doing little more than agree with Ryan. At one time, hearing Ryan speaking as though he were heir to the Sampfield Grange training operation would have bothered Kye. But Kye now knew that Ryan was not who he seemed.

Who the hell was Travis Byrne? And where was the real Ryan Urquhart?

33

On the unexpectedly mild February day of Curlew Landings' planned attempt at the Kingwell Hurdle, Kye found himself once again in the cab of the Sampfield Grange horsebox alongside the young man everyone had thought to be Mr Sampfield's second cousin.

Spring seemed to have arrived temporarily at the now busy Sampfield Grange yard. Nets of thin cloud were strung out across a bright blue sky, the remnants of a transparent mist which had placed a rapidly fading veil over the surface of the nearby hills when the red sun had first climbed above the horizon. With not a whisper of wind to stir it, the light fog had gradually thinned and risen as its moisture evaporated in the strengthening warmth of the morning. The yellowing sun had glared through the remaining mist, its light dispersed through the remaining water droplets. The peaceful mood of the developing morning had extended itself to Curlew Landings, who had loaded without trouble and had seemed well settled in for his important journey as the ramp of the box had closed on him.

With the approach of the Cheltenham Festival and Curlew Landings' entry in the Champion Hurdle on its opening day, the quality of the horse's performance in the Kingwell Hurdle at Wincanton racecourse was of paramount importance to the final decision as to whether Curlew would take his chance in the prestigious race. The young horse had already proved his ability by coming second in the Boxing Day Hurdle race at Kempton Park, and Kye knew that Merlin and Mr Sampfield were both of the view there was no reason why the horse should not repeat, or improve on, that performance at Wincanton.

Ryan, or Travis, had been instrumental in getting Curlew fit for both races, receiving praise from Mr Sampfield for his successful efforts. This success, Kye now knew, was not just the work of a naturally talented newcomer to the business of training racehorses. Travis Byrne was a professional jumps jockey in the

Australian State of Victoria – or at least he had used to be. Nowadays, he was disqualified.

During the drive back from Taunton races two weeks ago, Kye had decided to share with Jackie the information he had come upon through viewing Travis Byrne's British passport. Unexpectedly, Jackie had seemed already to know about the passport, although she had only caught a glimpse of the cover.

"Australian passports are blue," Jackie had explained, "So I knew there was something not right with it."

Neither Kye nor Jackie had had any idea what to do with the information they had discovered, and had discussed it endlessly when out of earshot of any other staff.

One option had appeared to be to confront Ryan, as they still thought of him, and to ask him directly what was going on. The drawback of this approach was that Ryan would realise that they had been snooping amongst his personal possessions and might well complain to Mr Sampfield. If he was really Mr Sampfield's cousin, and some innocent explanation for the presence of the passport could be provided, then Kye and Jackie would be in serious trouble.

A second option had been to report the matter to Mr Stanley and let him look into it further as he saw fit. Jackie had been particularly keen on this way forward, but Kye had had reservations. To him, it had seemed like reporting someone to the bizzies without giving him a chance to defend himself.

The third suggestion had been that they themselves should try to find out more about Travis Byrne and who he was. Maybe he had a presence on social media or something had been written somewhere online about him. It was a long shot, and they would have to find some excuse to borrow the kitchen iPad from Kelly, but at least it would buy them some time and perhaps arm them with some concrete information to report to Mr Sampfield or Mr Stanley.

Their fourth option had been to do nothing and to wait to see what happened when the Urquhart parents turned up at Sampfield Grange in five weeks' time.

In the event, it was the long shot which had produced the results they were seeking. But it had not helped them to decide what to do.

Having borrowed Kelly's iPad, ostensibly to research suitable races for Highlander Park for the purposes of a discussion with Mr Sampfield, Kye had typed in the name Travis Byrne, adding the words 'Australian horseracing' for good measure. He had been rewarded with a plethora of information.

Travis Byrne, it appeared, had been a young jockey, holding a 'B' licence to race over hurdles and jumps in the Australian state of Victoria. Travis had been found riding with a banned substance in his system, a finding which had been made after an anonymous tip off to the stewards at the racecourse where he was due to ride. Testing had proved the tip off to have been accurate and Travis had been instantly suspended pending further investigation. The investigation had led to the discovery of a more widespread drug dealing operation in which Travis Byrne was said to have played an integral part, apparently acting as supplier, not only to other staff in the yard of the racing trainer to which he had been attached since his days as an apprentice, but also to other jockeys at race meetings.

In vain had Travis Byrne's appointed representative argued at the disciplinary hearing which had suspended Travis's rider's licence that a proprietary soft drink brought by Travis Byrne to the racecourse that day had been spiked with the illegal drug. The charge that Travis had supplied drugs to others at the racing yard was unproven and had relied entirely on the testimony of two of his colleagues, who had reported Travis to their mutual employer, a racehorse trainer called Jack Tytherleigh. No fellow jockeys had been willing to testify against Travis, it was assumed for fear of incriminating themselves in the illegal drug use. The disciplinary panel would have liked to believe the promising young jockey, but the witness evidence from his respected employer and seemingly honest colleagues had been impossible to ignore. Travis had lost his licence to ride and had been dismissed from his position with the training yard with immediate effect. The police, fortunately, had decided that there was insufficient evidence to press criminal charges.

"Christ!" had been Kye's sole comment, on reading this readily accessible information, "No wonder he's changed his name."

"But what's the connection with Ryan Urquhart, and why is Travis here?" Jackie, equally surprised by the scandalous finding, had wanted to know.

Encouraged by their success, Kye had entered Ryan Urquhart's name into the iPad's search engine. This second search had been less helpful. It had told them that someone by the name of Ryan Urquhart had a degree in Veterinary Biosciences from the University of Melbourne but nothing more. This information had come up as one of many references to a lengthy report concerning Equine Nutrition to which Ryan Urquhart appeared to have been a contributor.

"That might not even be Mr Sampfield's relative," Jackie had said after they had tried to make sense of this new information, "It could be someone else with the same name. Anyway, if Travis Byrne is an Aussie, then why does he have a British passport?"

"He said he was here on a visitor visa and had to leave after six months," Kye offered, remembering the conversation during their journey home from Chepstow, "But that isn't a problem if he has a British passport. If he really was Ryan Urquhart with an Australian passport, then that would be right. But he isn't. Maybe the British passport is a fake. But why get it in his own name, then?"

"Perhaps the visa thing is just an excuse to leave when he's done whatever he came to do," Jackie had suggested.

"And what's that?" Kye had asked.

But neither of them could work it out. And so, they had reverted to the fourth option and waited to see what Ryan, or Travis, would do next.

"What's Veterinary Biosciences?" Kye asked his companion as the horsebox made its way East along the A303 towards Wincanton racecourse.

"What're you wanting to know that for?" asked Ryan, the name Kye had decided to continue to use for his work colleague.

"I heard Mr Sampfield tell someone that yez had a degree in it," lied Kye.

"Yeah, he's right about that," Ryan replied, "Uni of Melbourne. It's about animal biology to support vets. Horse vets in my case."

"Sounds interesting," replied Kye, hoping for more information.

"Yeah, it is," Ryan went on, "You get to find out all sorts about how horses' bodies work. I did a specialist project on racehorses. Nutrition was my main bag."

So we did find the right Ryan Urquhart, thought Kye to himself.

"All a while ago now, Kye mate," Ryan added shortly, "This Sampfield Grange outfit could do with a bit more of a scientific approach, I'd say. Just as well anyone can see just by looking that our Curlew's bang right for his run today."

The owner of the unscientific Sampfield Grange outfit had, as usual, driven alone to the racecourse, aiming to arrive there well ahead of his lorry and its passengers. Sam had been asked to lunch with Gilbert Peveril, who had also invited his friend Toby Halstock, the former owner of Curlew Landings. Toby retained a keen interest in the current progress of his former possession, not least for the purposes of placing bets on the horse.

Just before Sam had left the main house, Lewis had approached him to say that he had left a box of DVDs by Mr Sampfield's desk in the study. Sam had at first been mystified by this information until Lewis had explained that the material previously held on the ancient cassette collection in the drawing room had now been transferred onto these more modern digital video disks, and that Mr Sampfield could now view them on his computer whenever he had the time. Sam had thanked Lewis hurriedly and had said he would deal with the items when he came home after the races.

Lewis's announcement had reminded Sam that the blue envelope which he had found tucked into the cover of one of the cassettes had turned out to be empty. As the envelope had been sealed, it had seemed unlikely that any contents could have fallen out. Sam had eventually concluded that his mother had simply used the envelope as a note or label, the message on the front presumably referring to the video cassette into which it had been lodged. Sam had no idea which of the cassettes that could be, as he had not at the time even looked at its cardboard cover. Now any possibility of linking the note to its original cassette had been lost. He would just have to hope that the reference might become self evident once he was able to work his way through the collection on his computer.

The Kingwell Hurdle was due to go off at 2.45 that afternoon. Like Taunton, Wincanton was a mainly flat, right handed racecourse with a Roman circus shape. Unlike Taunton, the roughly oval course had wide ends, making the turns less sharp than at the smaller of the two Somerset courses, and at Wincanton a single circuit of the course was about one furlong further in distance.

As Sam entered the parade ring, having overseen the preparation of Curlew Landings by Ryan in the smaller pre-parade area, he found Toby Halstock and Gilbert in conversation with the dour Justin Venn. Notwithstanding the unseasonal warmth of the day, Justin was wearing a heavy green jacket and grey flat cap.

"Af'rnoon, James," said Justin Venn to Sam, "Oi wus tellin' yrr friends that y're 'orse is the one to be feared today. That jockey of y'rn does well on 'im."

"That's kind of you, Justin," Sam responded, courteously "Your horse looks in good shape as well, so we're not complacent at all."

Justin Venn nodded and moved away to speak to his own party while the horses began to come into the compact parade ring. His horse, Southern Cross, which had beaten Curlew into second place at Cheltenham in November was presently the favourite, and Sam's comments had not been made entirely out of politeness. There were a number of other excellent runners, all with good jockeys on them, most of them quite capable of causing an upset in the race.

The normally garrulous Toby Halstock, wearing a buff coloured shirt and green tie beneath his habitual tweed jacket, seemed as nervous as if he still owned the horse himself.

"Toby has quite a bit of money riding on young Curlew," Gilbert announced in a stage whisper, as Toby himself moved momentarily away to look appraisingly at Curlew Landings as soon as Ryan brought him into the parade ring. Curlew seemed to be in a chippy mood, looking around at everything he passed, the occasional snort emanating from his nostrils. Ryan strode forward alongside, a red baseball cap pulled forward over his eyes, ostensibly to shield them from the sun.

"Is that young man Curlew Landings' groom?" asked Toby, as he rejoined the other two men.

"He is," replied Sam, "Ryan rides Curlew Landings out every day. He's done an excellent job of getting him fit for this race."

"A member of the family too," Gilbert added.

"Oh?" queried Toby, "Your son, James, is he?"

"No, no," replied Sam hurriedly, "My cousin's son. From Australia, like my mother."

"I see," said Toby, in a knowing tone, "I was just thinking he might be about to step up as your assistant, what with your stable of top horses nowadays. I'm looking forward to hearing about them from Gilbert in the next few weeks."

Fortunately for Sam, Merlin joined the group at that point, wearing the distinctive red and green silks of Sampfield Grange. Toby immediately became interested in the detail of Merlin's planned riding tactics, and the conversation turned to other topics.

As Sam legged Merlin up onto Curlew's back, he could see Ryan continuing to walk firmly ahead of him. Would Ryan be suitable as a successor, he thought? Ryan was certainly a very talented rider, but was he really likely to be interested in training mostly point to point horses in a quiet country establishment?

The competitive six runner race started to the right hand side of the spectating enclosures. The pace on the good ground was fast from the outset, and Curlew Landings completed the first mile uncharacteristically sitting just off the two leaders, Rabbit Punch and The Squires' Tale. By the time the small field had passed the start point and was approaching the finish line in front of the thronged spectators there was still little to choose between the leaders.

"Rabbit Punch has made a mess of the second last," the commentator shouted, as a groan rose from those who had backed the tiring horse, "Southern Cross, Curlew Landings and The Squire's Tale are in a line going to the final hurdle."

Sam was not sure what would have happened had The Squire's Tale not fallen at the last obstacle, hampering Southern Cross and giving the unscathed Curlew a clear run to the finish. It was a victory, but it was far from clear cut. Southern Cross chased Curlew and Merlin stoically to the finish line, but the unlucky incident had made catching the swift Curlew Landings an impossible task. The excitement of the win was further diminished by The Squire's Tale being surrounded with the racecourse's dreaded green screens for a few minutes before the horse could be seen getting to his feet and walking away, apparently uninjured, led by a relieved groom. An equally relieved cheer rose from the watching crowd.

"Toby's cash is safe," noted Gilbert, sounding pleased, as Merlin returned to the winner's area and jumped down onto the grass ready to remove the saddle, "Bit of luck for us that good horse falling when it did."

Justin Venn was magnanimous in defeat, shaking Sam's hand and saying ominously,

"We'll 'ave 'n at Chelt'nam, don' you worry, Sam."

"And we'll be good and ready for you, Mr Venn," Sam heard Ryan saying under his breath.

34

Sadie had declined the opportunity to join the party of attendants to Curlew Landings at Wincanton racecourse. She had instead offered to take the work ride out by herself that morning, thereby allowing Mr Sampfield to make an early start, whilst leaving her the time to move in to her new accommodation in the former chauffeur's flat above the Sampfield Grange garage. It was also, she said, a chance to make her re-acquaintance with her favourite horse, Tabikat. In reality, though, Sadie had just wanted to avoid coming face to face with Merlin ap Rhys again.

The chauffeur's flat had remained unused since it had been suddenly vacated by Isabella Hall almost a year ago. Then it had been a gloomy and poorly furnished place, but Kelly and Lewis had made rather more effort this time to make it a pleasant billet for Kelly's sister. The flat had been newly decorated and furnished, improved lighting and heating had been installed, and the shower room renovated. Any trace that Isabella Hall might have accidentally left behind her had been well and truly obliterated.

Even after these improvements, there was no television or internet connection in the flat, so Sadie had been obliged to watch Curlew's race in the company of Kelly, Lewis and Jackie in the Sampfield Grange kitchen. Watching the smartly turned out Curlew being led around the Wincanton parade ring by Ryan, Sadie asked the room in general,

"So tell me about Ryan. What's he like to work with?"

"Well, guess what, Sadie," replied Kelly, before Jackie could speak, "We think he's gay."

"Really? What makes you think that?" asked Sadie, sounding astonished, "He didn't seem gay to me when he stayed with us that night at the Dickses in November. He was all over one of the girl grooms in the evening."

"Mr Urquhart told Mr Sampfield on the phone that Ryan was gay," Lewis said, defensively.

"You shouldn't believe everything you overhear, Lewis," Sadie told him, a note of warning in her voice, "Anyway, I hear he's done a good job with Curlew, and that's all that matters."

"Bethany's just handed in her notice," Kelly announced, trying to change the subject, sensing that the comments about Ryan had not met with her sister's approval, "Her husband's got a new job and they have to move to Devon. Mr Sampfield's asked her to get that Mrs Purefoy to find someone to take over from her."

"Mr Sampfield could always ask Isabella Hall to come back," Sadie said, offhandedly, as she watched the televised image of Merlin cantering Curlew Landings the short distance towards the Kingwell Hurdle start, the usual tight feeling clutching at her throat as she watched Merlin ride. Try as she might, she still could not see her unfaithful former lover without experiencing a mixture of rage and sadness. Fortunately, over the last ten months she had become well practised at hiding her emotions where Merlin was concerned, even when she had had to lead him out on Fan Court.

Sadie had hoped that by now, she would have got over her longing for Merlin, but this had not happened. Luke Cunningham had proved a pleasant and attentive boyfriend, but she had not found being in bed with him to be the exhilarating experience she had enjoyed with Merlin. It wasn't just the exciting sex that she missed. Merlin had been maverick, disrespectful and funny whereas Luke was urbane, reserved and, it had to be said, a bit dull.

Sadie had been shocked and upset by the revelation that Merlin had been questioned by the police in relation to the murder of a Liverpool sex worker. She could not think why Merlin would be involved with someone like that, let alone implicated in such a serious crime. Listening to the more recent reports from Hornblower Online and other virtual outlets about the nefarious activity of Santiago Alvarez, a painful wound had re-opened itself in Sadie's carefully guarded heart. She had had no difficulty in recalling that it was the apparently wronged wife of this sleazy footballer who was in bed with Merlin in the video clip she had found on Merlin's mobile phone. Did Merlin have something to do with this footballer and his wife, she wondered? If Merlin was having an affair with his wife, then surely she was an adulterer like her husband? But Santiago had made no such accusation.

"Isabella Hall?" Kelly repeated, bringing Sadie out of her moody reverie, "We thought she'd gone, but Lewis saw ....."

The rest of Kelly's sentence was lost, as Sadie and Jackie became too engrossed in watching Curlew's highly important race to engage further with the discussion.

"Curlew's not at the front," Sadie observed, as the horses pressed their urgent way along the back straight, the remnants of the morning fog still visible amongst the bare branches of the trees which stood in a sloping dip behind the course, "That's new."

"They're going pretty fast," spoke up Jackie, quickly, "This is a real test for Curlew, holding his own with this pace. But he can do it. Ryan's got him going really well here at home."

As the horses reached the final two obstacles, even Kelly and Lewis were shouting and calling out encouragement to the moving image of Curlew Landings and Merlin. They all gasped as Rabbit Punch fluffed his jump at the second last, then gasped again, even more loudly, when The Squire's Tale came down at the final hurdle, he and his jockey sprawling across the track in front of Southern Cross. Then Sadie and Jackie were riding every step of the run in with Merlin as he pushed Curlew Landings to the finish line.

"Curlew Landings wins the Kingwell Hurdle!" shouted the voice of the racecourse commentator, "Southern Cross comes home second. Third is Rabbit Punch."

Lewis had needed to remain patient before he could share the information which had been on the tip of his tongue since the start of the race. Curlew's win soon generated televised interviews, first with Merlin, conducted whilst Ryan was leading Curlew along the horsewalk with Merlin on his back, and then with Mr Sampfield, who was asked if Curlew would be going to the Champion Hurdle. Eventually, Lewis was able to say, "I saw Isabella Hall ages ago near the Charlton Arms. And I reckon she's with Mr Stanley again."

"Mr Stanley comes here sometimes to hack out with Mr Sampfield," added Kelly, not wanting to be left out, "So we think maybe she's not gone after all."

"She was watching me riding in the point to point at Cuffborough just before Christmas," Sadie replied, unexpectedly, "She looks a bit different now – she's grown her hair and changed the colour too – but I knew it was her because of the bike. It was the same one she had when she was here."

Isabella Hall would have been surprised to know that she was still a topic of interest in the Sampfield Grange kitchen. Isabella too had watched Curlew's race and had been ecstatic to see him win.

"I wonder if we will be invited to the Cheltenham Festival to watch him run?" she said to George Harvey who was tapping on the keyboard of his slim laptop computer at a small desk on other side of the sitting room.

It had been over a month since Frank Stanley had informed them in that very room about the denial of service cyber attack which had been launched on Ardua Industrie S.p.A. The attack itself had turned out to be a half-hearted affair, easily repelled by the company's in house cyber security team. Had it not been for the demand for the Mark 2 version of the Astrak flight system software, it might easily have been dismissed as a random attack from any malign group of online crooks trying to hold a company to ransom through wrecking its computer systems. The cyber attack and its ransom demand had simply been ignored whilst Frank Stanley had waited to see what the attacker would do next. So far, the attacker appeared to have done nothing.

"That means we do nothing too," George had told Isabella, when she had asked him earlier in the week what was happening. "We have set out our position now and the next move is up to him."

"Wasn't that D o S attack the last move?" had objected Isabella.

"No," George had said, shortly, "We made the last move by ignoring it."

"Run the plan by me again," Isabella had requested, "It might help me understand what you and Frank are doing if we got this ridiculous game-playing business straight in both our minds. Not to mention explaining why TK is involved."

George had sighed theatrically, but had done as she had asked.

"As you already know," he had said, "The fake air accident reports which appeared in April and May last year came through the computer in Frossiac which we used as a route to destroy Egzon Paloka's systems. As Frank explained in Faratxa, following Egzon's death the person who replaced him made use of that route to post the fake accident reports. Frank's people's assumption was that the individual concerned did not know that this was the means by which Egzon's systems were attacked. I think that might have been true at the beginning, but we are fairly sure now that the author of the reports eventually worked it out. So, he or she stopped using it for a few months.

"I guess that surviving in the Paloka operation, which has gradually been falling apart ever since the death of Aleksander, was not a comfortable ride. One wrong move, and you're dead, that sort of thing. Frank was wondering if our perpetrator, who seemed to want to damage the reputation of either Ardua Industrie or Astrak Avionics, or both, was even still alive. We needed to find out, because, as Frank said, the strong suspicion was that this person was after the rebuilt Astrak flight system software. Why else would they have selected Old Warnock airfield for the fake report? It had to be someone who understood the parameters of the live flight testing operation. Frank thought he knew who that was."

"Keep going," Isabella had prompted, as George had stopped to shift his stiff left leg to a more comfortable position in front of the office chair on which he had been sitting, "I'm with you so far.

346

Frank explained most of this back in May in Faratxa. At least here we don't have those over-zealous Mallorcan jailers minding our backs any more, although I definitely preferred the weather there."

"You'll remember," George had continued after a pause, as though getting his thoughts in order, "That I went to Frossiac a few months ago and checked on the Vacher place. The wine museum is now a bike hire shop, as I told you, but the same desktop computer was still there, apparently untouched. Guy Vacher didn't have a clue about what had really happened last year and went on using the computer after the police there had finished with it. So, I put a listening bug into the system."

"Yes," had said Isabella, impatiently, "And it showed that nothing more came through the link. So this person isn't using it any more. So what does that mean? Maybe it means that that person is dead along with the Palokas."

"We don't think so," George had replied, "Because someone took a jolly good look at the little bug - someone who was working at the other end of the route. It could have been the same person who sent the fake bulletins or it could have been someone new. We didn't know. But what we did hope was that whoever it was would assume that whoever had put it there was the same person who had destroyed Egzon's systems."

"And ...?" had prompted Isabella.

"It was a bit of a bluff," George had said, flatly, "We had a pretty good idea by then that we had found the missing Dominik Katz, the main creator of the original Katz:i software and would-be owner of the now defunct Croatian company Katz:i d.o.o. Young Mr Katz must have been well known to Egzon Paloka, as he was one of the top designers of commercial defences against cyber criminals such as Egzon. Egzon must have taken him into his own operation, and then he got Egzon's job when Egzon died. The next step for us was to try to draw Dominik out into the open, but not to frighten him off. It would have been easy enough for him to go to ground somewhere else. So we needed to challenge him. Get his interest, like we did with Egzon."

"So the next step was faking that accident at Old Warnock airfield," Isabella prompted.

"And mentioning the Mark 2 version of the Astrak software in the report," added George, "Then we ramped things up by having Arturo telling the world that the Katz family were crooks, and reporting that Lara Katz, Dominik's sister, had lost her job and ensuring there was information on the internet about someone called Lara Katz who was a sex worker. Only Dominik Katz would react to those stories. If it was someone else doing this stuff, someone who had somehow found out about the rebuilding of the Katz:i software by Astrak, then these pieces of news would have been of no interest to them. But we did get a reaction, although it took longer than we expected.

"That day when Frank was here, he told us about the half-baked cyber attack on the Ardua systems and the attacker demanding the fully developed version of the latest Astrak software as a ransom. That was Dominik accepting our challenge, letting us know who he was. He wasn't actually expecting us to give him anything at this stage.

"We already had our next move planned. The death of Lara Katz had been scheduled for reporting on the same day. But that is when something we really hadn't expected came into the equation."

"Merlin ap Rhys," had supplied Isabella with an exasperated sigh.

Isabella remembered George's careful summary of events, as she now watched the jubilant jockey being interviewed on the television following his success at Wincanton.

"Do you think he'll get Sadie back?" she suddenly said aloud.

"What?" asked George, who had not been paying attention to the television coverage.

"Well that horrible Hornblower girl from Stevie's old school has really nailed randy Señor Alvarez," Isabella went on, half speaking to herself, "But that doesn't help Merlin get Sadie back."

"Frank will think of something, you can count on it," George reassured her, "But it was an incredible stroke of luck that Merlin had been involved with the sex worker Lara Katz. As you know, we had an entirely different purpose in mind for Meredith and Katseye, which didn't need to involve Merlin. But the coincidence of the names of the horse and the software was just to good to ignore."

"I think you and Frank are getting too clever for your own good," Isabella remarked, "And getting TK involved in all this too....."

"That's an Army decision," George reminded her, tersely, "She's needed."

"I know," Isabella sighed, "She's at the airfield again today. I just wish this would all be finished."

"It will be," replied George, levering himself up with his stick to come to sit beside her, "At Cheltenham. On Gold Cup day."

35

Had Dominik Katz been listening to George Harvey's summary of their complex online dealings with each other, he would have been feeling very pleased with what he had achieved. Dominik was fairly certain that he had pushed his online opponent into the position which he had intended, but he also recognised that the opponent was at least as competent as Dominik in the art of subterfuge and deceit.

Dominik Katz had not until recently been entirely sure of the true identity of his opponent. He had always been acutely aware that Egzon Paloka would have made many enemies in his online dealings: other criminal operations hoping to move into Egzon's territory, legitimate businesses simply wanting to protect themselves from attack, and the law enforcement agencies of any number of countries whose citizens had suffered at the hands of the vicious criminal activities of the Palokas. The real opponent could even have been disguising his or her true identity by attempting to appear to be one of the others.

It had been the apparently genuine accident at Old Warnock airfield in November which had put Dominik on the track to the correct identification. Such an event could not have take place without the knowledge of a Government body. The airfield was owned by the British Government. Dominik had checked.

The appearance of the opponent's faked bulletin concerning the accident, together with the associated press conference staged by Arturo Ardizzone, had at first simply infuriated Dominik. In his initial rage, he had assumed that the Italian manufacturer, disappointed and frustrated at the dramatic loss of one of his company's innovative aircraft, was brazenly attempting to blame Katz:i d.o.o. for defective software and the consequent damage to the reputation of Ardua Industrie S.p.A and its products. But once Dominik had calmed down, he had started to think more clearly. He had played chess for many years with his sister, and was himself a successful poker player. His opponent's minimal action of installing a listening device in the French computer a few weeks earlier had suggested to Dominik that he was dealing with someone who was playing a more careful game than the staged and emotional reaction of Arturo Ardizzone might suggest.

The AAIB Special Bulletin issued in November had been clearly a fake, but the accident itself, which had happened on a dark and wet evening in poor flying conditions, had looked real. Dominik had found pictures in the British and Italian news media showing the aircraft burning on the runway. Police, fire engines, ambulances, and a helicopter were all in attendance. No-one had been allowed near the airfield until the next day because of the danger of explosion of oxy-acetylene gas cylinders, one report had helpfully added.

Why should the opponent, one who was possibly working for the British Government, produce a fake report of a genuine incident? Why should the fake report reproduce specific phrases which Dominik himself had previously used in his own faked work? Why had the Bulletin been sent through the tortuous route of Egzon's wormhole? If the placement of the harmless listening device in France had been a message to indicate to Dominik that he was being watched, then it seemed that the fake AAIB Bulletin was another message. It was not only asking if he was still there, but whether he was Dominik Katz. In addition, it had put him on notice that the development of the Artificial Intelligence system was progressing, through the reference to a Mark 2 version of the software on the doomed aircraft.

The opponent had evidently expected to provoke Dominik Katz to react in some way. Dominik's reaction was therefore to do nothing, or at least nothing that his opponent could detect.

The location of the November crash at Old Warnock airfield had interested Dominik. Either he had previously deduced correctly that this very airfield was being used to flight test the Astrak software, or else his deduction had been erroneous but the opponent was trying to make Dominik believe that it had been correct. Dominik had therefore devoted some time and effort to working out just what trick his opponent was trying to play on him.

Having already established that the facility was owned by the British Government, Dominik had set out to learn more about how the remote airfield was used in practice. This process had taken Dominik some time. Not only did he have his unpleasant work for the quickly imploding remnants of the Paloka criminal empire to occupy him, but he had little idea where to look for current information on activities at an obscure English airfield. At the time he had first selected the location for use in his own fake report, his researches had told him that the airfield itself had no website or other published online information, although he had seen from the aerial photographs he had studied that it appeared to be frequented by drone owners, model aircraft flyers, and microlighters. References to the remote airfield had helpfully appeared in online walking and cycling guides, evidently being part of the route instructions to those who enjoyed these pastimes.

Studying these online photographs once again, Dominik had identified a number of vehicles parked alongside the airfield. These must belong to the individuals who were operating the drones, model aircraft and microlights, he had concluded. Deploying every device he could summon from his extensive array of digital tools, Dominik had eventually managed to enhance the images sufficiently to read some of the registration plates of the parked cars. One vehicle had been particularly useful. It had been a white van with prominent black lettering on the side, which had read Colvin's Garage, Motor Repairs MOTs and Servicing. Beneath this information had been a telephone number and an email address.

Dominik's hope had been that the Old Warnock drone flyers, of which the owner of the white van appeared to be one, would upload the digital footage they had captured with their drones onto their home computer systems. Armed with the information gleaned from the side of the van, it was not difficult for Dominik to hack into the poorly protected computer at Colvin's Garage and to discover that the owner, one Graham Colvin, who appeared to have at least as much enthusiasm for viewing online pornography as for drone flying, was doing exactly that.

Unknown to Graham Colvin, he had become, during the next few weeks, Dominik Katz's metaphorical eye in the local sky. Unimaginatively, Graham had usually visited the airfield at least three times a week to fly his drone, and Dominik had soon built up an extensive picture of activity in the nearby area. The aftermath of the crash on the runway had been extensively recorded, the burnt out airframe of the Altior 10 remaining in place for several days as the AAIB inspectors pored over it.

Dominik had taken careful note of the people who had arrived to inspect the destroyed aircraft. Unlike James Sampfield Peveril, who had only briefly viewed the airfield from afar from the back of Caladesi Island on the day following the accident, Graham Colvin had meticulously watched and recorded all the work on the wreckage. Dominik had been particularly interested in a group which had arrived on more than one occasion in an elderly looking vehicle more suited to rough terrain driving. They did not appear to be either inspectors or airfield users. They had simply appeared periodically and had occasionally spoken with the crash investigation team. The group consisted of a young woman, usually wearing a black quilted jacket and jeans, a tall grey haired man leaning on a walking stick, and a second man, who did not always join them, but, when he did so, was usually wearing a dark coat and a brimmed hat.

Could these people be his opponent, wondered Dominik. Did they know they were being watched?

The digital tools had once again done their clever job at enhancing the images Dominik had procured from the Colvin computer and he had soon managed to read the registration plate of the sturdy vehicle. Hacking into the Driver and Vehicle Licensing Agency database of UK car registrations, he had discovered that the Land Rover Defender was the property of a Captain Tabitha Katherine Stonehouse. Further research had revealed her to be an Army officer in the Corps of Royal Engineers. This piece of information had been gleaned from the website of a girls' public school to which Captain Stonehouse had been invited to speak about her work with military aircraft in the field.

The discovery that a British Army officer was amongst the group interested in the wreckage on the runway at Old Warnock airfield confirmed what Dominik had suspected for some time. The advanced pilotless fly by wire system on the little Altior 10 aircraft was not being developed simply to be a rich man's expensive toy. It had military applications, and perhaps not only to fixed wing aircraft.

That is the reason they are so keen to find me, Dominik had told himself, triumphantly. When he had walked away into oblivion and a new career as a cyber criminal, he had taken with him the source code to complex and expensively commissioned software which might in future be installed in military aircraft used in real conflicts. It was software which an enemy, be it a terrorist army or hostile government, would certainly be interested in acquiring, probably at any price which Dominik cared to ask.

So, Dominik had continued with his thought process, if this was a reason for these people to want to find and, presumably to silence, him, it was also a reason for removing his sister, Lara, also a risk to them, from the development project. But surely they would have needed to make her removal worth her while and not just to dismiss her?

Sitting back in the soft white leather chair which had replaced the reinforced black contraption previously occupied by the obese Egzon, Dominik's thoughts had returned to his lost sister. Like him, she appeared to have become someone operating outside the norms of society. What she was doing was not, he believed, illegal. But it was certainly not a respectable occupation, even if it had the potential to pay her well. Why should his brilliant sister, who presumably could have had any job she wanted, with her sharp intellect and University of Cambridge education, be working as a glorified prostitute? It had not made sense to Dominik.

Lara's Services, the website which Dominik's little cyber spy had eventually found, was clearly a genuine and properly set up female escort business operating in Liverpool. The security surrounding the online booking facility was some of the best Dominik had encountered and he could well believe that his sister had been responsible for the design. It was impossible for anyone to penetrate, other than with an encrypted password issued by text to a mobile phone with a known owner. And even then, there were a number of sophisticated verification algorithms applied to the log in procedure to detect and eliminate scam callers, frauds and hackers. Dominik had considered posing as a client but had soon realised that this would be impossible without a mobile phone linked to a contract with a UK based network supplier. Failed attempts to register with Lara's Services and online hacking activity might well be traceable back to him.

Returning to the accumulating amount of dull material emanating from Graham Colvin's drone, Dominik had decided to concentrate on the activities of the female British Army captain. He had become more confident that she and her male colleagues knew nothing of what he was doing to follow their activities at Old Warnock airfield. It had seemed highly unlikely that they could guess that some dim-witted garage mechanic's toy drone was being hijacked by Dominik to serve as a spying device. The debris from the crash had been cleared from the small runway within a week of the accident and work had been quickly undertaken to replace the damaged surface. Astrak Avionics and Ardua Industrie had clearly been keen to resume their testing work as soon as possible.

Unhelpfully, though, nothing more had seemed to happen during December. Hacking into various aviation enthusiasts' personal sites to find images of Gloucestershire Airport had not shown Dominik any sign of activity there with any replacement Altior 10 test aircraft. At Old Warnock, Dominik had noted only that Graham Colvin had started sending his drone further afield around the area near to the village of Warnock. Although unhelpful in one respect, merely showing such things as horses being exercised on some nearby hills, it had by chance shown Dominik the location of the house in which Captain T K Stonehouse appeared to live, when her Land Rover Defender had been by chance captured on the drone's camera. Shortly after this discovery, however, the drone had either failed or Graham had become bored with flying it, as no images had been posted on his computer for several weeks.

Dominik had used this unplanned hiatus to review the earlier images held in Graham Colvin's messy desktop machine, those which had been taken during the period preceding the November crash. Gaining a picture of the current activity at the little airfield had been essential, but the movements during the period leading up to the incident might tell him more about how it might have affected the ongoing work by Astrak Avionics and Ardua Industrie.

A significant finding had been that the airfield had been organised a little differently before the accident had occurred. In particular, the arrangements for storing and parking the few resident aircraft had appeared to have changed. A couple of elderly single engine aircraft, neither of which the drone's recordings had ever captured in flight, two regularly flown microlights, and a home built gyrocopter had appeared to be the only craft kept at the little airfield.

The aircraft parking arrangements had, though, been altered following the November crash, perhaps to keep parked aircraft at a safer distance, Dominik had initially thought. But there had been something else which had been different. The two small aeroplanes which he had never seen in use had something different about them too.

It had not been long before Dominik had arrived at a startling conclusion. One of the aircraft had no longer been an elderly and obsolete hobby machine. It had been a new Altior 10. Carefully painted in dull colours and with a tatty looking cover hauled over its fuselage, this aircraft had replaced one of the genuine old timers formerly languishing on the asphalt parking apron. As far as Dominik could tell, this substitution had been effected at around the time of the crash at the airfield - the time when it was dark and raining and the place had been surrounded by emergency vehicles, and no-one else had been allowed near. It was not only the report of the crash which had been a fake. So had the crash itself.

Dominik had scarcely had time to consider what this finding might mean in terms of his dealings with his opponent when the tatters of the Paloka operation had finally collapsed. The well guarded house in Tirana in which he had been stationed had become no longer a place of safety either from the law enforcement agencies or rival criminal operations. The police and their crime fighting allies across Europe had previously selected easier sections of the extensive operation to target and had left until last what had been the unassailable fortress at the heart of the vile family enterprise.

Dominik's ancestors had had much experience of fleeing from people who wished them ill. The difference, though, was that they had been ordinary citizens escaping persecution, whereas Dominik Katz was now an internationally hunted criminal trying to escape justice. But the effect was the same. Dominik had needed to get out, and quickly. Characteristically, he had prepared well for this inevitability. His nasty online dealings on behalf of his criminal controllers had enabled him also to amass a valuable Bitcoin stash for himself. He had had three fake passports made in different names – one Italian, one British and one American.

Leaving Tirana and Egzon's powerful flight deck would mean compromising his ability to battle with this online opponent. Dominik had needed to set up an alternative operation elsewhere, somewhere from which he could continue to manoeuvre his opponent into the position which he wanted. He would announce his personal presence in the new location by launching a denial of service attack on the Astrak Avionics IT systems, an attack which his opponent would have no difficulty repelling, but which would serve as a warning. As usual it would be routed via Egzon's wormhole.

Carefully setting up in Egzon's soon to be useless systems a timed series of viral explosions, which would both cover his online tracks and also wipe out most of the cyber capability of the fallen Palokas, Dominik had used his Italian passport to book himself onto a flight via Rome to Carcassonne.

36

During the busy two weeks leading up to the Cheltenham Festival, Sampfield Grange inexorably became a focus of media interest for a number of reasons, not all of them welcome ones.

Sam privately thought that Stevie Stone was at least partly responsible for this not entirely unforeseeable development, having had Tabby Cat tell the Smart Girls who watched her vlog to keep a good look out for the three Festival contenders which had emerged from the formerly obscure point to point yard in Somerset. A helpful kitten-voiced explanation of the differences between point to point racing and racing under Rules had quickly followed. Jayce had not helped matters by tipping Tabikat to win the Gold Cup on the final day, and, rather more cautiously, telling the Smart Girls not to rule out Curlew Landings as a potential winner of the Champion Hurdle. The Sampfield Grange landline was frequently engaged by insistent callers, ranging from racing journalists to the local press, asking an increasingly agitated Bethany for interviews with Mr Sampfield Peveril, or, failing that, with one of his staff.

Freelance TV crews and photographers regularly turned up at the gates of Sampfield Grange, hoping for pictures of the prominent Gold Cup and Champion Hurdle contenders being exercised. Drones had been spotted over the gallops by the work riders, the ugly machines appearing to have been sent out from Old Warnock airfield and other nearby locations to obtain aerial footage of the two stable stars. Tabikat's ante post price had been shortening ever since his victory at Cheltenham at the end of January whilst Curlew Landings' more recent success in the Kingwell Hurdle had also put him amongst the current favourites.

Katseye had been initially of less interest to the racing media, his career in mainstream British racing having been much shorter than that of his popular stablemates. Katseye's win on Festival Trials day at the end of January had been preceded by two second and one third places, whilst his earlier excellent winning form had been gained entirely on the less prestigious Irish point to point circuit. Added to that, the decision as to which race to run him in at the Festival had been left until late in the day, leading to further uncertainty about the usability of the various ante post odds.

The intensity of focus on Katseye had, though, sharpened very suddenly when it had been announced that Arturo Ardizzone had bought the gelding. The publicity which had surrounded this change of ownership had seemed to Sam to be rather excessive in relation to the purchase of a relatively little known Novice hurdler, but the Italian businessman was clearly not a man to fight shy of promoting both himself and his personal interests. A feature had appeared in one of the UK racing papers, profiling the wealthy and successful racehorse owner from Italy who was now becoming involved in National Hunt racing in the UK and Ireland. Arturo Ardizzone had quickly resolved the uncertainty surrounding the race in which Katseye would be competing at the Cheltenham Festival by declaring, in response to a direct question, that Katseye would run the three mile Novices' Hurdle which would take place immediately before the Gold Cup race on the final day of the Festival.

Sam had been surprised and irritated to hear of this announcement only through a telephone call from Meredith Crosland, who seemed to have appointed herself as the main channel of communication between Sam and the new owner. Mrs Crosland, as Sam still preferred to think of her, had called him on the day preceding the racing paper's feature to tell him of Mr Ardizzone's wishes for the horse. Mrs Crosland had been defensive but unapologetic in the face of Sam's politely concealed annoyance at having matters so abruptly taken out of his hands, saying that Mr Ardizzone had consulted both Merlin ap Rhys and Feanna Foley before making the decision, and that she had naturally assumed that James, as she had continued to call him, had been consulted at the same time. Sam had merely commented through gritted teeth that the horse had not run over a three mile distance before, in response to which Mrs Crosland had stoutly replied that the horse had in fact been very successful over exactly that distance in Ireland. It had been impossible for Sam to argue with that statement, but he had felt stung by Mr Ardizzone's apparent lack of respect for his trainer's role in making decisions about Katseye. It would now be difficult for Sam to do anything other than enter the horse for the designated race without appearing to have fallen out with the influential owner.

Merlin ap Rhys had been a frequent visitor to Sampfield Grange throughout February and would continue to be during the early days of March. Merlin had a number of rides at the Festival, including that on the Dicks yard's Fan Court, who was due to run in the Arkle Challenge Trophy Chase on the first day. The unsavoury publicity which had surrounded Merlin during January, in relation to his evident connection with the murdered Liverpool sex worker, had suddenly become of interest again, as the police had made a new appeal for information and possible witnesses, no progress having yet been made in identifying the killer. Fortunately for Merlin, Santiago Alvarez's grubby status as an erstwhile client of the murdered woman had previously provided plenty of scurrilous material for the mainstream tabloids and sports media, but Merlin, whose exact connection to the dead Lara Katz had never quite been explained, now came to public prominence in his capacity as the jockey of the favourite for the famous Cheltenham Gold Cup. As a result, his black BMW was followed by paparazzi every time he approached Sampfield Grange, even in the early hours just after sunrise.

Having been unable to contact the elusive Arturo Ardizzone himself, Sam had consulted Merlin at the next available opportunity to verify the reason for the reported statement that Katseye was to run in the three mile Hurdle race on the final day of the Festival. Merlin had quickly nodded his head in agreement.

"I always said that we 'adn't got to the bottom of 'im, Mr Sampfield," Merlin had stated, firmly, "'e'll do well over that distance, and the competition doesn' look as tough as in the other races. I thought that new owner 'ad talked to you about it, any'ow."

Following the announcement, Katseye's price for the three mile race had started to shorten, especially after Feanna Foley had been featured in the Irish racing press, expressing her confidence in Katseye's chances of success in the event. When Sam had eventually succeeded in contacting Arturo Ardizzone himself, the Italian had apologised charmingly and profusely for the premature announcement, blaming himself for the oversight, but hoping that Mr Sampfield Peveril would agree with his preferences concerning the horse. Sam had been left feeling that he had been deliberately manoeuvred into declaring Katseye for this particular race, but had been entirely unable to understand why, or even by whom.

Walking briskly along the stone flagged path from the house towards the yard on a sharp and breezy morning in the first week of March, Sam could see his staff and horses assembled on the well-swept paved area outside the boxes, tacked up ready for the morning's exercise. The warm stone of the buildings with their dark moss-encrusted slate roofs stood out starkly against the bright blue of the sky, which seemed to have been scrubbed clean by the serrated edges of the drying wind. There was a zest in the sunlight, which seemed to poke its way even into the shadowed places beneath the eaves of the buildings and to strike sparkles from the remaining traces of moisture on the tops of the walls and hedges surrounding the yard. The string of well bred horses, led by the dark half brothers Tabikat and Katseye, the lighter Curlew Landings close behind, looked enthusiastic and well prepared to make their athletic way up the slopes above the rambling old country house. It was a scene which had been repeated many times in the yard over the years, but had never until now included such highly distinguished equine company.

Sam was proud of his support team. Not naturally a demonstrative man, he had had to hope that his quietly expressed thanks for their efforts on his behalf and that of the horses, had been fully understood. Sadie had shown the professionalism which she had always promised, seamlessly taking over the daily work with the calm and powerful Tabikat, whilst continuing to keep in touch with the newly returned Amelia Dicks over the final stages of the training at her father's yard of the talented Fan Court. Ryan, although somewhat withdrawn of late, had continued to work quietly and effectively on the enthusiastic Curlew Landings, patiently answering a stream of well meaning enquiries from Gilbert Peveril, made on behalf of his friend Toby Halstock. Jackie had followed conscientiously all of her employer's directions for her riding work on Katseye, often asking Ryan for additional comment and input, all of which Ryan had given freely and with a level of knowledge which had surprised Sam. Kye, now that Highlander Park was no longer a major focus for the small equestrian enterprise, had shouldered the burden of the ongoing work of the yard, organising the work riders in keeping the temporarily forgotten pointers fit. Being at the back of the string and the last out of the yard on the morning ride, he had borne the brunt of the shouted pestering by the racing spies who had surrounded the premises each morning. Fortunately, Lewis and Kelly, emerging eagerly from the main house, had proved particularly keen to help by providing a wealth of useless information and uninteresting gossip to the unwelcome visitors. Even Merlin, with his multiplicity of other riding commitments, had made himself available as much as possible to Sam, and was unstinting in his praise of his three rides.

"Couldn' ask for anything better, Mr Sampfield," Merlin had said, "I tol' you before that you've got a great set up 'ere. There's other jockeys'd tear my arms off to ride these three 'orses at the Festival."

Sam, occasionally lying awake at night, had felt slightly fraudulent when receiving such praise, knowing that most of Tabikat's training had been carried out at the Meaghan yard, whilst Katseye's success was to a large part attributable to the efforts of the Foley family. Only Curlew Landings was all his own work. Sam's main task was to keep the three Cheltenham Festival contenders fit and sound. A lot could go wrong between now and the second Tuesday in March.

As the string of horses and riders made their leisurely way up the steep track, the winter mud now hardening in the curved divots made by the horses' shoes, they passed behind the sunlit buildings of Sampfield Grange, and a feeling of anticipatory calm seemed to Sam to enfold them all. The clattering of the tack and the occasional snort of a horse were the only sounds to compete with the chirping of small and invisible birds in the hedgerows, where the spiked blackthorn was already in creamy bloom. In the wet verges, the remnants of the hardy white snowdrops had long passed away and been replaced by the customary purple and yellow crocuses and taller daffodils. Once on the top gallop, the riders saw the distant sea glint grey and gold beyond the newly awakening fields. The shapes of the horses worked their methodical way along the hilltop, the breezy air filling their lungs and making the riders' youthful cheeks glow red.

Sam had scarcely ever felt happier than he did that morning. It was the calm before the coming storm, he thought, and vowed to make the most of it.

No sooner had Sam seated himself in the breakfast room, having left Caladesi Island to the attentions of his work staff, than Lewis appeared in the doorway.

"Mr Sampfield," he announced, importantly, "It's Mr Urquhart calling from Singapore, he says."

Feeling irritated, not for the first time, at the inconvenience of having no extension to the house phone in the breakfast room, Sam was obliged to go into the hall to take the unexpected call. Fearing that there was bad news concerning his mother's health, Sam approached the large telephone table with trepidation. But Teddy's megaphone voice had reassured him at once.

"James, we're sticking here in Singapore for a few days," Teddy had shouted, "Things to get sorted. We'll come on to you a bit later than planned, if that's OK. Sorry for the muck up with the arrangements."

"Not at all, Teddy," Sam replied, "Is there a problem?"

"It'll be right, James, no worries," Teddy responded loudly, not really answering the question, "How's .. er .. Ryan doing?"

"He's become an invaluable member of my team," Sam told his cousin, meaning every word, "He's helping me prepare one of the favourites for the Champion Hurdle next Tuesday. And you'll both be watching that race live from my friend Helen's box."

"That's good to know, James," boomed Teddy, suddenly adding, "Tell the boy not to stress, things'll be right. We've got his back now. See you Monday morning, James. Tessa sends her love."

Sam hardly had time to say goodbye before Teddy cut the connection.

The Sampfield Grange staff were all tucking in hungrily to their breakfast when Sam came into the warm kitchen. Everyone turned to look at their employer expectantly.

"Mr and Mrs Urquhart won't be here until Monday morning," Sam told Kelly, "And your father, Ryan, asked me to tell you 'not to stress', as he put it. I imagine he thought you might be worried about their arrival being delayed."

All eyes then turned to Ryan, who ran a quick hand through his tousled fair hair, and simply said,

"Bonzer. Thanks, Mr Sampfield."

Jackie and Kye stole quick glances at each other. They had not expected that the young man they had come to believe was not Ryan Urquhart would be so unruffled by the prospect of the imminent arrival of the real Ryan Urquhart's father. Lewis and Kelly were equally intrigued, knowing, as they thought they did, that Ryan was estranged from his father because he had declared himself to be gay. But Ryan's guarded facial expression told none of them anything.

"Are you looking forward to seeing your Mum and Dad, Ryan?" asked Kelly, curiously.

"Sure am," Ryan replied, firmly, "Not clapped eyes on them for ages. I bet they'll love Curlew."

Unaware of the unspoken speculation buzzing in the air of the kitchen, Sam returned to his breakfast and then moved into the study. He had decided to attempt to view the stack of disks which Lewis had left there on the day of the Kingwell Hurdle and to

364

which he had not yet had the opportunity to return. The delayed arrival of his cousin had now given him a little more time to see whether they contained anything the Australian relatives might find of interest.

Sam had never viewed a DVD on a computer before, but, guessing correctly that inserting one of them into the slot in the processor would be the first step, he picked the top disk from the pile and pushed it in. A list immediately popped up on the screen as the computer recognised the presence of the newly introduced medium. Laboriously working through the words on the screen, Sam could see that they were titles describing such things as point to point venues, horse trials and equestrian shows. Recognising the name of Cuffborough, followed by a date from about thirty years ago, he clicked on the file, and was rewarded with a video recording of himself as a teenager, riding one of his father's long dead pointers over the finishing line. The moving images were far from perfect, but the quality and clarity of them surprised him. Long buried memories reassembled themselves in his mind as he clicked on file after file, finding images of his mother, his father, Helen and her mother, the Sampfield Grange horses and dogs with which he had grown up, and the pointers that he had ridden to competition success in his earlier years. There were pictures of the mellow old house, the well tended garden and the gallops, and sometimes the voices of his parents and various now retired or deceased grooms and other staff could be heard.

Sam had seen some of these recordings before, but it was at least fifteen years since they had been last released from their cardboard sleeves. The old cassettes themselves were stacked under the new, much smaller, disks in the large cardboard box, and Sam eventually realised that whoever had copied them had attempted to cross reference them to each other. The slim disks evidently held more information that the bulkier plastic cassettes, so that the contents of three or four of the originals had been transferred onto a single disk. The cassettes had been numbered by hand with a biro from one to 35 in total, and the disks were labelled 1 - 4, 5 - 9, and so on. The difficulty was that the old cassettes were not numbered chronologically, so the recordings which Sam viewed jumped randomly backwards and forwards in time.

So engrossed was Sam in working through the old images that he hardly heard the ringing of the mobile phone which lay on the desk next to the computer. Very few people knew the number of Sam's mobile phone, but one of those few people was Frank Stanley. His name, which even Sam had no difficulty reading, was flashing up on the little screen of the phone.

"Good morning, Sam," Frank started, a businesslike tone to his voice, "I trust that I haven't caught you at a bad time."

"Not at all," Sam responded, feeling unusually communicative, "In fact, I was just looking through some old video recordings of my mother's. You'll recall she was very good with her camera – or camcorder I think it was called – and she had left a lot of old material behind. I had completely forgotten about it until recently, but Lewis has had it recorded onto computer disks for me to look at. I thought my cousin Teddy and his wife Tessa might like to look at some of the recordings. Maybe you'd be interested too, Frank. You'll remember some of the horses and the people, I'm sure."

"How is your mother?" asked Frank, unexpectedly, "The last time I saw her was when she banished me from your company."

Sam blanched. In his enthusiasm for the old memories, he had forgotten that that terrible occasion was probably Frank's abiding memory of Sam's stern mother.

"I doubt she'll even remember that now, Frank," Sam told his friend, trying to mitigate his tactless error, "She's suffering from dementia and lives in Australia again nowadays. These recordings really are the only record of what she used to do with me and my father and the horses. They're a limited substitute for her lost memory, I suppose."

"I shall have to have a look at them sometime," said Frank, politely, "But I actually called to let you know the outcome of my enquiries into the reported threats to Brendan Meaghan and to thank you for your help with Katseye."

"What do you mean, help with Katseye?" asked Sam, wrong footed by Frank's statement, "This isn't a repeat of the business with Tabikat last year, is it?"

"Not really," Frank replied, "But we have an issue to deal with at the Festival on the final day and it is important for Katseye to be among the entrants then. I do realise that you would have been unhappy that Arturo took the decision out of your hands concerning Katseye's race."

Sam was silent for a while.

"I'm not going to ask, because I know what you will say, Frank," he eventually began, "But does whatever it is involve Isabella Hall?"

"I can't discuss anything with you, but I can tell you that Isabella won't be at the Festival on Gold Cup day this year," Frank replied, carefully.

"Well, if she needs a job," Sam said, not entirely jokingly, "My office manager is leaving."

Frank simply laughed and said he would tell Isabella.

"More seriously, what about the issue with Brendan Meaghan?" asked Sam, glad to realise that Frank was not seriously upset about his reference to the video recordings and the memory of Sam's mother.

"Nothing for us to worry about, Sam," Frank answered, dismissively, "A personal issue from long ago. The *garda* has been informed. But Brendan wanted Tabikat out of harm's way, to be on the safe side. Tell me, how is Tabikat doing? Will he win the Gold Cup this year?"

By the time Sam had concluded his conversation with Frank, it was past midday and Sam had still not paid his usual morning visit to the office in the yard. Walking through the kitchen on his way outdoors, he found that Kelly had left the kitchen TV running, ready for the imminent arrival of the yard staff for their lunch. A news item referring to Cheltenham racecourse caught his attention.

A company of travellers had broken into the parking area with their vehicles during the night and had set up camp there.

37

"*Bonjour, Guy,*" said Marcel Lambert, "*Et comment va t'en, aujourd'hui?*"

Guy Vacher looked warily up from his seat on the red canvas chair by the canal to see the local police officer who had just arrived at the entrance to the bicycle hire shop. The early March temperature in Frossiac was rather warmer than at Sampfield Grange, whilst soft rain had earlier speckled the still waters of the brooding canal. There was no warmth or softness in Guy's expression.

"And what can I do for you, Marcel?" he asked, not returning the other's greeting, "More trouble for the Vachers, is it?"

Marcel Lambert sighed.

"You understand, Guy, that your brother and his associates committed a serious crime," he said, mildly, "I am a police officer. It is my job to bring such people to justice. Even people I have known since childhood."

Guy shrugged and said nothing as Marcel pulled out a photograph from the breast pocket of his uniform jacket.

"Have you seen this man here?" Marcel asked, brusquely, "Did he come into your premises?"

Guy stared at the picture for a few seconds.

"Yes," he replied, "This man was here maybe three weeks ago. Why?"

"Why was he here? Did he ask to use the computer in the shop?" persisted Marcel Lambert.

"Why do you think he was here?" asked Guy, sourly, "He came to hire a bicycle. This is a place when people do such things. It is how I make my living now, Marcel."

"What records do you keep of those who hire the bicycles?" asked Marcel.

"Well, as I recall," Guy told him, beginning to realise that there was something serious about Marcel's spate of sharply spoken questions, "This man was Italian, although he also spoke good French. His details are in the computer in the office. I asked to see his passport for identity purposes and he typed all the information into the computer for me."

"This man used the computer himself?" repeated Marcel, taken aback, "But why? Can you not operate it, Guy?"

"Yes, of course, but he was in a hurry," Guy told the police officer, "So whilst I prepared the bicycle, he entered the details himself. I checked them afterwards against the passport. He asked me to check that everything was correct. It was."

"Show me this record, please, Guy," Marcel instructed.

An hour later, Frank Stanley received the report that an Italian called Nico Gatto had hired a bicycle in Frossiac on a date in early February and had later dropped it off at another hire station further along the Canal du Midi nearer to Carcassonne. The same passport had subsequently been used at Carcassonne airport to book Nico Gatto on a flight to Rome, the city from which it appeared that he had originally arrived. Further enquiries had revealed that a hotel in the citadel of the Cite de Carcassonne had a photocopy of the same passport, as the holder had stayed there for an extended period during January, eventually leaving in the first week in February. The scanned picture of the passport was enclosed with the report sent to Frank.

George Harvey, consulted by Frank Stanley by phone, could confirm only that the date of the bicycle hire predated by almost three weeks the date on which the little bug in the Frossiac computer had suddenly started spewing out uncontrolled and meaningless rubbish which had threatened to clog up the UK monitoring station.

"I think," said George, with a sigh, "That my little spy has been corrupted. I can try to check, but my guess is that our man installed a timer that day in Frossiac, which he set to start its work two days ago and produce all this gibberish."

"The man calling himself Nico Gatto also booked onto a flight from Carcassonne to Rome," Frank commented, "We're trying now to find out whether he actually took the flight. My guess is that Nico Gatto had ceased to exist and that Dominik Katz has been using another name and passport. We are going to have to wait until he shows himself again."

"Do you think he will?" asked George, dubiously, "Now that he's got away, he can surely do anything he wants with what he already knows. He may not have the fully developed Astrak application but surely he stole the basis of it from Ardua when it was still in its original form as Katz:i? It could be rebuilt by someone competent from that existing source code."

"Domink Katz won't be able to find a buyer for a half finished product," Frank asserted, "At the very least, they'd expect to have his services to do the work to complete it. And he'd be putting himself in great danger by agreeing to work for the sort of people who are likely to want this stuff. Not to mention the fact that he's a wanted criminal. It won't only be legitimate law enforcement agencies who are after him, either. There will be bounty hunters from any number of countries, not to mention the various people who will start to suffer as a result of his probable destruction of the old Paloka systems before he left Tirana. So, he's in a lot of peril from many quarters. Dealing with us is actually his best option. Beyond a shadow of a doubt, he'll be in touch."

"You sound very confident, Frank," George replied, "I'll let you know if anything other than rubbish comes through the Frossiac link. But what can he possibly want from us that we would be prepared to give him? You are not going to hand over the latest Astrak software in a million years."

"Safe passage, a new identity, lifetime protection for him and his family, immunity from prosecution, money for life, the chance to work in legitimate cyber security again," recited Frank, as if counting the items off on his fingers, "We have a lot to offer."
"And what if he doesn't want any of those?" asked George, "What if getting the Astrak software is his only price?"

"Then we'll have no choice but to kill him," replied Frank, baldly.

Dominik Katz had rather enjoyed his brief time on the run as Nico Gatto. The stay in the cold but attractive surroundings of the fortified citadel within the picturesque Aude city of Carcassone had enabled him to re-establish his peace of mind and to start to think through his next moves.

As Frank had surmised, Dominik's situation was unsustainable. It would not be long before the damage caused to Egzon's inherited systems would make itself felt across its dispersed criminal client base. Arms dealers, people smugglers, gambling syndicates, drug traffickers, money launderers, cyber attackers across Europe, and even further around the world, would not only lose the internet based systems which had previously supported their evil activities, but they would also find those same systems booby trapped with malware when they attempted to reinstate them. Dominik could at least provide that service to their many victims whose pitiable plights he had not only had to ignore, but whose misery had been in part directly caused by him through his own work for the Paloka family.

Dominik recognised that he had put himself in great personal danger and with no obvious allies to help him. The law enforcement authorities would certainly take him in if he surrendered himself, but he knew that there was no guarantee of his safety even in prison. He was only too well aware of what had happened to Konstantin Paloka, the evil father of Aleksander and Egzon, who had been murdered in a British prison, no doubt on the instruction of the British authorities themselves. So, he needed to secure lasting protection, and from a powerful source. But first he needed to make himself invisible so that he could start his negotiation when he himself was ready. He did not want to be discovered before he had achieved the strategic position which he now needed.

So, Dominik had deliberately created a time delay. By the time his opponent, now clearly characterised in Dominik's mind as the British military and Government authorities, had been led to Egzon's wormhole in Frossiac, they would be three weeks too late. The only difficulty was that he had had to visit the location personally to set up the decoy, as he no longer had access to the wormhole through the existing route from Tirana. It had been the work of seconds to re-set the listening bug to do the job he wanted, whilst the unsuspecting French cycle shop owner was preparing the hired bike.

Frank Stanley had been right about what Dominik wanted. But Frank had carefully omitted one item from the list which he had recited to George Harvey. Dominik also wanted the death of Arturo Ardizzone and his aircraft company with him. He also wanted the death of whoever had killed his sister, and, as far as he could see at the moment, the only known suspect was the man called Merlin ap Rhys.

Nico Gatto had never boarded the flight to Rome from Carcassonne. Instead, a British passport holder called Dominic Kitson had taken a flight to London. Dominik did not want to make it too difficult for the opponent to trace him, and the existing three week delay might well be enough to give him the time he required, but the second change of identity provided an additional smokescreen which would enable him to feel more secure.

Dominik had already purchased a state of the art laptop computer on his original visit to Rome's Fiumicino Airport after he had fled Tirana. Sitting at the narrow desk in the featureless room of an anonymous budget hotel in Kensington, Dominik had hacked into the computer systems of one of the London universities, prepared to use its services through which to make his initial strike of a cyber attack on Astrak Avionics. Like the previous attack on Ardua

Industrie S.p.A, this would be easily repelled by the in house team, but designed to let his opponent know of his presence. The route back to the University concerned was cleverly camouflaged, but not so carefully that it could not be uncovered eventually.

Working to create his new cyber hacking capability whilst enjoying the multiplicity of tourist attractions of London had been a comfortable and even enjoyable existence during the dismal weeks of February when the opponent would have assumed him to be still elsewhere. It was during that time that something occurred to change Dominik's plans. He learned that the hated Arturo Ardizzone had bought a racehorse. It was not just any racehorse. It was called Katseye, an English sounding version of the name of Dominik's father's defunct company. Dominik had no doubt that Arturo Ardizzone had done it to taunt him.

Intrigued and angry, Dominik had quickly researched the horse Katseye on the internet. He had quickly discovered that there were many websites and online services devoted to British and Irish horseracing, all filled with highly detailed information, mostly aimed at individuals interested in gambling. Dominik knew a lot about gambling from his time overseeing the Paloka systems in Tirana. For him, though, gambling had been simply an actuarial exercise undertaken to ensure that the systems he had controlled would always have the statistical advantage over the gullible people who used their money in such a dull and pointless manner.

Dominik had soon amassed a number of useful facts about Katseye. That he was a black horse of six years of age with form in Irish point to point races, whatever those were, prior to coming to England to race under Rules, was not of any interest to Dominik. What was of much interest, apart from the recent purchase by Arturo Ardizzone, was that the horse was kept and trained in a grand looking place in Somerset, called Sampfield Grange. Somerset was a name which Dominik recognised. It had not taken him long to find out that Sampfield Grange was situated in the area he had viewed from Graham Colvin's drone, close to Old Warnock airfield where the disguised Astrak equipped Altior 10 aircraft was being kept.

Furthermore, the impressive Katseye was due to compete in a race at a prestigious horseracing event called the Cheltenham Festival. Arturo Ardizzone had announced this fact himself, even confirming the date and time of the race. Dominik had heard of Cheltenham too. It was where Astrak Avionics was based and the nearest airfield was Gloucestershire Airport, the other end of the flight test route for the Altior 10 aircraft and its advanced flight control system.

When Dominik later learned that Merlin ap Rhys was the name of the jockey who would be riding Katseye in the race, the plan which had been forming in his mind began to crystallise. His opponent would never guess what he was about to do. After all, he had only just thought of it himself.

Turning back to his laptop on the hotel desk, Dominik accessed the unwitting host University's IT systems and started to hack a new and untraceable route through to the little computer in the Frossiac bike shop.

Next, he decided, he would go out and buy himself a drone.

38
Monday

On the day prior to the start of the Cheltenham Festival, Teddy and Tessa Urquhart arrived at Heathrow on the red eye flight from Changi International Airport in Singapore. With them was their son, Ryan Urquhart, who looked, in contrast to his robust parents, tired and drawn. The Urquhart family's hired Volvo made speedy progress along the M4 and M5 motorways and by midday was pulling in through the open gates of Sampfield Grange. The weather that day was still and quiet, with motionless grey cloud hanging over the peaceful English countryside which was awakening at last from its winter sleep. A hopeful pale sun gleamed out briefly between the gaps. After the brightness of Queensland, though, the day seemed dark and depressing to the Australian visitors.

Everyone at the Sampfield Grange yard had been in a state of feverish anticipation that morning. Curlew Landings was as ready as he could ever be to run the race of his life the following afternoon. Sam had received calls from many friends and acquaintances wishing him luck. Toby Halstock had even come personally to Sampfield Grange to check for himself that the horse was fit and well. Sam privately feared that the erratic Toby had staked a large amount of money on Curlew and hoped that he would not be disappointed, or, worse still, rendered penniless the following day. Helen had called to confirm the arrangements to host Gilbert Peveril and his wife Philippa, as well as Toby Halstock and the Urquharts in her box the following day.

"This is so exciting, Sam, darling," Helen had told him, "Curlew Landings has turned out to be such a star. I shouldn't be surprised if he goes off favourite once people see him in the parade ring with your cousin's boy leading him up."

Lewis and Kelly had hardly been able to contain their excitement at the impending arrival of the Urquharts. Jackie and Kye were more fearful. They liked the young man who had lived and worked with them for over five months and did not want anything unpleasant to happen to him, not least because of the effect it might have on the carefully prepared Curlew Landings.

The object of their interest had mucked out Curlew Landings' box as usual that morning. Sam had prescribed that Curlew's only exercise that day should be a leisurely walk up to the gallops and a short canter to loosen him up and ensure that he was breathing effectively. Rachel Horwood, the equine vet, had called in to check Curlew over, providing her more scientific analysis of the horse's state of readiness for his competition. The absence of such scientific facilities at the old fashioned Sampfield Grange yard itself had already been the subject of earlier comment by Ryan - or Travis.

The Sampfield Grange staff were walking together towards the kitchen to their well earned lunch when Teddy Urquhart manoeuvred the silver Volvo into its parking space. Sam had seen the car mounting the slope from the road and had emerged from the front door to greet his long distance travelling cousins whom he had not seen for several years. Lewis and Kelly came out from the boot room door to stand on the step. The remaining staff turned round to look curiously at the arriving vehicle.

First out from the car was Tessa Urquhart. A tall and strong woman with blue eyes and tanned skin, she spotted Sam first and went to embrace him with a quick fierce hug.

"Where's Travis?" she asked, "Thank you for looking after him, Sam."

"I'm here, Mrs Urquhart," spoke up the voice of the young man whom Sam knew as Ryan, the Australian twang now no longer so exaggeratedly evident in his voice, "And I'm safe too. Mr Sampfield and his people have looked after me well. I couldn't have asked for better."

Behind Tessa, a dark haired young man leapt from the back seat of the Volvo and ran forward to add his greetings, clapping Travis, as he had suddenly become, on the back and shaking his hand.

"And I'm safe too," he said, "We're going to get those bastards, Trav."

"I hope so," said Travis, suddenly sinking to his knees on the path, whilst everyone else watched, dumbfounded by the mysterious pantomime, as he buried his face in his hands, "I'm all done in with this.

Whilst Tessa and the new young arrival comforted the kneeling figure, Teddy turned to Sam.

"We owe you an explanation, James," he said in his usual booming tones, loudly enough to be heard by everyone on the premises, "You've saved this boy's life by all accounts – and my son's."

"But I thought he was your son," Sam replied, bewildered by the turn of events, staring at the kneeling group in the yard. The horses peered out interestedly over the half doors of their boxes at the unexpected and strange activity. Even Bethany was standing unmoving in the office doorway, looking perplexed.

"No, this is my son, Ryan," clarified Teddy, pointing to the dark haired boy who had arrived with them, "He came on with us from Singapore. The lad you have been looking after for us is called Travis, Travis Byrne. His father used to work for me. He's British."

As Sam struggled to formulate a response, and the Sampfield Grange staff gaped in silence at their employer and his suddenly much more interesting family, Tessa Urquhart stood up.

"We could all do with a cup of tea," she announced, authoritatively, "You especially, cousin James. You look like you've seen a ghost."

"I almost think I have," Sam replied, weakly.

It was into the middle of this dramatic tableau that Merlin ap Rhys at that moment drove his smart black BMW sports car. He had promised to make a detour to speak to Sam on his way to Cheltenham, where he would be staying for the week in his usual shared rented house in the village of Prestbury, close to the racecourse.

"Christ!" Merlin exclaimed, leaping from the driver's seat, "What's wrong with Ryan? 'as somethin' 'appened to Curlew Landin's?"

The sudden intervention allowed Sam to recover his voice and to gather his scattered wits.

"Curlew's fine, Merlin," he said, firmly "Let's all go into the house and I can try to understand what this is all about. Kelly, get everyone some lunch as well as the tea that Tessa has requested. Mr and Mrs Urquhart, Ryan and .. er.. Travis will join me in the drawing room. You can bring the tea in there, and some sandwiches or something of the sort. Merlin, would you mind eating with the staff whilst I get this sorted out?"

As Merlin, conscious of the presence of Sadie amongst the assembled staff group, was about to suggest that he would leave and return later, Travis quickly rose to his feet and spoke up.

"I'd like Merlin to hear this," he said, "He ought to know too."

Once the mostly family group was seated with tea and sandwiches before them in the drawing room, Merlin having become a mystified extra in the drama, Tessa carefully started on the explanation.

"This young man," she said in her forthright Queensland tones, "Is Travis Byrne. His father worked for us for years on the cattle station. He looked after our horses - after your mother's time, though, James. Travis and Ryan were brought up there together, along with quite a few other kids, so the two of them have always been good mates.

"Travis's dad, Tommy Byrne, was British, like a lot of people in Australia. He was a good bit older than Travis's mum, Kirsty, and he died when Travis was sixteen. We looked after Kirsty and Travis on the station for a while, but Kirsty wanted to go back to

Melbourne where her family lived. So they left us, and Travis went to work for a local racing trainer as a stable hand.

"The boys kept in touch, even so, and when it came time for Ry to go to uni, he chose to go to out of State to the University of Melbourne. We thought he might be a vet, but Ry really wanted to work in a lab, still with horses, mind, so he did his degree in Veterinary Biosciences. By that time, Travis had done a great job for the training yard and was a start out jockey with a big trainer called Jack Tytherleigh. I expect you've heard of him, James? You too, Merlin?"

Both Sam and Merlin nodded, saying nothing.

"Have I told it right so far, boys?" Tessa paused in her narrative, looking at the two young men who were sitting silently on the large sofa, their teacups and food plates untouched. By contrast, Teddy, slumped into a comfortable armchair, had a ridiculously diminutive plate carefully balanced on his lap, several sandwiches heaped upon it.

"Pretty much, Mum," her son Ryan responded, "You want me to tell it from here?"

As Tessa nodded and reached for her china teacup, Ryan went on.

"When I got to Melbourne, Trav and I hooked up again. I used to go to the races a lot, saw how he was doing, took friends from my course with me to watch the horses, drank plenty of beer, that sort of thing. We had a good time for a few years.

"I did my degree OK, then went on to do research. In my first postgrad year, I had to do a work placement and write up a practice-based dissertation. That means you go and work somewhere that's relevant to what you're studying and use it to produce a report based round a real work activity. I was – still am – working on equine nutrition, specifically for racehorses. So my tutor got me a placement at Travis's workplace, Jack Tytherleigh's set up. I guess they thought some untrained student couldn't be much of a problem to them."

"But Ry was a problem," Travis cut in, "Because he uncovered something that we weren't supposed to know, what no-one was supposed to know, about how they were feeding some of the horses. It was pretty complicated, and I don't pretend to understand it, but basically they were being doped with performance enhancing drugs, like the human athletes that try to cheat in big competitions. Not common drugs, but weird stuff coming out of the Far East, made out to look like harmless herbal things. But they weren't.

"So Ry went back and told his tutor what he suspected. Next thing I know is that when I go to ride at Moonee Valley one day, a steward fingers me for a drugs test. I wasn't that much fussed because I knew I hadn't done anything. But they found cocaine in my urine sample. It had come out of a bottle of juice that they found when they searched my bag.

"So I was suspended and then it went to a disciplinary hearing. It was all over the racing papers – still is. It's still all over the internet too if you search for my name. Not only that, some other people in the yard gave evidence against me, said I was a drug dealer. The lawyer who helped me did his best but it was no good. Jack Tytherleigh is a powerful man. So I lost my job and my jockey licence too. They wouldn't let me appeal without new evidence, and I didn't have any.

"It wouldn't have been so bad if it had stopped there. I could probably have found another job doing something else, maybe here in England with my British passport. I've got two, the other one's Australian but I didn't want to use that."

"We got threatened," cut in Ryan, brusquely, "Over the internet. On the phone. Stuff through the mail. Warned not to take it any further or say anything. Someone had a go at my tutor too. Threatened her kids. She's a single mum. We were all pretty scared."

"I'm not surprised," interjected Sam, "Tytherleigh would have been desperate. Any trainer could face a lifetime ban if he was found guilty of doping his horses. It would have ruined him."

"Well, we just decided to cut and run," Travis continued, "Get as far away as we could. So I came to the UK and Ry here went off to Thailand with some mates. Trouble is, I had no money or anywhere to stay. So Ry came up with the idea of me pretending to be him. He'd never met you and we thought I knew enough about him and his family to busk it for a while until we could work out what to do. I thought I could pay my keep by helping out with the horses. I was going to tell you, Mr Sampfield, I truly was. But I just didn't dare in case it got back to Jack Tytherleigh that I was here.

"And then I started working with Curlew Landings and I thought you wouldn't let me ride him if you found out I was a banned jockey. I've never been on a horse like him. Honestly, Mr Sampfield, he's a real beaut."

"And to finish the story," Tessa said quickly, as Travis broke off, apparently unable to speak, "Ry knew we were coming here, and we'd find out anyway. So he called us in Singapore and we stayed there for a few days talking about things. We said we'd try and help get this sorted. We got hold of Travis's lawyer and he said he'd help too. But he needs evidence and everyone is too scared to talk."

"An' I thought I 'ad problems," Merlin suddenly spoke up, having remained silent throughout the telling of the unsavoury story, "You lads 'ave really been shafted. No wonder you did such a good job with exercising Curlew, er.. Travis. It did come as a surprise to me that you were such a good work jock. Now it makes some sense."

"Tell me, Travis," said Sam, thoughtfully, "When you say you're a banned jockey, does that mean that your licence has been revoked? How far does that revocation extend? Is it just the State of Victoria?"

"That's right, Mr Sampfield," replied Travis, "But I guess if I applied for a licence in another State, they'd know about all this and wouldn't give me one there either."

"And are you banned from working at or entering racecourses in Victoria, too?" persisted Sam, as the others all looked at him, wondering what he was trying to find out.

"Working, yes, but I'm not banned from attending as a spectator," Travis said slowly, "But I wouldn't dare go near a racecourse in Vic in case I was recognised. I wasn't too keen about leading your horses up here in England in case it was on TV in Australia and someone recognised me. That's why I always wore a hat. I would've have worn sunglasses too but that would have looked like I was crazy with the weather here being as it is."

"What are you trying to get to, James?" asked Tessa, bluntly.

"Whether I can let Travis lead up Curlew Landings in the parade ring tomorrow at Cheltenham," Sam told her, "I can't conceive how a ban by Racing Victoria, the authority which will have issued Travis's jockey licence, can stop him leading up a horse, unpaid, at a race here in England."

"You'd still let me do that, Mr Sampfield?" asked Travis, incredulously, "I thought you'd be mad."

"If by mad you mean angry, I am angry," Sam told him, more forcefully than Merlin had ever heard the trainer speak, "But not with you. And, in any case, the last thing I want is for anything to interrupt Curlew's preparation for the race tomorrow. He's used to you being his groom, and I want it to stay that way. Once this week is over, I'll make some calls. I don't know anyone in Australian racing, but I know people who do. This sort of thing is totally unacceptable. Even if you and Ryan are wrong about the doping, there are perfectly legitimate ways for the authorities to look into such a matter."

"Thank you, Mr Sampfield," said Travis, simply, his eyes filling with tears, whilst the real Ryan Urquhart sighed with relief and said, "I told you he'd be right with it, Trav."

"Very well," went on Sam, in the same authoritative tone, "Now, you go into the kitchen, Travis, and talk to the other staff. They have a right to know who they've been living with. I should not be in the least surprised if they have worked some of it out for themselves by now, if you say it is all available to read on the internet. Telling them the facts will stop them making up something even more lurid for themselves. Perhaps Ryan might like to meet them too."

As Travis and Ryan left the drawing room to face the inquisition that was no doubt awaiting them in the kitchen, Sam turned back to his cousins.

"I need to have a short discussion with Merlin," he told them, "Then Merlin can get on his way. And after that, I'd like you to tell me how Mother is."

39

Tuesday

Sadie impatiently twiddled the dial on the elderly radio in the horsebox cab.

"There must be something worth listening to," she told Travis, who was sitting quietly in the passenger seat, "You have a go, Travis. I know there's a Cheltenham radio station for the races, but we'll probably have to get closer to the racecourse before we can hear that."

Curlew Landings had been carefully prepared and loaded into the lorry as soon as it got light that morning, with the intention that Sadie and Travis would have no need to worry about possible delays caused by any heavy traffic near the racecourse. Having avoided most of the early Bristol commuters, the lorry was making unhindered progress North along the M5 towards Cheltenham. Mr Sampfield, they knew, would be following behind them soon in the Range Rover together with the three members of the visiting Urquhart family.

Travis's back story, related once again in the Sampfield Grange kitchen to an enthralled audience yesterday, had been received with initial disbelief by Sadie, Lewis and Kelly. It had come as less of a surprise to Kye and Jackie, whose main reaction was relief that the truth about Travis Byrne had now been explained. After the details of the unpleasant story had been picked over several times and had been treated with suitably outraged exclamations of shock and sympathy at the injustice of what had happened, Lewis had been able to wait no longer to ask the one question to which he had not yet received an answer.

"Ryan, I mean the real Ryan," Lewis had started, awkwardly, "No offence, but is Travis here your boyfriend?"

"Jeez, that's a funny question, Lewis," had responded Ryan, taken by surprise, "What makes you think that?"

"It's just that, well, I thought I heard Mrs Urquhart, your mum that is, telling Mr Sampfield that you were gay," Lewis had stuttered, looking embarrassed.

"Lewis, Trav here is just a mate from when we were kids," Ryan had told him, "My boyfriend, as you call him, is back in Phuket, enjoying himself, waiting for this mess to get fixed. You been earwigging my mum's phone calls to cousin James, have you?"

"Of course not," Lewis had replied, hotly, "The house phone's in the hall. It got left off the hook."

"Let's go and see Curlew," Sadie had suddenly intervened, jumping up, safe in the knowledge that Merlin's car had disappeared down the drive some time ago, "I expect we've all got things to do, with guests here and big races coming up."

Travis was now doing his best to get the horsebox radio tuned into a station they could listen to, as he and Sadie carried Curlew Landings towards his destiny in the famous Champion Hurdle race. Elsewhere on the M5, Sadie knew, would be the Dicks horsebox, taking the haughty Fan Court for his attempt to win the Arkle Challenge Trophy.

Travis eventually hit upon a news radio station wrapping up a sports bulletin, which at least mentioned the Cheltenham Festival, but seemed to be mainly about football. Just as Sadie was about to suggest that the radio should be turned off, something the newsreader said caught her attention.

"And in other news," said the newsreader, "Disgraced Premier League striker Santiago Alvarez is in hot water yet again. Hornblower Online, which exposed the faked videos made to cover up Santi's cheating on his wife Abby, announced this morning that this may not have been the whole story. Rumours circulating on Twitter say that there are more videos, this time videos faked to make it look as if other men are having affairs with Abby. The identities of these other men have not been revealed, but they have been told that their faces have been superimposed over Santi's own face in videos he made of him and his wife together.

Whoever they are, we bet they're not happy about that! We'll bring you more on that story when we have it."

"Christ, how could a bloke do a thing like that?" muttered Travis, as the newsreader handed over to the weather forecaster, "So he cheats on his wife and covers it up, and then tries to make it look like she's cheating on him. What a drongo."

As the day's unpromising weather forecast was read out, mentioning cold winds and intermittent rain for the rest of the day, a similarly cold feeling was slowly creeping its way into Sadie's heart. If she had understood the report correctly, videos of Abigail Alvarez in bed with her husband had been altered to make it look as if she was sleeping with someone else, and more than one someone else at that. Her husband had done this to protect himself in the event that his own unfaithfulness to his spouse was discovered, perhaps so he could make damaging and false accusations against her. Sadie didn't know what a drongo was, but the term sounded about right.

"Leave that radio station on for a bit, Travis," she instructed her companion, "It'll help keep me concentrating. We don't want to rattle Curlew around, do we?"

As Sadie had hoped, the next news bulletin fifteen minutes later had more information. The allegations were that three different men's faces had been faked into the videos and associated still images with Abigail Alvarez.

"At this stage, these are unproven allegations," the newsreader insisted, "But Hornblower Online claims to have received the faked video evidence this morning and says that it has been passed straight on to Abigail Alvarez's divorce lawyers. We don't know if the men concerned were previously aware that their faces had been used in this way. More news on this breaking story when we get it."

Could Merlin be one of those three men, wondered Sadie, trying to stay calm for the sake of her precious cargo in the back of the horsebox. She had never actually spoken to Merlin about the video she had found on his mobile phone on that April morning more than ten months ago in the cosy Chepstow bedroom. She had not returned the text messages Merlin had sent her. Merlin's attempt to speak to her at Cheltenham racecourse in November had been thwarted, first by the incident in the parade ring when Abigail Alvarez and her husband had been splashed by the upset water bucket, and later by Luke Cunningham joining her to watch the racing on the parade ring screen. After that, Sadie had made sure to avoid speaking to Merlin and he too seemed to have given up trying to communicate with her.

Could Merlin's questioning by the police in January have something to do with this new business, Sadie's thoughts continued, as she turned the horsebox off the motorway towards Cheltenham. The sex worker who had been killed had definitely had something to do with the nasty footballer. Was it her who had helped him fake all these videos?

Sadie was not a complex thinker and it was beyond her capacity to work this weird puzzle out. But one thing was clear to her. She had to know the truth. This meant that she had to swallow her pride and speak to Merlin. But it would have to be after Fanny's and Curlew's races, she decided. The horses were much more important than she was today.

Travis, still shell shocked from the events of the previous day, did not mind Sadie's silence on the journey. Travis did not know his new colleague very well and was secretly glad that she was clearly not the talkative type. It did not occur to him that she might have problems of her own.

The Arkle Challenge Trophy was the second race to be run that day. Sadie was no longer responsible for leading out Fan Court, having had to hand over her work to another member of the Dicks team, so there was no requirement for her to be in the parade ring. Amelia Dicks had previously invited her to join the Fan Court connections, but Sadie had quickly declined, not wishing, as usual, to come face to face with Fan Court's jockey and her erstwhile lover.

Merlin himself had arrived at the racecourse early, having decided to walk from Prestbury. He had received a text from his cousin Bryn in Chepstow that morning to confirm that the new set of faked video images had been sent anonymously to Hornblower Online that morning. The faking had proved more complex on this occasion, as it had required Merlin's face to be changed to that of Santiago Alvarez and then back again, but Bryn was confident that it would be very difficult for anyone to work out that Merlin's face was actually the original. Altering the other two recordings had been simpler, as they had merely had to replace Santi's face with those of two anonymous men whose images Bryn had taken from the internet. The raw material had, as before, been supplied to Bryn through Frank Stanley.

Frank Stanley had been blunt with Merlin about this second piece of clever video editing work.

"I've done what you asked, but this won't get your girlfriend back," Frank had said, "You're the only one who can do that, Mr ap Rhys."

At least Sadie might give me a chance to explain, though, Merlin had thought, as Frank Stanley had cut the connection before Merlin could reply.

Merlin looked briefly around for Sadie as he came into the parade ring in his purple and green colours to join the Todds, who were standing nervously with an equally edgy Ranulph and Amelia Dicks. Mrs Todd was swathed in a complicated purple wrap over a green coat, whilst her husband had simply opted for a warm black coat and his usual tartan scarf. Fan Court was striding arrogantly around the parade ring along with the seven other talented contenders, his lightning shaped blaze standing out in the dull light of the grey day. The seething racing crowds, the more sensible of them well wrapped up against the cold wind, were clustered excitedly several deep around the railings and up the steppings. There was still an excited hubbub following the conclusion of the first race, the Supreme Novices' Hurdle, which had been unexpectedly won by a long odds outsider, greatly to the glee of the bookmakers. Merlin had had no booking to ride in that race, so Fan Court was his first ride of the Festival.

Fan Court did not in the event win the Arkle Challenge Trophy, but he and Merlin came very close. A big Irish horse which Fan Court had never raced against before managed to get the edge over him in the final stages of the race, but the battle during the last half furlong caused those members of the crowd lucky enough to have seats to jump excitedly out of them. The two leading runners hurtled together towards the line, their necks stretched out and their ears laid back against their heads. The imposing Irish horse had been the odds on favourite, so the bookmakers had most likely been Fan Court's biggest supporters in those tense final moments. The grey Penalty Kick, having been sold to new and highly enthusiastic owners, had run into third place several lengths behind.

The Champion Hurdle was the fourth race on Tuesday's star studded card. Curlew Landings was not short of support in the parade ring, as Toby Halstock, dressed in his customary brown and green tweeds, had come down along with Helen and the Peverils from the heights of the Garratt box in the main grandstand to join Sam in the parade ring. Sadie had walked with a tight-lipped Travis down the soft black track which led past the Hall of Fame entrance and curved down the famous hill into the compact pre-parade ring. Curlew Landings himself had seemed highly aware that there was something special about today's race, and had bounced down the track, tossing his handsome head as if posing for the crowds. Once in the pre-parade ring, he had walked calmly enough for Travis, who had led him around, his heart feeling almost literally in his mouth, in front of a buzzing group of spectators crushed together in the viewing area, keen to get an early look at the impressive equine contenders in the famous race.

The atmosphere was no less frenetic in the much larger parade ring, which was surrounded by even more noisy spectators, now truly immersed in the day's exciting events. The good to soft going had brought out the best in most of the runners, and so far there had been no fallers, a single unseating, and only a few horses pulled up. The previously spattering rain had held off for the last half hour, and the chill wind had dropped a little. The conditions for the Champion Hurdle looked ideal.

After the disappointment of being chinned on the line by the Irish horse in the race named after the winner's famous compatriot, Merlin was absolutely determined that Curlew Landings would not be similarly beaten. Curlew had become a gritty competitor in his second season over hurdles, but his preference to run his races from the front meant that both horse and jockey were always under considerable pressure throughout their races.

The busy TV presentation team had made sure to speak to most of the connections clustered expectantly in the parade ring. One of them had also been positioned down at the start, ready to receive the horses when they arrived and to attempt to get a comment out of any jockey prepared to give one. Sam had quickly been spied and approached by the smartly dressed anchor woman, who had asked him, "You are both the owner and trainer of Curlew Landings, Mr Sampfield Peveril. You must be very pleased with the horse's performance this season. How do you rate his chances today?"

"We are very hopeful of a good run from him," Sam replied, cautious as always.

"And will he be setting the pace, as usual?" asked his interviewer, fishing for more information.

"Well, as you have just said, that's his style," Sam told her, "It really depends whether any of the others want to take him on at the start."

Thanking him, the interviewer had moved on to speak to Justin Venn, who was standing a few yards away, a flat grey checked cap pulled down over his eyes. Justin's face, as usual, gave little away.

"Southern Cross is in good order. We'll see 'ow he does," was his only comment.

When Merlin, clad in the red and green Sampfield Grange colours, was expertly legged up by Sam onto his talented ride, he could feel the excitement emanating from the horse's warm body.

"Good luck, Merlin," said Sam quietly, as Travis proudly led the horse out of the parade ring.

"Curlew's going off favourite," Travis called up to Merlin as they passed the big screen by the exit to the horsewalk, "And he knows it too! Sadie said she thought he was in with a great chance."

"Is Sadie here?" asked Merlin, having looked out once again for Sadie in the parade ring without success.

Travis, who knew nothing of the previous relationship between his new colleague and the successful jockey, simply replied quickly in the affirmative and released Curlew's rein to allow Merlin to canter the horse past the heaving and humming spectator stands.

There were ten runners in the Champion Hurdle. With more than a quarter of a million pounds on offer in prize money, the kudos of winning was not the only incentive to put in a good performance. The start was down at the bottom of the extensive course, not far from the row of expensive helicopters which had been shuttling in and out of the heliport, which in truth was little more than a large field, all morning. A number of curious dog walkers were peering over the boundary fence nearby.

Merlin was keen to get into the best position for a fast start and kept his eye carefully on the starter as the trilby topped man climbed the steps with his yellow flag in his right hand. As the flag dropped, and the massive crowd further up the hill let out a combined roar, Merlin sent Curlew powering up the slope toward the first hurdle. He could hear the pounding of hooves, the rattling of tack and the voices of his fellow jockeys as they slotted in behind the scurrying Curlew Landings.

Curlew flew over the first flight as if the devil himself were on his heels. Merlin was fearful that his enthusiastic partner would wear himself out before reaching the hill at the end of the two mile distance but there was clearly no stopping Curlew that day. Before long, the horse had pulled himself clear by six lengths, as the field passed the Chase jumps on their left side and approached the watching crowd packed into the viewing areas further up the hill.

"Curlew Landings is well clear of the field as they pass the stands," the commentator stated, unnecessarily, whilst a final cheer arose from the spectators on the far side of the track opposite the main grandstand, "Flights three and four now await the horses on their downhill run along the far side of the course".

Merlin could tell from the sounds behind him that the rest of the runners were close on Curlew's heels. His mount was not the only one who wanted to see the race run at a cracking pace.

"Merlin ap Rhys and Curlew Landings are still in control as they approach the fifth flight at the top of the hill," the commentator continued, his voice still calm and even. Watching in the parade ring, Sam could see Southern Cross and Rabbit Punch hot on Curlew Landings' heels. The Squire's Tale, which had fallen in the Kingwell Hurdle, was not amongst today's runners. Sam could see that the field behind Curlew was beginning to close up.

Travis was at the far end of the horse walk along with all the other grooms. His quiet manner of earlier had now been replaced by furious energy as he rode every step of the race with Curlew and Merlin, shouting and calling for the horse to keep going.

By the time the field crossed the sixth obstacle, Southern Cross and Rabbit Punch had cruised up to challenge Curlew Landings. Curlew's ears went back as Merlin urged him forward.

"The race is really unfolding now," cried the commentator, "There are three in line as they approach the second last.

Merlin could hear the swelling roar of the crowd as he and Curlew turned to climb up the hill. Curlew heard it too, and his ears swivelled forward like elongated radar dishes, as he tried to find another gear.

"Come on Curlew, *bachgen*, do it for Travis," cried Merlin, hardly knowing what he meant.

Like the bird after which he was named, Curlew Landings flew straight up the long hill, pursued by Southern Cross, whose jockey was determined to have revenge for the defeat in the Kingwell Hurdle. But Curlew was not to be caught. With a mighty leap at full stretch he shot over the final obstacle and streaked past the hysterically cheering spectators to cross the finish line clear of Southern Cross by about four lengths.

Merlin immediately stood, breathless and ecstatic, in the stirrups to salute the crowd. In the parade ring, Philippa Peveril and Helen Garratt were hugging Sam, as Gilbert thumped the back of Toby Halstock, who was trembling with relief and for once seemed to be unable to speak. Justin Venn came over to shake Sam's hand and to concede defeat. Down on the course, Travis was beside himself, grabbing the panting Curlew's rein as soon as he was allowed, a beaming smile over his youthful face, the recent ordeal at the hands of Jack Tytherleigh temporarily forgotten.

Sadie stood, jubilant, at the top of the hill above the pre-parade ring, watching Curlew Landings' and Merlin's triumphant return into the winner's enclosure, accompanied as was customary with by blaring music, Travis punching the air and grinning up at the winning jockey. With Sadie were an equally excited Amelia Dicks and an only slightly more restrained Luke Cunningham. Watching the screen, Amelia Dicks suddenly asked Sadie a question.

"That lad leading up Curlew" she said, "I recognise him from somewhere."

40
Wednesday and Thursday

The Charlton Arms rarely received American visitors. The dark haired and bespectacled young man who had arrived early on Wednesday morning had given his name as Damon Casey. Mr Casey planned to stay until Friday morning, he told the receptionist as she photocopied his passport, and then would be driving to Birmingham to meet his wife at the airport.

Dominik would have been intrigued to know that his comfortable room, which overlooked the picturesque crossroads outside the old coaching inn in the quiet settlement of Charlton, had once been occupied by one of the people he now regarded as his opponent. An outwardly calm Frank Stanley had waited with the agitated Isabella Hall in this very bedroom in anticipation of a confirmatory text message from George Harvey in Frossiac over a year earlier.

The polite and rather nerdy-looking Mr Casey had asked the receptionist the way to Old Warnock airfield. A member of his online drone flyers' chatroom, who had visited the UK recently, had recommended it, he said, as a good spot from which to obtain spectacular moving images of attractive English countryside. Dominik did not in fact need any directions, having researched not only this locality, but also that around Cheltenham and its famous racecourse using online maps and satellite imagery. He was merely laying a trail for later.

During the preceding week in London, Dominik had acquired more knowledge about British horseracing than he had ever wanted to know. The Cheltenham Festival itself had required little effort to research, particularly as it was due to take place in the very near future. He had browsed through a multiplicity of dull articles, betting forecasts and other pointless information about horses, jockeys and trainers. One tipster site had been particularly irritating, featuring a talking kitten, which gave out information through vlogs aimed at female racing fans, accompanied by a young woman with long coloured hair and an invisible man who provided the racing tips.

Annoying though Dominik found the digitally enhanced Tabby Cat and his human companions, the kitten had provided some of the most useful information in that one of the vlogs had included a face to face interview with Arturo Ardizzone, who had spoken enthusiastically about his horse Katseye, which Dominik already knew would be running in the third race on Friday, the final day of the Festival. In response to questions apparently from Tabby Cat, Arturo Ardizzone had confirmed that he would be personally present in the parade ring before and during the race, together with some of his senior staff from Ardua Industrie and expert collaborators from Astrak Avionics, which he said was a local company in Cheltenham itself. Another of the irritating vlogs had included an item on shopping in Cheltenham and yet another had showed Tabby Cat's human female companion standing on a windswept hill above the town demonstrating, without the need of a drone or other aerial spotting device, the complex layout of the racecourse when seen from the air.

Whilst still in London on Monday, Dominik had sent his disruptive, but far from fatal, Denial of Service attack into the computer systems of Astrak Avionics, routing it from a fake staff account at the unsuspecting University via the Frossiac wormhole. The resultant message which had flashed up in garish red letters on the screens of the horrified staff at Astrak Avionics had not asked for a ransom to be paid in Bitcoins, but had simply said REQUEST NEGOTIATION WITH ARTURO. LONDON. SATURDAY.

"I think my work is done," George Harvey had told Frank Stanley by telephone when George had called to confirm that this latest communication had been routed via Frossiac, "This last message has also destroyed my listening bug and has closed the route permanently."

"Then that suits our plans," Frank had confirmed, quickly, "You and Isabella can disappear back to your bolthole in the sun during the Cheltenham Festival. I believe that journalist has given up chasing Isabella since she has had Santiago Alvarez and Merlin ap Rhys in her sights, but we can't be certain. We'll stick to the plan with Meredith, just to be sure."

"Have you located our man, yet?" had asked George.

"We know he didn't make it to Rome from Carcassonne," Frank had told him, "He seems to have changed identities. We're checking all the flights out of Carcassonne now. We'll find him."

The elusive object of these searches had left London before anyone had even known he was there and was now stopping his hired car just inside the open gates of Old Warnock airfield. The windswept and barren facility, surrounded by farmland interspersed with narrow lanes lined with ragged hedges, was deserted on that Wednesday morning, and Dominik had the place entirely to himself. At least, he hoped so.

Walking across the recently repainted runway numbers, Dominik quickly approached the line of small aircraft parked on the further side of the field, just as he had seen them through the lens of Graham Colvin's drone. A quick review of the only nearby building revealed no surveillance cameras, nor had Dominik observed any by the gate. There was no perimeter fence on which to position any such equipment, and the overgrown hedgerows provided equally little opportunity. The only way of keeping watch on this airfield, thought Dominik, would be through the presence of a human guard or by mobile aerial surveillance. There was no sign of either.

Dominik had remembered the regular visits of the female Army captain in her elderly vehicle. He had made sure to pass by the house he had seen her enter when he had viewed the drone images, but today there had been no-one there and no sign of any vehicle either.

Would Arturo Ardizzone and his people at Astrak have left the newly sophisticated Altior 10 unguarded, wondered Dominik, standing at an apparently disinterested angle to view the line of unattended aircraft, trying to make it appear to any observer as if he were simply surveying the area in preparation for flying the drone which he was about to take out from his car.

The Altior 10, was not, of course, supposed to be there at all. As far as everyone knew, it had been destroyed in the fiery crash in the dark and rain of a November evening. No-one should come looking for it at Old Warnock airfield at all. The aircraft was at little risk of being successfully stolen, given the complex software on board, which no ordinary pilot would be able to operate. In any case, the paint job and tatty cover which formed the disguise were sufficiently disreputable to make the aircraft look unflyable, suggesting that no-one would be likely to risk their safety to steal what appeared to be an unwanted old flying crate. Indeed, such an insulting description was entirely appropriate to the aircraft which stood tiredly alongside. The little old Cessna was in a genuine and obvious state of disuse, given that its propeller was missing and one of its tyres was flat.

Returning to the car for his newly acquired flying camera, Dominik wondered whether other means to ensure the Altior 10's safety might have been put in place. Someone could, he supposed, attempt to vandalise it for spare parts, or just for the perverted amusement of causing damage, or even to steal the fuel which he had no doubt was stored in the aircraft wing tanks ready for a return flight to Gloucestershire Airport. These possibilities, though, seemed fairly unlikely in such a location, attended as it was on a regular basis by the microlight, gyroplane and model flyers, not to mention drone flyers such as he had now become, and passing hikers. There were enough unpaid guards, not to mention free sources of amateur surveillance, to make ill-intentioned people think twice.

Dominik was himself a highly ill-intentioned person as far as the aircraft was concerned, but his objectives were of a different kind than petty theft. Dominik planned to launch the endgame in his online battle with his opponent by flying his drone above Old Warnock airfield and the surrounding area. Whilst he was doing that, he would use the smartphone based control newly acquired by the innocuous Damon Casey in London, not just to steer the drone, but to provide the remote connectivity which would enable him to hack into the Altior 10's flight control system. The decoy which was the drone could fly for up to thirty minutes before it needed recharging, which was more than enough time for

Dominik's purposes. The clever Astrak software would have been hackproof against anyone else, but Dominik was not just anyone else. Designers always left themselves a back door.

Had Dominik Katz bothered to look later at the images which had been caught by his drone that day, he would have seen the busy Sampfield Grange horses, including his object of interest, Katseye, out on their regular exercise on the nearby sloping gallops. The euphoria with which the victorious Curlew Landings had been received on his return to the yard on Tuesday evening had quickly been replaced by a new focus on preparing Katseye and Tabikat for their challenging Friday races.

Curlew Landings had come out of his race well and without obvious injury, but had nevertheless seemed very tired. A still excited Travis had been assigned to take care of the returning equine warrior for the rest of the week, bringing the horse back slowly into light work and fending off the attentions of the many local admirers who had called at Sampfield Grange in the hope of meeting the new equine superstar. In the light of the worrying comment by Amelia Dicks, which Sadie had reported privately to Mr Sampfield so as to avoid alarming Travis, it had been agreed that the team to accompany the horses to Friday's racing would consist of Kye, Jackie and Sadie.

Teddy and Tessa Urquhart had hugely enjoyed their Tuesday experience at Cheltenham races, and had made friends with almost every guest in the Garratt box, with the result that they had been invited again for the racing on Friday. The Urquharts had driven back to Heathrow the following day to enable Ryan to take a flight back to Thailand. They would return to Sampfield Grange on Thursday evening after spending some time in London. They were not city people and the very short visit to the Big Smoke would be more than enough for the two of them, as Teddy had informed Sam in loud and decided tones.

Sadie, her usually clear mind still in turmoil, had had plenty of time to anticipate her prospective discussion with Merlin whilst she was working Tabikat through the final stages of his exercise regime. Merlin was busy with riding commitments on the second and third days of the Festival, although he had not ridden any more winners on either day. Fortunately for those whose horses he was due to ride on the final day, he did not appear to have picked up any injuries either, notwithstanding a dramatic looking tumble on the Thursday. Sadie knew that the soonest any conversation with Merlin could sensibly take place was on Gold Cup day, preferably after Tabikat's race. Sadie did not intend to instigate any difficult discussion which might disrupt the chances of her beloved Tabikat from claiming the famous prize which she considered that he completely deserved. So, she resolved to say nothing to Merlin until after the conclusion of his final ride. If nothing else, it gave her more time to think about what she wanted to say. It was a long time since she had last spoken to Merlin and she had to recognise that he might no longer wish to talk to her.

On Thursday afternoon, the geeky American known as Damon Casey was innocently flying his brand new drone once again at Old Warnock airfield, although in reality assuring himself that the Altior 10 remained unsupervised and that no-one had detected the additional instructions which he had entered into its flight control system the previous day. But nothing occurred that day either other than the arrival of a model aircraft flyer, who greeted him curiously, and the appearance of a leatherclad and booted motorcyclist who came to check on his microlight.

During the afternoon, Sam asked Bethany to download and print a copy of the list of declared runners for the next day's Novices' Hurdle race and the Gold Cup Chase. By this time, there was little more that the yard could do to get the two beautiful and athletic animals ready for their chances of glory. Their work was done.

Katseye's race would be the earlier of the two races to take place, being third on the afternoon's card. Working his way slowly through the list of names in his study, Sam wondered again at the wisdom of entering the horse in this particular race. Although there were twelve runners in the field, Katseye had been competing over a shorter distance all season, and only two of the other contenders were familiar to Sam. Admittedly, these two had both been well beaten by Katseye. But even Merlin and Feanna Foley had appeared to support the less well-informed views of

Meredith Crosland and Arturo Ardizzone in pressing for Katseye to take his chance over the longer distance. Sam was not unduly concerned that all the horses, which were mostly the same age as Katseye, were carrying the same weight, nor did he think that Katseye could not stay the longer distance. He simply did not like going into a race ill prepared. Katseye, he noted, was number seven in the alphabetical list. Seeing at least three Irish runners in the race, Sam decided he would find out whether the Foley family had any opinion to offer.

Many of the names of the next day's contenders for the celebrated Gold Cup Chase were familiar to Sam. As last year, there were ten runners declared, including Tabikat, whose name once again put him as number ten in the alphabetically arranged list. Former foes Macalantern, the present holder of the trophy, Less Than Ross, Harry Me Home and Stormlighter had reappeared to vie with Tabikat for the famous Cup. The single new entrant which Sam immediately recognised was The Page of Cups, whose trainer had had the strange altercation with Niamh Foley at Newbury. The horse had, though, been beaten by Tabikat at their two previous meetings that season. The remaining four horses were all Irish entrants, one of which, Uisce Dorcha, Sam thought he recalled as an entrant in the most recent running of the Punchestown Gold Cup. Once again, he thought, the Foleys might know more.

Sam had called the Enda's Farm often enough now to be able to return the familiar greeting of *Trathnona Maith* delivered in the soft tones of the young Enda Foley, the nephew of the man after whom the remote Irish establishment was named

"What do you think of the fields for tomorrow's races for your two, Genie?" Sam asked Eoghan Foley, once the latter had been called to the phone, "I should be particularly interested in your opinions of the Irish runners.

Eoghan Foley had clearly also been studying the race entrants and had no hesitation in putting forward a number of helpful comments about the runners' recent form, their preferences as to the going and type of track, and eventually concluding, "I doubt any of them could touch Tabikat now, barring bad luck for the horse in running. For Katseye I am less confident, but we are all expecting him to run well."

"I believe the Levy Brothers have taken a box in the grandstand this year," Sam replied, "So which members of your family will be joining me in the parade ring this year?"

"Niamh's daughter, Aoife, she has made the arrangements to fly us to that airport nearby Cheltenham in the morning," Eoghan explained, "Caitlin will be with me and also my niece Feanna. With your permission, the four of us will join you for both races. Aoife will not be attending herself, nor Danny this time."

"You hardly need my permission, Genie," Sam told him, amused at the other man's formality, "You bred these two potential champions yourself, as you know."

"Caitlin and I wonder if we could ask you a question," Eoghan said, rather carefully, "It may sound rather unusual."

"Of course," said Sam, somewhat mystified, "Please ask whatever you wish."

"We heard reports," Eoghan continued, slowly, "That there were travellers camped at the racecourse in Cheltenham. Do you know, are they there still?"

"Er.. er...well..," Sam hesitated, completely wrong footed by the unexpected topic of the question, "I did hear that information myself, but I think that the racecourse authorities said that the people had been moved on. We can check tomorrow morning, if you want. Is there some reason you need to know?"

"Not at all, we were just curious," Eoghan assured him, "We will look forward to meeting you again tomorrow."

As Sam put down the phone in the study, the reported threats to Brendan Meaghan for some reason came back into his head.

41
Friday

By eight o'clock in the morning of what promised to be a bright, still and clear March day, the events which were due to unfold on that eagerly awaited afternoon had already been set into motion.

The larger of the two Sampfield Grange horseboxes had left the yard, the de-mister blowing hard to prevent the breath of the three human occupants of the cab from steaming up the inside surface of the windscreen. The precious cargo which was Katseye and Tabikat was well wrapped and protected in the back of the vehicle, whilst Kye drove with the tense vigilance of someone whose life depended for the next two hours on his driving skill.

Damon Casey's rental car had made its way to Old Warnock airfield shortly afterwards. The occupant had stopped the car near the line of parked aircraft at the far side of the runway and had walked quickly around the dull-coloured aeroplane at the left hand end of the uneven row. He had unfastened the faded blue waterproof cover which had been fastened around the aircraft with black webbing straps, and had removed the tie-down cables by taking their hooks from the rings mounted under the wings. There seemed to be little danger of the aircraft being blown about today, as no breath of a breeze could be felt in the still air. Checking that no thief had secretly siphoned the fuel from the tanks in the wings, the car driver had left the tatty cover lying in a heap by the ragged hedge behind the parking line. If someone saw it from a distance, they might assume it had simply blown there on another day when the wind had been stronger. Satisfied that no-one had seen him, Dominik Katz went back to his car and drove off, following the same route as the horsebox had taken earlier.

A few minutes later, the smart green Range Rover containing Sam and the Urquharts had turned out of the gates of Sampfield Grange and headed swiftly towards the M5. Lewis and Kelly stood in the boot room doorway watching the party leave, whilst Travis, temporarily in charge of the yard, assembled the work riders and the remaining horses for their exercise in the strengthening morning sun.

*

By eleven o'clock, the Sampfield Grange horsebox had carefully entered the gates of Cheltenham racecourses and the two horses had been unloaded and installed in their temporary accommodation prior to their respective races. Spectators arriving early for the day's events, a few tanked up with the lager already being served with breakfast by the local pubs and bars, loitered alongside the red brick stableyard to watch the arrival of their favourite horses.

"Look, that's Tabikat," exclaimed the voice of a girl who was accompanied by a group of three young men wearing tight blue trousers and tweed jackets stretched over skinny shoulders, "Stevie Stone and Jayce say that he'll be the favourite for the Gold Cup and that we should put him in a forecast with Macalantern or The Page of Cups."

"What'd you know about it?" sneered one of the buttoned-up lads, "You been watching that kitten thing again, 'ave you? Those people don't know what they're on about."

"Well, they've made me a bit of money, that's all I know," replied the girl, defiantly, flicking her fake fur scarf back over her right shoulder, "Just 'cos you're always too pissed to use your little brain ..."

"That's telling them, Tabsi," muttered Sadie to a well rugged Tabikat, as she led him away from the lorry, "She's right. You're going to win this time."

Tabikat's own opinion on the matter was, naturally, unknown, so his purposeful, calm walk and regal bearing remained unchanged. But Sadie was sure he agreed with her.

Jackie quickly brought an equally even tempered Katseye into the yard behind Tabikat, a little disappointed to have learned by way

404

of her mobile phone that Tabby Cat and his human team were less certain of victory today for her gorgeous charge. Katseye was a truly impressive creature – a star in the making, Jackie was sure - but he had been in the limelight for a shorter time than his older half brother.

"We'll show them, today, won't we Big Kat?" Jackie whispered to the young horse, as they walked together, "You're the best horse in the race, whatever those people think."

Kye had been left with the task of shutting up the lorry and moving it from the unloading area into the main park. The memory of this same day last year reared up in his mind, suddenly clear and frightening once again. As he drove the lorry between the lines of trainers' vehicles, he could only hope that no-one would step forward to accuse him of shopping them to the bizzies. Almost as bad, one of the bizzies themselves, many of whom seemed to be armed this year, might stop him and say that Mr Stanley had changed his mind, and Kye was under arrest.

Kye did not breathe easily again until he was safe within the confines of the stables with his fellow workers and saw Mr Sampfield walking unhurriedly towards them.

*

By twelve o'clock, Dominik Katz was sitting alongside the golf course at the top of Cleeve Hill, above the exposed escarpment of golden rock which he had learned from his online research was known as Cleeve Cloud. He had left his car in a layby on the winding road below, alongside a couple of other vehicles, clearly belonging to the sort of outdoor walking enthusiast for which he was now hoping to be mistaken. Crossing towards a footpath on the far side of the uphill road, he had worked his way upwards, sweating in his unfamiliar waterproof jacket and sturdy walking boots, scrambling and trudging along the steep path which led to the track above the rock face.

Dominik was normally a sedentary man and the climb felt strenuous. When crossing the stile which led him to the foot of the steep track, he had noticed with interest a wooden sign which indicated that flying drones and model aircraft from the top of the hill was prohibited. Dominik had no intention of flying his drone, which he had left in the car, but he did have the smartphone-based remote control for the machine zipped into his inside pocket. When he took it out, as he would later, anyone watching would think he was simply either taking a picture of the panoramic view, or a selfie, or even just making a call.

Eventually arriving at the top of the challenging route, Dominik walked along the grassy track, looking for the spot which he had identified. Dominik had studied carefully the layout of the racecourse and its surrounding buildings and spectator areas. He had compared the position of the site, which he had learned was known as Prestbury Park, with the orientation of the walking route running above Cleeve Cloud. Eventually he had pinpointed on the map the exact position for his purposes. He needed both a good view towards the South and a clear line of sight to the racecourse parade ring. After a short time, he found the place he had identified, and sat down. There was nothing more for him to do now but wait.

*

At about twelve o'clock, Giles Penney, the now middle aged grandson of the man whose farmland had been requisitioned to provide a wartime airbase, drove his muddy blue pickup truck onto the Old Warnock field. Giles was the owner of the Cessna with the missing propeller, the aircraft which Dominik had briefly scrutinised earlier in the week.

Today was a red letter day for the stingy Giles. The original propeller had been damaged during a careless nose wheel landing some months earlier and the insurance company had agreed to pay up at last. A mechanic from an aircraft maintenance company was due to meet him at the field that day to assess the extent of the work required and to provide an estimate of the cost. Giles had previously removed the damaged propeller himself, reasoning that this might save him some money on the job, but had been told, too late, that he should have left matters as they were and that the assessor would come out to look at the propellerless aircraft where it stood. Mr Penney was not to attempt any of the work himself, the insurers said.

Giles observed the flat tyre on the nose wheel of the little Cessna with some annoyance. That too had seemed to have been a consequence of the bad landing. The strut in the nose wheel landing gear assembly had successfully taken the shock caused by the mess he had made of the touchdown, but the tyre looked as if it had developed a puncture, or else a damaged valve was allowing a leakage of air from the tube.

Pumping up a tyre was something which Giles was confident he could manage himself without permission from the insurance company. He had a tyre pump in his pickup, an electric model which would run from the vehicle's battery. He just had to create some space to get his truck close enough to the tyre to inflate from the pump.

Giles knew the owner of the strangely painted aircraft which stood alongside his own. She was a young female Army captain who seemed to have spoilt with weird camouflage what Giles could see was once a pretty nice aircraft. If he was not mistaken, it was the same type as the one which had crashed and caused the big fire last November. This one was obviously unused, as he had never seen it fly anywhere.

"The Altior 10s are all grounded since the crash," TK Stonehouse had said sadly, when Giles had asked her about it, "So it's going to sit here for a while. I don't want people thinking it's worth stealing. I'd appreciate it if you could cast an eye over it whenever you're up here. Make sure no-one's tried to get into it or anything. If anyone here needs to move it when I'm not around, there's a tow bar in the store shed over there."

The grounding of the Altior 10 seemed to Giles to have persisted for a long period of time but he had not recently seen Captain Stonehouse to ask her about progress with rectifying what was clearly a very serious fault on the aircraft type. Going towards the storeroom to fetch the towbar so that he could move her aircraft away from the place in which he wished to position his truck, he noticed that the rain cover had apparently blown off and was lying screwed up behind him in the nearby hedge.

The towbar was a carbon steel rod almost three feet long. One end was forked with a hook protruding inwards from each fork. At the other end was a T shaped handle. Giles brought the chunky implement back to the Altior 10 and slotted the two hooks into the matching recesses on either side of the nose gear assembly. Grunting a little with the effort, and hoping that the aircraft's brakes were not on, he used the handle to tug the machine forward and sideways several feet so as to create space for his truck. Leaving the towbar hooked in place, so as to be ready to push Captain Stonehouse's aircraft back into its usual place later that afternoon, Giles set about inflating the Cessna's flat tyre before the mechanic arrived.

*

At one o'clock, Merlin ap Rhys was standing in one of the staff offices at Cheltenham racecourse listening carefully to a briefing by Frank Stanley.

"I'll be in the parade ring with Meredith Crosland, Arturo Ardizzone and one of Arturo's technical colleagues," Frank told Merlin, "Obviously James Sampfield will be there as usual as the trainer and Jackie Taylor will be leading the horse up. There is no need for you to do anything different from normal, Mr ap Rhys. Greet everyone in the usual way and then go out and ride the race in accordance with Mr Sampfield's instructions. You'll be in the Ardizzone colours today, of course. They're green with a white chest motif, I believe, the nearest the BHA could get to the colours of the Lombardy flag."

"You could at least give me some idea what's going to 'appen," Merlin replied, crossly, "I talked Mr Sampfield into puttin' the 'orse into the three mile race, like you asked, an' I 'ave no idea why I 'ad to do that."

"I don't know what is going to happen," Frank Stanley answered, "I am sure you won't feel any better if I tell you that we have armed men watching the parade ring from the top of the stands – and in the crowds, too. But we may not need them. They're there to protect you and Mr Ardizzone, Mr ap Rhys."

"OK," Merlin said, feeling a bit sick, "I wish I 'adn't asked now."

"We'll all be pretty much in the firing line too, Mr ap Rhys," Frank replied, "You won't be alone."

*

At half past one, as the Cheltenham starter brought down his yellow flag for first race of the afternoon, the Artificial Intelligence pilot of the Altior 10 at Old Warnock airfield begin to run automatically through its starting checklist.

Giles Penney and the aircraft mechanic had had a difficult discussion during the previous hour. Giles had been theatrically shocked at the price he was quoted for the replacement of the propeller and associated work on his aircraft. He remained convinced that he was being overcharged. In vain had the mechanic reminded him that the insurance company would be picking up the bill, but Giles was more concerned about the effect that the size of the claim would have on the following years' premiums. If he could get the price reduced, it might be cheaper to pay for it himself.

Giles had eventually suggested that the two of them repair to the Horse and Groom in Warnock village in the hope of persuading the other man to come up with a better offer. The weary mechanic had no intention of doing any such thing, but had no objection to being bought a drink by this miserly skinflint of a client, deciding that he would eventually offer to discuss the matter further with his employer, knowing full well that the company would not deviate from its published prices.

The two men had duly left the airfield, the mechanic's van following Giles's dirty pickup truck.

When the Altior 10's checklist had been completed, the virtual pilot started the engine and taxied the little aircraft out towards the runway. A human pilot might quickly have realised that there was a problem. A bystander at the airfield would certainly have done so. But there was no human pilot and no bystander at Old Warnock at that time. The virtual pilot's checklist did not include a check on the unwanted presence of a towbar, the software's assumption being that any external check before starting would have been done by ground staff.

The Altior 10 taxied successfully to the nearby runway with the carbon steel towbar still attached to its nose wheel. The T shaped end rasped noisily along the paved surface, sending sparks flying upward, impeding the smooth forward movement of the aircraft. The invisible pilot added a little more power. Turning to line up on runway 25, the aircraft began its forward roll, even more sparks flying around it, whilst the hooks vibrated and strained against the nose gear assembly.

Exactly as Dominik had instructed the onboard pilot, the Altior 10 set off towards the North on its familiar test flight route to Gloucestershire Airport. As before, it would intercept and then establish itself onto the Instrument Landing System which would take it in to land on runway 27.

*

At two o'clock, Giles Penney returned to Old Warnock airfield and saw that Captain Stonehouse's aircraft had disappeared. Fearing that it had been stolen, although he could not understand how, he took out his ancient mobile phone and called the number the young woman had given him.

At five minutes past two, Frank Stanley's mobile phone pinged to indicate an incoming message, which read

Katseye live, TK.

At ten minutes past two, the second race of the final afternoon of the Cheltenham Festival went off, and a nervous Jackie, followed by a scarcely less edgy Kye, started to lead Katseye down to the pre-parade ring. The magnificent horse stalked imperiously down the rubber surfaced path from the brick built stables at the top of the hill, but there were few people other than a couple of red jacketed stewards to appreciate him. Everyone else was watching the live racing.

At half past two, the Altior 10 approached the interception point for the localiser. Dominik could see the aircraft in the distance towards the South, its black outline showing at about one thousand feet above the ridge of the hills overlooking the town of Cheltenham. It was close enough now for him to take control. Raising the smartphone enabled remote control, Dominik told the virtual pilot that it was no longer to fly the aircraft and that a human pilot was now taking charge of the flight from the ground.

"You have control," the onboard software immediately confirmed by text to Dominik's handset.

Instead of continuing with its previous instruction to intercept the localiser and to descend on a westerly heading with the glide slope procedure into Gloucestershire Airport, the little aircraft continued instead to fly towards the place where its new pilot was standing above Cleeve Cloud, overlooking Cheltenham racecourse.

*

The Novices' Hurdle race in which Katseye was entered was due to start at ten minutes to three.

Jackie led the handsome jet-coloured horse into the busy parade ring about fifteen minutes before post time, and the smooth oval path was soon full with all twelve runners. Each of the beautiful horses looked fit and imposing, their respective trainers having done their utmost to get them ready to show what they could achieve in the top class race.

Sam soon found himself in the grassy centre of the parade ring with the new owner of Katseye, who was now showing as third favourite at odds of 13/2 on the giant screen above the parade ring. Arturo Ardizzone, whose green and white silks Merlin would be putting on at this very moment, had brought with him an attractive and smartly dressed woman. He had introduced her to Sam vaguely, as "one of my most trusted staff" without, as far as Sam could tell, having mentioned her by name. The woman herself who was of medium height and wearing a smart grey coat and fur hat, had little to say, which made Sam wonder if she even spoke English. She wore large and fashionable dark framed glasses and Sam could see that she had thick blonde hair tucked up neatly under her warm headgear. Opening a small black handbag, she soon drew out a mobile phone, and thereafter seemed to take little interest in Arturo Ardizzone's effusive comments made to the roving TV interviewer about his talented horse.

Stevie Stone had been in and around the Press area for most of the afternoon, passing on Jayce's tips via the voice of Tabby Cat to the watching Smart Girls. For this race, though, she had been invited, apparently by Meredith Crosland, to join the Katseye connections in the parade ring. Meredith Crosland herself had come over to join the group standing with Sam, uncharacteristically silent and seemingly morose. Stevie Stone had put a comforting arm around Meredith's shoulders. Perhaps Mrs Crosland was regretting selling her horse to Arturo Ardizzone, thought Sam.

Unexpectedly, at least to Sam, Frank Stanley had followed Meredith Crosland into the parade ring.

"I didn't know you would be here," Sam told him, as his friend came forward to greet him, "This is a pleasant surprise, Frank."

"I couldn't really miss this race, Sam," Frank replied, somewhat obscurely.

Following the progress of Katseye along the parade ring path and hearing the hubbub of the gathering crowds of chattering spectators alongside the white railings, Sam spotted a familiar and unwelcome face in the Press area.

"I thought you had got rid of that journalist woman, Frank," he said, nodding towards the steppings to the left of the weighing room, where a red coated Jessica Moretti stood staring unashamedly towards them.

"She is the least of our problems today," Frank told him, shortly, "Stevie will deal with her, don't worry, Sam."

At twenty minutes to three, Merlin entered the parade ring clad in Katseye's new racing colours.

*

The Altior 10 continued to make its way at an altitude of two thousand feet toward Dominik. The ground where he was standing was almost one thousand feet above sea level, which meant that the aircraft would be a similar distance above his head on reaching the point at which he would direct it towards the racecourse. This required it to make a turn through about ninety degrees to the left.

Domink had checked that all his targets were in the parade ring, an area which was clearly visible through the binoculars which he had now taken from the side pocket of his jacket. He could see Arturo Ardizzone, standing arrogantly in the midst of a group of people who were shaking hands with the jockey who Dominik knew to be Merlin ap Rhys. Horses were parading in a large elongated circle around them, watched by thousands of people who were pressing around the area. It was a shame that their fun would soon end when Dominik flew the Altior 10 at full speed directly into the face of the hated Arturo Ardizzone, killing his rich friends and his racehorse, not to mention the jockey who had been involved in the murder of Dominik's sister.

The aircraft was almost overheard. Dominik initiated a steep turn left onto a compass heading of 260 degrees. Looking up, he saw the aircraft bank steeply above him as the software responded to the instruction from the handset.

Throughout the journey from Old Warnock to its current position above Cleeve Hill, the steel towbar attached to the nosewheel assembly had rattled and strained against the hooks. One of the forks was hinged to allow easy opening and removal of the device

413

from its place when the aircraft had been towed to its correct position. At three thousand feet during the flight, the airflow had pushed and tugged at the aircraft's metal burden, shaking it up and down and from side to side. The steep turn was the last straw for the overstrained pivot pin, which suddenly snapped under the extra loading. The hooks which had been holding the towbar in place were tipped suddenly out of the nose wheel gear assembly, finally releasing the towbar from its moorings. The towbar plummeted earthward.

Three kilograms of dead weight propelled earthward by gravity and the forward movement of the aircraft landed square on the back of Dominik's skull and shattered it to pieces, destroying most of his clever brain in the process. Dominik's body was simultaneously propelled violently forward and plunged over the edge of the rock face, tumbling over as it fell, landing with what was left of his head facing downwards in the grass and bramble filled gulley below. The smartphone handset shot from his hand and smashed into pieces against the stones at the bottom of the escarpment.

Recognising the signing off of the human controller, the Artificial Intelligence of the virtual pilot in the aircraft above Cleeve Hill immediately took charge of the flight once again. Reverting to its original instructions, it continued the left hand turn to take it back towards the localiser. Descending the glide slope in accordance with the published procedure, the Altior 10 made an uneventful landing on runway 27 at Gloucestershire Airport.

*

Katseye's race went off at the published time of 2.50. All twelve runners started the race, but only eight of them finished what became an attritional affair, mainly because of the speed at which it was run. Katseye was amongst the weary finishers, and did his new owner proud by defying his rank in the betting, and finishing in second place.

Jackie would have preferred Katseye to win, but had no objection to leading the horse towards the second place spot in the winner's enclosure, whilst excited racegoers gathered and pushed onto the steppings above her, ready to welcome the victor home.

"So what was that all about, then?" Merlin quietly asked Frank Stanley, who stood nearby, as the excited connections crowded around the steaming horse. Jackie was holding a yellow bucket under Katseye's dark nose, which was still puffing out the occasional snort of hot breath, whilst everyone else was patting the horse and hugging one another, "I thought something bad was supposed to 'appen to us 'ere."

"It seems that we have been fortunate," Frank replied, looking at Arturo Ardizzone's companion, who had come to stand beside him. She was holding out what looked like a highly sophisticated mobile phone to show Frank a text message.

Merlin's sharp eyes quickly took in the words on the screen.

Yr ac on taxiway. Plse move soonest. No test flight booking recd fm u. Regards ATC

The words made no sense to Merlin, whilst Frank and the woman simply looked at each other, questioningly. Frank realised that Merlin had seen the message and turned quickly to speak to him.

"Merlin, may I introduce Dr Lara Katz?" Frank said, "She and I are most grateful for your help today."

"Lara Katz?" asked Merlin, taken aback by the name, "But that's...."

"I am the real Lara Katz," said the woman, in a soft and accented voice, "The attractive young woman who you ..er .. met, Mr ap Rhys, was, like you, also helping us. She has a different name, you understand. I am sure that you will be pleased to know that she is not dead at all, as the helpful police have said. Her job for us was done, that is all."

"I'm very glad to 'ear that," replied Merlin, meaning what he said, "But if you 'ave no more use for me, I am goin' to weigh in now. I 'ave to ride Tabikat in the Gold Cup, as I expect you know."

As Merlin turned quickly towards the exit to the weighing room, carrying his lightweight saddle with him, a sudden disturbance broke out on his left hand side. Meredith Crosland and Stevie Stone had been been hailed from the Press area by a woman with frizzy black hair, who was clearly determined to stop them leaving the parade ring until they answered her questions.

"Hello, Stevie," called the woman loudly, a triumphant edge to her voice, "I bet you thought you'd got rid of me, didn't you?"

A number of people standing nearby turned to look at the source of the ill-mannered shouting. Fortunately, the presentation of the prize to the connections of the winning horse was about to take place in the little white stand situated in the winner's enclosure, and attention was generally focused towards that area.

"Hello, Jessica," Stevie replied, "I didn't expect to see you here. And I have no idea what you're talking about."

"Don't mess me around any more," Jessica replied, loudly, "I've run halfway around France and Ireland, not to mention mud-ridden horse training places and freezing racecourses, to prove that your family are liars. Your mother isn't dead at all. I bet your dad isn't either. How much were you all paid to keep quiet about that murder?"

More heads were quickly swivelling towards the aggressive speaker. A parade ring steward started to walk towards the group, signalling at the same time to a police officer who was standing near the weighing room into which Merlin had now disappeared.

Stevie and Meredith Crosland stopped together on the path and stared at the smirking Jessica Moretti.

"What on earth are you talking about, Jessica?" Stevie replied, sounding cross, "You know my mother is dead. And my dad too."

"Well, who's that then?" Jessica snapped back at once, jabbing an accusatory finger towards Meredith Crosland, "That stable girl at the horse place in Somerset was told to get rid of me so that I wouldn't recognise her when she came to see her horse that morning."

"I see," replied Stevie in a calmer voice, "Sorry Jess, but you have been really barking up the wrong tree this time. Allow me to introduce Meredith Crosland. She's my mother's sister. And my aunt."

Epilogue

Sam sat alone in his study at Sampfield Grange looking out at the damp sheep grazing in the wet paddock. In his hand was the last of the DVDs onto which the obsolete video cassettes had been copied. Sam was still finding it difficult to concentrate.

The incredible moment that Tabikat had won the Cheltenham Gold Cup had been the most overwhelming experience of Sam's life. The stream of reporters and wellwishers, and the messages and calls, which had swamped Sampfield Grange in the last two days had shown no sign of abating, as everyone wanted to see the victorious horse back in his quiet rural home.

Tabikat had been the favourite for the Gold Cup for at least a week beforehand and had remained so when the race went off at its appointed time of half past three. Sam had been joined in the ring by a very different group of connections to those who had appeared to support the horse last year. There had been no sign of Daniel Levy or TK Stonehouse, nor Isabella Hall or George Harvey.

Stevie Stone had been involved in some kind of shouted altercation with the unwelcome journalist who had badgered Sam, which had resulted in the woman being asked to leave the Press area. The incident appeared to have involved Meredith Crosland too, and she and Stevie Stone had soon left the parade ring together, accompanied by Arturo Ardizzone, whose female companion seemed to have already taken her leave, together with Frank Stanley.

This year, Sam had found himself in the welcome company of Eoghan Foley and Caitlin, together with Caitlin's sister Niamh and her daughter Feanna. The family had been enthusiastically pleased by Katseye's performance in the preceding race, Feanna having commented that she was sure the gelding would make up into a great Novice Chaser next season. Sam had dared to ask why she had not come down to join him for Katseye's race, in response to which she had given the rather mystifying answer that Mr Stanley had advised against it. So the Foleys had watched Katseye run from the comfort of the box which had been made available at the expense of Levy Brothers International.

Tabikat's first appearance in the parade ring had produced an audible buzz of growing anticipation from the excited spectators who had been packed several deep around the rails, desperate to get a glimpse of all the gorgeously turned out horses. Sadie, her blonde hair tied primly back into a pony tail, her blue eyes shining with excitement, had stepped out proudly alongside her highly popular charge. Tabikat had worn his usual air of calm authority, nodding his dark way gracefully around the parade ring, as if he were a king acknowledging loyal subjects.

Glancing around in case of any unexpected late arrivals to the party, as had been the case last year, Sam had noticed a sturdy looking man with shoulder length grey-streaked black hair, who had appeared to be trying to attract Caitlin's attention. The man had looked like a gypsy, Sam had thought rather dismissively, and had wondered if Caitlin would acknowledge him.

At home now on Sunday at Sampfield Grange, Sam could scarcely remember his discussion before the race with Merlin, wearing his blue silks with the gold stars. Sam recalled watching the horse disappear grandly under the stone bridge leading to the track, Merlin perched up on his broad back, Sadie's pony tail bobbing as she walked. The parade of the horses before the heaving stands had seemed to take place in slow motion, with Tabikat's name the last of the ten to be called. On the screen above the parade ring, where most of the runners' connections had elected to remain during the race, he had watched Sadie release her hold on Tabikat and say something to Merlin, her chin tilted up towards him. Merlin had nodded in response, then had turned Tabikat to the left to canter down the hill.

Sam had quickly realised that the Foley party had been completely confident that Tabikat would win this year. They had been right. Tabikat had travelled like a dream throughout the race, Merlin scarcely having to move a muscle until the final moments of the contest. Macalantern had led the field for much of the first circuit

419

but by the time the field had turned for home, Tabikat and The Page of Cups had motored up from their earlier mid-division positions to challenge him. With two fences left to jump, Tabikat had become a clear leader and had stayed on determinedly to win the famous race by two lengths from The Page of Cups. Macalantern had had to be content with third place.

As Sam had waited in the winner's enclosure under the eyes of a growing crowd of noisy supporters massing together on the steppings, he had seen Niall Carter, standing close to the post marked with a sign for the second placed horse, come forward to shake the hand of Eoghan Foley. Caitlin had stood quietly at Eoghan's side, until she had stepped forward to kiss Niall Carter on the cheek and to motion her sister forward to do likewise. Whatever had occurred to make Niamh so angry with Niall Carter at Newbury racecourse had clearly been somehow resolved, thought Sam.

As Merlin had brought the triumphant winner into his rightful place at the winner's station, Sam had become aware that the scruffy man who had tried to attract Caitlin's attention had now forced his way down to the front of the stepped area and was standing by the rails nearby. Caitlin had at last given him her attention.

"*Felicidades, Catalina,*" the man had called out to her, "*El nieto de Maria?*"

"*Si, Arnaldo,*" Caitlin had replied, promptly, a response which appeared to satisfy the strange man, who had smiled, uttered the single word *bueno* and had then shoved himself upwards through the crowd to disappear from sight.

The presentation of the diminutive Gold Cup and the interview afterwards had both passed by like a brief dream. Sam had been acutely aware of the deafening noise from the spectators, Tabikat's unusual background having made him immensely popular with both the Irish and English support contingents. Sam had seen Merlin stop to speak to Sadie after having collected his share of the prize and posed for the necessary photographs, which had required the former lovers to stand together next to Tabikat's victorious nose for a time.

"I'll come an' watch you at Cuffborough on Sunday, if you'll let me," Sam thought he had heard Merlin say. Sam had not heard Sadie's reply, but would be able to find out for himself that same afternoon, when Sadie was due to ride the promising Indian Rocks for Sampfield Grange in a point to point race at the usually muddy Cuffborough course.

Pushing the remaining unwatched DVD into the slot on the computer, Sam saw that this disk contained only one file. On opening the file, he was surprised to realise that it was the oldest of all the recordings which had been saved from the old video cassettes. The images flitting across the computer screen showed a couple of young teenage boys riding two of Richard Sampfield's smart pointers over the jumps on the top gallops. Sam's father was pictured issuing authoritative directions to the riders, and Sam could hear the Queensland tones of his mother, calling out from her position behind the camcorder – or perhaps it was even a cine camera, given the age of the recording - to indicate the shots that she wanted.

The two teenagers were James Sampfield Peveril and Frank Stanley. The schooling session apparently complete, the friends dismounted their horses and walked with them towards the camerawoman. Sam could hear his father's almost forgotten voice shouting something from afar and his mother laughing in response.

"My son James and his friend Frank," Raldi's proud voice announced from the speakers of the computer, "Sampfield Grange's top team!"

ABOUT THE AUTHOR

Harriet Redfern was born in the North of England but has spent most of her life living and working in London. Her longstanding passion for National Hunt racing was originally inspired by watching televised race meetings whilst doing the family ironing on winter Saturday afternoons. This entertaining distraction from the housework soon became a serious pastime as her children grew older, and included a brief, although rather unsuccessful, excursion into racehorse ownership. Harriet is also a qualified pilot and aircraft owner and can be found in the skies whenever the weather is good. Now retired from her career in the University world, Harriet lives and writes in Cheltenham.